A Rose Blooms in the Desert

A Rose Blooms in the Desert

⅄⅄⅄

Alan Messing

ISBN-13: 9781540899279
ISBN-10: 1540899276
Library of Congress Control Number: 2016920564
CreateSpace Independent Publishing Platform
North Charleston, South Carolina

To Mom and Dad
Thank you for a great life.

CHAPTER 1

The Blitz

⅄⅄⅄

THIS IS DEFINITELY THE BEST part of the job. It was a beautiful summer day and the road was clear, so I opened up the throttle and let the old German NSU motorcycle go as fast as I could. That didn't last long, as I was coming up fast on my unit. I was part of the Twenty-Seventh Infantry Division of the Krakow army assigned to defend southeast Poland. I was just a corporal but was lucky to be assigned to Major Paloski, the division commander.

I was a flag signaler, in charge of communicating his orders to the infantry by waving colored flags. Each series of flags sent signals to the troops in the field. My job was to position the infantry, tanks, and other vehicles and artillery pieces. We spent our days running drills. I followed the commander's orders by raising the correct series of flags, expecting the troops in the field to move accordingly. I heard about other divisions with some form of radio telephones allowing various division segments to speak directly to each other, but these were scarce throughout the Polish army. We were poorly supplied, and the new communication equipment was not likely to reach us anytime soon.

I was not exactly on the front lines. Generally, I was in an elevated position on a hill behind the battle. Frankly, we had never been in a battle in the nearly four years since I began my conscripted service. I was nineteen then, and now I was three months away from being discharged and ending my service. My plan was to go home and join my family lumber business.

As I sped up the dirt road approaching the encampment, I saw my friend Yitzchak coming up fast. I hit the brakes and skidded to a stop. "Where have you been?" he asked. He was an infantry private on the front line, but we were from the same town of Pysznica. He was a childhood friend, and he was clearly jealous that I had a cushy job with the commander. "How come you get to take a nice Sunday drive through the countryside while we march around in circles, eh?" he asked.

"I ran an errand for the commander." I tried to be vague.

"Was it a secret mission?" he asked sarcastically.

"Not so secret, he needed some supplies," I said, knowing that this would lead to no good.

"What supplies does the commander need that the rest of us don't?" he asked indignantly.

I said, "OK, but keep your mouth shut." I opened one of my saddlebags and showed him the three bottles of good Russian vodka, strictly forbidden by the Polish army code of ethics, which was usually ignored by most officers. "There are three more on the other side."

He just looked at me and started laughing. "You officers really know how to live." He chuckled, knowing full well that as Orthodox Jews we were looked at as second-class citizens by the Christians in power, who would never have a drink with us.

In fact, we suffered much anti-Semitism. As a private in basic training, I took many beatings at night by my comrades as the only Jew in the barracks. They would wait until I was asleep and hit me with the barrels of their rifles. My only protection was my thin blanket. The officers on duty would break up the fight but would never reprimand the soldiers, so it happened quite frequently. Somehow my sergeant allowed me to take an officer's exam, and I was able to earn a promotion to corporal and an assignment with Major Paloski. The beatings stopped, as the officers had bigger issues on their mind. I suspected Yitzchak still suffered those beatings.

"What do you hear about the Germans?" Yitzchak asked, losing his humorous attitude.

"They are amassing on the border," I replied just as seriously. "Our reconnaissance officers have confirmed this. Major Paloski is out-of-his-mind angry. He keeps sending messages to General Szylling for reinforcements, but the only answer he gets is that they are more concerned about the Russians and are sending the bulk of the troop reinforcements to the eastern border with Russia. Hopefully they are right and we won't have to find out if our training is any good. I have to get back and complete my secret mission. Please take care of yourself."

We shook hands. I cranked up the NSU and headed back to deliver my load.

The next morning, Major Paloski called a meeting at 0800 to review the latest intelligence from the border. The news was not good. The Germans were bringing in more troops, artillery, and tanks. They had closed off several roads and turned them into landing strips for supply and attack planes. There was not much doubt they were planning an invasion. Again, the commander's pleas for additional troops and armaments were ignored. He advised that the week before, the Germans and Russians signed a nonaggression pact, agreeing not to attack each other in case of war. We knew Poland was stuck in the middle between two superior forces. The Polish commanders could only fortify one border well so they chose to protect the eastern front instead of the German border. As it turned out, it didn't matter, but at that time, we felt abandoned.

It was August 31, 1939, three months before the end of my service, and now we were on the brink of war.

At 0400 the next morning, we awoke to the sound of airplanes. At first, I thought we were getting reinforcements, but then the alarms sounded. We were being attacked. I knew the Nazis were coming, but I didn't know how fast. When I arrived at my position, it was too late. The planes were bombing and shooting at our front positions. In the background came endless tank attacks and artillery shelling, followed by troop carriers. The battle was swift and fierce. I could see our men in the distance falling to their deaths. The position of the troops no longer mattered. They came from the front and the sides. They looped around our position. Our artillery was ineffective, seemingly bouncing off their tanks. There was death everywhere. After a few hours, the fighting edged closer to our position. I could see our men fighting hand to hand, blood and limbs scattered everywhere, with few Nazi casualties. I was in shock. I never imagined we were so unprepared to face the enemy we knew was just over the border. I felt so guilty that my friend Yitzchak was probably dead or injured, and I was back safely overseeing the destruction. I had grabbed my rifle with bayonet attached and headed toward my NSU bike to join the fight when the commander ordered a retreat. The battle was lost, and we had to retreat to the east to defend Krakow.

I signaled the troops that remained that the retreat was on. As we left, more casualties were inflicted on us. The ruthlessness of the Germans was shocking. Killing, it seemed, was as important as taking territory.

We began our march toward Krakow. It was hard to imagine that any defense we put up would be successful. We marched all night and into the next day. On the afternoon of September 3, we halted and could not believe our eyes. We were marching right into another German division. They did an end around and surrounded us.

Now it was every man for himself, and I would join the fight. I expected to die, with only my Karabinek WZ 29 rifle and as many rounds as my saddlebags would hold. It was an eight-millimeter German-designed gun with a bayonet affixed to the front. I'd had this rifle since I entered the army. I kept it clean and serviceable. I was a pretty good shot, ranking high in all my drills. The problem was, I only shot targets, not actual people. None of that mattered. We were in the fight of our lives, and I had to try to fend off these Nazi bastards who were taking my country.

We retreated over a bridge and took our positions on the eastern side of the river. We had no time to dig a trench. We took shelter behind vehicles, trees, anything to give us cover. What was left of our artillery was positioned and manned. As we looked out over the bridge, we began to see a cloud of fog flowing across the river. Someone started yelling, "They are smoking us out!" The Germans had used the smoke as a diversion to move across the bridge to attack. I do not recall who fired the first shot, but it seemed to happen within seconds of the smoke appearing. Our artillery shells began flying. Bullets were flying everywhere. I could see enemy tanks moving at us through the cloudy air in the distance and heard the sound of the German artillery. Shells began dropping and exploding around me. We continued our retreat toward Krakow. After a while, I took cover inside an abandoned warehouse about one hundred meters off the main road, with several dozen other soldiers I did not know. The building, although abandoned, was filled with boxes and farm machinery ready for sale or delivery and gave us plenty of places to hide. There were windows in the warehouse, but we could not see much of what was happening outside. The noise was deafening, and we could feel the vibrations from the bombing. We had men perched at each window so we could shoot if attacked.

After about two hours of continuous shelling, we looked out from our perch and saw vehicles and artillery blown to bits. The German tanks were closer now, and we could see the Nazi troops advancing. We were scared, knowing that the odds of surviving were small, let alone winning the battle. As they got in range, we used our hidden position to surprise the enemy and began firing. We all began shooting at the same time. I could not tell if I actually hit any of the Nazis, but I could see some enemy soldiers falling. I began to feel exhilarated that we possibly had a chance to win this battle. As an Orthodox Jew, I often thought about how I would feel about killing another person. I recalled a conversation I had with my cheder morah, a religious school teacher, about the Ten Commandments. Christians believed the sixth commandment was "Thou shalt not kill." The Jewish translation was "Thou shalt not murder," a justification for fighting battles throughout Jewish history. Now it was my turn, and killing the enemy was not only allowed; it was my duty to fight for my country and—although I didn't know it at the time—the survival of the Jewish people.

Once the German infantry troops realized they were under attack, those who were not dead or wounded looked for cover and began shooting at us. The firefight lasted for several hours, and we seemed to be holding our own, even though we had casualties. In order to get a better shooting position, the private next to me jumped out from behind the tractor that was shielding him and pointed his gun through a window that had already been shattered by enemy fire. He got one shot off and fell beside me; two bullets had seared through his head. The blood was everywhere, but I had no time to react. I had to keep shooting and stay under cover.

We were hungry and exhausted, but that seemed not to matter. We were soldiers fighting for our lives. As the sun starting going down, we were losing light and low on ammunition, and the shooting suddenly stopped. Had we killed the enemy? Had we won the battle? A few of us came out of our hiding places to see what was going on. There was a hum of engines that seemed to get louder. As we looked out, there were two tanks perched outside the warehouse. Clearly the Nazi infantry called for help—and it arrived.

I screamed, "Look out and cover up!" I crawled back inside and under the tractor. The tanks began firing on the building. After about fifteen or twenty shells, the top of the brick building began to crumble and the roof caved in. The rubble fell on and around us. The tractor I was under began to break apart but protected me enough to survive the debacle, although the floor caved in below me and I fell into the hole it created.

After the crumbling stopped and I realized I was alive and not hurt, I crawled out of the hole in the floor that was created by the collapse. As I emerged, I saw that some of my fighting mates were crawling out as well. Some men were crushed and clearly dead. They were scattered throughout the warehouse. Then I looked at the edge of the rubble, and what seemed like a hundred German soldiers were standing there, pointing rifles at us. They were screaming in German, which I didn't fully understand, but they clearly wanted us to come out of the building. They gathered us up and had us lie on the ground facedown. They gathered our weapons and threw them in a pile.

What would happen to us? Would they take us prisoner or just shoot us and leave us for dead? While we contemplated our fate, we could hear the marching of soldiers and humming of vehicles traveling down the road toward Krakow. My heart sank as I realized I would die here and that nothing could stop this powerful army taking over the country. We were the last line of defense, and we were defeated.

Suddenly I heard what was clearly a German officer barking orders to our infantry guards. This was it. We were dead.

Suddenly the guards began to walk off. They joined the march down the road to Krakow and left us lying there. I got up, as did the others, in bewilderment. They took our weapons but left us whole. Did they show mercy because we gave them a tough fight? Did they think us insignificant insects that were no threat to the mighty Nazi army? Regardless, we were alive and free. The Nazis disappeared in the distance.

CHAPTER 2

Now What?

⅄ ⅄ ⅄

FIVE OF US SEEMED TO congregate as the rest of the surviving soldiers dispersed and disappeared. We ranged in rank from private to major. None of that mattered now. The war was over for us. We were somewhere near Wroclaw, just east of the German border, about three hundred kilometers from Krakow. For all we knew, we were now living in Germany. My thoughts immediately turned to home and family. Somehow my mission was now to go back to find and help protect them. As it turned out, my new mates were all from towns on the main rail line between Krakow and Lublin.

I grew up in the little town of Pysznica, approximately two hundred kilometers northeast of Krakow. It was a small town of about five thousand people, with a small, tight-knit Jewish community of about two hundred. We were observant Jews, left alone except for occasional anti-Semitic remarks and signs. My family owned the local lumberyard, and I had hopes of finding everyone home and everything normal. Now the question was how to get there without being caught or shot. We agreed we needed to stay off the main roads and hike through the farmlands. It could take weeks to walk the more than five hundred kilometers. The first thing we needed was food. We began our trek through the farmlands that were plentiful in southwestern Poland. Soon we came upon a farmhouse that seemed to be bustling with activity as if nothing new was happening around them. I knocked on the front door. A middle-aged woman answered. She was clearly the lady of the house.

She looked at our torn uniforms and immediately knew we were in need of assistance. "Wait here," she said and disappeared into the house.

A few minutes later, a man appeared and asked us why we were there.

"My name is Corporal Marcus of the Krakow Army," I said.

We each introduced ourselves. There was Private Borkowski, Private Adamski, Lieutenant Nowicki, and finally Major Michalski.

Major Michalski jumped in and said, "We are soldiers who fought off the German attack, and we are regrouping to a new position. We are in need of supplies and food, and I expect you to fill the needs of my men immediately."

The farmer was clearly annoyed at the major's arrogance. He seemed well aware of the German invasion and knew we had nowhere to regroup. "My name is Kaczmarek," said the farmer. "You are welcome as my guests. If you intend to try to attack this farm, know that my men are well armed and you will have battle on your hands."

Didn't this so-called major see we had no weapons? Kaczmarek saw right through us. I replied that we were honored to be his guests and would gladly accept whatever hospitality he could provide. We had been in a brutal battle and were starving. I pulled the major aside as the other men went inside and admonished him. "Are you out of your mind? You should not take such a hard stance with these kind people. You are no longer my superior. The battle is over! The army is over!"

He looked at me sternly. "You're a coward. We still are at war, and you are a soldier. You will listen to my orders. We will get supplies and move out to defend Krakow!"

"Did you see what happened out there today?" I responded. "We are not in the army anymore. If it turns out we are still conscripted, I will gladly accept my court-martial."

"You're a traitor," he barked. "If I had a gun, I would shoot you in the place where you stand." He turned away in disgust and walked off. I went inside to see if they had any food.

It turned out the farm was manned by the farmer, his wife, two sons in their late teens or early twenties, and a teenage daughter, hardly a match for five well-trained and desperate soldiers, but he clearly saw our condition and bluffed us into submission.

Regardless, Kaczmarek was true to his word. We were able to bathe in a nearby lake while the women prepared a meal of vegetables, potatoes, and various meats, some of which was pork, strictly forbidden by the Jewish dietary laws. What I did not know was that those dietary laws would be broken many times in the next few years.

We ate our fill and told stories, including details of our experiences in the recent battle. The family was terrified of the potential consequences of the German occupation, but for now we were all safe and well fed. The war was for another day. Then the farmer offered to let us stay the night and made an odd request. As a former soldier of the Polish army, he collected anything military. He asked for our uniforms and any medals or military-issued supplies that we might have retained. In exchange, he would provide civilian clothing and a few zlotys each for our journey.

This created a stormy debate among me and my fellow soldiers. "This is treason and desertion, punishable by death by firing squad," declared Major Michalski. "If any of you accept this offer, I will personally lead a squad of men to hunt you down and bring you to justice."

I looked at him in disbelief. "Did you see what happened out there today? Did you see the power of the German army, the tanks, the airplanes, the well-trained and equipped infantry?" I became irritated. "Do you still think there is still a Polish army after today?" I was now being condescending. "You are a fool if you think you are going to walk out there and rejoin Polish soldiers who will repel the invasion. The Polish army is finished and nonexistent after today."

The major stood up, gathered his things, and screamed, "I will see all of you in front of a firing squad!" He marched out the door, never to be seen again.

I turned to my new best friends and said, "Look, the battle is over. We have to get home to our families. This will be the best way to blend into society and not be noticed by the German invaders. You are welcome to join Major Michalski, but I am staying here." We talked this through for a little while. They all saw the major as delusional and soon agreed that they wanted to get home. We were eager to get some badly needed sleep and get on our way in the morning.

I awoke at first light and was excited to start my journey. I laid out my uniform, shirt, jacket, trousers with baggy thighs, and high leather boots. They were dirty and torn, but they could be repaired. I had the soft hat that came to a point in front. I had no need for a helmet in the normal role I played. It was a miracle my head was still on my shoulders. I had a half-dozen medals, including the cross of merit and a steampunk medal. These were fairly common for soldiers who completed competency drills. They certainly were not for bravery in battle, since I was only in one—and it was our last.

I put on the civilian clothes Kaczmarek left for me, nothing fancy and not a great fit, but I was happy to take off the uniform I had worn for three years in an army that was totally defeated in a few days. It seemed almost funny that Poland had an army after seeing what the Germans did to us.

Mrs. Kaczmarek made us a wonderful farm-fresh breakfast. My comrades all looked like civilians now, and we were ready for our journey home.

Home was approximately five hundred kilometers from there, and the route would take us through Krakow if we followed the main roads. The Polskie Koleje Państwowe, the Polish National Railway, had a line from Wroclaw to Katowice. That would take us approximately two hundred kilometers toward home and one hundred kilometers from Krakow. We had enough zlotys to go that far, if the trains were running. Kaczmarek agreed to drive to the train station in Wroclaw but warned he would turn around at the first sign of danger. We all piled into the back of his old pickup truck. He took as many dirt roads as possible to try to avoid any German soldiers. I was struck by the beauty of the Polish countryside, with its rolling hills and greenery. It was not yet fall, so leaves had not begun to turn. Fall was my favorite time of year, but there would be no time this year to enjoy the colors.

When we arrived at the Wroclaw station, the German army presence was very noticable. They seemed to be observing all aspects of the operation, taking notes about the locomotives, the passenger cars, and the freight cars that often were attached to passenger trains. They were even studying the ticket booth clerk. Private Borkowski commented that it looked like they were about to take over the railroad, a prediction that came true just days later. We had no identification, so if any German soldiers stopped us, we would have some explaining to do.

We hopped out of the truck and said our good-byes to Kaczmarek. We thanked him profusely for taking us in and sending us on our way. We joked about Major Michalski, wondering where he wound up spending the night. We wondered if he found any Polish soldiers who wanted to try to defeat the mighty Nazi war machine.

Luckily the German soldiers were still observing and not interfereing with the trains, so we bought our tickets. The train to Katowice was scheduled to leave in two hours, so we had to blend in and not get noticed. Maybe it didn't matter now that we were not soldiers any longer, but we did not want them to know we had been Polish army and deserted.

We strolled around town like tourists, looking at shop windows. Some of the shops were closed, and the people on the street were few, clearly affected by the German occupation.

As we walked through town, we came upon a commotion in the main square. A large group of Chasidic Jews were gathered. Above them was a large sign ordering all Juden to report for transport. I was confused about what was happening. We stopped to watch. These were religious Jews who were in traditional Chasidic dress, as they had worn for centuries. They were all in black pants, long coats, hats, and white shirts. They had the traditional pais, long sideburns, and beards.

Why were they singling out these harmless people? They spent their days learning Torah and studying ancient Jewish texts. They were all gathered, men, women, and children, with suitcases, as if they were going on a trip. Then they lined everyone up and separated them into groups. Young men to one side, women and children to the other, and the elderly were placed in a separate group. They were equally bewildered. They were loaded in separate military transport trucks, which then drove off.

I heard some anti-Semitic comments from my mates. “Filthy Jews,” one of the privates whispered. I knew I needed to keep my mouth shut.

All I could think about now was getting home. I didn’t know what was going on, but I knew I had to get home and soon. We were taught how the Jewish people had been targeted and persecuted throughout history, going back to biblical times in Egypt, but Eastern Europe had been a safe haven where Jewish culture had thrived and an entire Yiddish culture had grown strong, paticularly in Galicia, the district in Poland where I grew up. It was unimaginable that the invaders trying to take over a new country would take the time to worry about a few Jews. I needed to get home.

We headed back to the train station.

CHAPTER 3

Must Go Home

⅄ ⅄ ⅄

THE TRIP FROM WROCLAW TO Krakow was reasonably uneventful. We sat in coach seats in separate cars so as not to attract attention. My car was mostly filled with a variety of families, older couples, and some well-dressed businessmen. Those conversations I overheard were about one thing: What would life be like under Nazi rule?

One couple traveling with two small boys believed life for their children would be better under the Nazis. "They are farther advanced than anything we have even thought about, and I am sure they educate their children to a much higher level," said the father.

The mother was not so sure. "Yes, but look how cold and brutal they are. Why did they invade Poland if we are so backward and weak? What can they get from us that they don't already have?" No one really knew why they were there.

Another elderly couple was talking behind me. "Did you see how they were gathering the Jews?" asked the woman. "Why were they taking them away?"

"I'm sure they had their reasons. Those religious fanatics are dangerous and control all the wealth in Poland," said the old man, like he actually knew something.

His wife responded, "And the women and children too?"

He had no answer. There was little any of us understood about what was happening. I just sat and stewed.

We arrived in Krakow about three hours late. We stopped several times, as Nazi soldiers walked through the cars looking for something—what, I have no idea, but it was nerve-racking living through it. They were clearly in control of southeastern Poland.

When we arrived in Krakow, it was midmorning, and the four of us gathered at the station to discuss our next move. We noticed the same thing we saw in Wroclaw: Nazi soldiers watching the station and other parts of the train operation.

We were low on funds, so we were not going to take any more trains.

Now it was time to hike. Our military training would be very useful. We routinely went on forty-kilometer hikes in our army drills, carrying full backpacks and rifles. It would take a few days to get to Pysznica. I was getting anxious to see what was going on there.

Off we went. We headed northeast, staying off the main roads. The countryside outside Krakow was beautiful. It still was warm and summery, and the rolling hills and farmland were green and lush. The Nazis had clearly taken over the cities, but the countryside appeared to have been left alone. The route was dotted with small towns along the way, and we were able to spread our remaining zlotys to buy meals of boiled potatoes, borscht, and other staples to keep us going. At each stop, the talk was only of the invasion. The Nazis were making their way across the country, occupying the major cities and moving toward the smaller towns. There was also talk among the townspeople of cold-blooded mass murders of anyone who protested the occupation. Again there was talk of gathering Jews, stripping them of all possessions, and transporting them to some undisclosed destination.

Since we were hiking through farmlands and woods, it took us longer than we imagined. For several days, we hiked and looked for food.

We slept in barns and under the stars. Some of the farmers were generous with their food; others were not, but we were able to get what we needed. Finally, we reached Nisko, the destination of two of my compatriots, Borkowski and Nowicki. When we reached the outskirts of town, we saw Nazis patrolling the streets, and we thought it best that we say our good-byes there so Adamski and I could avoid the town and move on. We were only about twelve kilometers from my home. Adamski would leave me there and head to Lublin, which I was sure was crawling with Nazis.

Along the way, we came to the banks of the San River, where I used to swim with my friends as a child, right up until entering the military. We took the opportunity to bathe ourselves in the fresh river water, as we had not bathed since leaving the farmhouse in Wroclaw. Of course, I did not want my mother to see her son filthy returning from the war. At this point, neither she nor my siblings would have any idea if I was alive or dead.

I gave Adamski a big bear hug and thanked him for his loyalty. Then I headed into Pysznica. It was eerily quiet, and I was thankful that I did not see any German patrols, although there were quite a few local policemen strolling through the streets.

It was Friday afternoon, exactly one week since the invasion, and I was not only excited to see my mother, brothers, and sisters, but I was looking forward to spending a real Shabbos in my home with my family and close-knit Jewish friends. The last time I was home was back in February when I returned for my father, Avraham's, funeral. He had died suddenly, we think, of heart failure. He was a big, imposing figure to me who had started our family business, the local lumberyard in town. He was much older than my mother, over twenty years. I had a half brother, Henry, who was from a previous marriage and fifteen years older than me. I did not see him often.

My father married my mother, Hinda, after his first wife passed away. My mother was only nineteen and very beautiful, and the older Avraham swept her off her feet. He was tall, handsome, and well established, and she didn't know what hit her. I don't think her parents approved, but she fell in love. I was the firstborn, the oldest of six children, and the apple of my mother's eye.

I had five siblings, three sisters and two brothers. After me were two girls, Rivka and Naomi; then a boy, Yossel; then a sister, Chava; and then the youngest son, Benjamin, only fourteen years old when my father died. My dad was sixty-five when he had Benjamin. He got plenty of kidding from the other men in town for being quite virile. My mother worshiped him and was devastated when he died.

She begged me not to go back to the army after the funeral, but I had no choice. My older sisters and brother stayed with her to manage the business. Now that the war was over for me, or so I thought, I could go home to help the family. I was excited, and the Nazi invasion was the furthest thing from my mind.

I grew up in a Yiddish house. We spoke proper Polish for business and dealing with the secular world, but at home and in our little shtetl, our community of roughly two hundred observant Jews, we spoke, read newspapers, and learned Torah in Yiddish. We were generally separated from the rest of Polish society and wanted it that way so we could practice our observances without outside influences. This of course was incongruous with the fact that in order to live we needed to interact with the outside world.

Eastern-European Jews had spoken Yiddish for centuries, and while it had mostly German origins, our version had Polish, Hungarian, and Russian words thrown in. The region of Poland we were from was Galicia, and we were known as Galicianas among Eastern-European Yiddish-speaking Jews. Outsiders saw our lives as fanatical and weird, but we knew who we were and were happy and comfortable in the knowledge that we gained from study and devotion to God.

My conscription to the army was the first time I had left the shtetl for long periods of time and was forced to put aside my beliefs, religious observances, and the laws of Kashrut, dietary laws, that were the basis for my existence for the first twenty years of my life. This was very uncomfortable, but I decided early on that in order to survive the outside world, I would conform the best I could and not flaunt my Jewish observances. I still said prayers three times a day, as always, but only to myself and not in public. I was a bit fearful of the outside world and was not looking for a bullet in the back from some anti-Semite.

As I walked through town, things seemed quite normal. People were on the streets. Businesses were open. It didn't appear that the German invasion had reached Pysznica. Perhaps we were too small to worry about.

As I reached the lumberyard, I saw my sister Rivka and my brother Yossel closing up for Shabbos. I was sure my mother and my other sisters, Chava and Naomi, were home cooking and the shtetl was abuzz with everyone getting ready.

I stood there and watched them, and as they locked the gate that covered the entrance to the yard and office, they turned around, saw me, and screamed "Meyer!" in unison. They ran over and gave me such tight hugs I couldn't breathe, but they were welcome nevertheless, and tears were running down all our faces.

"Momma will be thrilled to see you. She has been worried sick since the news of the invasion!" cried Rivka.

"There are stories of horrible treatment by the Nazis of all Poles but especially Jews," said Yossel. "This has also given Poles justification for anti-Semitic acts. Our shop was attacked last week by a group of young men who set part of the yard on fire. No one was hurt, thank God, but our small Jewish community is very scared."

Rivka jumped in. "Let's go home. It will be a great Shabbos now that we are all together."

We took the thirty-minute walk, which seemed more like five minutes as I related the events of the past week, a story I knew I would have to repeat several times in the next few days.

Arriving in the shtetl, we passed some of the men rushing home. As we walked by the shul, a few men already dressed for Shabbos were entering, probably having an early Talmud discussion to get in the mood.

We lived in one of the nicer houses in town. My father, being older, had run a successful business for many years despite the obstacles put before him, but the local authorities were determined to keep Jews from being successful. He knew how to endear himself to them and overcame their special taxes and permits needed to allow a Jew to have a thriving business. His death was a great blow to us all, but somehow the family had been keeping things together.

As expected, I walked in and chaos ensued. My sister Naomi saw me first. She was my favorite, and I was hers. She looked up to and spoiled me, and I loved it. She was busy preparing the gefilte fish, chopping up the pike and fashioning it into oblong shapes to be cooked. Chava was cutting up carrots for the tsimmes, and Rivka immediately jumped in and started peeling potatoes.

Fortunately for me, men were spared the drudgery of household chores. Men were supposed to work, make money, and study Torah and Talmud. However, with me in the army and Papa passed, the girls were also helping run the business. They never questioned the traditions and happily did what they had to do to survive. Now that I was home, I would take my rightful place managing the lumberyard.

Of course, when Naomi shrieked at my appearance, Momma turned around. She was in her early fifties, a very young-looking, beautiful woman. My father used to say that the first time he saw her he was hooked and was determined to marry her. As he was so much older, she had no interest in him. Several young Jewish men in the shtetl were interested in her, but unlike many other young women, she was in no hurry to marry.

Hinda was from a poor family in the shtetl. Her father, Moshe, was a revered scholar and taught cheder, the religious studies school, teaching young Jewish boys Torah and Talmud. Avraham was mature, reasonably successful, and made his intentions clear. In time, he won her heart. She looked up to him, and he treated her like a queen. The problem was that he was so much older and too close to her father's age. Moshe and her mother, Leah, were against the marriage. They began looking for a shitach, an arranged marriage, with one of her younger suitors. That became problematic once others found out she was in love with Avraham. They were married in 1914, and I came a year later. Hinda had the remaining five children over the next ten years.

Momma turned around and began to cry. Growing up with so many women, I was used to this, which happened every time I came home from the army. Everyone knew I was home for good now and was just letting it show.

She washed her hands, as she was preparing the chicken Benjamin brought home from the shochet for roasting. The kitchen smelled of chicken soup, and all was right with the world at that moment. Momma came over, hugged me, kissed me on both cheeks, and said, "Thank God you are safe and home." Then her disciplinarian side took over, and she added, "Now go clean up and get ready for shul."

Actually I couldn't wait for the peace and serenity of Shabbos after the past week.

Although many Jewish men had beards, which were very useful for stroking while contemplating the many deep issues presented in the Talmud, I never did. I was happy for the opportunity to shave the weeks' worth of stubble, and the hot bath made me feel like a mensch.

Putting on my Shabbos clothes was another ritual I relished. Black pants, jacket, and white shirt were unremarkable, but when topped with my black fedora hat, all made the weekly ritual special.

Benjamin, Yossel, and I made it to shul just in time for mincha, the afternoon service. The shul was the center of the shtetl. It was relatively small, reflecting the size of the small Pysznica Jewish community. It was a narrow four-story building. The shul was on the bottom floor. This was where the men davened (prayed) and learned Torah and Talmud. At the far end was the bimah, a stage of sorts, where the ark with the town's Torahs was stored. In the center of the sanctuary was another bimah where the Torah was read and at times services were conducted. On the second floor was a balcony where the women sat during Shabbos morning and yom tov (holiday) services. The top two floors had classrooms. This was the cheder. This was where I learned of the traditions and rituals of Jewish life. As I got older, the Torah and Talmud dominated my education. The Talmud was the basis of all Jewish law and defined what was acceptable in Jewish life. It did not just define laws but chronicled the arguments between the great Talmudic minds over the past centuries. Many of the debates were quite heated and taught me that you must question everything and that there is often more than one right answer. However, as I learned in the army and from the German invasion, questioning those in power can be dangerous and needs to be measured.

The gabbai ran through mincha in about ten minutes. That service belonged to Friday, a weekday. We had to wait awhile until it was dark enough to begin the Shabbos ma'ariv service. The tradition was to wait until three stars were visible before we were sure that sundown had occurred and the next day was upon us. While I sat there, I began to think that Momma was gathering the girls to light Shabbos candles. As I daydreamed, two of the men in the congregation stopped to talk to me.

"Meyer," said Mr. Gross, "how did you get home?"

Before I could answer, Mr. Lubin said, "I have not heard a word from my Yitzchak. Have you seen him?"

I told him the story of how I saw him the day before the attack. What I didn't tell him was that it was unlikely that he survived the battle. I really did not know what happened to him, so I thought it better not to speculate.

As I began telling them the story of my escape, one of the men got up to the bimah in front to lead the ma'ariv service and began to sing, "Shalom Alechem," the traditional song to welcome Shabbos. I couldn't remember a Shabbos I welcomed more than this one. It also gave me the chance to say kaddish for my father. It was the traditional prayer of mourning that Jewish men said for the loss of a father and mother for eleven months after death. I took the opportunity to think about how much I missed and admired him as I said the words, and a tear came to my eye. I had not said it since I went back to the army after burying him. It required a minion, ten Jewish men, and I never ran into ten Jews at the same time in the Polish army.

After ma'ariv, we all walked to our respective homes to share Shabbos dinner with our families. As my brothers and I arrived at home, I could see the Shabbos candles burning through the window. When we walked in, there was chaos as my sisters were setting the table and bringing out the wine and challah. As the oldest male, I was now the man of the house and took my position at the head of the table to say Kiddush, the blessing of the wine and hamotzi, the blessing over bread.

Now we could eat the wonderful dinner they made. As expected, I was the center of attention, as they wanted to hear of the battle and how I survived and journeyed home. I was more interested in their lives and what they knew of the war.

I told the entire story of the German invasion and the overpowering might of the Nazis. My mother and sisters were horrified by my involvement in the actual battle, but the boys were thrilled and now looked at me as a hero. I certainly did not feel the role. I also told them how I believed they were taking over the railway and how I witnessed the gathering of Jewish families.

Momma and Rivka were following the news accounts in the daily Yiddish newspaper, the *Forward*. They reported that the Nazis were taking over the major cities, seizing homes and property, and executing anyone in their way. There were also reports of their focus on Jews, getting help from the local Polish authorities to identify them. They also reported that people who wanted to leave were taken prisoner. They wanted to know if I thought we should try to leave.

"Where would we go?" I asked. "We have Russia on one side and Germany on the other." We agreed to stay and try to have a normal life as long as possible.

"God will watch over us," said Momma, and we finished dinner in silence, not sure we believed we would be safe.

Yossel chimed in. "Since next Wednesday is Erev Rosh Hashanah, we have a lot of deliveries to make before yom tov. We better rest up good this Shabbos because we have a lot of work to do on Sunday." We agreed to focus on the family business.

The next two weeks were joyous, even though danger was looming around us. After Shabbos on Saturday night, the younger people gathered and had some good social time. The boys and girls were clearly flirting with each other, while several parents were taking evening walks, keeping an eye on the proceedings.

Sunday was a full day of work. We had a full schedule, as there was some construction going on in town. It was natural for me to step in, as I always worked with my father growing up. At lunchtime, my sister Naomi came to bring me lunch. Momma always assigned her to be my caretaker, and frankly I loved the attention. She was protective of me and told me how all the girls I had talked to the night before were no good and I should stay away from them. We ate together and became very close.

That afternoon, I was visited by the landlord who owned the property that the lumberyard was on. In fact, he was the single largest property owner in the town of Pysznica and, I suppose, the wealthiest man in town. He was tall, blond, and very handsome. He rode a beautiful white horse, definitely not Jewish. All the girls always noticed him. Interestingly he was never in the company of a woman but seen around town with several men. There were whispers of homosexuality, but we kept that to ourselves. Actually Mr. Szweda was very good to our family. He helped my papa start the business and never showed a hint of anti-Semitism. He came to the funeral, wore a kippah my father had given him, and was clearly shaken by the loss of an old friend.

He came over to see me. "Meyer, welcome home. I am so glad you survived the attack. I hear the stories of Nazis seizing land, and I am afraid they will eventually come here." I knew he was right.

He continued, "I just want you to know that if they come, I will do everything in my power to protect all the business owners who have been so loyal to me. We cannot defeat them in battle, but perhaps we can convince them that they are better off letting our town thrive."

I just shook my head and responded, "I am afraid from what I saw they will not listen to anyone. They are on a mission to take control of everything and will not stop until they do."

Mr. Szweda shook my hand very tightly and said, "Take care of your wonderful family and stay safe." He turned around and left, probably continuing to visit his other customers.

We continued to work for the next couple of days until Wednesday midday, when we closed to go home and prepare for Rosh Hashanah.

CHAPTER 4

A Rose Blooms in the Desert

⅄⅄⅄

When we arrived at home, as I expected, the smell of roast turkey and vegetables filled the house. Momma was cooking the traditional fare and enough for the three full days, since Rosh Hashanah ends on Friday night and we go right into Shabbos. The boys and I prepared ourselves for shul while the girls helped Momma in the kitchen. I was enjoying the routine that I'd missed for the last four years, but when I got to shul, the mood was somber.

Rabbi Unger, who was about sixty years old, had a very long white beard, and was bent over quite a bit, began to speak in Yiddish. "My friends, on this new year, we ask God for a sweet year and for forgiveness for our sins. But we live in very troubled times. The Nazis have invaded our country and are taking over in the big cities. Last year, they expelled all Polish Jews from Germany and sent them back to Poland. Now they are here, and there is danger everywhere. As their influence grows, the Jewish people are being targeted not only by German soldiers but also by anti-Semitic Poles, who use this as an excuse to inflict pain and suffering on the Jewish people. We must stay together and cling to our beliefs, continue to study Torah, and daven with kavone and koved, fervor and dignity, to ask for Mashiach, the Messiah, to come, so we may all live in peace and beauty."

I leaned over to Yossel. "Mashiach better have better airplanes and tanks than the Nazis."

Mr. Lubin turned around, put his forefinger up to his mouth, and whispered, "Shhh!"

I immediately stopped talking, as I didn't realize I was disrupting him as he listened intently for some comfort. He still had not heard from Yitzchak and feared, as I did, that he did not survive the battle. When Mashiach came, they would be reunited, so I showed respect and sat in silence. I daydreamed through the rest of the speech but woke up when the chazzan, the cantor leading the service, got up, and we all began to sing the Rosh Hashanah tune leading up to the barchu.

The rest of Rosh Hashanah was uneventful, although everyone was uneasy about the future of Poland and the Jewish people. We all went to shul the next day, but as we sat down to eat afterward, I raised an issue that created a big argument.

"We should think about leaving Poland for Russia or at least the Russian-controlled area of Poland. The Nazis are taking over all the land they can, and we are targets for whatever they plan to do."

Momma became very irritated. "We cannot just pick up and leave. We have a business, a home. This is where we live, and we are not moving."

Chava agreed. "What happens if we leave everything and we cannot get into Russia? The Russians do not treat Jews any better than the Poles. What is the point?"

"The point is, I think Mr. Szweda would buy the business and the house, and we could use the money to start a new life in Russia," I responded.

Momma put her foot down. "We don't know if the Nazis will even bother with us. We are staying."

We finished eating in silence. Yossel, Benjamin, and I made a half-hearted attempt to sing a few traditional songs, zamiros, but quickly benched singing the after-meal prayers and rose from the table. The girls cleaned the table.

Later, Naomi came to me. "If you think we should leave, I will follow you and settle in Russia."

I looked at her and said, "We both know the answer. I cannot leave Momma and the rest of the family. Papa is dead, and I am the man of the house. We will stay and hope for the best."

The rest of Rosh Hashanah and Shabbos was quiet, in that we had no more uncomfortable discussions. We buried our heads in the ground like onions and ignored the looming danger ahead.

As I rode my bicycle to work on Monday, I noticed quite a few mounted policemen patrolling the town. Pysznica was generally a quiet town, and the police were generally low key, although corrupt. For a Jew to remain in business without prejudice, Papa made regular payments for "permits" to several key police officers and local civil servants. When Papa died, they kept coming around, and Momma knew the routine and kept the money flowing. I suspected the heavy presence of the police might result in a visit today.

Surprisingly, the first visit came from Mr. Szweda. He looked very nervous. "Good day, Meyer. How was Rosh Hashanah?"

"Very nice," I said. "It is great to be home and celebrate with the family. It felt as if life were normal, but it is clear that things are far from normal. What's with the police?"

Mr. Szweda came around behind the counter and pulled me back into the office. "The Nazis bombed and invaded Stalowa Wola last night."

Stalowa Wola is a large industrial town about seven kilometers west of us, across the San River. It's the largest town in the region, with a new steel mill that had just opened recently and an ammunitions storage facility only known to army officials. I knew about it because of my army position, but obviously it was discovered by the Germans.

"The police are out as a reaction to the German attack," said Szweda. "I honestly do not know whose side they are on, and I am not sure they know. I don't think they will fight against Poland, but they blow with the wind, so who knows?"

I asked, "Have they taken any action?"

"Not yet," said Szweda.

As we were talking, we had our chance to get some answers straight from the horse's mouth. Two of Pysznica's finest rode up on their mounts. I did not know these guys, but Szweda did. "This can't be good," he said.

"My name is Officer Kozlowski, and this is Officer Wojciechoski. We understand this business is owned by Jews."

I replied sheepishly, "Yes, that is true."

"We have just been advised by the Stalowa Wola County Police that a new tax has been imposed on Jews and homosexual businesses, and you are to pay us ten thousand zlotys immediately," said Kozlowski.

When he said *homosexual*, he looked directly at Szweda. That answered that.

I responded, "I do not have so much money in the store, and business has been slow. I will need time to raise it," hoping they would move on over the next few days.

Szweda jumped in. "I own this property and many others in town and have no knowledge of such a tax."

"Then your tax will be much higher, homo!" screamed Kozlowksi. With that, he used his nightstick to break everything on the counter, scattering the files I was working on, and began hitting the cash register.

I yelled, "Stop!" and leaped over the counter to grab him. I knew attacking an officer was dangerous and illegal, but I just reacted. He was big and strong, but my military training surprised him, and I got in a few good punches. I saw Szweda lying on the floor from the corner of my eye, probably laid out by Wojciechoski. As I turned to help, I felt a sharp blow to the head. That was the last thing I remember.

I woke up in jail. Szweda was waiting for me outside the cell. He bribed the officers to let me out. I was outraged and told him we needed to report Kozlowski and Wojciechoski to their superiors.

Szweda looked at me like I was crazy and started laughing. "Their report said that they came in to buy some wood planks, and you tried to cheat them. When they protested, you started to fight. You're lucky to be alive. A Jew fighting policemen is not smart. They left me alone, as they know I still have connections with the police chief in town."

I confronted him. "Are you a homosexual?"

He looked at me very uncomfortably. "No one has ever come out and asked me," he said, whispering. "I hear the comments people make. Yes, I have relations with men. The Nazis hate me as much as you, so we are brothers in this war." He continued, "Now get your brothers, clean up the store, and close it up for the rest of the week, if you know what is good for you."

We took his advice. When I got home, everyone was waiting. "Where were you when all this was going on?" I asked my brothers.

Yossel replied, "Benjamin and I were taking inventory in the back of the yard. When we heard the commotion, we ran in the office and saw you get dragged out by the police and draped over one of their horses. Szweda stopped and told us he would take care of things. He seemed to be in some pain but told us to go home and wait for you."

Momma yelled, "You are fighting with police? Are you crazy?"

I explained what happened and that the police were taking advantage of the Nazi invasion of Stalowa Wola, and it was just a matter of time before they came here.

Over the next two days, we all cleaned up the mess. The windows were smashed, and many of the fixtures, shelves, and products were destroyed. The cash register was opened, and the few hundred zlotys we kept in the store were gone. We cleaned up, locked up the store, and went home. Yom Kippur was coming Friday night, so we looked forward to asking forgiveness for our sins during the past year. Oddly, the police were not patrolling the shtetl. This gave me a chance to heal a bit from the beating I took.

On Friday, we prepared for the fast of Yom Kippur. We ate lightly, and all went to shul for Kol Nidre, the prayer asking God to let us pray with those who have sinned during the year and that ushers in the holiest day of the Jewish year. It is a great spectacle, as the Torahs are removed and the chazzan begins the emotional chant. While Yom Kippur is a solemn day, the idea is to be uncomfortable—no food, no leather shoes. For me, it was a chance to totally focus on the moment, get absorbed in prayer, and forget about the outside world.

After services that night, there was nothing to do, so everyone went home quietly, went to sleep, and arose the next morning to return to shul to spend the entire day in prayer. Yossel, Benjamin, and I went early. Momma and the girls would come later, as was our tradition.

As we walked up to the shul, several men were congregating outside. "Look what the goyim have done!" cried one old man.

"What a shondah!" cried another.

There were broken windows and swastikas drawn on the outside walls. There were writings of "Dirty Jew" and "Kill all Jews" as well. Clearly the anti-Semites, who were numerous throughout Poland, were being encouraged and emboldened by the Nazi presence, and clearly the police would do nothing. We all went inside and began the Pizukei Dezimra, the opening prayers, while some of us, including me and the boys, cleaned up the broken glass and looked for any scraps of wood and cloth to cover up the broken windows. I would come back after yom tov with proper materials to seal up the windows until they could be replaced.

The rest of Yom Kippur was uneventful, but while we pounded our chests as we listed all our sins during the Al Chait and bowed and laid on the ground during the Aleinu, I leaned over to Yossel and asked, "Why do we need forgiveness when the sins against us are much greater than anything we have done?"

The next day, it was back to work, but something was different. As we closed the shop for the day and headed home, we noticed a lot of new faces in the shtetl. Several Jewish families arrived—some with luggage, some just with packages—but clearly they had been displaced, and they were looking for a place to stay.

When I got home, Momma was out in front of the house, talking to a family.

"My name is Jonah Goldin," said the eldest man. "The Nazis have evicted us from our home and business in Rozwadow. Most of our neighbors are fleeing east to the Russian-controlled territories, but I am not well and am hoping we can find a room to rent and stay here."

Momma replied, "We have a full house with seven of us, but I am sure we have some neighbors who would be happy to have your family stay with them."

I suggested Mr. Lubin. "I know a man whose son I served with in the war is missing in action. He may be very interested in having a family live with him."

Momma weighed in. "Why don't you come in for dinner, and we can help you find a home."

"Thank you so much," said Mr. Goldin. "We have had a difficult trip. This is my wife, Shayna. These are my children. My eldest daughter, Miriam; my other daughters, Pearl and Ruth; and my sons, Leibish and little Shlomo, who is six years old," said Jonah.

Inviting them to dinner was a great idea. The three young girls were very pretty, but I was immediately drawn to Miriam, the eldest, who I learned was nineteen years old. She was tall, just as tall as me. She had long brown hair and was slender and shapely. Her little brother Shlomo was clinging to her and was obviously very shy. Miriam looked at me and smiled, and I knew I wanted to get to know her. Naomi, my protector from all females, saw the exchange and gave me a dirty look.

Rozwadow was a suburb of Stalowa Wola. It was essentially a shtetl with about two thousand observant Jews, ten times the size of our little town. If they chased all the Jews out of Rozwadow, none of us were safe living here, just on the other side of the San River.

The girls were able to whip up some food for the two large families, which I thought was quite amazing on such short notice. After dinner, I took Jonah and Miriam over to meet Mr. Lubin, while Shayna stayed back at our house with the children. Mr. Lubin was widowed, and now, sadly, he'd probably lost his only son. He answered the door immediately.

"Mr. Lubin," I began, not knowing how he would react, "this is Mr. Goldin and his daughter Miriam. The Nazis have evicted them from their home in Rozwadow, and they are looking for a room to rent. I immediately thought of you."

Lubin invited us in for a cup of tea. Messer's. Lubin and Goldin seem to hit it off. Mr. Goldin was a colonel in the Austrian army during World War I, where he became a heavy smoker. Lubin offered up some cigarettes. Smoke filled the room as they shared their stories of war, pain, and loss.

They seemed content to keep talking, so I asked Miriam to take a walk to show her the town. She agreed immediately, obviously as bored with the conversation as I was. I asked her what happened in Rozwadow that led them here.

CHAPTER 5

Miriam's Story

"I REALLY HAD A WONDERFUL childhood, but the last year has been very difficult, and now we are homeless." Miriam began to cry and asked, "How does that happen?"

I took her hand and said, "It's all right; you are safe now." She calmed down a little. She looked at me with her big brown eyes, and I felt a shock go through my body. Showing affection in public was forbidden, but she squeezed my hand and said, "Thank you."

She continued, "Even though we lived in the shtetl, I was allowed to go to public schools with the goyim. Many of my parents' friends thought it was horrible, a shonda, that we could go to school outside our little world, but my parents were determined to give us a Polish education so we could get along in the world while maintaining our religious observances. This was quite progressive in our town. We spoke Yiddish in the house but Polish outside and for business. It was actually a good experience, even though I did see a lot of anti-Semitism from the children. I had some non-Jewish friends, but some of my classmates were clear that they would not talk to me. They never said anything but would turn away when I walked by. Clearly this was something they were taught by the adults.

"In the shtetl, we lived separate from the rest of the world, but in public school, I was allowed to interact with the goyim, although we were taught not to get too friendly.

"Later I went to a trade school, where I learned how to sew. I am quite good with a needle and thread, which became useful in the family business.

"Most of the people in the shtetl were quite poor, but my father owned a grocery and liquor store. When I turned sixteen, it was time for me to get to work, so he got me a sewing machine and I began to take in mending work. I even made some dresses for the local women. It was fun, and I was helping the family. In 1936, we moved into a beautiful new house. We enjoyed life. We were able to balance Jewish life with being part of the Polish society.

"That all changed in the last year. The Poles in Stalowa Wola became more vocal about their hatred for Jews. Signs were posted by local officials to boycott Jewish businesses. I thought that was crazy and no one would listen. But in fact they did. Our business got so slow that we started closing on Fridays and Sundays and early on the other days.

"In recent weeks, we were attacked by locals breaking windows and taking whatever they could when we were closed.

"Finally, last week, the Nazis started bombing Stalowa Wola. The Nazis took over the town and marched into the Rozwadow shtetl on Yom Kippur. They ordered all Jews to leave immediately. We were shocked. How could they? What did we do to them? This was our home. We spent our entire lives there in peace, working, praying, living our lives, and not bothering anyone. We gathered with our neighbors and refused at first.

"A group of German soldiers and Polish policemen marched into the shtetl and picked a bunch of random homes, maybe ten, maybe twelve. They arrested the families who lived there and dragged them to the center of town under guard. The Germans gave the orders, and the Polish police carried them out. Then they marched through the streets announcing that all residents of the Rozwadow ghetto must come to the town square immediately. There were approximately two thousand Jews in the shtetl at that time.

"A big crowd gathered in the town square. They built a platform, where we saw the families gathered. I knew some but not all. A Nazi officer stood up with a loudspeaker and announced, 'The German army and Nazi party are now in charge of the region of Stalowa Wola. All Jews must leave this town immediately and leave all belongings and valuables behind. To show the importance of these orders, we will show what happens if you do not leave in forty-eight hours. These Jew criminals will be punished for all to see.'

"With that, fires began to rage all around us. They burned down the homes of these poor people. The owners and their families were in the square, including women and children. As the fires were smoldering, the officer announced that owners of these homes were criminals and that the punishment was death. Shots rang out. We could not see who did the shooting from where we were, but we could see those poor people fall to their deaths. They killed them all for nothing."

She began to cry again. "I'd never seen a dead person. It was horrible. Blood everywhere. We were ordered to bury them. My brother Leibish joined them to help. My father is ill and could not help. We knew it was hopeless."

I put my arms around her and hugged her tight.

"I feel safe for the first time in a long time," she said.

"I don't know what to say," I said softly. "I tried to get my family to move east to Russia, but Momma would not leave."

She continued, "My father is ill. He is weak from severe stomach issues. His legs are swollen from gout, and he is in pain when he walks. He also has this horrible cough, which I tell him is from smoking, but he doesn't believe me. After that, armed soldiers and police began to roam the streets as we and our neighbors gathered our belongings and left. Most of our neighbors were headed to Russian-controlled Poland, but Father cannot make the trip. We gathered anything of value that we could carry, gold and silver jewelry and money. We took some clothes, and we left our beautiful home and our business and crossed the river to the closest town with Jews we could find. Here we are, and I have no idea what will happen to us."

"For me, I am glad you are here," I said. "I will do everything I can to help you and your family. Let's get back to Lubin's house and see if you have a place to stay." I was thrilled to have a new friend. I guess we were gone a long time. By the time we got back, the whole family was at the Lubin house, moving in.

"Where were you?" asked Shayna.

"We just took a walk," Miriam said defensively.

I said good-bye and headed home.

"Where were you?" asked Naomi when I got home.

"I just met the girl I am going to marry," I responded.

Naomi yelled, "Some poor homeless girl shows up at your door asking for help and you are ready to get married? Are you mishuga? Momma, did you hear this? Meyer wants to get married."

"I didn't say I wanted to marry her now; I just like her," I replied.

Momma laughed. "Everybody calm down. No one is getting married today."

It was back to work the next day. Business was slow. It seemed the boycott on Jewish businesses had spread. I was working on the books, but my mind was wandering. I had never felt this way before. Then, as if a dream came true, Miriam walked into the store.

"Hello, Meyer," she said, flashing a beautiful smile. She was wearing a plain blue dress, but it fit perfectly and showed off her beautiful curvy figure.

I was clearly smitten. I stood up to say hello and banged my knee on the desk drawer. I had to do everything in my power not to scream out in pain, but she knew I was hurt and came over to see if she could help. As I was telling her everything was fine, Naomi walked in with her daily lunch delivery for me and the boys.

"What is she doing here?" asked Naomi quite angrily.

"I just came by to thank Meyer for his help finding us a place to stay," replied Miriam. "Can I help you with the food?"

"No." Naomi was nasty.

I called her into the back. "What are you so angry about?" I asked.

"I hate her," she spewed.

"Why? Because I like her? Jealous? Be nice," I begged.

"Fine," she said as she stormed away.

Miriam got the message. "Thank you, Meyer. My family appreciates everything you did for us. Please come by so we can all thank you."

I took that as an opening and said, "I will come by, but mostly I want to see you again."

She smiled, said good-bye, and left.

Naomi just rolled her eyes and said, "Here, eat your lunch so I can go home and throw up."

After work the next day, I took Miriam up on her offer and stopped in to see the Goldins. Mr. Lubin came out to greet me. "Thank you for introducing me to the Goldins. It's nice to have people in the house, and Shayna and the girls are good cooks, so things are working out great."

Well, that was unexpected. "It looks like everyone is doing well," I said.

Miriam came out and said, "Please come inside." She grabbed my hand, and I felt a shock go through my system.

Inside, Mr. Goldin was sitting in the living room, reading the Yiddish paper, and Mrs. Goldin came out of the kitchen when Miriam went in to tell her I was there. Mr. Goldin was weak but struggled to stand up to shake my hand.

"Thank you for introducing us to Mr. Lubin. When we came, we had no idea if we would be able to survive what the Nazis did to us, but thanks to you, we are here. Mr. Lubin tells me you are a fine young man. He is heartbroken about his missing son, but he has nothing but good things to say about you."

"Thank you," I said, somewhat embarrassed.

Mr. Goldin continued, "You know I was in the Austrian army during the Great War. Galicia was part of Austria before Poland was formed at the end of the war in 1918. I held the rank of colonel and led men to their deaths in battle. I know what you went through when the Nazis attacked, and I am proud that you fought bravely and happy you were able to come home. I guess we are all lucky you were here to help us."

Now I was really embarrassed but grateful for his words.

"Would you like to join us for dinner?" asked Mrs. Goldin, as she had clearly taken over the household.

"Thank you, but I am expected at home. I have to help my brothers put up our sukkah tonight. It would look bad if the owners of the lumberyard did not have a nice sukkah." I laughed. "I hope you will visit us and eat in our sukkah this week." With that, I turned to leave.

"Meyer," called out Mr. Goldin. He struggled to get up from his chair. He grabbed a nearby cane and my arm. "Let's talk," he said as we walked outside. "Miriam likes you—a lot. You are all she talks about. I expect she is the reason you came around here today. These are difficult times, and you two cannot think of romance or marriage. We do not know what will happen to any of us. I am weak and will not be able to fight off the Germans when the time comes. I am glad you found each other, but I want you to promise me that you will protect her as best you can if needed."

I was shocked. I had just met her, but he saw right through me. I had to respond, "I will take good care of her. I liked her from the first time I saw her. I plan to see her a lot more. Thank you." With that, I skipped and danced home, very proud of myself. She liked me, and I liked her. I never felt this way about anyone, but Mr. Goldin was right. It was terrible timing.

When I got home, Naomi called out, "How's your girlfriend?"

Does she have spies out watching me? "Great," I replied. "She likes me, and I plan to see a lot more of her, so get used to it." That shut her up.

The boys had all the lumber laid out behind the house. The sukkah was to be built as a temporary dwelling that reminded us of how our ancestors who were freed from slavery in Egypt lived as they wandered through the desert. All the families in town had their own design and architecture, using whatever materials they had and could afford. We drove eight ten-centimeter-by-ten-centimeter wooden posts into the ground, two and a half meters in height, in a rectangular shape. We secured them on top with five-centimeter-by-ten-centimeter planks that were nailed to the top, tying the posts together. We then covered the sides all around with canvas sheeting, leaving only an opening for the doorway, framed with additional five-by-ten planks. The top was covered with branches and leaves we gathered from the woods nearby. The roof was supposed to be open to the elements so sunlight and moonlight could come through. Unfortunately, it meant that rain and wind could also come through.

The idea was to actually live in the sukkah for eight days. That meant sleeping and eating your meals. As young kids, we would usually spend a couple of nights sleeping there, but the minute it got cold or rainy, we would sneak into the house and crawl into our warm beds. We did try to eat our meals in the sukkah.

Once we finished building it, the girls came out, and we all decorated it with flowers, fruit, and Jewish stars and other symbols. It was a great project that brought the family together. Chava picked up the lulav and etrog from the shul that morning, and we were now ready for Erev Sukkot, which started the next night.

On Thursday, the first day of Sukkot, we went to shul as always. Mr. Lubin came with Mr. Goldin and his sons and sat near us. We davened peacefully but with great urgency. Our world was collapsing all around us, yet somehow we expected our prayers to be answered and the Nazis and Poles who were persecuting Jews would cease to be our enemies. Hindsight says that was foolish, but prayer was our strongest weapon at that time.

Regardless, I invited the Goldins and Mr. Lubin to lunch that Shabbos, for obvious reasons, and they agreed. After shul on Shabbos, we walked to our house. I led them all to the back, where the sukkah had been prepared for a sit-down lunch for the fifteen people. It was quite crowded, but I made kiddush, the blessing over the wine, and then we all squeezed into our seats while the women began serving food. They all kept their eyes on me and Miriam, wondering when we would make our escape from the meal and disappear. We didn't disappoint. Miriam rose and grabbed some soiled dishes to bring back into the house. On her way back out, I grabbed her arm and guided her out of the yard and down the street.

"Meyer," she protested, "let me tell my parents I am leaving."

"Don't worry; they know what we are up to," I said glibly, and we strolled down the road. I felt nervous as we walked to the edge of the road near a wooded area. I wanted to get some privacy with her.

I stopped walking and took both her hands in mine. "Miriam," I said softly, "I can't stop thinking about you. I think you like me as well. Even your father told me so."

"He told you? I am shocked that he would even notice," she said.

At that moment, I pulled her close and kissed her. She started to push me away and then put her arms around me, and we kissed for a very long time.

"This is so wrong," she said. "Our world is crumbling all around us. It's not right for us to behave this way. What would your mother think and your sister who hates me?"

With that, we both started to laugh hysterically and couldn't stop. Finally, I calmed down and said, "I think I am falling in love with you."

"You're crazy," Miriam replied. "I hardly know you."

"I think you are falling in love with me too," I insisted.

"Take me back; this is crazy. You are crazy to think of love at such a time," she insisted.

I kissed her again. She didn't resist.

CHAPTER 6

Rebellion

⅄ ⅄ ⅄

THE REST OF SUKKOT WAS a blur but delightful. Miriam and I spent every possible moment together, sneaking off into the woods whenever possible. Each time, we would go deeper and deeper into the wilderness to escape the realities of the occupation. Her skin was soft, and her body was firm, a beautiful combination of youth. While the air was beginning to chill, we kept warm, making love draped in blankets I sneaked out of the house. We believed the world was coming to an end, and the modesty we were taught as children was buried deep in our memories. We did not speak of marriage. We did not speak of tomorrow. Only today mattered, as we did not know what would happen tomorrow.

Thursday night was Simchas Torah, the last day of Sukkot and the celebration of finishing the annual reading of the Torah. The men of the shtetl celebrated hard, dancing in the street with all the Torahs and drinking schnapps into the night. Even the children took part in the celebration. I took little Shlomo into the fun and gave him a little sip of my drink. He loved it. He was the apple of Miriam's eye, and she wanted me to keep an eye on him. She would not be happy that I got him a little drunk, but we knew our way of life was about to change so we allowed ourselves a little extra. The festivities lasted all night and all day Friday. Soon it would be Shabbos, and we all needed a true day of rest.

Sunday, it was back to work. Business was slow, as the boycott of Jewish businesses spread to our little town. As the days passed, we talked about cutting back on the hours and maybe even closing completely. As we were contemplating what to do, Mr. Szweda rode up, carrying a big case.

"Hello, Meyer," he said in a quiet, solemn voice as he placed the case on the counter. He took off the cover and revealed a radio. No one I knew in the shtetl had a radio, and I had only rarely seen one. Mr. Szweda said, "They have been making announcements all day that I want you to hear."

He plugged the radio in and turned it on. It took a minute to warm up. Mr. Szweda said, "I am tuning in to the local Stalowa Wola station. Every thirty minutes, they are making an announcement that all in the shtetl need to hear."

Orchestral music was playing. I looked at Mr. Szweda and said, "What announcement are you talking about?"

He replied, "Just wait a few minutes."

The music went on for about ten more minutes while Mr. Szweda sat quietly with his hands over his face. While it was going on, Yossel and Benjamin came into the office.

I interrupted them as they were asking what was happening. "Sit down, boys. Mr. Szweda says we need to listen to this."

Finally, the symphony ended and an announcer came on. "The following is an announcement from the German Nazi Party. On September 30, the president of Poland, Ignacy Mościcki, and Władysław Raczkiewicz, the speaker of the senate, have resigned their posts and, along with other Polish leaders in the senate, have fled Poland. As a result, Poland is now part of the Third Reich of Germany. Due to the glorious victory of the army of the Third Reich, the people of Poland have been freed from the tyrannical and criminal government of the Republic of Poland and will now be part of the strongest, most advanced nation in the world, led by the great chancellor Adolph Hitler." With that, the announcement ended and another voice came on the radio.

"This is the part you need to hear," said Szweda.

"This is Frederick Bronski reporting. The following announcement is for the residents of the Stalowa Wola district. Effective immediately, the soldiers of the Third Reich and all Polish law enforcement officers have full jurisdiction over all Polish citizens and businesses. You must obey all orders received from the authorities. In addition, there are special rules that apply to Juden throughout the district. The Juden have been found to be responsible for most crime throughout the Third Reich, including 34 percent of drug peddling, 47 percent of robberies, and 82 percent of international crime organizations. Most live in ghettos, which are filthy and unkempt, even though they are all in business and very rich. Some are hiding among us, assimilating into Western society, dressing like us and shaving their beards. They must be found and controlled. The following rules will now be applied to all Jews in the district. All Jewish-owned businesses will close immediately. All assets of Jewish-owned businesses will now be the property of the Third Reich, and Nazi-assigned agents will be in charge of those assets. All residents of Jewish ghettos will be restricted to those areas. They will be identified and must not leave their designated areas. All Jews who live outside the ghettos will be relocated to the nearest ghetto and will be restricted to those areas. All Jews able to work will make themselves available to the authorities on a daily basis for labor assignments at the discretion of the authorities. This is Frederick Bronski reporting."

"God Almighty, what are you doing to us?" I said to no one in particular.

"They're going to kill us all!" yelled Benjamin.

Yossel looked at me and declared, "We must fight them. I have friends who have weapons, and we are ready to fight. Meyer, you must join us. You have military experience, and we need leaders."

I replied, "I've also seen how the entire Polish army buckled under the overwhelming might of the Germans. Now they also have whatever

Polish army and police are left at their disposal. We cannot go to war and defeat them."

Yossel snapped back, "So are you giving up? Are you just going to let them march in here and make us slaves, like our ancestors in Egypt?"

I was very perturbed. "We don't have a choice. It's about to happen whether we like it or not. We cannot defeat them, but I agree that we must try to organize an underground and try to survive and help our families survive. In the meantime, let's take anything we have here that is of value and bring it home. Then go tell your friends I will join you and set a meeting to discuss how to organize our efforts."

Mr. Szweda unplugged the radio and put the cover on. "This will be the last time I see you all for a long time. I have to go into hiding. I am a homosexual, and the Nazis have declared war on me as well. I am also about to lose all my properties, so I must gather my valuables as well and flee. I wish you all long life and hope we all survive this."

I embraced him in a bear hug. "Thank you for all your help. You supported my father and family and have been very good to us when other Poles turned us away. You are a good man, and we all need to survive this."

Mr. Szweda replied, "Good luck to all of us," and with that, he left.

We took the cash we had in the store and all books and records we did not want to leave for the Nazis. We had saws and other tools we used to cut wood and build prefabricated structures for our customers. We loaded pushcarts we had with all of these items and began the trip home. Maybe we could sell these. Obviously all our lumber inventory had to be left for the Nazi thieves who were coming to take over. While we kept busy loading our possessions, my thoughts were on our uncertain futures, as we were hated by all now in power. Why would the Germans invade Poland just to make the Jews miserable? We were good at that ourselves.

We pushed the carts into the shtetl, and a few people who saw us stopped to ask what was going on. I realized the good and pious Jews of Pysznica had no idea what was about to happen. I told all I saw to meet me after ma'ariv, the evening prayers, and I would explain it to all. "Bring all you know, as our lives are about to change."

We passed the Lubin house, so I stopped in to tell them as well.

Miriam saw me coming and answered the door. "What are you doing?" she asked, as I was sweating from pushing the cart.

I pulled her aside. "We heard a radio announcement from the Nazis. They are taking over our businesses and are making us workers for their use, slavery. I am asking everyone in the shtetl to come to shul tonight so I can explain. Please tell your father and Lubin."

She did not get upset, which surprised me. "After they chased us from Rozwadow, I knew they were ruthless, and nothing would surprise me. I knew we would not be safe for long here, although I wanted to believe that we would. I will let them know." Miriam went inside, and I rejoined my brothers for the final push home.

When we arrived, we pushed the carts into the backyard, where the sukkah was still up. Momma, Rivka, and Chava came out to see what was going on. I asked them to wait in the sukkah and went inside, where Naomi was cleaning the kitchen. "Come outside," I said. She saw the seriousness on my face and followed me out. We all sat in the sukkah while I explained the radio broadcast we had heard earlier. Chava began to cry uncontrollably. Benjamin put his arms around her and hugged her, trying to calm her down. Momma, Rivka, and Naomi were stoic and calm.

"We should have headed to Russia when Meyer suggested it," declared Naomi defiantly.

Momma sat quietly, almost acknowledging she was right.

"It's too late now," I replied. "The countryside is crawling with Nazi soldiers and Polish sympathizers. We will stay, resist, and try to survive as best we can. Hopefully the stories we hear are exaggerated and we can survive this."

With that, I went inside to try to decide what I was going to tell the people of the shtetl that night.

As it became dark, we all went to the shul. They were finishing up ma'ariv. Most of the town and a few people I did not recognize showed up. The Goldins were all there. Miriam sat with her parents and her siblings, close to the front. I cannot remember a time when men and women sat together in the shul. I got up in front and began to speak in Yiddish. "Chevra, friends. Today I heard some very disturbing news on the radio, an announcement by the government that will affect all our lives in the future." I quoted the announcement word for word as I remembered it. It would likely be reported in the Yiddish papers tomorrow if they were being published. In recent days, the papers sometimes came and sometimes did not. I assumed some form of authority would come there soon, and I wanted to let everyone know we were all in danger and that they should prepare the best they could. "This is all the information I have, and I would like anyone who has any other information to share it with us."

A young man came up. He was a stranger and clean shaven. He could pass for German. "My name is Oskar Hart. I just arrived from Stalowa Wola, where I was employed as an accountant in a German firm. The Nazis have taken control of the city, and the announcement you heard is being implemented. I escaped before I could be captured. Although I have assimilated into German society, I have been known to be Jewish, and no one is safe from these murderers. They are working their way east and should be here soon. My plan is to flee eastward, hopefully reaching Russia before they capture me. All interested may join me."

At that moment, several young men from the shtetl rose and began to shout that we must resist the invasion and that Hart was a coward. Clearly the resistance movement that Yossel talked about was beginning to manifest itself. Among the shouters were Leibish, Miriam's brother, and Yossel. I looked at Miriam, and she was just as shocked as me that this was happening.

Leibish seemed to be speaking for the group. "We cannot allow these Nazi criminals to take our homes and businesses and take over our lives. We must fight. We are organizing all the young men in the shtetl, and we will keep the invaders out any way possible."

Oskar shouted back, "The Germans are way too strong for a few hotheads to challenge them. They will kill you and your families. Trying to escape is the only smart action we can take."

I knew he was right, but the boys were determined to make their presence known, and their screaming got louder. The elders in the room tried to get their children under control. Miriam helped her father stand up. He turned to Leibish and told him to sit and be quiet. They began arguing with each other. Everyone was either angry or scared, and it was turning into total chaos. I felt that I had caused this tumult, but we had to face the imminent danger to our lives.

At that moment, the doors to the shul burst open, and a group of Polish policemen entered, carrying rifles and pistols and pointing them toward the crowd. No one seemed to notice, and the shouting matches continued. I recognized the two officers who had trashed the lumberyard, so I knew what they were capable of and that this could be a disaster. As I got up to warn the people, the sergeant who seemed to be in charge fired his rifle through a window above the bimah, and glass rained down on some of us. That got everyone's attention, and the crowd quieted down.

The sergeant walked up to the bimah, where I was standing, and addressed the crowd. "All Jews of Pysznica are now under the jurisdiction of the police and the Nazi Party. You must not leave this ghetto and stay in your homes until you are given further instructions. We will have officers posted at every exit of the ghetto, and anyone caught trying to escape will be shot. Now everyone is to leave this building at once."

I was worried that Leibish and Benjamin would start a brawl and get themselves killed, but they didn't. The officers started poking some of the people who were not moving fast enough for their liking. Slowly but surely, everyone began filing out of the shul. Leibish helped his father up, and they hugged as he rose. He was emotional, and I was afraid he would do something stupid. I walked out with my mother, who was hanging on to me for dear life. She was scared not for herself but for her six children. Miriam held hands with Shlomo and would not let go as he tried to run around and get away from her. I so wanted to comfort her at that moment but held back and walked home with the family. There was not much to say or do, so we all sat together for a while, trying to comfort each other. Eventually we went to sleep.

The next morning, we woke up to blaring loudspeaker announcements. I could not make out what they were saying, so I went outside. It seemed like I overslept, for when I went out, the whole shtetl seemed to already be lining the street.

"What is going on?" I asked Momma.

"The Nazis will arrive tomorrow. Listen. They keep repeating the announcement," she replied.

Sure enough, there was a police truck cruising the streets with a loudspeaker, announcing, "Juden of Pysznica, by order of the ruling Nazi Party, you will all become subjects of the Third Reich of Germany. Under the dictum of the government in Berlin, all Jewish-owned businesses and assets owned by those businesses are now the property of the Third Reich and will be assigned managers. Tomorrow a group of Nazi officers and oberscharführers, senior squad leaders, will arrive in Pysznica to advise local authorities on how to carry out the new edicts. Tomorrow morning, at oh eight hundred hours, all able-bodied Jewish men between the ages of sixteen and sixty are to gather in front of your synagogue for inspection and assignment to new jobs. Anyone who tries to leave the ghetto or disobeys these orders in any way will be punished. Police officials will be posted throughout the shtetl twenty-four hours a day. We urge all residents to stay in or near your houses."

One minute later, the announcement started again.

We went inside. Yossel was incensed and very animated. "We can't sit around and let them make us slaves. Leibish and I are organizing a meeting as soon as it gets dark at the Lubin house. Mr. Lubin is with us one hundred percent. His son was murdered by those bastards, and he can't stand that more of us will meet the same fate."

I looked at him and shook my head. "I'll be there, but I'm telling you I will not allow any crazy suicide missions. If we are going to resist, we have to be careful or you'll get us all killed."

It was late November and starting to get dark early. About 6:00 p.m., Benjamin, Yossel, and I walked over to the Lubin house. The streets were quiet, no sign of police. The front door was unlocked. The living room was packed with about twenty young men from the shtetl, the Goldin family, and the three of us. I went over to Miriam, who now had a look of horror.

"My brother wants to singlehandedly fight the Nazis," she said.

"I know." I said nothing else.

Once everyone was settled, Leibish stood in front of the group and preached forcefully. "The Nazis will be here soon. There are reports all over Poland that they turned Jewish communities into slave labor camps and have taken everything. We must not let this happen to us. A group of us have gathered rifles, handguns, and ammunition, and we will fight them and keep them out. The weapons are hidden in an abandoned barn near the woods. We need volunteers to help us for the cause."

Before I could interrupt, Mr. Goldin shouted, "Boys!" and slowly stood up with all his strength. "The Nazis came to us in Rozwadow, and with lightning speed and strength, they confiscated our homes and our possessions and sent us out from our town with nothing. A few determined boys and a few guns are not going to deter them. Better to surprise them with small attacks than try to meet head-on in battle."

"I agree," I chimed in. "We cannot destroy them, but maybe we can make them think we are more than what we are."

"How do you suggest we do that, Mr. Soldier?" said an annoyed Leibish.

I replied, "Snipers. A well-placed group of hidden shooters can take out a few soldiers and put them on their heels. We need hiding places for the weapons as well. Nothing in anyone's homes, as that would put everyone in danger. We can also make some fiery bombs, Molotov cocktails, which can be set to blow up vehicles and buildings. This will be extraordinarily dangerous, and we might all get killed, but this may be better than what they have planned for us."

Miriam looked at me in horror and cried out, "You're going to turn these boys into murderers?"

"Not murderers," I insisted. "We are killing to protect our lives, just as Jews have done for centuries."

Leibish interrupted. "This is too little, too late. We must meet them as they arrive outside the shtetl and open fire and defeat them."

Oskar Hart, our German-looking stranger, stood up and said, "Even if you are successful, they'll bring in double the number of soldiers and kill you all."

Leibish snapped back, "If we do nothing, we will die anyway. Who is with me to attack?"

No one stood with Leibish.

Yossel stood up. "I'm with Meyer. Let's arm ourselves and chase them out."

At that moment, I felt sick at the prospect of my dear brother taking up arms. About a dozen other young men stood up to join us, including Leibish, who shook my hand, and we had our sniper force. I had no idea if any of these kids had ever shot a gun before, but I would do my best to teach them in what little time we had.

The meeting broke up, and Miriam came over in tears and gave me a hug. She looked into my eyes but didn't have to say anything. I knew what she was thinking, and I loved her too. The new Pysznica army gathered and headed to the barn where the weapons were hidden. It began to rain as we arrived, but there were kerosene lamps in the barn, which we lit. There, lying under a canvas sheet, were about twenty Polish Karabinek WZ 29 army rifles, just like the one the Nazi soldiers took from me during the blitzkrieg, and fifteen Pistolet WZ 35 handguns, also Polish-army issue, with caches of ammunition to match.

"Leibish, where in the world did you get these?" I asked.

"I found them," he replied evasively.

"You found them?" I replied sarcastically. "Where?"

Leibish said, "On the way out of Rozwadow, I noticed a rifle sticking out of an abandoned barn much like this one. A few days after we got settled in Mr. Lubin's house, I mentioned the gun I saw at the barn. Lubin asked why I didn't take it. I told him my parents would not have allowed me to stop. We were all anxious to get as far from Rozwadow as possible, so I let it be. I told him I was thinking about going back to get it. He said he would go with me, so one night after everyone went to sleep, we hopped on bicycles and headed to Rozwadow. I knew about where the barn was, not far across the San River, over the same bridge that brought us here. It was about twenty-five meters off the road, but I had noticed it walking by. Sure enough, it was still there as I saw it. When we got to the barn, we went in. It looked like a Polish army squad abandoned all their gear and deserted the army. In addition to these guns, there were uniforms and boots and things. There were also pushcarts used by the abandoned farm. We loaded what we could in the pushcarts, including the bicycles, covered them with these tarps, and headed back here. We knew we would have to be home before we would be noticed, so we stopped on this side of the river, ditched them in the woods, and rode home before anyone knew. The next night, we did it again. This time, we made it back before morning. Lubin knew of this abandoned barn, so here we are. We told no one until tonight."

"I give you a lot of credit for getting all this here, but I'm afraid our rebellion will not last long," I said in a defeated tone.

We began our training session.

CHAPTER 7

The Hammer Comes Down

⅄⅄⅄

Our group of volunteers were between the ages of sixteen and twenty-five. There were thirteen, including me. There were only two others who had military training, Henry Grossman, who was a private in the Lodz Army, and Nachman Herschell, who was a private in the Modlin Army. They were both in fierce battles in the first few days of the invasion and somehow survived. The Lodz Army was defeated defending the Lodz region, just north of where the Krakow Army was based. The Modlin Army was assigned to defend Warsaw and had to retreat as the German forces overran them and marched into Warsaw, resulting in the exile of the current government. We shared our stories. None of us could claim victory, but we were proud to have served our country, even though the majority of our brothers in arms would have been just as happy to put a bullet in a Polish Jew as any German soldier, which I never understood. We each took a group of volunteers, assigned them a rifle and pistol, and showed them how to clean and load them. I had Benjamin, Leibish, and two others. Yossel was in the group with Nachman.

As we removed the bolts and cleaning rods from the guns, I could see the fear in the faces of the new recruits. They were determined to learn how to transform from being students learning the teachings of Talmud and Torah to killers in a matter of hours. They learned all the parts of the rifles and pistols. They learned which parts had to be removed for cleaning, how to clean them, and how put them back together. The next lesson was how to load them and which bullets fit each weapon. By the time we finished lesson one, it was midnight. Each sniper had a rifle and pistol assigned to him. We decided to sleep in the barn, get up at dawn, and start lesson two: how to shoot the damn things. We spread out as much as possible. It was cold, but we had hay and tarps to try and keep warm. As I settled in, I was filled with thoughts of dread. "This is insane. We're all dead men." I consoled myself with the thought that we had no choice. Better to die fighting than as pacifists. All those thoughts kept circling in a loop around my head. Finally, I fell asleep.

The next thing I remember was Benjamin yelling, "Wake up, Meyer! I want to shoot these things."

Sure enough, the sun was coming out. Everyone was milling about. I arose, and we gathered out back. Henry and Nachman gathered our students and lined them up. Henry found some cans and boxes and set them out about twenty-five meters as targets. We were several kilometers from any homes, so no one would hear us. The weapons were loaded from the night before, and it's a wonder no one shot themselves. No time for safety.

We lined them up and began with the rifles, the weapon of choice for professional snipers. The shooting began. We should have been aiming at the barn because none of them could have hit it. A couple had their eyes closed. The recoil of the rifles knocked down a couple of the younger boys, including Benjamin. They reminded me of when I started my training. I stopped them and showed them some techniques, how to stand, hold the gun, aim, and squeeze the trigger. I saw my fellow teachers doing the same thing. Good old Polish military training. Not much good against the Germans. "Stop it," I told myself.

I lined them up again. This time, they took more care. Of my four protégés, two actually were pretty good, including Leibish. They even hit the target a few times. The other two were getting better but not great. I let them shoot fifty rounds each. We had plenty of ammunition, but who knew how long we would be able to hold out.

We gathered together after the shooting ended. "Remember, hide the guns somewhere away from home," I instructed, and off we went.

Benjamin, Yossel, and I found a spot in the woods not far from the barn. We hid the weapons and ammunition behind a fallen tree and covered them up with branches and leaves. Then we headed home. We didn't speak a word. We just walked briskly back to the shtetl.

Momma must have seen us walking up to the house. She stood at the door. "Where have you been all night?" she demanded. "I heard about your meeting from Miriam and that you organized some sort of militia."

I replied, "Yes, everyone is scared, and we want to defend ourselves. We spent the night teaching Benjamin, Yossel, and others how to shoot guns that Leibish had gathered from his trip from Rozwadow." I was mostly honest but conveniently left out the sniper discussion.

"Well, we are stuck here for better or for worse now," Momma quietly continued. "We don't know what the Germans have planned for us, if anything."

"If anything?" I snapped back. "They all hate us. The Germans and the Poles. Now they have the power and the authority to do what they want with us. We must find a way to fight back! Listen to me. I know this is hopeless…"

Just then, Naomi came into the house. "Come see what's happening!"

We went out and found both German soldiers and Polish policemen scattered along the main road. They were brandishing their weapons and telling us to go to the main square in front of the shul.

When we arrived, it seemed that the whole town was gathering. Apparently Polish officers were going from house to house, ordering all Jewish residents of the Pysznica shtetl, or ghetto, as they were calling it, to gather in front of the shul. It seemed that they were headed to our house when we walked out at Naomi's insistence. Some of the people were walking on their own, and some were being pushed along or had guns pointed at them.

Mr. Lubin and the Goldin family were among the last to arrive, mostly because of Mr. Goldin's ill health. One of the German soldiers started pushing him pretty hard. Lubin started yelling at him, and Leibish, always the hothead, jumped the soldier to get him off his father. One of the Polish officers hit him with his nightstick, and Leibish fell to the ground. Miriam picked him up as Ruth helped her father take his place in the lineup.

It was hard to tell how many soldiers and police were in attendance. Certainly most of Pysznica police force was there, probably about fifty men on horseback. As far as German soldiers we saw, a few vehicles included a couple of soldier transports. Maybe fifty Nazis. A force of a hundred armed men, for a total Jewish population of less than three hundred people, including women and children. This seemed like very overwhelming odds.

Once everyone was gathered around the square, a German officer and the Polish police captain stood in the center with megaphones. The German spoke, and the Polish captain translated, "Jews of Pysznica, Poland is now under the rule of the German Third Reich and the Nazi Party. Under German law, now the law of Poland, Jews are to be laborers of the state. We will assign labor to all men, women, and children able to work. You will own no businesses, no assets of any kind. You must surrender all valuables to the Third Reich. This includes money and gold or silver of any kind. You will be issued identification cards special for Jews. You must carry these at all times and show them on request. You must not leave the confines of this ghetto. You must not have any contact with non-Jews unless given special permission by a German or Polish officer or ordered to do so by an officer. You will remain in the houses you occupy. No German would live in such filth, but know this: these houses are the property of the Third Reich. You must stay in these houses except when ordered to work by an officer. Any activity deemed to be a crime will be punishable by immediate death by decision of any German officer. You must never congregate or be in groups of ten or more for any reason. There will be no prayer in groups of ten or more, as we know you do. This is also a crime punishable by death. Leaving the ghetto without permission is punishable by immediate death. Each person in this ghetto must report to the gathering place formally your church directly behind us at twelve hundred hours tomorrow to be assigned work and receive your identification cards. This is the new headquarters of the force overseeing the ghetto. I am Colonel Roeder, the oberscharführer of this ghetto."

The oberscharführer and Captain Sobiech, the local police chief, started walking around, looking at all the faces and talking to each other. Many of the women were crying, and the men were crying out to God. "How can you do this? What do you want from us?"

Our way of life was over. Our traditions gone. No more would we celebrate the exodus of the Jewish people from slavery in Egypt on Pesach. We were beginning a new era of slavery. How long would it be before our exodus? As our new slave owners got to us, Captain Sobiech looked at me and said, "This is the family that runs the lumberyard. We can use them." Then they moved on.

We all stood still. Naomi whispered to me, "Can we leave yet?"

"No," I said. "Not until they dismiss us."

Then there was a commotion. They were pushing a group of men into the center of the square. Among them were Mr. Lubin and Leibish. The others were a varied group of different ages.

The oberscharführer spoke. "So you know this is serious, these ten Jews are congregating together. This is in violation of the law."

With that, ten Polish officers drew their pistols and at close range fired shots into their heads. They all fell. They fired several more shots as some of the bodies were convulsing, not unusual even if they were dead. These were heartless killers who wanted to strike fear in their captives, and as far as I could tell, they succeeded.

Shayna Goldin screamed, "Leibish!" Others were screaming and crying.

The oberscharführer screamed, "Silence!" as German officers began shooting in the air. "I order the members of the families of these criminals to take the bodies and dispose of them as you wish. Now the rest of you go to the pigsties you live in and report tomorrow at twelve hundred hours at Nazi headquarters."

The murderers and the rest of the soldiers and police force then moved back as the family members, distraught with sorrow and total shock, trembling with fear and an outpouring of emotion, ran to the bodies of their loved ones. I turned to Momma and the girls and told them to go home. I took Benjamin and Yossel and told them to come with me to help with the bodies. Poor Mr. Lubin had no family, and we would be there for him.

Mr. Goldin stayed back, not having the strength to move. Shayna stayed back with him. Miriam and her remaining siblings stood over the lifeless body of Leibish. She was frozen in place standing over him. "They murdered poor Leibish. I can't believe they could do this." She cried uncontrollably.

I put my arms around her. I did not know how to comfort her but tried, just saying, "I'm so sorry."

Leibish and Mr. Lubin were obviously chosen because of the protest they made when they were brought to the square. No dissent would be tolerated. If we wanted to live, we would have to learn and follow the rules.

The rabbi came over to talk to us about what to do with the bodies. There was a room in the shul that we used for chevra kadisha, the ritual for preparation of dead bodies for burial. According to Jewish tradition, burial usually took place within twenty-four to forty-eight hours, depending on the day and time of death. Funerals were forbidden on Shabbos. During the period between death and the funeral, there was usually a voluntary committee that cared for the body. My father served on the committee in charge of this depressing task, but it was a great mitzvah. Many family members of the deceased volunteered to help. I was a mitzvah for them and helped some with the grieving process. The basic duties were threefold: to thoroughly clean the body of dirt and any blood or other bodily fluids that may be apparent; to dress the body in white linen shrouds for burial and place the body in a plain pine casket, which was immediately and permanently closed; and to watch over the body. Someone should be with the body at all times.

The police guards would not allow us to use the shul. I told the rabbi of the abandoned barn that earlier was the training ground for our sniper force, which was already defunct.

We agreed to move the bodies there. The Polish officers wanted the bodies out of the square. They provided a truck, which we loaded with all the bodies. We moved them to the barn. A very somber procession of grieving family members followed the bodies to the barn, where we would clean them the best we could and prepare them for burial. I went to the lumberyard, which was abandoned at the time, and took as many supplies—including pine coffins, which we kept in stock, and shovels—as we would need to bury our brothers and friends. It was starting to get dark. Other members of the community came to the barn to help us prepare the bodies. It was now dark, but we all kept at it until we were finished preparing the bodies. We did not have access to white linen to dress the bodies, but each family member brought some clean clothing for each of the deceased. Ruth brought something for Mr. Lubin. The authorities seemed uninterested in our efforts. This was lucky, as we had quite a gathering to attend to the bodies. We were all in shock and spoke little while we prepared them.

Once we were finished with the bodies, a few women, including Miriam and Chava, agreed to stay with the bodies. Ruth went back to the house to tend to her parents and baby brother. Naomi went home to help Rivka tend to our mother. They were all admirably trying to hold back the tears. A group of men, including me, Benjamin, and Yossel, headed to the cemetery to dig the grave. We agreed to dig one massive grave where the bodies could be laid to rest together with dignity.

We also agreed to hold the funeral at 9:00 a.m., before we had to report to the Nazis. Several people were assigned to spread the word. We hoped our overseers would agree to let us have the funeral.

We spent several hours digging the grave. Sometime in the early morning hours, we dragged ourselves home and got some sleep.

In the morning, Naomi woke me up. It was time to go to the funeral. Momma came to see me. "Meyer, I am so afraid for all of you. Please promise me you won't let your brothers try to get revenge for yesterday."

I agreed. "I want us all to live. Killing one German will mean death for our family. I will make sure Benjamin and Yossel don't do anything stupid." I knew they looked up to me. They weren't hotheads like Leibish. Poor Miriam. I didn't know what to do to help her.

The cemetery was crowded. I think the whole shtetl was there. We also had other attendees. Several Polish police officers were watching the proceedings. I saw the two who trashed the lumberyard. They were the only cops I knew. I went up to Kozlowski. "You know me," I said in a quiet tone.

"Yeah," he said. "You gave me a black eye. I didn't expect a good punch from a Jew. Where'd you learn that?"

"The army," I replied. "I served with the Krakow Army. I tried to keep Poland free. I'm not that different than you."

He looked at me and said angrily, "You're a Jew. The Nazis have a problem with Jews. I do too."

"I noticed," I said. "Are we going to be able to have our funeral?" I asked respectfully.

"This gathering is illegal," he said firmly but then continued, "Those Nazi bastards are brutal, and we have been ordered to obey them, but today they are not here, and we won't interfere. Life will get worse for you."

I actually thanked him and went to the crowd. We stood graveside as the rabbi began to speak. He tried to remember the victims of this brutal murder in a positive way to give the families some comfort. Frankly I wasn't listening. Kozlowski's words were ringing in my ear. What did he mean when he said life would get even worse for us? It was pretty horrible now. My thoughts then turned to Miriam. Shlomo was hanging on to her for dear life. He was just a little boy and watched his older brother, to whom he looked up, shot in the head in public by a brutal, murderous police officer. He must be so confused and horrified. I went over to try to console the Goldin family.

Mr. Goldin was particularly angry. "I blame myself. If I could have traveled to Russia, Leibish would be with us. What right do they have to do this to us?"

"I don't know," I replied sheepishly. I had no answers and plenty of questions.

The rabbi spoke about each of the victims, whom he knew personally. He gave a wonderful tribute to Mr. Lubin, who, after he lost his beloved wife and son, became very generous in helping families in need and of course taking in the Goldins, refugees from the Nazis. His generosity affected me, as it allowed me to be with the woman I wanted to spend the rest of my life with. I would always remember him.

After he finished speaking, the male mourners said kaddish, the prayer to remember the dead, then we all grabbed the shovels and filled in the grave while the cries and screams of the widows, parents, and siblings of the dead filled the air. The Polish officers watched in silence. After the grave was filled, the crowd broke ranks and headed home. The mourning period would be very much shortened, as we had to report to the Nazis at noon. Me, Momma, and the rest of the family walked the Goldins to their adopted home and sat with them while they tried to make sense out of what happened.

"I told Leibish not to make trouble when they came to the house and told us to come to the square," said Shayna. "Lubin was angry about his son, poor man. He yelled at the officer, then Leibish joined him. I knew it was a mistake, but I never imagined they would murder him in front of the whole town. They are godless. What threat are we to them? I don't understand. They have the whole country. What threat are the Jews to them?" Mr. Goldin was distraught. He felt responsible. "We have been chosen by God but hated by everyone else. It's been that way for three thousand years. If it's not the Christians or the Muslims, it's the godless bastards like the Nazis. They based their whole civilization on our Bible, and all they do is blame us for it."

CHAPTER 8

Slavery

⅄ ⅄ ⅄

I DON'T KNOW WHAT SADDENED me more, burying my friends and landsmen this morning or watching the procession of the people I grew up with to meet with their masters to determine their fate. True to their word, the Nazis were all set up inside the shul. The pews were torn out, and the ark was gone. What did they do with the Torahs? I hoped someone took them and hid them, but more likely they were confiscated.

Everyone in the shtetl reported as ordered. The group was somber and seemed to have their spirits broken by the murders. They stood in line and said nothing. All the family members stood together. Mama gathered us all, and we met up with the Goldins. As I got closer and started to hear the conversations, it became clear that the Nazis were only interested in manual labor. Anyone with a usable skill would work at their trade if needed. Those without a useful trade were assigned to work cleaning and repairing roads, bridges, and sewers, whatever was needed. With winter setting in, all outdoor work would be brutal, dangerous work.

The Goldins went first. Clearly Jonah Goldin was in no position to perform manual labor and was quickly dismissed. His wife, Shayna, told them she was his caretaker and was dismissed as well. Shlomo, who was six, was told to stay with his parents. Miriam described her skills as a seamstress and dressmaker. She was ordered to immediately report to a tailoring facility on the other side of Pysznica. Pearl and Ruth were ordered to line up with a group of other women who were going to be used as workers in a textile mill.

It was finally our turn. We were in no rush. The German officer didn't even look at us. "Surname?" he asked gruffly.

"Marcus." I spoke for the family.

"Address?"

I responded.

"Occupation?" He still did not look up.

"Lumberyard owner," I replied.

"You own nothing, Jew." He looked up at me as if I were a criminal. In his mind, I was. "You will report to the Pysznica Lumberyard for immediate duty."

Benjamin and Yossel were also assigned to the lumberyard, as I expected. Momma and the girls were all assigned to the general laborer group at the same textile factory. I felt we were the lucky ones. They would work inside, and we could get shelter from the bad weather and do what we knew while many of the younger and older men were being assigned to hard labor outdoors on the road and rail workforce.

Benjamin, Yossel, and I were escorted by a local cop to the lumberyard. There Kozlowski was waiting for us.

"You work for me now," he said with a victorious satisfaction. "Consider yourself lucky. I asked for you. You know this business. The Nazis want to use this lumber to feed their construction needs. You will be here every day. No Saturdays or Jew holidays off. They will pay nothing. Just take what they want. You will tell them what we need, and they will send it. From where, I don't know. They control everything now. You better fill every order on time. Nazis don't like to wait, but they like to kill."

"How will we live?" Yossel asked.

Kozlowski jumped right on that. "All you Jews have money hidden away. You'll be fine. Pay me, and I'll get you what you need. You better keep what you have hidden. Nazis are thieves too."

"It sounds like you don't like being controlled by the Nazis either," I said.

"Just do what I tell you, and we'll be fine," he snorted. "Here are the orders for today." He handed me one of my own order sheets. "I have to check in on my other businesses. Get to work, and don't leave until I tell you." With that, he left us alone.

Benjamin turned to me. "Let's get our guns and kill the bastard."

"That's a death sentence for us," I insisted. "Besides, I promised Momma I would keep you alive. Now let's get to work."

We spent the next several hours gathering the sheets of wallboard and other lumber and brought it into the cutting area. We cut the lengths to order and were short some pieces but made do with what we had. We cut the lumber to order and placed the order on the loading dock. We had no idea who would pick it up or when. As we worked, we talked and wondered what Momma and the girls were going through. We hoped they were being treated well. When we finished the order, we went inside and began to fill out an inventory supply order that we needed to keep the yard stocked. Somehow, we magically expected the Nazis to fill the order. By the time we finished, it was dark and we were ready to leave, but Kozlowski was clear that we could not leave before he came back. We sat around and began to contemplate our fate.

"What will happen to us?" Yossel asked in an exhausted voice.

"I don't know," I replied. "I suppose as long as we can work and stay out of their way, they will keep us alive. I don't know how long this can last or how we can escape, but we must find a way to stay alive."

Benjamin jumped in. "We must fight back. Yossel is right to want to fight. How can we let them do this to us, our mother, our sisters, and not fight when we have weapons ready?"

"Here we go again," I replied, trying to stay calm. "How many can you kill? One, three, even five before they shoot you dead and turn their guns to our entire family? No, we must be patient and find a time and place to fight back. I hope that day will come."

We stayed quiet after that and sat for another two hours trying to figure out if Kozlowski would ever come. Finally, a truck pulled up to the loading dock. Two German soldiers and Kozlowski jumped out. "Jew!" he shouted.

I hated that bastard. We went over and loaded the lumber on the truck while the two Nazis smoked cigarettes, laughed at us, and kept yelling, "Faster, Jews!"

While we loaded, I tried to ignore the comments. I thought about trying cigarettes in the army given to me by one of the officers. I took a puff, swallowed the smoke, and began to cough uncontrollably. I could remember the officers laughing and calling out, "Look at the weak Jew!" I never tried again after that and in fact never understood why so many would smoke those things. A lot of men did and seemed to enjoy it. Many of the soldiers smoked constantly. They smelled from it, and I just didn't get it.

Once we finished, Kozlowski said, "Be back at oh-seven hundred." He jumped in the truck, and they drove off, laughing and carrying on.

We dragged ourselves home. As we approached the house, we saw Momma and the girls walking home from the other side of the road. They were helping Chava along. She was limping as she walked.

"What happened?" I asked.

"They hit her," said Rivka.

Momma explained, "They put us and the other women in a military truck and took us to a textile factory in Stalowa Wola. They put us on the assembly line, sewing pieces of military uniforms. Chava didn't work fast enough. A policeman pushed her off her chair and hit her leg over and over until she screamed in pain. Then he dragged her up back on the chair and screamed at her as she tried to work. As I got up to help her, I was pushed down with a gun to my head and told not to move. I think her leg is broken. They wouldn't let me look at her until they let us go and brought us home. Let's get her inside."

Everything in my being wanted to find the son of a bitch who hit her and kill him. Again, this would be instant death for all of us, so I had to repress those feelings. I was afraid Benjamin or Yossel would lose control.

As Momma tried to wrap Chava's leg, I went to check on Miriam. She seemed to fare better than the others. "They have me making a wedding dress. One of these Nazi murderers actually has a woman marrying him. There is nothing like a free wedding dress made from Jewish slaves."

I'd never seen Miriam angry before. We all were.

She continued, "I heard what happened to Chava. I am sorry."

I replied, "It seems we are lucky she is alive. I am afraid this is how life will be for a while."

The she came up to me and kissed me, more passionately than ever before. We embraced for a long time. She would not let go. It felt wonderful. This was not proper for an unmarried Jewish couple, especially in front of the family. We did not care. We kissed as if the world was about to come to an end. Finally, I heard Shayna yelling at us—what she said I have no idea—but we were startled and let go. We went out for a walk. There was little comfort we could find in our predicament. Our routine observances were gone. We didn't know how we would feed ourselves or keep warm during the winter. We had nothing but each other to make this bearable. We stayed out all night, using the infamous barn as our refuge from the world.

When the light broke, we kissed and headed for work. I stopped at home to bathe and change clothes. When I got there, Naomi met me at the door. "Where have you been? I woke up and you and Benjamin were gone."

"Benjamin?" I said. "I was not with him. When did he leave?"

Naomi replied, "I don't know. He was here last night."

I knew exactly where he went. I stormed out of the house again and found him right where I knew he would be. He was loading up his guns, about to head off to get revenge.

"Benjamin!" I yelled. He turned around, startled, and pointed his rifle at me.

He was seething. "Don't try to stop me. I'm going to kill the bastard who beat up poor Chava."

"No you are not," I said firmly. "Even if you get him, they will make an example of you by killing you in public like Leibish, and even worse, they could kill Chava for good measure. You will accomplish nothing."

"I have to do something," he shot back. With that, he turned and ran off. I ran after him and tackled him in the open road. We struggled as I grabbed his rifle. It went off. We both stopped for a second and realized neither one of us was shot. Benjamin sat on the ground and began to weep. "I have to do something."

"We have to find another way," I said, having no idea what that was. We put the guns back and headed to the lumberyard.

Kozlowski was waiting for us. "You're late, Jews," he said, trying to provoke us. Yossel was there already.

"What happened to you two?" Yossel had no idea what we had been up to.

"We'll talk later," I replied.

"Being late is punishable by death," threatened Kozlowski.

"Everything is punishable by death," I said sarcastically, regretting it once the words came out.

Kozlowski let out a big laugh. "I like you, Jew, plus I need you to get these orders ready. You're lucky I'm in a good mood. I had sex last night, and it was a good time."

"Good for you," I said. Looking at the orders, I continued, "We don't have enough to fill this order. Are they building the Taj Mahal in Poland?" My sarcasm knew no limits.

"Don't worry, the delivery is on its way," said Kozlowski. "Our German friends are very efficient. They are building a palace for the regional Nazi commander, and you are the lucky ones that get to fill the orders. Meanwhile, clean this place up!" Then he left but assured us he would be back.

As we were getting the yard ready for the delivery, Benjamin told Yossel the story of how I found him this morning. Yossel was pretty level-headed and agreed with me that it was too dangerous. Luckily I was able to avoid the subject of where I was last night, although they would have enjoyed hearing the story.

Sure enough, within an hour Kozlowski was back, escorting a very large truck filled with lumber. They pulled into the yard, opened the truck, and Kozlowski said, "Jews, get to work." This was a huge load, bigger than anything we had handled before. Just as yesterday, Kozlowski and the driver stood around, smoked cigarettes, and bragged about their sexual conquests while we unloaded the truck and stacked the inventory into piles. Winter was now here in full force. It was cold, windy, and starting to snow. This was something the three of us had done all our lives, so it wasn't that unusual. The difference was that there was no money exchanging hands. There was no food to buy or coal to heat our homes.

The Germans seemed happy to let us work until we starved or froze to death. We had our money and jewelry hidden away, and so far, they were safe. Luckily our father had no trust in the Polish bankers, known to confiscate Jewish assets, so he invested in gold and diamonds and kept any cash we saved hidden as well. We would have to figure out how to get what we needed to survive as time went on.

The work went smoothly after that. We filled the order, the truck picked it up, as they did the day before, and Kozlowski seemed happy. He had offered to get us supplies if we paid him, so here was my chance to ask.

"So I hear there is a black market where there is food and supplies available for a price."

"Yeah, you could say that," he said, avoiding the direct question.

"So how would one go about buying from this market?" I could be evasive as well.

He replied, finally being direct, "Give me a list of what you want. I'll bring whatever I can get, and you'll pay whatever I tell you it costs. Of course there will be a little something for the effort."

"Of course," I replied. I wrote out a basic list of groceries to see if this would work and handed it to him.

"This should be no problem." He laughed. "I'll see you tomorrow."

When we got home, Momma and the girls were not there. We scrounged around for something to eat and found some leftovers from the other night. Clearly the pantry was empty, and I hoped that Kozlowski would come through with his promise.

After we ate something, we walked over to the edge of the shtetl, where we knew they would be dropped off. Sure enough, the military truck was there. All the women were loaded in the back of the truck, stuffed in like sardines, including Chava. We went over and helped the women off. Benjamin and I got up in the truck to carry Chava off. All the time, there was a German and a Pole pointing pistols at us. She was in terrible pain. She never should have left the house. We all walked home. We carried Chava, but no one spoke a word. They seemed exhausted. It was a long day with hard labor, and it was no wonder they were exhausted. But when we got home, we learned what was really happening.

As soon as we were behind closed doors, Naomi turned to me and spoke angrily. "They're beating Chava all day, and there is nothing we can do about it. Every couple of hours this one huge, mean German guard comes over to her, knocks her on the floor, and beats her with his nightstick. He hits her on her broken leg, and she screams in pain. She is an example for the rest of the workers to keep working and work faster and harder, or the same will happen to them. They are killing her, and we have to watch."

Naomi was tough and did not cry, but Momma was in tears. "Even some of the Polish guards tried to get him to stop, but he pushed them aside and continued to hit her. They say if she can't work, they will kill her." We carried her to bed and tried to make her comfortable.

When we came out, I tried to give them some good news. "Our Polish overseer will get us groceries and supplies if we pay him a profit. We should get some food tomorrow. At least we won't starve on the few rations they give us."

Benjamin, who was uncharacteristically quiet, chimed in. "Great. We'll be well fed while they work us to death and beat our sister." Then he stormed outside, slamming the door behind him.

I just looked at everyone and said, "He'll be OK." Then I left.

Of course everyone knew where I was going, to see Miriam, my only comfort in this crazy world we were in.

When I arrived, Miriam was on her knees tending to her father. Still in mourning for Leibish, the house was somber. They welcomed me in. Miriam showed no signs of difficulty, but I had seen Ruth and Pearl get off the truck from the textile mill, and they were witness to Chava's beating.

"How's Chava?" asked Pearl.

"She is sleeping. She's in lots of pain. I am afraid she cannot take much more."

Miriam got up and kissed me on my cheek. How can something so simple feel so wonderful?

"I will continue to mourn for Leibish until I have no breath left," said Jonah. With that, he rose and began to say kaddish. He was stoic, but I knew he was in deep pain over all that was happening to his family.

After that, Miriam and I left. Neither of us could wait to escape to our hideout in the woods. "How are you holding up?" I asked.

Miriam replied, "I'm fine. They are leaving me alone to make the wedding dress and dresses for the mothers and sisters. They may as well all get in on it. They came for fittings today. They acted like they were in a dress shop in Paris. They were all laughing and carrying on as if all was right in the world. Actually, it was a good distraction. They were actually respectful, asking my opinion on how they looked. They were ugly beasts in my eyes, but I complimented them and treated them like customers. When they left, I saw that I was being watched by an officer. I remembered my place and was back to reality. Then when I came home and heard about Chava and saw how my sisters were being mistreated, I felt terrible that somehow I have been spared some of their pain."

We buried ourselves deep in the back of the barn under horse blankets. We kissed and held each other. We fell asleep from our exhaustion, holding on to each other.

When we awoke, it was light out, and I knew we were late for work. We realized it was Shabbos. There was no more Shabbos, so we got up and said our good-byes.

I went straight to the lumberyard. When I arrived, Kozlowski was pacing the floor. Yossel was there, reviewing the day's orders, but I did not see Benjamin.

"You're late, Jew!" Kozlowski yelled in a booming voice.

"It's only thirty minutes. I had family business," I replied.

Kozlowski continued, "And where is your no-good brother? We have a lot of work to do today."

I looked at Yossel, and he just shrugged his shoulders. "I don't know," I said.

"I should not give you these groceries I got for you, as punishment," he replied.

I looked over and saw a box filled with items, including milk, cheese, and bread. It was about half of what I asked for, but I was not going to complain. "I have zlotys to pay you with. It would be a shame to let it go to waste." I knew his greed would win the day.

"OK, but it will cost you fifty zlotys," he said.

I knew it cost him about twenty, but I was in no position to argue. I paid him and put the groceries in the back room.

"Where's Benjamin?" I turned to Yossel.

"He was gone before I woke up this morning," he replied.

"Let's go. We need this order filled, and the two of you will have to do it, no excuses," Kozlowski bellowed.

We got to work, but I knew Benjamin was up to no good.

About three hours later, Benjamin showed up. Kozlowski had gone.

"Where were you?" I was angry but more worried.

"I was busy," he said in defiance.

"What did you do?" I demanded.

He pulled me and Yossel aside and whispered, "I got him. I took out two of those Nazi bastards. I am sure one of them was the big one who beat Chava. I got there before sunrise and waited for them to arrive. There were only two Germans. The rest were Poles. I shot them before they went into the building. They were definitely dead. The Poles began to look for me. I was hidden in the bush. I took off and swam across the San River. I dropped the guns in the river, but once I got across, I did not see any officers. I went home, changed my clothes, and here I am."

He was very proud of himself. I have to admit, I was proud of him too. Maybe Chava would be safe. But I knew that the Nazis would not let this go without consequences. "Are you crazy?" I chided him. "You know they will search for the killers everywhere and will not stop until they get revenge."

Yossel jumped in. "I wish you had told me; I would have gone with you. I would have loved to shoot those bastards. Good for you."

"We have to do something," he argued. "Besides, they have lots of workers in Stalowa Wola from all parts of the region. They have a big search on their hands."

I had no words. I finally said, "Let's get to work."

CHAPTER 9

Futility Has No Limits

⅄⅄⅄

We continued to work quietly. Maybe we should have celebrated Benjamin's heroism, but we all knew there would be consequences. The Nazis seemed to have an unending thirst for building materials. In our old world, business would be booming. Papa would have been excited about our new business growth. Unfortunately, the world had changed. We had to remember this was no longer our business. We were back in ancient Egypt. All the Passover Seders where we celebrated the freedoms of Jews from slavery were a joke. The only difference was that the Nazis liked killing more than the Egyptians. My mind was just wandering, but now I knew what it was like to be a slave.

We all seemed to put everything out of our minds temporarily, and we cut wood like never before and started to put together the day's order for pickup.

Late that afternoon, Kozlowski showed up. "I see you boys have been working hard today. The Nazis will be here soon for the pickup. You are making me look good to our guests. I may have to cut my profit on your supplies." Kozlowski let out a big laugh. He was really enjoying the power he had over us. He was a second-rate, corrupt policeman whose greed was even greater than his hatred for us. Now he had the power of life and death over us. He could be judge, jury, and executioner and would probably get a medal for killing lowly Jews.

The Nazi pickup was right on time as always. We loaded the truck under their watchful eyes. They always kept their guns drawn. I can't imagine what they were afraid of. We were hungry and working day and night. Did they think that somehow we would attack them? Once they left another truck with new inventory of wood arrived, driven by a couple of other Nazi officers, who got out of the truck and immediately drew their guns. As usual, the three of us unloaded the truck as the driver, his guard, and our guard stood smoking cigarettes and laughing over their evil exploits. Kozlowski thought these guys were his friends, but he was just being used like the rest of us and they looked down on him as well.

I just could not wait for this day to be over. I wanted to go home and hear what happened at the textile plant today, and I wanted to see Miriam. Finally, the lumber delivery was off loaded and put away, and we were ready to leave, when Kozlowski came over.

"Boys," he said, "two Nazi officers were murdered today outside the textile plant where your mother and sisters work. The Nazis have no idea who did it, and they don't like surprises. They don't think Jews have the guts or the ability to shoot officers. They worry that angry Poles are doing this. Anyway, they are bringing in the Gestapo to investigate, and I am sure they will interview everyone who works there. Tell your mother and sisters that if they know anything, they better tell them. These guys have a nasty reputation."

"We will," I responded. With that, we left.

When we got about two hundred meters down the road, I pulled over and looked at Benjamin. "I know you are feeling very proud of yourself right now, but I am telling you that you cannot tell anyone anything about this. Not even a hint. Momma and the girls cannot be asked to keep a secret from the Gestapo."

Benjamin replied, "I understand. I just had to stop the beatings. I hope it did."

I turned to Yossel. "That goes for you too. Not a word to anyone!"

He just nodded. I think they were genuinely scared about what was happening. I continued, "Look, I don't think Kozlowski connected you being late this morning with the murder. Hopefully he won't. I am sure he would love to impress the Nazis by solving this. Let's go home."

When we got home, we found Chava lying on the sofa, covered and half asleep.

"What are you doing here?" asked Benjamin.

"I can't take the pain," she replied. "Let them come and kill me. It can't be any worse. I told Momma to go without me. I can't work anyway and won't sit there and wait for my beatings." She was defiant.

Benjamin looked at me, and I knew what he was thinking. He was dying to tell her that he killed her attacker, but I just shook my head and he backed off.

Chava spoke again. "I have been sitting here all day waiting for some Nazi goon to come in and drag me out by my hair and who knows what else. I have been imagining my death by torture all day, but no one ever showed up. Maybe they forgot about me."

"Or maybe they were distracted." Benjamin couldn't help himself.

I cut him off. "We heard from the Polish officer who oversees us that there was an incident at the plant. Two guards were killed. Maybe Momma will have some more details." I gave Benjamin the eye, and he shut up.

Chava asked, "Can I get some water?"

Yossel jumped up. "I'll get it." He was a good boy, and he loved Chava, who took care of him as a baby. Even when she was five years old, if there was a baby in the house, she would push her way in and ask to hold the baby. She would not take no for an answer and usually got her way. We had such a wonderful, close family. It was so painful to see the suffering everyone was going through.

"How is the leg?" I asked.

She lifted up her skirt to show me the bandage around it. She was all black and blue around the bandage, and it was twice as wide as her other leg.

"It's broken in at least three places. They won't let me see a doctor in town, but Dr. Lansky, who lives in the shtetl, came to look. He wrapped it. There is internal bleeding, and he is afraid I may have a broken pelvis, which is why I cannot stand up at all." She began to cry. "I can't believe this is happening. What did we do to deserve this? Dear God!"

I wished I could comfort her, but I had no answers. "Let me put some ice on it for the swelling." I went into the kitchen. While I was getting the ice pack together, I heard Momma, Rivka, and Naomi come home.

I came out with the ice pack for Chava. They all seemed in a good mood. "Well, we had an interesting day," Momma started.

I looked at Benjamin, and he wiped the smile off his face. "Tell us," I said.

Momma began, "We met the truck as usual for the trip to Stalowa Wola. We left Chava home, as we agreed she was in too much pain to travel and work, and so we took the chance that they would forget about her. Well they didn't. The Polish guards that drove us took a roll call. They knew that Chava was hurt, but when they called her name and she did not answer, they were not very forgiving. They wanted to know where she was. They wanted her there because they knew the German guard wanted to use her as a victim to keep the rest of us in line. They also knew that with his anger focused on her, he would leave them alone. They were afraid of him too. I told them she was in pain, could not walk, and needed to rest at home. They were angry and demanded that we go get her. When I refused, they slapped me across the face. It knocked me down, but it did not hurt bad, and I stood right up. The two guards stood there arguing with each other for quite a while. One argued that it was important to have the full complement of workers, even if one was lame. The other argued that it was more important to have the delivery of workers on time, even if it meant they were one short. They did not have time to drag Chava out of the house and bring her all the way to the edge of the shtetl. There was no way they were driving their precious truck through the shtetl.

"They finally decided to leave without Chava and bring their workers to the factory. As we got close to the factory, we stopped short. We could not see outside, so we sat for several minutes. We were all abuzz about what might be happening. We heard the guards talking that they didn't know what was going on either. One got out of the truck to find out what was happening, presumably the one not driving. He came back after what seemed about fifteen minutes. We sat quietly so we could hear what they were saying. One guard told the other that there was a random shooting outside the factory entrance. Two German guards were killed, and they were investigating and had not yet removed the bodies. We knew there were only two German officers assigned to this plant, including the one who beat Chava every day. If this were true, then our prayers had been answered. We sat on the truck for a long time. It was freezing outside, but we were packed in the truck so tight that we kept each other warm. After at least an hour, the truck started up, and we began moving. Finally, we were told to get off. Outside we could see all the other trucks unloading and bringing the workers from all over the county who were enslaved from other Jewish communities.

"When we got inside, instead of being led to our work areas, we were gathered around the factory floor and told to remain standing. Two Nazi officers we had never seen before stood in front, and one began to speak. He said, 'We are investigating the murder that took place early this morning in front of this facility. Two German officers who were assigned to manage this factory were shot from long range and killed, with two shots each. The killer or killers have escaped, and we are looking for them and their weapons. When we find them, they will be put to death immediately. If any of you have information about the death of these two fine officers, you must tell us now. If you do not and we learn you knew something, you will also be put to death.'

"With that, they lined us up outside one of the offices and began to interview each worker one by one. This is when I got scared that I would have to explain why Chava was not in attendance. I told the girls if they asked about Chava to say they didn't know where she was and to ask me. I didn't know what I would tell them, but I would have to make it up. I went first.

"One of the Germans was asking the questions. One of our Polish guards was also in the room. 'Your name?' he asked. I told him. 'I see you are from Pysznica. Do you know anything about these murders?'

"'No,' I replied, not wanting to say too much.

"He continued. 'I know all the women were being transported here when the murders occurred and were not involved directly, but I believe you know something more than you are telling me. I see you also have three daughters working here. Is that correct?'

"'Yes,' I replied.

"'Are they here?' he asked.

"'Two are here, right behind me,' I replied.

"He said, 'I was told by the guards that one of your daughters was hurt badly and was near death when she was taken from here yesterday. Is that correct?'

"I replied, 'Yes, she is near death.' He seemed to accept that and just told me if I learned anything that I should report it immediately. With that, I left. It seems that the police did not expect women to know too much, and frankly none of us did. I did not hear anything about Chava the rest of the day."

Naomi said, "I was next, and he only asked me if I knew anything. When I said no, I was dismissed."

"Same for me," said Rivka.

"After that, we were told to go to work, but frankly the women were talking about what took place, as were the guards, and little work got done," said Momma.

I looked at Momma and calmly lied, "Our guard told us there was a murder, and he said that the Gestapo would be called in to investigate, so I suspect we will hear more about this. But I am glad the bastard who beat Chava is dead and she can stay here and recover." With that, we had something to eat and I headed out to see Miriam.

On my way out, Momma stopped me. "Meyer," she said, "I must to talk to you about disappearing with Miriam all the time. We still live by the values of our traditions, and it is not proper for you to spend your nights with someone you are not married to; plus, we have no idea what will happen to any of us, and you may be setting yourselves up for a great disappointment."

"Momma," I responded, "if these were normal times, we would be planning a wedding. I have grown very attached to her. She gives me comfort at a time when we don't know whether we will live or die tomorrow. I will always be here for you and the family, but I need to spend time with her." With that, I kissed her and went on my way.

The days started to blend together. We didn't know what day it was. Shabbos was a distant memory. We had no day of rest. We worked from dawn until late at night, going home to the rest of the family, who were doing the same. We continued to buy supplies from Kozlowski, who was enjoying his newfound income from us and others he was ripping off. Actually we learned that after he got us started in the morning, he would then go to all the other businesses he was overseeing. He would deliver groceries and supplies to some of them if they had any money to spend. I am sure he had to share the profits with some of the other officers. He was becoming a one-man black market. It may have been bigger and more organized, but we only saw him on a daily basis, starting to wear nicer clothes and some nonregulation jewelry. Without the black market, we would've been starving, like many of our neighbors, whom we tried to help as much as we could. Our misery began to become routine, and we fell into accepting our fate. The one exception was that Miriam and I spent as much time together as we could. I had some jewelry put away that I wished I could give her, but we had pooled all our valuables to be used as payment for food. The Goldins did the same, and I was able to use my black-market supplier to get them food as well. It was enough that we were together. We held each other tightly whenever we could as if it were the last time we would ever see each other.

Things stayed quiet and routine for several weeks. One late morning after Kozlowski left to make his rounds, three men in black uniforms paid us a visit. They were clearly German officers but different than the gray-clad German soldier.

"Guten tag," said one of the men.

"Hello," I said. "Our German is not very good."

Another officer stepped up and began to speak in Polish. "My name is Officer Huber. We are detectives with the Gestapo, investigating the murder of two of our officers at a textile plant in Stalowa Wola a few weeks ago. They were shot from a distance of fifty meters with a military rifle. Who is Meyer Marcus?"

"I am," I said, responding apprehensively.

One of the other officers pulled up a wooden chair and placed it in the middle of the store. "Please sit down. We have some questions for you." I sat. Huber continued, "Who are these other men?"

I replied, "These are my younger brothers."

"You are Jews. Let me see your identification."

We showed him our ID cards, which we carried all the time. Benjamin and Yossel were told to sit in the back of the room while one of the other Gestapo officers stood by them.

Huber continued, "I understand you were an officer in the Polish army. Is that correct?"

"Correct," I answered.

"What was your rank?" he demanded.

"Corporal," I responded, not having any idea where he was going with this.

"What division were you in, and where were you based?"

"The Krakow Army, assigned to defend the western border with Germany."

"Your puny army was no match for the mighty German war machine," he said with great pride. Did he come here just to tell me that? Then he continued, "Did you receive weapons training in the Krakow Army?" It became clear where he was going.

"Yes," I responded.

"What kind of weapons?" he asked calmly.

"Karabin rifles and standard-issue pistols," I said calmly.

Then he suddenly pointed to one of the other officers and said something in German. The officer stepped outside and came back a few seconds later with a rifle and handed it to Huber.

"Like this rifle we found at the bottom of the San River?"

I heard a gasp from Benjamin and Yossel, who were watching the proceedings.

He continued, "We believe this is the murder weapon. We believe the murderer dropped the gun in the river on his way back to Pysznica. We believe the murderer is someone with military training who could shoot someone from fifty meters." His voice grew louder. "You have a sister, correct?" he said, pressing his hand against my head.

"Yes, I have three sisters." I tried to stay calm.

"We understand that one of the German officers who was murdered punished your sister for poor work."

I replied, "She was beaten, and her leg was broken."

"So, you decided to get revenge by stealing this rifle, crossing the San River, and waiting for our two heroic officers to come to work. You shot them in cold blood and fled, dropping the rifle in the San River to hide your cowardly act. Correct?"

"No," I protested. "I was here at work, as I am every morning at sunrise."

With that, Huber took his Lugar pistol and rapped me across the face. The blow gashed the side of my face, drawing blood and knocking me down. One of the other Nazis picked me up and put me back in the chair.

"Admit it. You are a Jew murderer." Huber wanted to kill me on the spot for murder.

"No," I insisted. "I was here."

He bashed me again. This time he knocked me to the ground and began to beat me with the barrel of the rifle while another Nazi held me down. As I was about to lose consciousness, I heard Benjamin scream, "Stop it! I killed them! I shot those two Nazi bastards!"

The beating stopped. The third guard held Benjamin and Yossel at gunpoint. Huber walked over to him and said, "I think you are just trying to save your brother."

I mustered up enough strength to agree. "Yes, he is just a boy, never in the army. He never held a gun in his life."

I wished Benjamin would shut up, but he continued his confession, "I did it; punish me. Meyer had nothing to do with it."

It seemed that Huber believed me and hit Benjamin over the head with the barrel of his Lugar. Benjamin fell to the ground unconscious but alive. I was thankful they shut him up.

Huber turned and walked over to me, lying in pain on the ground. "Now you will pay for your crime, Jew." He knelt down and pointed the gun at my head. I was too scared and hurt to move.

Just then Kozlowski walked in, returning from his collection rounds, only to find the Gestapo about to kill his best customer. "What is going on here?" Kozlowksi asked, as he was startled by what he found.

"Who are you?" asked Huber indignantly.

"I am Officer Kozlowski of the Polish police, and I am responsible for this business and these people."

Huber responded, "This Jew murdered two German officers at a textile plant in Stalowa Wola and must be shot."

Kozlowski surprisingly defended us. "I am familiar with this murder, and these men were here working when the murder took place. They are doing important work for the construction of the new homes and offices for the Nazi officers commanding this region. Unless you have specific evidence that he is the murderer, you must leave at once." As Kozlowski was talking, Benjamin was waking up.

Huber seemed impressed. "Are you saying you are absolutely certain that these men had nothing to do with the murder?"

"Yes," said Kozlowski emphatically.

Huber walked up to Kozlowski, stood right in front of him, and responded, "We will leave, but if I find out that you are lying, I will come back and hang you right next to all these filthy Jews."

With that, Huber picked up the rifle that Benjamin used to kill the two Nazis, and he and his two henchmen walked out the door.

I pulled myself up onto the chair they had used to interrogate me and got myself together enough to say, "Thank you for saving my life," to my Polish overseer.

He turned to Benjamin. "I know it was you. You were late that morning. I always suspected, but it did not suit me to turn you in. I couldn't care less about those two Nazi thugs. I am making an impression with the regional authorities, and they let me make good money in the meantime in the black market. I get them things they can't get themselves. A small price to pay for being in business. They don't need to know I am harboring a murderer. Those Gestapo goons were bluffing. They had no real proof, just looking to get the case closed and go back to Germany. I do give them credit for finding the gun, but that may have been a guess too. Now you need to prepare the order for pickup tonight." With that, he turned and walked outside, probably wondering whether they would come back for him.

Once Kozlowski left, Benjamin and Yossel ran over to me.

"I am so sorry. I was ready to die for what I did, but I could not bear to see you killed," said Benjamin.

Yossel got a wet towel and wiped the blood from my face and mouth.

"I am actually glad you shot those two bastards. They deserved to die for what they did to Chava," I said, now wishing we had killed more of them. Other than losing a tooth and aching all over, I had no major injuries, no broken bones, and felt OK to try to work. The boys seem to work twice as fast as normal, while I dragged behind, but sure enough, we were ready when the truck arrived. Kozlowski was actually surprised we got it done.

"It's the least we could do for what you did for us today." I was actually sincere and thankful.

Kozlowski said, "This is the last time we will speak of this. Just remember I am not your friend. You are my assets, and if you fail, I will kill you myself."

That brought me back to reality.

We dragged ourselves home after we were done, practicing our story to make sure we left out the fact that Benjamin actually did it. When we got home, we didn't get the chance to tell our story. There was a commotion, and Dr. Lansky was tending to Chava, with Momma hovering. I pulled Naomi over and asked her what was happening.

"Chava is very sick. She developed a very high fever. The doctor said she developed an infection from internal bleeding. They talked about amputating her leg, but Dr. Lansky is not allowed in a hospital and he does not have access to a sterile place where he can perform surgery. Plus he is not a surgeon."

Just then, the doctor and Momma moved away from Chava. I asked the doctor how she was.

"I'm afraid there is nothing I can do for her. She has an infection, probably in her pelvis from the internal bleeding she suffered during the beatings. I thought about taking the leg, but that might not be enough depending on where the infection is. She needs serious surgery that I cannot perform and cannot get access to. What happened to you? You look like you took a beating yourself."

"It's nothing," I replied.

Momma noticed too. "What happened to you?"

"I'm fine. We'll talk later," I said. "Dr. Lansky, what can we do to help her?"

He replied, "I gave her morphine to help her sleep. I am afraid I have to be careful with that. I only have a small supply and cannot get any more, but she should sleep for a while."

Benjamin and I sat up all night with her. We were distraught. After all, Benjamin killed to try to save her. The beatings were too much. Do these Nazis have any feelings at all, beating up a poor, defenseless woman? They all should die.

By morning, Chava was dead.

CHAPTER 10

In Mourning

⅄ ⅄ ⅄

We sent Yossel to get the doctor, but we knew Chava was gone. When Dr. Lansky arrived, he confirmed it. I had seen a lot of death since the Nazis arrived, but this was the first time I cried. I cried like a baby. We all did. Chava was so sweet and good. Everyone loved her. She was beautiful and only eighteen when she died. How could they be so cruel? She died from her injuries, a child, a young, sweet life wasted.

Momma was draped over Chava's lifeless body, screaming. She was so strong for all of us. I never saw her break down like this. She was devastated. No one should lose a child this way. What was worse was we had no time to mourn. It would be light soon, and we were expected to work. I had to pull Momma away from Chava and explain that the Nazis had no sympathy for our loss. They would not allow us to mourn, to bury her with dignity, to sit shiva, to gather a minyan to pray, or to say kaddish. We would have to do this at night in secret. Now, Momma, Rivka, and Naomi had to meet their transport to Stalowa Wola, and the boys and I had to get to the lumberyard. Momma understood and gathered herself. All we could do was clean Chava a bit and cover her in blankets. Even the doctor had to get to work. We would tend to Chava that night.

I tried to speak to all of them. "We must survive this. They will beat us. They will starve us. They will work us to our deaths. We must stay strong. We may be slaves all our lives, or Mashiach may come and we may be saved. We must stay alive so we can be saved. Let's go to work and take care of Chava tonight."

Working that day was total misery. We were inconsolable. The revenge that Benjamin had exacted on that Nazi masochist could not even put a dent in our grief for poor Chava. Even Kozlowski felt pity for us. He was not his usual boisterous, demanding self when he heard the news. He knew that even though he was profiting from all of this, he was still a slave to the Nazis also and could be snuffed out if he rubbed one of them the wrong way. True to his word, he did not mention the interrogation from the day before.

"Listen," said Kozlowski, "I know you are distraught. Lord knows killing your sister accomplished nothing for those goons, but we have to get the order ready for tonight and take in the next load of lumber. I'm going to stay here today and give you guys a hand. Today I work for you. Don't get used to this, and don't tell anyone else."

Was he becoming a human being? I wondered. In fact, he was very strong and helped us a great deal that day. He put down his gun and nightstick, rolled up his sleeves, and was quite adept at lifting and carrying piles of wood. He left the cutting to us, but we were actually motivated to forget about our troubles and get busy. Of course when the delivery truck arrived, he straightened out his uniform, picked up his weapons, and acted like the Nazi ass-kisser we knew him to be. We weren't sure whose side he was on. He may not have known which side he was on either.

After work, we arrived home first. Chava was where we had left her, wrapped in blankets. Walking home, I secretly fantasized that she would be sitting on the sofa, laughing about how she faked her death to fool those German bastards, but instead she was as we had left her. Benjamin, Yossel, and I lifted her and put her on a push cart we had from the yard. We were taking her to the barn that had become our makeshift morgue. As we got on the road, Miriam came running up to us. She wrapped her arms around me and give me the tightest hug. She wouldn't let go. I had to push her away after a while, as I actually could not breathe. Benjamin and Yossel turned away, not knowing where to look.

"I'm so sorry." Miriam held herself back from crying. As we pushed a little further, we could see Momma, the girls, and Miriam's sisters, Ruth and Pearl, coming toward us. Once Momma realized what we were doing, she fell down and began to cry again. Naomi helped her up.

Miriam looked at her and said, "Me and my sisters will take care of Chava tonight. You should go home and rest. We should bury her tomorrow as we did Leibish."

I added, "She's right. The boys and I will prepare the grave for her. We will let the rabbi know and anyone who would like to attend."

With that, Momma, Naomi, and Rivka headed home. The rest of us took Chava to the barn and got her situated. Then we left her in Miriam's hands and went to dig the hole.

The word had gotten around. Nachman and Henry, my training partners, came to the barn to see how they could help. We went to the cemetery and dug the hole in three hours. Everyone went home, but I wanted to stop and see how the girls were doing with Chava. Miriam greeted me with another hug, and I held her tightly. We gave each other comfort in this terrible time of sorrow. I felt so much love for her at that moment, I never wanted to leave her side.

"Go home and get some sleep," she said. "Chava is taken care of, and we have to bury her at oh seven hundred so we can get on with our day." She was so right. I kissed her good night and headed home.

The next morning, we all gathered ourselves and headed to the cemetery. The whole shtetl seemed to come, and Rabbi Unger led the service. He was distraught, as we all were, as so many of our young people were being murdered by our masters. He gave an impassioned sermon in Yiddish, praying to God to save us from this horror, this nightmare. He was angry yet powerless. Our fate was in God's hands completely.

We buried Chava with dignity. Our grief was bottomless. Benjamin and Yossel held Momma. Naomi, Rivka, and I held hands during the service. Miriam stayed with her parents and gave us our space. As Chava was lowered into the grave, Benjamin, Yossel, and I recited kaddish. There were no Nazis or police around to object. Momma, the girls, and many in the crowd were crying. We were of course trying to deal with our loss, but the Jews of Pysznica were in grief for our way of life. Also what would happen to the rest of us? The men filled in Chava's grave with dirt, and we began to disperse.

Momma grabbed my hand and said, "I want to know what happened to you yesterday."

"We'll talk tonight, and I'll tell you the story," I advised.

We went to work. Kozlowski was back to his old self. "I have some new supplies for you, boys," he boasted. "Time to pay up. No discounts for dead sisters!"

Benjamin lunged at him, but I grabbed him before he could hit him.

"I knew you were a murderer. Now pay up before I turn you over to the Gestapo," growled Kozlowski.

"I'll pay you," I said, "but we all want to kill you right now. We buried Chava this morning."

"Not my problem," Kozlowski growled louder. "It's a new day, and I love the smell of zlotys." He was drunk with greed. "Besides, the Gestapo solved the murder, so they're not interested in you anymore."

"Who did they get?" asked Benjamin.

"All I heard was a group of Jew terrorists. Now here is the order of the day. Get to work." With that, he was out the door, no doubt to make his rounds and collect his precious profits.

"That bastard!" Benjamin yelled. "I would have killed him with my bare hands!"

"Great," I said. "First of all, he is twice your size, and he would have killed you. And if by some miracle you would have killed him, it would be a death sentence for all of us. Now let's get to work."

Once Benjamin calmed down, we tried to focus on the work, but thoughts of Chava kept rushing forward. The work was mindless, although we had to be careful not to saw our fingers off. When Kozlowski came back, no doubt with his pockets full, he was in a good mood, plus we had the order done, so he could kiss up to the Nazis picking it up. We finished up and went home.

We waited for Momma and the girls to get home. When they arrived, the Goldins were with them to make a shiva call. Momma was so sad, crying as soon as she walked in. When we saw her, we all started to cry. Miriam sat next to me and held my hand.

Since no one was talking, I decided to tell the story of how I was accused of the murder of the guard who killed Chava and only hoped Benjamin would keep his mouth shut. "The day Chava died, we were visited by the Gestapo, who accused me of killing those two officers at your plant—" I started to say.

Momma looked up and interrupted. "That's why you were so beat up yesterday. What happened?"

I continued, "They thought since I was in the army and had military training, and they knew about Chava's beatings, that I was the one who killed them. They were going to beat it out of me when Kozlowksi came in and vouched for us, and they left."

Benjamin stayed silent.

Naomi chimed in. "Well, we witnessed what they do to real murderers today. Right after we got into the factory this morning, they called us out in front of the building. There was a group of Nazi soldiers and two men in black uniforms."

"My Gestapo friends," I said.

Naomi continued, "They had ten men, definitely Jewish, blindfolded and standing in front of us. They have a thing about having ten men. I have no idea who they were or where they came from. Then one of the men in black spoke. 'These ten Jews are responsible for the murder of the two hero soldiers that guarded this facility. So you know that we will not tolerate any action against our soldiers, these men will be executed here and now,' they said and forced these poor men on their knees and shot them in the back of the head one at a time. These poor men, I am sure, had families who don't know what happened to them."

"Oh God!" Benjamin cried out and fell to his knees. "What have I done? Chava is dead, and now ten innocent men have died for what I did."

Everyone was speechless. I picked up Benjamin and put him on a chair. He composed himself and told his story the same way he told us the morning of the shooting. He recounted how he had found the guns and told of our entire training session and how he was so uncontrollably angry about Chava that he walked to the plant in Stalowa Wola, shot the officers, and then came back, dropping the guns in the San River, and went to work. He confessed the whole affair. Now he felt responsible for the deaths of ten innocent men.

Mr. Goldin stood up with great effort, clearly in pain. He spoke with great conviction. "Benjamin, you are not responsible for the deaths of those ten men. I watched those Nazi killers come into Rozwadow and kill innocent men just to intimidate us into leaving. These men were killed to intimidate the workers at the textile plant. We are at war with these people with overwhelming strength. You are the only man I know who has had the courage to fight back in the name of your beloved sister. I, for one, am proud of you."

Momma disagreed. "You could have gotten us all killed. It was foolish to give in to your desire for revenge and kill in the name of Chava.

I am happy that Chava's killer is dead, but we must have hope that we will survive this horror."

Miriam jumped in. "How can we just wait for them to kill us? We must fight them." There was an old joke: put ten Jews together, and you'll have fifteen different opinions. This was no different.

I was clearly of the same opinion as Momma. "What good does it do to fight a stronger enemy head-on and achieve certain death? We kill two; they kill ten. I agree with Momma," I said, not sure I actually believed it. "We must survive this terror. After all, they can't kill us all, can they?"

Mr. Goldin responded, "Jews are such a target by the Nazis and Poles. Imagine that killing all the Jewish people will ultimately become the goal of Hitler and the Nazis. Would it then not be better to die fighting?"

"Who could imagine such a thing?" I responded.

The argument went late into the night, with no resolution. Momma and I were clearly in the minority. Everyone would have to follow his or her own path. Either way, it would be unpleasant for all of us.

Chava was on all our minds, but we continued our work schedule without incident for several weeks. Kozlowski was draining the family funds. We pooled our resources with the Goldins, and we were able to get enough to sustain ourselves at the bare minimum. Many of our neighbors were starving, so we helped them out as much as we could, but we knew once our funds were gone, we would not be able to sustain ourselves.

We settled into the routine. Work from dawn until dusk and sleep at night. During this period, Miriam and I became closer. We no longer cared who saw us carry on. We knew every thought we each had, and we started finishing each other's sentences. We were as one. We promised we would marry if we survived. We were happy for the few hours at night we spent together and miserable during our days of servitude.

This was now our lives. We had little information of the outside world. We knew there was war throughout Europe, and the Nazis were winning was all we heard. As long as we could stay inconspicuous, perhaps we could emerge and have a life once the war was over.

Our dreams were all we had to hold on to. We were numb from our lot in life and for many months put our heads down and did what we had to do to survive.

Many months and even years came and went. You lose track of time when you have no milestones. No weekly Shabbos or holidays to mark the New Year or passing of seasons. No celebrations of life events—weddings or bar mitzvahs. Even birthdays were forbidden. There was only work, dreams of freedom, and occasional visits to Chava's grave to place a stone to commemorate our visit. Maybe we could endure this and come out alive.

CHAPTER 11

Everyone Has Limits

⅄⅄⅄

As the day's work was ending, Kozlowski came by with our weekly order of supplies. We had become more and more careful to buy only what we absolutely needed to survive. We didn't know how long we could last with what we had. We and the Goldins were barely able to get what we needed through our black-market contact. There were others in the shtetl who seemed to have their own access to the black market, but some did not and were visibly suffering. We tried to help those in need as much as we could, but we were not going to reveal our source. Aiding the Jews was illegal, and we could easily lose access to our lifeline if it became known where we obtained food.

Regardless, people in the shtetl were getting sick from malnutrition, contracting infectious diseases like pneumonia, and dying. Others went to work and never came back.

One night, Henry Grossman came to the house totally distraught. "I am looking for my father. He and my mother were taken to work on road projects. Last night, she came home, but he didn't. No one will tell us what happened. We have to find him."

Since we were not allowed to leave the shtetl, it would be difficult to sneak around at night and find out what happened.

"I will ask our overseer at the lumberyard and see what he can find out," I offered.

"Thank you, Meyer," replied Henry. "I'm going to sneak out tonight and see what I can learn. I have an idea where they were working."

"Good luck," I replied. "Be careful out there. If they catch you, they will kill you." He shook my hand and left.

The next morning, when Benjamin, Yossel, and I were headed to work, we ran into Henry, obviously coming back from his search. "Did you find him?" I whispered.

He just shook his head.

"No sign of what happened?" I asked. "I'll check with Kozlowski," I said before he could respond and walked on.

As promised, when we arrived, I pulled Kozlowski aside. "My friend Boaz Grossman is missing. He was working on the roads south toward Nisko. Can you ask around?"

"If he was out digging roads, he's probably dead. I'll ask," he said without any emotion.

We got our orders for the day. It was big and would take several days to finish. It seemed that there was no end to the need for construction material. As long as this was going on, we would have plenty of work.

"We will need more raw wood to finish this," I said. "Why so much?"

Kozlowski snapped back. "Since when do you ask questions, Jew? You'll have an extra delivery today, if you must know. The Nazis are bringing in thousands of German settlers to occupy different areas of Poland. It looks like they intend to stay."

"Maybe it will be good for your business," I said somewhat sarcastically.

"Hardly," he responded. "I can't risk doing business with the Germans. I need Poles and Jews to keep this going. More Germans makes this difficult; plus, they will be taking jobs from Poles, putting them out of work. It's a good thing I have you rich Jews to keep me busy." Somehow, he thought that was funny and laughed out loud. "Now get to work. I'll check on your friend." He turned and left.

Around noon, two large trucks came to deliver our supplies. They were both full. Kozlowski wasn't there, which was unusual. The trucks were early, and no doubt he was making his collection calls. It didn't matter; we knew the routine. Benjamin and Yossel got up into the truck. They handed me the wood and other supplies and guided them onto the hand carts. We then pushed each load onto the dock. Once they left, we would organize it into inventory. Even the Nazis were impressed with our efficiency. By then, we were experts at our jobs but always remembered we were slaves to murderers.

The Nazi officers were particularly talkative. Our German was getting better, and we each overheard bits and pieces of their conversation. I was pretty alarmed at what I was hearing, but none of us reacted. We continued the unloading process. We looked at each other and knew we had a lot to talk about when they left. We finished truck number one and moved on to number two. The driver and guard on the first truck hung around while we unloaded the second. They continued their discussion while chain smoking cigarettes. It seemed as if smoking was a requirement in the German army.

They finally left. We had to get the delivery for pickup that night. But first we gathered in the office to talk about what we'd just heard. Benjamin started.

"Did you hear what they were talking about? Thousands of German families are coming to settle in the area. They know they do not have places for them to live."

Yossel added, "And they can't build enough to cover them. They are going to kick out Poles and Jews so they can take their houses."

"How can they kick us out and expect us to work for them at the same time? It makes no sense," I said.

Yossel added, "I also heard them talking about sending those who can work to Germany and those who are old or sick to other camps where they can be dealt with. What does this mean? I don't understand what will happen to us."

"Look," I said, "these were low-level Germans talking about rumors they heard. Let's see if Kozlowski knows anything when he gets back. Let's get this order filled."

We went back to work, but I had a very uneasy feeling about what was going on. I wanted to sound reassuring since the boys looked up to me, but I wondered if this had anything to do with Boaz Grossman disappearing. We spent the next four hours getting the night's order together, anxiously waiting for Kozlowski to show up.

He finally walked in, just as the truck arrived to pick up the order. "Hello, boys. Everything in order?" he asked, like he had something to do with managing us.

"Yes, sir," Benjamin said angrily. "The order is ready and waiting to be loaded."

As we were loading the truck, I could hear Kozlowski boasting to the two German officers who were standing around having their obligatory smoke. "Look at my efficient operation. When you need your order, my workers have it ready."

I wanted to throw up.

The German officer put him in his place. "That's because we demand it! If the order is not ready, you and your Jews will be punished!"

The other one chimed in. "Or worse!" He laughed pretty hard.

Finally, they went on their way, and we were able to sit down for the first time all day.

"Well, I guess we are done for today." Kozlowski must have had a good collection day.

"Not so fast," I said.

Kozlowski was taken aback.

"Did you hear anything about Boaz Grossman?"

He responded, "Not specifically, but I was told that someone in the Nazi ranks decided that they needed workers to help with the Nazi invasion of Russia and the men working on the Nisko roads were loaded into trucks and headed East. Given the cold weather and the hard conditions up there, I doubt that you will ever see your friend again."

"Oh" was all I could say. This was very disheartening. I wasn't sure what I was going to tell Henry.

"I have another question," I added. "We overheard the Nazi officers talking about the Germans who are coming to settle here, displacing Poles and Jews from their homes. They also said they would take those who can work to Germany and those who cannot they would gather into camps. What does that mean?"

Kozlowski looked at us and paused for a minute. "I've heard the same thing. This is bad for both of us but probably worse for you. They look at you as property and believe they can do what they want with you. Send you anywhere to work. Look at your friend being sent to Russia. As far as camps go, they run an efficient operation, so anyone they don't need, they don't keep, if you know what I mean. This is bad news for me too. If they take you and my other business-assigned workers away, they won't need me, and they will shut down my side business."

Yossel responded, "That will cut off our food supplies and give them excuses to kill more of us."

Benjamin jumped in. "We have to do something. We just can't let this happen!"

I stared him down. I still didn't trust Kozlowski enough to let him know what we were thinking. Benjamin got the message and stopped talking.

"Listen," Kozlowski began, "I have been as big a Jew hater as there is in Poland, but I never bargained for these Nazis coming in here and taking over our lives. There has been a lot of talk about groups of partisans all over Poland taking up arms and hiding out to avoid capture and slavery. Not only Jews but Poles whose lives are being destroyed by the Germans, just as you heard today." He took a deep breath and continued as we listened intently. "If, and only if, these German settlers show up in Pysznica and close us down, my suggestion to you is to gather up your families and any and all valuables you have and go deep into the many square kilometers of woods around the town and develop camps where you can hide out. I will provide you with supplies through my connections, even guns you will need to protect yourselves, but you will have to trust me to know where you are."

"Why are you doing this?" I asked.

He responded, being totally honest. "For my survival and my family. This will be my income until things change. I don't love you Jews that much." He laughed.

Benjamin declared, "I would rather live with the slimiest creatures in the woods and die fighting than let those Nazi bastards treat us like property and do what they please with us."

"Benjamin, for once, I agree with you. This may actually be the best thing we can do. Let's see what happens," I said.

"Just so you know," Kozlowski warned, "if you should suddenly disappear without my knowledge, I will hunt you down and kill you myself."

"I think we understand," I responded.

As we walked home, Benjamin couldn't have been more excited. "I knew this would not get any better and we would have to fight or die. We should gather all the families of the boys we trained as snipers and head into the woods. We don't need Kozlowski. We have weapons. We can take what we need and kill Nazis in our way."

"Take it easy." I tried to stay calm. "There are not enough of us to fight anyone. We will need more guns than we have. The women will have to learn to shoot as well. We can get some supplies from local farms and shops, but if Kozlowski can be trusted—and that is not certain—it will be less risky if we use him to get us what we need." I continued, "Let's tell Momma and the girls, then the Goldins, then let's reach out to Nachman and Henry to help organize." I had to tell Henry about his father, so I was sure he would agree, but I was still agonizing as to whether we could trust Kozlowski.

When we got home, Momma and the girls were already home. We didn't realize how late we were. We had something to eat and told them we had to talk about the latest developments.

I laid out in detail what we had heard, what Kozlowski suggested, and what we thought happened to Boaz Grossman. Benjamin and Yossel both were enthusiastic about being partisans and fighting the Nazis. The big question was, do we need and can we trust Kozlowski?

The girls looked to Momma to react. "I don't want to leave my home, my life. As bad as things are, we are still together in our home that your father and I built for you." She began to cry. "I miss him. We need him now, and he is gone."

Yossel went over and hugged her. "I miss him too, but if we don't leave, they will take away our home and who knows what they will do with us."

Naomi jumped in. "I don't want to go to that factory anymore. It reminds me of Chava every day and what they did to her. Give me a gun. I'll shoot some of those Nazis."

"That's my girl!" cried Benjamin.

That gave us all a good laugh.

Rivka made it unanimous. "I'm with Naomi. I don't know what else to do."

Momma was still skeptical. "How are we going to live in the woods? Like animals? How will we get shelter? I'm too old for this."

I replied, "First of all, I think we have a little time. We are not going ahead with this until we know the Germans plan to change our situation. Also I am not sure how we will live. I think we should get a group together and scout a location deep in the forest where we can set up a camp, have some protection from the weather, and get access to farms and the town to get supplies. Let's hold off on Kozlowski for a while, although I am feeling we can trust him as long as we are paying him. He has an obsession about keeping this black-market business going."

"OK," said Momma, "I will trust your judgment on this."

We were all in agreement. Next I headed to see the Goldins. Benjamin and Yossel went to see Nachman and Henry. When I arrived, Jonah was standing outside talking to a neighbor. It wasn't unusual for me to show up late at night. After all Miriam and I spent as much of our free time together as we could, but tonight was different. We weren't going off for our long walks. When I walked into the house, Miriam was helping her mother clean up after dinner. Little Shlomo was there also.

"Good evening," I said.

Miriam came over and kissed me on the cheek. "I'll be ready in a few minutes," she said.

"I need to talk to the whole family tonight," I said firmly.

"What is going on?" asked Shayna.

"Some new disturbing developments have surfaced, and we have to make some plans," I responded. "Can we all get together in the living room?"

"I'll get Jonah," said Shayna. "Miriam, please get your sisters."

Within a few minutes, they were gathered. "What's the emergency?" asked Jonah.

I began to again tell the story of what we overheard the German officers say about the German settlers displacing Polish and Jewish homes, how Boaz Grossman was seemingly shipped to the Russian border, and Kozlowski's confirmation and suggestion that we all hide in the woods as partisans. This time, the story seemed crazy, even for me, and that was exactly what Jonah Goldin believed.

"This makes no sense. They rely on Jewish labor here in Pysznica to do all their dirty work. Why would they displace us and gather up people for transport?"

I replied, "All I know is they are bringing in thousands of Germans to settle in this area, and they need places to live. We can't produce enough houses to put them in, so they will take what they need. The Germans will take the jobs from the Poles, and we will all be shipped out somewhere else if we can work. If not, who knows?"

Shayna protested. "Jonah cannot go anywhere. His legs are so painful that he can hardly walk. It just gets worse."

"I can do what I need to," Jonah snapped back.

"When is this going to happen?" asked Ruth.

"I don't know," I replied. "One week, maybe two, if it happens at all. We have to prepare. My brothers are talking to some of the boys with military experience. We will look for a location and gather what we need to set up camp."

"How will we get supplies and food?" asked Miriam.

Again, I responded, "We can pay Kozlowski to get some of what we need, but we will have to trust him with our location. The rest of what we need we will have to steal. We have some guns, and Kozlowski will get us more. This will not be what we are used to. We will have to survive like animals and be criminals. We have to defend ourselves as many of our ancestors did before us. Now it is our turn. We may have to kill to survive."

Miriam said, "I will do what is necessary. We have to fight back."

Ruth and Pearl agreed.

Jonah put his hands over his face. "How did we come to such a place? I wish I was healthier, but I will agree to go along the best I can."

"I will let you know if we have to do this," I said somberly.

I got up and left the house alone. As I was walking toward home, coming the other way were my brothers, Nachman, and Henry.

"I can't believe what is happening here," said Henry. "The boys told me what you heard happened to my father. I am so upset. I hope he makes it back, but in the meantime, I am ready to join the partisans and take some control back of our lives."

Nachman jumped in and said, "Me too. My family will join if necessary. Also I think you should work with this Kozlowski guy. We will need all the help we can get. Maybe we can meet him away from the camp and not give him our exact location."

"That's worth a try," I responded. "We need to find a campsite now and have it ready in case we need it. We should also try to recruit more of our snipers. The bigger the group, the more money we will have to pay Kozlowski. Who will be able to look for a site? We have to work all daylight hours. It will be hard to scope out the site at night."

"We'll do it," said Henry. "Nachman and I are on the same road detail, and we usually have a couple of hours of daylight before we get picked up."

Nachman agreed. "It may take a couple of days. There are a lot of areas I can think of where we used to disappear and play as kids. We know the territory, and we can go in deep and not get lost."

"Great," I said. "It's settled. Let's meet at my house after work the day after tomorrow and see what you have found."

We headed home after that, but I did not sleep very well that night. I kept wondering how we would pull this off.

The next morning, we headed to the yard as usual but with a new purpose. On the way, I said to Benjamin and Yossel, "We need to think about some supplies we can use to build the camp. We will need to dig trenches, and perhaps we can get some lumber to build some shelters. It will be very simple, but we should put some posts and plywood sheets aside and figure out how to get them later."

Benjamin replied, "Agreed. After Kozlowski leaves for his usual rounds, let's start to stockpile small amounts in different parts of the yard so no one gets suspicious."

"Good," I said.

When we arrived, Kozlowski was waiting and seemed very nervous. "So?" he asked. "Did you consider my proposal?"

"Yes," I said without hesitation, "In fact, we have scouts looking for a suitable location for when the time comes, and we will likely recruit several families to go with us, so you will have more people to supply." I saw no reason not to agree, even if we wound up disappearing without him. I also did not have any intention of telling him our exact location regardless. We would find a place to meet.

"Good," he said. "Don't waste time. I hear the Germans are settling in Lublin, and people are being evicted. They may be here soon."

"We will be ready," I said with confidence I did not really have.

Kozlowski left, and we started gathering all the supplies we thought we could put aside without being noticed. Regardless we would have to sneak in at night to get the goods out when the time came. Frankly, Kozlowski probably would help us, but it was better not to take chances. The good news was that we still had the keys to the yard gate and the office, as Kozlowski was not always there in the morning to greet us. He was violating his orders, but that seemed to be his nature. We would try to take advantage of that. We must have been pumped with adrenaline, as we were able to handle our little outside activity and fill the order in time for pickup that evening.

That night, I gathered the family once again and gave them an update on the plan. I told them that it was likely that we would be leaving our home in a week or two and that we should think about what essential things we should take to make do in the harsh environment of the forest. No one wanted to hear it, but we all agreed to get ready. I did the same with the Goldins. Miriam wanted to help set up the camp when we found a spot, and I thought that was a great idea. She was strong willed and determined, and she would need to learn to handle a weapon. Being in love would be on hold for a while, and we both knew it. We needed every man, woman, and child to become a soldier in our little army.

The next day, we continued our mission to gather what we could, like squirrels getting ready for the winter. I was looking forward to seeing what Nachman and Henry had found for our new home.

CHAPTER 12

Ready or Not

⅄ ⅄ ⅄

THEY WERE RIGHT ON TIME and were smiling. They were very excited. "How did it go?" I asked.

"We found two sites we think will work," Nachman replied.

Henry said, "But there is one we really think is perfect. It's about five kilometers southeast of here, deep enough in the woods to be hidden but close to several farms where we can get food. There is a clearing where we can dig trenches and put up tents. There is also a stream nearby where we can get water and bathe."

"That sounds good," said Benjamin. "Can we see it?"

"Yes, let's go tonight," said Nachman. "We have some good torches we can use to light our way."

"Let's go," I replied. "Yossel, please go home and let Momma and the girls know we are looking at a campsite. They need to know this is really going to happen, and soon."

"I will," said Yossel, and he took off. So did we.

As we walked, I asked Henry, "How are your mother and sister doing with the news of your father being sent to Russia?"

"They're both so sad," Henry replied. "There is lots of crying, not only for Papa but for our whole situation and way of life."

I pressed. "Are they ready to make the move to the camp?"

"Like the rest of us, they have no choice if they want to live," he replied.

Nachman said, "My parents are ready as well." Nachman was an only child.

"Have you spoken to any of your sniper students about joining us?" I asked.

Nachman replied, "I have two families coming, the Levines and the Fishers, an additional eight people."

"I have one additional family coming, the Wachtels, and there are five of them," Henry added.

"So how many is that?" I asked.

Nachman did the math. "There are thirteen, plus Henry's three, and my four makes twenty, plus you and the Goldins make thirty-two."

"Good," I said. "Let's think about that as we set up the camp. We will need to feed all those mouths. We will also need more guns and ammunition."

We reached the site in less than one hour, which would be good if we had to make a fast evacuation. It was as Henry and Nachman described it—deep enough in the woods where we would be hard to find but close to local farms. I would have to find a nearby location to meet Kozlowski. There was a clearing that had obviously been used for camping by the locals. The trees were tall, and there was room to dig trenches and build some structures to keep us dry. Someone had already built a fire pit that we might be able to use.

"Mazel tov, boys. You have found the perfect spot," I declared.

Henry replied, "I knew this place. My father and I used to spend nights here sometimes in the summer. We built the pit."

"Great," I said. "Let's hope no one else finds this place before we need it. I have been gathering supplies at the lumberyard we can use to build some small huts for the families."

Nachman replied, "I have access to an old truck. When can we get them?"

"Tomorrow after we load the day's order for the Nazis. Kozlowski will leave, and we will have free reign of the yard."

"Great," said Nachman. "We'll see you after dark."

We then headed home. "Benjamin, I want to stop at the Goldins and tell them about the camp."

"You mean you want to see Miriam." He smirked.

"Yes, that too," I admitted.

He replied, "You stop. I will go home and fill everyone in on the latest plan."

"Thank you," I said. When I got to the house, Miriam and her mother were arguing.

"I'm not leaving the family. Papa is sick, and you need my help," she declared.

Shayna replied firmly, "If we have to leave this house and live like animals in the woods, at least you will be able to hide out safely with a roof over your head."

Miriam shot back, "I will only go if the worst happens and we have to run. Also I am taking Shlomo with me. I need company, and he is attached to me."

Shayna argued, "He's only eight now and will get in your way. He does not know when to be quiet. He will say or do something that will give you away, and you will both get killed."

"I don't care. I want him with me!" she cried. I had never seen her so determined. She held her own, and Shayna agreed.

"What's going on?" I asked Jonah.

Before he could answer, Miriam jumped down my throat. "I'll tell you what is going on," she said. Everyone else except Shlomo suddenly cleared the room. Miriam took a deep breath and spoke. "A woman and her daughter came into the dress shop today. The girl was about my age, and she was getting married and needed a dress."

Miriam looked at me curiously, like she was wondering when it would be her turn to be married. I just listened.

She continued, "At some point the girl asked me, 'Aren't you Miriam Goldin from Rozwadow?'

"'Yes.' I looked at her.

"'I am Stephania Dombeck,' she said. 'We went to school together.'

"I had no idea who she was. 'I don't remember you.'

"'We had classes together, but I did not speak to you because you were a Jew,' she replied as her mother looked away. 'I am sorry for that. I do not understand why the Jews are hated so much in Poland, and now the Nazis are here and are killing and enslaving your people. I think it is wrong, but I am glad to see you are working, making beautiful dresses, and doing well.'

"I looked around to make sure I wasn't being watched and said, 'Well, that is not exactly my situation. My family and I were chased from our homes in Rozwadow under threat of death. They murdered people from our shtetl to scare us out. We gathered what we could and moved to Pysznica, where we found a kind man who took us in and let us live in his home. The Nazis eventually came to Pysznica and have turned us into slaves. This job is a slave job because I had the talent to make dresses for women marrying Nazi officers and they needed me. They pay me nothing and send me home when I am done. Now the Nazis are threatening to chase us from our homes again.'

"Mrs. Dombeck came over after hearing my story. 'Poor, sweet girl,' she said. 'No one deserves to live this way. We were taught that the Jews were the devil. They killed Jesus and were not to be trusted. Now I see the real devil lives in Germany. His name is Hitler, and he calls his disciples Nazis. We can only hope the rest of the world wakes up before the Nazis take over everywhere. I want to help you if we can. If you ever need a place to live, you can hide in our house. We have a basement that you can stay in. It is illegal to hide a Jew, but we will do it if you need us. We will keep it a secret. My dear, you are the first Jew I ever met, and I want to help you.'

"With that, she wrote down her address, and they said good-bye and left. I didn't know what to make of such an offer. Can I trust them? Do they really feel bad about what is happening? Maybe they see the Poles are being treated almost as badly as us, and this is their way of fighting back. Anyway, I was confused, so when I got home I told everyone the story, and Momma immediately decided I should go and leave everyone here."

I was devastated. All I could think of was that she would disappear and I would never see her again. "It's a great offer," I said. "Poles are worried. Even Kozlowski, a great Jew hater, actually feels like he wants to help us. He disguises it by making it about money, but I believe he doesn't like to be told what to do by Germans and this is his way of rebelling."

"You can send me away so easily?" she asked angrily.

"No," I said, "I want you to stay with me. I want everything to be normal and live a normal life, marry you, have children, and run my lumberyard. But that is not the way it is now. If we get forced to leave our homes and live like animals in the woods, who knows if we will survive? Once we stop showing up to our slave jobs, we will be hunted down. We will have no time for being in love. You know it, and so do I. It doesn't matter what we feel, just what we need to do to survive. You have a chance to disappear into the world and you need to take it. What good will it do if we all die together?"

She was not happy with me, but she knew I was right. "Isn't it time for you to go home now?" She was clearly irritated.

"Yes," I said, kissed her on the cheek and left.

As I walked home, all I thought about was Miriam, the one positive thing that came out of this was now lost. I had to focus on getting our camp set up quickly. I had no idea how long we had to get ready. I also realized that my whole purpose for stopping at the Goldins was to tell them about the campsite. It would have to wait.

When I arrived at the house, Momma, Rivka, and Naomi were discussing what to take if we had to move quickly. They sounded like they understood that we had to take as little as possible. We needed something to cook in and eat with but just enough for the six of us. They picked out what we would take from the kitchen.

I couldn't help but join the conversation. "No fancy clothes. We will not be going to Shabbos dinners."

They laughed and understood what was about to happen to us. Tomorrow we would start to build our new home.

In the morning, we got to the lumberyard as usual. Kozlowski was there ahead of us, earlier than usual. That was not a good sign.

"How's your search going?" asked Kozlowski first thing.

"Good," I responded. "We have a site. We need a few days for setup, but we will be ready. What are you hearing out there?"

Kozlowski advised, "Yesterday Nazi soldiers went into Lublin and arrested Polish farm owners and their families, not Jews. They are taking their houses to give to Germans coming in to settle there."

I asked, "Are they shipping people to Germany, as we overheard yesterday?"

"I don't know for sure, but yes, they are arresting the people and sending them somewhere," he replied.

"What about the Jews?" I asked. "If they are not bothering the Jews, then we don't have to run into the woods."

"Are you crazy?" asked Kozlowski indignantly. "Whatever they are doing to the Poles, they will do ten times worse to the Jews. You may have a few days, but they will come for you. Where is your camp?"

"It's about five kilometers east of Pysznica, but we have a slight problem."

"What's that?" asked Kozlowski.

"Some of our group are worried about letting a Polish policeman know where we are hiding. On the other hand, I have convinced them that you will help us, and they get it."

"What the hell are you talking about, Jew?" He was angry now.

I replied calmly, "We want to work with you, but we will have to work out a location close to the camp where we can do our business. Having you come into the camp will be a problem. The good news is that this will be good business for you. We already have thirty-two people signed up to join us. We will need guns and other supplies. All the families have some money, and you will be our only supplier." I knew the prospect of more zlotys would calm him down.

"That works for me." Kozlowski beamed. "I don't want to step into your stinky camp anyway."

"Good," I said. "Keep me informed so we can make the move when we have to."

Kozlowski gave us our orders for the day and said, "I need to go and make my collection calls early today. I may lose some customers soon, and I don't want them to owe me money when they get taken away." Then he went on his way.

We started the day by gathering more supplies for the camp. Henry and Nachman were bringing a truck that night, and we wanted to make sure we had a full load. We would be pretty well equipped to deal with the elements.

"Do we really need all this wood and supplies?" asked Yossel.

"Yes," I said, "we will have over thirty people, some older and sick, like Mr. Goldin. We will need shelter from the elements, and we could be there a long time. It will not be easy for those like you who were not trained in the military."

"I think it will be fun, an adventure, and finally we can be human beings instead of slaves, living by our wits," added Benjamin.

"This is not a game," I snapped at them both. "This is life and death. It's about survival. I hate those Nazi bastards, and they should all die."

"Now you're talking," declared Benjamin.

Yossel jumped in as the voice of reason. "Let's calm down and get to work. We still have to get this order filled and get it out so we can start to work on the camp."

"Good point," I said, and we immediately buckled down.

The day went pretty quickly. The order was routine, and we worked well together and got it on the dock and ready to go before Kozlowski got back.

"Very impressive, boys," he said, walking into the office in a good mood. "I'm not sure what will happen to these businesses once the Nazis chase you away. They want slave labor, but they also want to kill Jews. It makes no sense. I heard that they are rounding up Jews in Lublin and sending them away, as they are Poles, but on different trains and to different places."

I mumbled, "It's just a matter of time until they visit us again."

"Right you are," answered Kozlowski.

At that point, the delivery truck pulled up to get the order. As we were loading the truck, I could hear Kozlowski asking the German drivers about the plans to bring settlers to Pysznica. I didn't hear the answer, so I would have to ask Kozlowski when they left. I asked the boys if they heard anything, but they didn't. Finally, the truck was loaded. We shut the doors. The drivers got in and off they went. I knew we didn't have a lot of time before Henry and Nachman were to come. We had it timed. They were to be stationed two kilometers down the road, west of the lumberyard, which was the route the delivery trucks usually took. Once the truck drove by them, they were to wait fifteen minutes for Kozlowski to leave, then they would come. We would load the truck and head over to the camp to unload and start building, but I had to ask what he just learned.

"Kozlowski," I called out as he was about to leave.

"What?" he responded.

"I heard you talking to the drivers about settlers coming to Pysznica," I said. "What did they say?"

He replied, "All they know is that once they finish cleaning out Lublin, they will head south in this direction. They had no idea about the time it would take to get here, but they will likely come at least to Rozwadow, as there are jobs, and probably here to take over the farms."

As we were talking, a truck pulled into the yard. "Shit," I said softly. They couldn't wait the fifteen minutes. They had to come now.

"What's this? There are no more trucks expected tonight," Kozlowski muttered to himself. He went out to see who they were. As he got closer to the truck, he pulled out his revolver and quick as a flash jumped up on the foot rail, swung open the door, and pointed the gun at Henry's head, as he was behind the wheel. "Get out and put your hands where I can see them. What are two Jews doing driving a truck? You have broken the law and will be punished."

"Wait," Benjamin cried out, as he got outside first. "They are with us, friends of ours." He could have been a bit more creative.

I jumped in. "They work with this truck, and they were just going to give us a ride home tonight as a treat."

Kozlowski laughed. "You're a lousy liar, Meyer. Do you think I am an idiot? Do you think I didn't notice your little piles of cut wood, hammers, nails, and supplies scattered around the yard? Did you think I didn't know what you were doing? When are you going to learn to trust me?"

"Look," I replied, "we are fighting for our lives, our survival. I seem to have to tell everyone that today." I looked at my brothers and continued, "The less you know about our little venture, the better for you. We want to do business with you, but I am sure you do not want to get caught helping those evil Jews hide from the Nazis."

"Screw the Nazis." Kozlowski was defiant. "I'm leaving now. Do what you came to do." Then he left.

Henry and Nachman were in shock.

"Is that guy for real?" asked Nachman.

"He's an egotistical lunatic," added Henry. "Are you sure we can trust him?"

I replied, "As long as we can pay him, we can trust him. Now let's get to work."

Benjamin and I got in the back of the truck. Yossel directed them to follow him as he walked to each of our piles in the yard. Once they backed the truck up to the pile, the three of them jumped out and handed us the various wood pieces and plywood sheets and supplies, and we carefully piled them in the truck so we could fit as much as possible. We repeated the exercise five times until the truck was full.

When we arrived at the site, it was lit up with torch lights and there were lots of people milling around.

"What's going on here?" I asked, totally baffled.

"Surprise," said Nachman. "We thought our new community should be here to start setting up the camp. We mapped out the site and picked spots where the seven families can set up a shelter for themselves."

"Very nice," I replied as I looked at the schematic they had prepared. "Is there enough room in the clearing?"

Henry replied, "It will be tight, but there should be enough room where each family can be together and have privacy from the other families."

"It will be tough on those who have not had experience living this way, but the rest of us can help them get acclimated," said Nachman.

"In fact," added Henry, "when I went around talking to people about coming tonight, most were very excited but not because we were setting up a camp in the woods. It was because this will be the first time in two years they will have any kind of freedom. They would not have to report to grueling, thankless jobs where they are hated and treated like cattle. In their own way, they would become freedom fighters and finally do something to fight our captors, even if it means death. Your precious Miriam was the first one here, with her sisters and brother, and they are ready to work."

I said, "Let's get everyone together and meet to discuss the plan. We all have to be in agreement or there will be nothing but fighting and difficulty putting this together. If we are not helpful and respectful of each other, this could be dangerous for all of us."

"All right," said Henry, "let's spread the word and meet in the middle of the clearing in fifteen minutes. Meyer, you start the discussion, and we will chime in as needed."

I immediately went over to see Miriam. "Welcome to our new home," I said, trying to get a laugh.

"If this is the best you can do, I'm going to have to rethink our relationship," she snapped back without missing a beat.

"Is your family here?" I asked.

"Momma and Papa are home," she said. "He is not feeling well, but he is determined to come join us here when we have to move and not give up the fight. After all, we were kicked out of our home a long time ago. My sisters are here, as is Shlomo."

I had to ask the next question. "Are you coming with us, or are you going to live with the family in Rozwadow?"

"I don't know yet. Momma wants me to go and said I can take Shlomo. I don't want to leave them or you, so we will see how it goes. I will stay for now, but the invitation is open."

"Good," I replied. "Gather your family; we will meet in a few minutes."

Next I saw Naomi and Rivka talking to Benjamin and Yossel. "I guess you know the plan by now. Where is Momma?"

"Home," said Rivka. "She is packing; she wants to take everything. We'll have to help her leave some things behind."

Just then we noticed everyone gathering in the center of the clearing. "Let's go," I said, then started walking to the front of the group.

"Hello, and thank you for coming tonight. We all know why we are here, but Henry, Nachman, and I are trying to organize this camp so we all have what we need and we all agree on how the camp will be set up and organized. First, I will tell you what I know about the latest news. I hear that Nazi soldiers have arrested Polish farm owners and their families. They are being taken from their homes and sent to Germany to work camps. I have also heard they are gathering Jewish families, separating the young and healthy from the old and sick, and are sending them on trains. No one knows where. Supposedly they are making room for German civilian settlers who are coming to occupy parts of Poland. We also have heard that they will head south toward Rozwadow and will eventually arrive here. We want to be ready with this camp if and when they arrive."

David Fisher stood and said, "I have heard that they will not hesitate to kill anyone who resists, right on the spot, Pole or Jew."

I continued. "It's important that we know the desperation of this situation that is forcing us to take this action."

Benjamin jumped in. "We should have done this long ago and done what we could to fight these bastards."

I tried to get back control. "Well, we are doing it now. Nachman and Henry have mapped out the clearing and assigned each family a spot where you can put up a hut, dig trenches, or whatever you would like. Each location is measured by number of people, so larger families get a bigger area than smaller families. Benjamin, Yossel, and I have brought some supplies to help us build shelters to help protect us from the elements. We will provide what we can and try to get more if needed. We must also all work together to help each other, as some of us have more building skills than others. Henry and Nachman will mark each area for each family, and you will be limited to that area. We will have a common area in the middle, where we will build a fire pit. Next, we have some weapons and ammunition, but everyone in the camp should have at least one gun. We have a supplier who can provide weapons as well as food and other supplies. He is a Polish officer with ties to the black market. We have agreed to get supplies as needed. He will not know the location of the camp. We will meet at a point about two kilometers away when we need him. We can also supplement what we need from local farms. Does anyone have any questions?"

"Yes," said Miriam, "when do we start already?"

"Right now," I replied. "I will stop talking and turn it over to Henry and Nachman. Let's get to work."

CHAPTER 13

Shelter in the Storm

THE GROUP FOLLOWED HENRY AND Nachman around the camp. Nachman said, "We figured about fifty square meters per person, plus fifty extra meters so we could have enough space to sleep, sit, and not step all over each other. This means a family of six would have three hundred and fifty square meters to use. A smaller family of four would have two hundred and fifty meters of inside space. This would allow us to have room for seven huts inside the clearing, with room in the center to gather and have a fire pit."

"We will get to know each other very well." Naomi laughed. "Can we at least build a wall between the boys and the girls?"

I replied, "We can build a mechitzah. We will live like partisans. Trust me; this is better than the army. I give these boys a lot of credit."

No one protested too much. We all knew what was at stake. Henry and Nachman thought this out very well. The first area was ours. They used the measuring tape we brought from the lumberyard to measure the 350 square meters we were allowed and marked it off with sticks and branches found nearby. Next to us were the Goldins. I liked the sound of that. They would have the same 350 square meters as us but with four women and two men instead of three and three.

They continued to mark off the rest of the families' areas while we and the Goldins went to gather some shovels, hammers, nails, and posts we would use to set up around the boundaries of each shack we would soon live in. We were able to take two shovels per family and limited amounts of other tools that we would share. We decided that the two families would work together to build the two shacks.

Miriam, Pearl, Ruth, and Shlomo came over to us. Miriam said, "None of us are very experienced in building. Let us help you build your house, and then we can all build ours. What do you think?"

In our world, men usually did the manual labor outside the home, and women were homemakers and raised the children. Our traditions were already out the window, and we would need every woman, man, and child to do his or her part, both as builders and as partisans, to keep us all alive.

"Yes, that is a great idea. Having four more pairs of hands working will make the whole thing go faster," I responded.

Everyone agreed, and we headed over to the supplies. I sorted out the tools, shovels, ladders, hammers, nails, and such, and Benjamin and Yossel started handing out posts. Henry, Nachman, and I agreed that the first thing we should do was dig a trench about three feet deep and build a little below ground. Should we be found and there was shooting, we would have a bunker to give us some protection. We grabbed four shovels.

We worked all night. It was actually quite joyful and exhilarating, as we were taking matters into our own hands, working for our own benefit, not as Nazi slaves. We dug the trench the full length and width of the footprint we had agreed upon. We then dug holes and sank posts two meters high every meter around the perimeter of the lot. Then we put up plywood walls and a roof to cover the dwelling. We then framed the inside so we could have separate rooms for the men and women and a small common area, just as we planned. The dwelling would have dirt floors and no indoor plumbing. We would get water from a nearby stream and live closer to nature than anyone wanted to. This would be a very stark existence that none of us were used to. Our current lives were luxurious compared to the simple animal-like existence we were about to embark upon. We were all exhausted. We finished our new home and started digging the Goldins' trench.

We all needed to go home and try to get an hour's sleep before heading to our day jobs. Before going home, Miriam and I walked around to see how the other families were doing. No one had finished an entire dwelling, although Nachman and Henry were both giving pointers to the other families and helping them.

"Tell your sisters that you were all fantastic," I told Miriam.

"We all worked hard, and each of us pulled our weight," she replied.

My brothers were both hardworking and skilled, but the women from both families hardly missed a beat, digging, hammering the walls together, and just carrying heavy loads. Once we were done with the Goldins' hut tomorrow, we would help the others finish. We had no idea how much time we had.

Nachman came over to me and said, "I think we need more supplies. We are running out of plywood. We have everything else."

I looked around. "We will try to gather up some from the yard. Can you get the truck to come pick it up?"

"Yes," replied Nachman. "I'll be there after dark. We are done for tonight."

I walked Miriam home. On the way I asked her point-blank, "Are you going to take up those people's offer and move in with them in Rozwadow?"

"I don't know," she replied. "My parents think I will be safer away from the Jewish community, and they like the idea of me taking Shlomo."

"Won't it be hard to leave your family behind and go off into an unknown world?" I asked.

She was upset. "I don't want to leave them. Papa's condition is getting worse, and my place is with them." We were quiet for a while. "And you. I love you. I want to be with you and never leave you." She began to cry, and I tried to comfort her.

"I love you too, but this is not our time. The world is crazy. We may all die or live. I have no idea. All we can do is live day to day. If you can survive by leaving, then you must leave. I will find you someday, I promise."

We embraced, and she whispered in my ear, "Let's both promise that if we are free when this horror is over that we will look for each other and not stop until we know for sure what happened to the other."

"Amen," I replied.

With that, we continued our walk to her house. I kissed her goodbye and left her there.

Everyone was asleep when I got to the house. The sun would come up in about an hour. There was no point in trying to sleep. I just sat there thinking about what was happening to our lives and wondering if the Russians or some other European power could stand up and defeat Germany or if we all were going to die trying.

I closed my eyes for a few minutes. The next thing I knew the sun was up.

"C'mon, Meyer, we need to get to work," said Benjamin. He and Yossel were up and ready to go.

"I guess I was sleeping," I said, trying to wake up. I got myself together, and we headed to the yard.

When we arrived, Kozlowski was there waiting for us. "They're coming" was all he said.

"What do you mean?" asked Yossel. I knew what he meant.

"The Nazis, idiot," he replied, annoyed. "They are moving in this direction from Lublin and are gathering Jews as well as Poles they are displacing."

"When will they be here?" I asked. "Maybe tonight, maybe tomorrow—soon," he replied.

"We are ready to move tonight. We need some guns and ammunition in addition to food and supplies for the thirty-two of us," I said.

Kozlowski put his business hat on. "Very good. I will gather some supplies today and meet you tonight at midnight. Where will we meet?"

I replied, "Follow the Sportawa Road about five kilometers east of the Pysznica shtetl. We will meet you on the road, and we will ride into the woods and show you where we will meet in the future. We will flag you down with torches as you drive by. The road should be otherwise quiet at that time."

"Good," said Kozlowski. He started to leave.

"What about our orders for today?" I shouted as he was walking out.

He turned back and began to laugh. "Seriously, don't you get what is happening? There are no orders for today. The Nazis are busy preparing to ruin your lives. You better get moving." Then he left, leaving me, Benjamin, and Yossel with our mouths hanging open.

This was really happening. Henry and Nachman were not coming until after sundown, and I assumed the women went to work as normal.

Yossel said, "I guess we better get our supplies together."

"Right," I replied.

We went into the yard and gathered the plywood we needed to finish the camp. We gathered some extra posts, tools, and whatever else we thought would be useful and piled them near the front gate.

By then it was nearly noon, so we decided to head to the shtetl and see if we could start preparing the house to leave. As we walked from the lumberyard, we noticed some unusual Nazi-soldier vehicles on the roads. They were not headed our way or even concerning themselves with us, but it seemed to me they were headed to join others for a potential operation, surely one that included us.

As we got home, we ran into Henry and Nachman driving their truck. I still had no idea where they got it, but it would come in handy. They stopped when they saw us.

Henry shouted, "Meyer, hop in! We are bringing our things to the camp. They let us leave the road crew. Our guards were all ordered away for something. We saw troops gathering outside town. It looks like we are next."

"Yes," I said, "we heard the same."

"Let's get this load to the camp then go by the lumberyard and get the supplies we prepared."

I got in the front seat.

Benjamin said, "Yossel and I will go to the house and get everything together. We are prepared and know exactly what to take. Come back to the house after you get the yard supplies delivered."

"Great idea," I replied, and off we went.

The camp was as we left it. We unloaded the truck and started for the lumberyard. "Whose truck is this, anyway?" I asked.

Henry and Nachman looked at each other and laughed. Henry spoke. "It belongs to the road crew we work on. They just leave a couple of trucks parked along the side of the road at the end of the day, so we decided to help ourselves a few times, and no one noticed. The only issue is stopping for petrol, but we have been able to fill up without question so far."

"It would be nice if we could keep this for a while," I said without really thinking.

The boys laughed louder this time.

"Do you think we are going back tomorrow?" Nachman chuckled sarcastically.

I started to laugh. I finally got the joke.

We went to the lumberyard, passing numerous Nazi and Polish military vehicles on the way. They didn't pass a glance at us. We filled the truck with all the supplies and headed back to camp.

By the time we got back from the camp and arrived at my house, it was early evening, and everyone was home. When we pulled up, Naomi came running out. "Meyer, we were sent home early too. Our guards were called away, and we were told to gather our things and get into the transports. We are ready to make the move tonight."

When I got into the house, everything we agreed to take was piled up in the middle of the living room. The only real furniture we would take were mattresses and a couple of chairs. The rest was clothes, bedding, kitchen items such as plates, silverware, and pots and as few personal items as we could afford to take. Of course, we also took anything of value that we could trade or sell.

By the time we loaded the truck, it was dark. Everyone piled in the back, and we headed off to our new home. "Before we leave I want to stop at the Goldins," I said. I could hear the groans from the back of the truck. "Just for a few minutes!" I yelled back.

When we stopped I jumped out. Jonah saw me on the way in. "Meyer, we are ready to move. When the girls came home, they told me they were let out early, and they saw troops amassing nearby. I know what that means, so we are gathering our belongings. Miriam is not home yet. She must not know, so we will fill her in when she gets here."

"Very good," I said. "We have access to a truck. We are headed to camp with our things, and we will unload everything and come back here for your stuff and the family. Give us a couple of hours. We will have a long night ahead of us. We have to build your shelter when we get there first thing."

Then Jonah embraced me and said, "You know I am not doing well, but I will use whatever I have left to help in any way I can." He kissed me on the cheek and said, "Go; we are running out of time."

As I walked out of the house, Miriam was walking up the street. When she saw me, she ran over and asked, "What is going on?"

I grabbed her by the arms and just said, "Go talk to your father." I let go and jumped back in the truck, and Nachman put it in gear.

When we arrived at the camp, it was raining lightly. The ground was a bit muddy, and it would make it more difficult to continue the move and finish building the other structures. We all got out of the truck and started to unload all we had brought into our new home. When I came back out, Momma was standing there, and she began to cry.

"What will become of us?" she cried out. "How can we survive in this hovel and filth all around us?"

We all stopped what we were doing and gathered around her. None of us were thinking; we were just doing. Yossel and Benjamin both put their arms around her and tried to tell her things would be fine. Naomi went over to her and said, "Momma, if we stay in the house, the Nazis will come and throw us out. They will take us and send us who knows where and probably separate us."

I jumped in. "At least here we are hidden and free. It will be hard and dangerous, but we are together, and we will try to survive until a miracle comes to save us. Maybe Mashiach will come in our time of need."

Momma looked around at us and said, "I'm all right; let's get to work."

We all took a moment to look around at each other. I wondered if the family would survive. We had already lost Chava. None of us could bear to lose another member of the family to these barbaric murderers.

We put our heads down, unloaded the truck, and brought everything inside. It was going to be crowded. Henry and Nachman left to go help their families finish their building and unpacking. Benjamin and I left the others to finish organizing the house, got in the truck, and headed to get the Goldins.

When we arrived, Jonah was outside having a cigarette and getting wet. "We're ready to go."

I backed the truck up to the door, and Benjamin and I went in. They were in fact ready. We began loading the truck. Miriam organized an assembly line. Benjamin and I jumped in the truck to position everything so we could get it all in. We finished in about an hour and a half. We helped get Jonah and Shayna in the front seat with me, and everyone else climbed in the back. Jonah had not been to the camp yet and couldn't wait to see it.

As we approached, I turned off the road as usual. "The ride is going to get a bit rough," I warned them. "Hold on."

They did. We drove through the brush deep into the woods. It was extremely dark. After a few kilometers, we saw the torch lights, and we arrived at the camp.

"Fantastic," said Jonah. "You've done a great job." He climbed out of the truck himself, getting a big shot of adrenaline. He suddenly had a spring in his step.

Everyone got out. I walked over to Jonah. "Over here is your site," I said. "We dug the trench. Now we have to complete the building before we can unload the truck."

"Let's get to work!" yelled Jonah exuberantly as the rest of the family gathered around. The rain also stopped, and the sky was clearing. The ground was good enough that we could start digging the posts. I went to get the rest of my family as Benjamin led the Goldins over to the stockpile of materials and tools.

When I walked in, Rivka said, "So, Meyer, what do you think?"

"Looks great," I said.

There was more room than I expected when I'd left. The two bedrooms were set up with mattresses on the floor. They put up shelves they cut up from scrap pieces of wood so we could store some clothes. The rest of the living area was one room, where we had a chair for everyone, a small table, and a neat pile of dishes, silverware, and pots separated for meat and dairy. It was unlikely that we would find kosher food, but we were determined to keep our traditions alive and do the best we could.

"A real balbatish home. Who remembered the mezuzah from the front door?"

"I did," said Momma proudly. "We are still Jewish, no matter how hard they try to stop us."

"We need to help the Goldins build their home," I said, interrupting the momentary glee. Everyone got up and went outside. Nachman and Henry had come over and were digging holes for the posts. Benjamin and the entire Goldin family, including Jonah, were carrying lumber and setting it alongside the trench.

"Nachman! Henry!" I called out. They stopped digging and looked up. I continued, "We have to go meet Kozlowski. You both should come. He is bringing guns, and you should help me check them out before we buy them."

"Agreed," said Henry.

"He will also have a truckload of food and other supplies that we need to bring back," said Nachman.

Benjamin and Yossel jumped in and started to set the posts as we headed out to the road where I told Kozlowski to meet us. It was getting close to midnight.

We lay hidden in the woods for about a half hour. A few cars passed but were going too fast to be Kozlowski. About 0100 hours, we could see some headlights in the distance moving very slowly. That could be him.

"I'm going out and see if that is him," I said to them. "Keep an eye on me in case it's not him."

I waved down the truck with my torch. The truck stopped, and sure enough, it was Kozlowski. I called the boys over. We got in the truck and directed him a few hundred meters down the road and told him to pull off into a clearing behind some bushes. We all got out into the night.

"This is the first time I have seen you out of uniform," I said, trying to break the obvious tension in the air.

"I'm off duty. Besides, a uniformed officer making such a delivery would be shot on site," he replied firmly. So much for lightening the mood.

"Let's see what you have," I said, trying to get on with it.

We walked to the back of the truck. He started pulling out guns and boxes of ammunition. He had about fifteen rifles and pistols, which we recognized as standard Polish-army-issue WZ 29s and 35s, just like the guns Leibish found abandoned. It looked like the entire Polish army had abandoned their weapons. The three of us started to examine them. Some were in very poor condition, very rusted. They looked like they had been underwater. I wondered if Leibish's rifle was among them. We picked four rifles and two pistols out of the group. We also took all the ammunition.

We tried to negotiate the price, but Kozlowski was firm. He had other buyers, and we had no other suppliers. Supply and demand. All the families agreed to pool their resources. Henry volunteered to be treasurer. Each family gave two thousand zlotys to start, and Henry had discretion on how to spend it. We also purchased some food that Kozlowski brought. It was hardly enough to feed thirty-two people.

"I will be back in a couple of days with more food," he said.

"We need to use your truck to bring what we bought back to camp. I will stay here with you until they return," I informed Kozlowski.

"Fine," he said, "but you boys better not take one thing that doesn't belong to you."

"We won't," said Henry as he and Nachman got in the truck and left.

"Let's meet at midnight in this exact spot in two days," I said.

"How long do you think you can hide out here from the Nazis?" he asked.

"I have no idea. We have no plan beyond this. We are lucky we found this place and had time to make camp," I said.

Kozlowski looked at me and said, "These Nazis are evil bastards. I see them gathering anyone they don't like and killing them or shipping the young and strong somewhere to work. They are well organized and well equipped. No one, including me and my family, are safe from them. You may be safer here in the woods than I am trying to do their bidding," he said. "All I can do is obey their orders, watch their evil, then get drunk at the end of the day to try and forget. I was taught that Jews caused all the evil in the world, but I would rather live with you than them any day of the week."

"Things have certainly changed since the day you beat the crap out of me in the lumberyard," I said, hoping to get a laugh.

I did.

"Life was more fun when you were the bad guys," he said, laughing.

Thank God the boys returned with the truck. I was tired of babysitting this guy. Next time we would bring our truck.

"Here is your stuff, safe and sound," said Henry as they jumped out of his truck.

He looked in the back anyway to make sure he wasn't cheated. "Good," he said, "I'm off." We all shook hands. Kozlowski got in his truck and left.

"We are going to have to supplement his supply," said Nachman.

"We can use our new weapons to raid some of the local farms and stores," said Henry.

"We will turn into everything we were always taught not to be. We will be thieves to survive. Let's hope we don't have to be murderers too," I said pensively.

Nachman replied angrily, "If there are Germans in our way, it's not murder. We are in a war. They will kill us if we don't kill them."

"I know, but I don't have to like it," I replied.

"None of us like it, but we will do what we must," said Henry. We walked quietly back to camp.

When we got back, the Goldins' dwelling, the last to be finished, was pretty well along. The posts were set; the side walls were up. Benjamin, Miriam, and Ruth were framing out the inside while Jonah supervised. Yossel and the rest of the two families were working on framing the roof. The roof was tricky, as we had to work on ladders. The rest of the families came out to help, but there were many cooks in this kitchen. The three of us jumped in to finish the roof, and we were done about 0300 hours. Then it was a matter of unloading the truck with the Goldins' belongings. They got the bedding materials out of the truck and left the rest for the morning. It was time for all of us to get some sleep. The good news was that we were free. The work we would do tomorrow would be for our benefit only. There was great satisfaction in this, although it was very scary for all of us.

The six of us crowded into our new home. It was cold and damp, but it was our salvation for the time being. Tomorrow would truly be an adventure. All the torches were turned off, and we tried to sleep.

CHAPTER 14

Freedom Costs

⅄⅄⅄

As light began to leak into the hut, I awoke and went outside. I took a deep breath and realized I was no longer a slave. I didn't have to go anywhere. My mother and sisters would not be gathered onto a military truck, sent to a textile mill, and forced to work in horrible conditions without rest, overseen by the brutal masters who killed my poor sister, Chava. Now they were free and safe.

As my head cleared from my morning fog, reality set in. Just outside these woods was likely death for all of us. Soon about thirty people would not report to their forced labor jobs and would be branded criminals, sentenced to immediate death by an all-powerful occupying force filled with mindless murderers.

"So, Meyer, we're here. Now what?" I turned around, and it was Naomi.

"Good question," I responded. "We need to get everyone together today to figure out what we have and what we need to live here and be independent from the outside world."

We took a walk around the camp. There was life in all seven of our wooden-frame huts. Nachman, his parents, and his friends the Fishers were starting a fire in the pit. Kozlowski had provided some fresh chicken eggs, and they were planning to cook some up for breakfast. The fire felt good, as it was bone-chilling cold overnight. We didn't have heat in our little houses. We would never survive the winter unless we figured out how to get some heat. Slowly but surely, the rest of our little band of partisans gathered in the middle of the camp around the fire and brought some food to make breakfast. We would be very intimate together and would have to find a way to get along. The Goldins were out, and Miriam and I broke away to have a quiet breakfast together.

"How are we going to feed and care for thirty-two people?" I asked rhetorically.

Miriam responded, "Your guy Kozlowski would have to come every day. We are going to have to go out and get supplies elsewhere, but if we get caught, that is the end of us."

"You're right," I said. "We may have to do some uncomfortable things to stay alive."

"We are going to need someone to lead and make decisions. That should be you," she said.

"I'm not sure," I responded. "Henry and Nachman can lead as well. Let's go back and talk this through with the rest of the group."

When we walked back, Jonah was speaking to the assembly, and they were listening. He looked like a leader to me.

"Meyer," he said when he saw me, "when is our next delivery from your black-market contact?"

"Tomorrow at midnight," I responded.

"Henry says that you discussed supplementing his deliveries by raiding the local farms," said Jonah.

"Yes," I said, "we don't know how much he will bring, and we don't want to run out of money. His prices keep going up."

"I agree!" cried Jonah. "We need to develop attack teams of three or four people who can go out and attack several targets at once. I would like Meyer, Nachman, and Henry to come up with a plan we can implement in the next few days."

I looked at Miriam. She looked just as shocked as me. We never saw Jonah so animated and aggressive. Actually he was our highest-ranking and most-experienced military leader, but it was still a shock to hear this man who was in so much pain take such a leadership role.

Just as I was processing all of this, the other side of the argument came to light. "Jonah, what are you talking about?" yelled Shayna. "You are sending these children to steal at gunpoint and make them as evil as our enemies!"

"This is a war and a matter of survival," Jonah snapped back. "If we are going to live, we have to fight! These are not children. They are grown men and women, and they are now soldiers in our army."

Momma chimed in. "We just don't want to lose more of our children. Some of the farms have been taken over by Germans. They won't like being targets of robberies."

"We should kill those Nazi murderers." Jonah was on fire. "It's the only way we will truly be free."

"I agree with Poppa," said Pearl.

The debate ensued. There was overwhelming support for Jonah's militant position.

David Fisher said it best: "Throughout history, Jews have been in military battles against overwhelming odds. The Assyrians, the Babylonians destroyed the first temple; the Romans destroyed the second temple. Then there were the great victories of the Maccabees, the story of Purim in Persia. There are many more. Now it is our turn. We must fight, even if it looks hopeless. We do not know what God has in store for us, but we cannot just sit around and wait for the Nazis to find us. Right now our survival is our fight. I am committed to do what Jonah believes is the right path."

It was settled. Nachman, Henry, and I went to plan our attack force. "We have thirty-two refugees, but how many partisan fighters do we have?" Henry asked.

"My question," I said, "is how many people do we want to put out there to risk their lives for the benefit of the community? My view is, we should not put more than half the camp residents on the team at one time. I am thinking four teams of four partisans, well trained and armed. We should limit this to the young adults and pick the most competent and in good health. From my end, we can count on my brothers and sisters, so that's five including me. Also the three Goldins—Miriam, Ruth, and Pearl—are all capable. Shlomo is too young. That's eight, although we may want to leave one from each family back if possible."

"My father was in the army and is a pretty good shot," said Nachman. "He wants in."

I looked at him and said, "But that would leave your mother alone."

Nachman laughed and replied, "I think they are OK with that. Being in such close quarters is not making them any happier together. Momma is very close to Mr. and Mrs. Fisher, and they will take care of her if the worst happens. He is insisting on being involved, so that is two of us."

"That's good," said Henry. "My sister has to stay with my mother, who is so upset about my father, so I will be the only fighter from my family. That makes eleven. We need more."

"Three of the Wachtels can join," Nachman said. "I will speak to the Fishers and Levines. There are four among them I believe are old enough to join. That makes a total of eighteen. We should train everyone and put them in teams. We should always leave at least three armed members to protect the camp while the teams are out."

"Very good," I said. "We are agreed. Let's go review this with Jonah. Then we should gather the group, divide them into teams, issue weapons, and provide training to whoever needs it."

We reviewed the plan with Jonah. He wanted to make a few adjustments. "We should divide the group into three teams, each team of six led by one of you, our most experienced fighters. Let's put the names of the teams down before we meet with the group. We can always adjust if needed. We can make three attacks simultaneously. Each attack team should be a team of four. The remaining six team members should remain here in reserve. It will be your call on who goes on the attack and who stays. We should divide family members as much as possible. Meyer, Miriam cannot be on your team for obvious reasons." He laughed loudly then continued, "Now you three go off and divide up the teams; then let's gather everyone to discuss the next move."

I must admit I was pretty impressed with Jonah's commanding presence. Gone was the man in constant pain, and here was a man with a renewed sense of purpose. I knew he was still ill, but he had been able to repress the pain for now. I saw where Miriam got her strength.

Henry, Nachman, and I went off again to pick our teams, just like we did when we played soccer as kids. I knew I wanted Naomi and Benjamin on my team, but we needed to split up the families. "How should we do this?" I asked.

Nachman replied, "Let's just pick one at a time and pick until we are done."

"Let's start with two; then we can go one by one, to speed things up," I said with an ulterior motive.

"Good idea," said Henry. "You may as well go first since you already know who you want, right?"

"Right," I admitted. "I want Benjamin and Naomi to start."

Henry jumped in. "I'll take Nachman's father and Miriam."

Nachman took Yossel and Jack Levine. Jack was the Levine's oldest son. I didn't know him well, but he seemed like a good choice. We continued to pick one by one until all were chosen. In addition to Benjamin and Naomi, I chose Pearl Goldin, Ari Fisher, and Joel Wachtel, all eighteen and under and inexperienced. They would need some training, which Benjamin and I would lead.

We went back to review the choices with Jonah, but it was already late and we would have to meet in the morning. Jonah had exhausted himself and was asleep. Miriam and I took a walk. We hadn't spent any time together since the move to the camp began. Neither of us was thinking much of romance. I told her about the plan and that she would be on Henry's team.

"I don't want to rob or certainly kill anyone," she said.

"We don't have much choice. We will have to do what we must to live in this crazy world," I replied.

"I know," she said. "Momma and Papa still want me to take Shlomo and go live with the Dombecks. You know I love you, right? I don't want to leave you or them."

"I know," I said. "I love you too. I want to marry you, but it will have to wait. If you have a chance to live in a safe home, you should jump at the chance. I will find you when the time is right. How many times do I have to tell you that!" I didn't mean to yell at her, but she needed to do what she could to live.

"For now, I am staying here," she said abruptly.

I walked her back and kissed her good night on the cheek. It was time to try to get some sleep. Our first day of freedom was over.

I woke up early, before it was light, and went outside. Henry was already stoking the fire and talking to Jonah. "Good morning," I said to the two of them.

"Good morning," replied Jonah. "Henry was just sharing your teams with me. They seem good."

"They will need training," I replied. "We have some new recruits who've never shot a gun."

Jonah looked at me with glee, "Well let's get started. Gather up the families, and let's get them to agree to the plan."

That's exactly what we did. Jonah took the lead. "Meyer, Nachman, and Henry have developed a great plan to help us get through this very difficult time. It will mean sacrifice from every able-bodied man and woman in the camp. These three men have military experience and will lead teams of six people each to get the food and supplies we need to survive. I will oversee and advise the teams. Many of you will be asked to volunteer. No one will be forced to do anything you don't want to do, but I must say that the Nazis are ruthless killers, and they have corrupted many Poles. If we do not fight to survive, we will surely die at the hands of these butchers. Are there any questions?"

"Yes," said Momma, "I have questions. I thought this Kozlowski was going to get us the supplies we need. Also, how are we going to get the supplies you are talking about without getting us all killed?"

I had to answer this one. "Momma, we can't rely on Kozlowski alone. We have no idea what he will be able to bring. His prices keep going up. He will wipe us out of any valuables we have, and that will leave us destitute. It's better that we fend for ourselves now rather than wait until we are forced."

Jonah jumped in. "We are going to target the local farms, and that means using force. We are going to train everyone to use guns safely, and we may have to use them. If we do this right, no one will get killed, and we will get what we need."

"God help us!" cried Momma.

We announced the teams, and there were no complaints. All the team members understood the situation and were very willing to learn and participate. Henry, Nachman, and I had dug a trench outside the camp, where we buried the weapons and ammunition and covered them with a tarp, topping it off with tree branches and brush to keep them hidden. Each of the teams gathered as we uncovered the stash. We handed each team member a rifle and pistol, just as we had done before, and took a stockpile of ammunition.

Then the teams separated. We had designated spots for each of our teams to get together and train. Benjamin was the only one on my team who had trained with our original sniper force. I wanted Naomi on my team because she was my favorite, always took care of me, and was tough as nails. I knew she would be great at this. We started the same as before—taking apart the guns and learning to clean them. Naomi picked it up quickly. Benjamin helped the others. We spent several hours working on the guns. They were all in reasonably good shape. That was enough for the first day. I wandered over to see Henry and Nachman, and they were done as well. I reminded them that we were meeting Kozlowski at midnight.

"How did it go?" I asked.

"Good," said Nachman. "Everyone is willing. Some are slower than others, but all will be ready. We will be shooting tomorrow."

"Same for us," said Henry. "Everyone knows the importance of what we are doing and are all pretty smart."

"Good," I said. "I will stop by and tell Jonah."

Henry laughed. "Don't corrupt my teammate Miriam. I need her focused and ready tomorrow."

"Don't worry," I said and then left.

I stopped at the Goldins', but Jonah had already gotten a full report from his daughters. "I don't like my girls as soldiers," he said quietly.

"I know," I responded. "It goes against our entire way of life."

Jonah was clearly disturbed. "One day they are behind a mechitzah, separated from men, and now they will be fighting alongside you."

"I know," I said. "The world has changed us. Someday I hope we will be able to get back to our traditional ways, but we have to live through this nightmare first."

"It's one thing to send men under my command into danger but my daughters? Please try to protect them," he pleaded.

"We can't afford to lose anyone," I responded. "We will be careful." I tried to be encouraging, but we both knew we were in for trouble.

"Do you think I want this?" Miriam had overheard us. "I never imagined in my wildest dreams that I would be learning to shoot guns and steal food from people. I've seen them murder at will. They killed Leibish and beat Chava to death. We all know what we have to do, and we will do it."

That shut us both up.

I went to find Henry and Nachman. It was almost time to meet Kozlowski.

We arrived at the meeting spot fifteen minutes early in the truck. Kozlowski was waiting for us. He was not happy. "Those bastards are sucking up everything for the army and the occupiers coming here. There are shortages of everything—food, gas, and all supplies. The black market is drying up. I have some things for you, but it's not enough and the prices are higher."

We took a look in the truck, and the load was pretty light. There were some fruits and vegetables, some flour, some fish, and some other food stuffs, but it was a fraction of what we needed to supply the seven families we had responsibility for.

"Will you be able to continue to bring supplies?" I asked.

"Yes," he responded. "The black market will continue, but finding supplies will get more and more difficult. I will cut down the number of people I supply. Your group is my biggest customer, so I will get all I can as long as you can pay my prices." He meant he planned to clean us out of everything we had.

"We want all you can give us," I said. "Let's agree to meet every other night, and we'll see what you can get us."

We transferred the load to our truck, and then he left.

It was quiet on the short drive back to camp. As we arrived Henry broke the silence.

"We have no choice now. We have to get these kids trained quickly and plan an attack. I think we should plan an attack of three farms on the same day and use the truck to take whatever we can get."

I responded, "Let's get this load distributed and everyone shooting tomorrow. The three of us should sit down with Jonah and plan the attack. There are several farms within ten kilometers, and we should scout them out and try to find those with the most supplies and the least risk."

"Agreed," said Nachman. "Let's be careful not to get us all killed."

We shook hands, hugged, and went to get some sleep.

CHAPTER 15

Independence Is Hard

⅄ ⅄ ⅄

It was very strange seeing women holding and firing weapons. Even in the army, women were relegated to nursing and office work. I have to admit Naomi was pretty tough. I knew the recoil from the rifle was hurting her shoulder and knocking her a step back, but she stayed on her feet. We set up some empty boxes and cans as targets. Naomi, Pearl, Ari, and Joel all did reasonably well for beginners. We did not have the time or the ammunition to turn them all into marksmen. My hope was that we would never have to fire a shot but that the threat of the loaded weapons would be enough to scare the farmers into turning over their food and other supplies.

We shot for about two hours. Benjamin and I opened up the sessions, giving some basic tips on aiming toward the target and squeezing the trigger to hit it. It took our four rookies a while to get the feel for the weapons, both the rifles and pistols. Once they did, and after a few rounds, they seemed to pick it up and get better. We would clearly have to repeat the exercise on a daily basis. We would have to get our hands on more ammunition. After the shooting session, I had them take apart the weapons and clean them again. This would become part of their daily routine.

While we were working on the guns, Pearl asked, "So what are we going to do with our new skills?"

I hesitated. "We are going out in the next day or two and start getting our own food and supplies. Our trusty friends here," I said, holding up my pistol, "will help convince the locals to share their bounty with us. We are going to meet with your father later to talk about the plan. We don't plan on taking everyone at the same time. Some will go, and some will stay here and guard the camp."

Joel jumped in. "I'm ready; let's go kill some Nazis already."

"Me too," said Ari.

The girls just looked at them like they had two heads.

"I'll let you know as soon as we decide on the plan," I said, before the fight broke out. Too late!

"Are you crazy?" yelled Naomi. "We're not killing anybody. We will get what we need and leave the people alone unless we are attacked."

"She's right," I said. "Our mission is to feed and clothe our community. That is all we are going to do. We don't even want to be seen if possible, but if needed, we will defend ourselves. We are in no position to get into a gun battle. You are not that good. Today was the first time you shot a gun. The Nazis are trained killers."

"Idiots," declared Naomi.

"Enough," I said sternly. "We are on the same team. Let's act like it."

The boys were looking for action but got the message.

"Fine," said Ari. "Let's get on with it."

"Good, I want you to put the safeties on and keep the guns nearby at all times. Be ready to go into action on my orders."

When we got back to the camp, Jonah was sitting by the fire. He looked up when he saw me, and then we both looked toward the other side of the camp as we heard gunfire, so clearly the other teams were still working.

"We've been hearing this all morning from around the camp," said Jonah. "Shayna and your mother have been yelling at me all morning for encouraging this. We went to the truck to distribute what you brought last night. Not nearly enough for the whole camp."

"Exactly," I said. "This is why we have to act."

"That's what I told them," Jonah said, exasperated. "We've lost our children; I don't blame them for being angry. They don't want to lose anyone else. I don't either, but I don't know what else to do."

"I'll talk to Momma, but I don't think it will help," I said. "Let's get together when Nachman and Henry get back. It's time to start."

I left Jonah and the warmth of the fire and went to find Momma. "I hear you're upset."

"Of course I'm upset," she said. "You know, when you went to the army, I was awake nights worrying about what would happen to you. I was thrilled when I got a letter telling me you were all right. But this is much worse. All my children are walking around shooting guns and are going out looking for trouble. This is torture for a mother."

"I know." I chose my words carefully. "Trouble is all around us; we cannot hide from it. You taught us how to be good, moral people. We will be as careful as we can and not hurt anyone needlessly. We will not take any chances that will put us in danger. But danger may find us anyway. We have to find a way to survive. That is what we must do above all."

"Just be careful and look out for your sisters!" she cried. "You're all I have in this world."

We embraced and held each other tight. I started to cry too. I loved her so much. The world is such a terrible place. You forget that it doesn't have to be that way when you are stuck in an impossible situation. Life was great once and would be again. That was all we could hope for.

"Meyer!" I heard Nachman outside.

"Coming," I said. I kissed Momma on the forehead and said, "I have to go."

Nachman and Henry were waiting outside.

"How did it go?" Henry asked me.

"Not bad," I said. "The boys think they're going out to defeat the whole Nazi army. The girls are much more grounded and can handle themselves with guns, I might add. How about you?"

Henry said, "All I can tell you is I told Miriam to imagine the target was you with another woman. She didn't miss. That box was like Swiss cheese."

"Very funny," I said.

"I'm not kidding; she's good. Don't get on her bad side."

Henry and Nachman laughed hysterically. They loved to tease me about Miriam.

"Let's go see Jonah," I said, not laughing at all.

Jonah was back in his hut, eating something. "Come in, boys. I've been waiting for you. How are your teams coming along?"

Nachman said, "Honestly my team knows enough about guns not to shoot themselves, but I wouldn't want to put them in front of the German army."

"Hopefully we won't have to," I said. "They just need to look scary enough to get these farmers to give up their stuff without a fight. In fact, we should try to sneak in and out and when they are gone or asleep."

"How are we going to manage that?" asked Henry. "How are we going to have more than one team attack and bring back what they get? We only have one truck."

"I've been thinking about that," said Jonah. "What if we put three teams of three in the truck with a driver. We find three farms in close proximity. The driver drops off team one a few hundred meters from the target. Then the driver goes to target two, then three, and drops off the teams. Each team gets one hour to gather what they can. The driver then meets them where they were dropped off, picks up the other teams, then all get brought back to camp."

"That sounds very risky to me," I said. "What if they need more time? What if they need less time? What if they can't get back to the drop point for some reason, like they can't carry what they take? What if they get pinned down somewhere where we have no way to communicate?"

Henry agreed. "Why don't we do one at a time and have the truck as part of the team?"

Jonah replied, "We have thirty-two people to feed. We have to do something big because we cannot do this every day. We'll get caught for sure."

"It would be nice if we had German field radios, which I saw when they attacked," I said sheepishly.

"Do you think Kozlowski can get some on the black market?" asked Nachman.

"No way." I laughed. "He can barely get a dozen eggs at this point. I'll ask, but let's not count on it."

"You are right," said Jonah. "We cannot do a large operation without communication. Let's send out one team at a time. We will have to target different locations and act quickly so they cannot anticipate our moves."

"My team will go first," I said. "We will need a team of four, including a driver. We will be ready to go tonight after dark."

Afterward, I gathered the team and told them we were going that night.

"What's the plan?" asked Naomi.

"We are going with one team at a time," I said. "We will be a team of four. One driver and three to gather what we can. We will go at twenty-two hundred hours. Hopefully they will be asleep and we will get in and out without a problem. The team tonight will be me, Benjamin, Ari, and Pearl. Benjamin will drive."

"I thought you wanted me on the team," Naomi protested.

"Two from one family is enough," I said. "We do not want to put everyone at risk. You will go next time."

"Fine," she said, but she was not happy.

"Benjamin, get the keys to the truck from Nachman, and let's go look for our target for tonight," I said.

"Sure," he said and was off in a flash.

We drove by the shtetl to see what was happening to our homes and neighbors. The streets and homes were abandoned. Other than a few German soldiers patrolling the area and a few military vehicles, there was nothing. We went by the shul. There was no activity.

"Let's drive through town," I told Benjamin, who was driving.

"We shouldn't be out here," Benjamin said. "It's dangerous. Let's find our farm and get back to camp."

"Let's drive through town; then we will move on," I responded.

I didn't know what I was looking for, but we found it when we rode by the train station. About fifty of our friends and neighbors were boarding a train. There were soldiers pointing guns at them. They were being loaded onto freight cars, not passenger cars. There were men, women, and children, and they were going willingly. What would happen to them? As we drove by the station, there were dead bodies of three young men being thrown in the back of a truck by Nazi goons. We could not see who they were, but Benjamin saw a yarmulke on one of them. They must have tried to fight the evacuation.

"Let's go," I said.

"Good, happy now?" Benjamin was annoyed.

"I had to see if Kozlowski was right. I had to see if they are they coming for us. Now we know," I responded.

Benjamin was madder now. "I knew we were in trouble. We didn't need to risk our lives to see that! We need to be smarter."

"All right, all right, let's find our farm." I was very disturbed by what I saw. Were they going to kill us all? Why would they? What threat did we pose to the strongest force in the world? This made no sense. All we could do was try to live. Maybe by living we beat them.

"Meyer!" shouted Benjamin.

"What? I was daydreaming," I responded.

"Look, the Dudek farm," said Benjamin. "The house and barn are close to the road. We can be in and out quickly, plus I have been inside delivering lumber."

"Good choice," I said. "Let's go home and get ready."

I had to talk about what I saw to anyone who would listen. We all needed to understand the danger that was outside the camp and the importance of our survival. That was what I did. I started with Momma and my sisters. I then went and got Miriam and asked her to help me gather the rest of the camp together. An hour later everyone was gathered by the fire pit.

I began to speak. "For the first time since we have been here at the camp, Benjamin and I went out to Pysznica and the shtetl. What we saw disturbed me, and I wanted to share it with you. All of the homes in the shtetl have been evacuated or abandoned. There are German soldiers roaming the streets, and it looks like they are being prepared to be occupied, just as Kozlowski told us would happen. Then we drove into town and saw dozens of Jews, people we know from the shtetl, being loaded onto a freight train to be sent who knows where. We also saw three dead Jewish men who had been shot being thrown into a truck by Nazi soldiers. I have no doubt that if we had not taken the action of creating this camp, we would also be dead or imprisoned. I don't know why we are being targeted by the Nazis, but we all know how Jews have been targeted throughout history, and if we are to survive, then we will have to do whatever we need to live until this nightmare is over. I know we have all talked about this before, but we should never have any doubt that what we are about to do, which goes against everything we have learned all our lives, is right and necessary. Does anyone have any questions or objections?"

Everyone looked around at each other, but no one said anything.

Finally, Jonah chimed in. "Meyer, I think everyone understands and is ready. Is your team ready?"

"Yes," I replied, "the Dudek farm is first."

"Then let's get started," said Jonah.

We met at the truck right at 2200 hours. Nachman and Henry met us as well. They were to ensure that the camp was guarded while we were out. My team was there. We checked our weapons and were ready to go. "I want to make one change," I said. "I will drive. Benjamin knows the Dudek farm. He has been inside and knows the layout. He will lead the mission."

Pearl sat in the passenger compartment with Benjamin, and Ari rode in the back as I got behind the wheel.

As we pulled up close to the farm, I turned off the lights and the engine, and we were able to coast down the hill to get close to the barn. The barn and house were dark. The farmers generally went to sleep early and rose early.

Benjamin, Pearl, and Ari took their loaded pistols and left the truck. They climbed through a window to get into the barn. I could see light from their torches as they moved around the barn. It was eerily quiet, and I was growing impatient. After about fifteen minutes, the barn door opened. They began to bring out boxes, egg crates, and some cans. I got out of the truck to help them load when we were interrupted.

"Stop!" came a voice from behind the barn. There was a rifle barrel pointing at us. I pulled my gun out, but we were totally exposed, and he was hidden behind the sidewall of the barn. Someone could get hurt or killed. Suddenly Benjamin put down what he was carrying and walked toward the threat.

"Mr. Dudek, it's me, Benjamin, from the lumberyard."

Dudek came out from behind the wall. "What are you doing here?"

I kept my gun pointed. I had no idea what he would do. We were robbing him, and I might still have had to kill him if he looked like he would shoot.

Benjamin responded, "We are hiding from the Nazis, who are gathering Jews and killing us at will. We have a group trying to survive, and we need to feed and clothe them. We don't want to hurt anyone, but we will if we have to. Also, we hear the Nazis are taking over the local farms, so we have to be prepared to fight."

Dudek put his gun down. "I'll help you. No need to steal. The Nazis have not come here yet. Mrs. Dudek and I sent our children to relatives in Russia. I know the Germans will come. You can come here for eggs, milk, even chickens, and I have some more supplies in the house. I'd rather give them to you instead of having the Nazis take them. You can't come here every day, but if I am still here in a week, come back and I will have more for you."

I saw Benjamin in a new light. He was my hero. I did not want to fight anyone. He was brave to take control with a gun pointing at him at short range. We found a valuable ally, and maybe we needed to rethink our military view of this. On the other hand, we could have just as easily run into hostile Poles or Germans. We could not trust or count on anyone but ourselves.

We loaded the truck with what he had. Then we drank a toast to the end of Nazi occupation, thanked him profusely, and left. People like Dudek would never drink with Jews, but we had a common enemy now, and some Poles were becoming our friends.

We came back to camp. It actually looked imposing, with a group of armed guards patrolling the perimeter. If you didn't know these people barely knew how to shoot a gun, you would be scared to enter the compound.

We unloaded the truck and distributed what we got. We were very thankful for the supplies, but showing up at Dudek's would not be enough. We got off easy, but team number two would have to go tomorrow.

"How did it go?" Jonah surprised me from behind. "Sorry to make you jump. I am glad to see you all home safe and sound."

"It was a piece of cake," I responded. "Too easy. We have a new best friend. He will help us all he can. I only hope the other teams will find friends out there. There can't be too many."

Jonah replied, "I agree. You all did good tonight. Go get some sleep. We are just getting started."

All I could think about was that Henry's team was up next. I knew he would take Miriam.

It had been raining lightly during our mission. Suddenly it felt like the heavens opened up and the resulting downpour was so strong we all began to head for shelter. Within an hour, the campground became a mud pit, and water was flowing into the hut. We tried to lift everything we could off the floor, but we would be soggy for a while. I had an uneasy feeling. The next day, I sought out Henry, who was meeting with his team. When the meeting broke up, I went over to him and asked him to tell me his plan.

Henry was happy to share. "Nachman and I found a large farm that looked well supplied. Mr. Herschell, Miriam, and I will go tonight. I'm still deciding on a driver."

"I'll drive," I responded immediately. "The roads are wet, and I know the area well. You need someone experienced to help."

Henry responded, "You've done your part. Let me do mine." He paused. "Are you worried about Miriam?"

"Yes," I said, "I don't want anything to happen to her."

"All right," he said, "I'll feel better with you there anyway. I hope we make a big score tonight so we don't have to do this every day."

"Kozlowski is coming tomorrow night anyway, so we should take a day off," I replied.

I felt better too. Even though we had an easy time last night, most other Poles and certainly Germans would not be so friendly.

I saw no need to tell anyone I was going. It would be easier to tell the family afterward. I went back to check on the hut as the rain continued. Everyone was struggling to keep dry. We were all soaked, and the floor was muddy. There was not much we could do but deal with it. The day dragged on, and it got dark. The rain finally stopped, and I went out to meet Henry and his team. He chose not to tell them until I arrived.

Miriam knew right away why I was there. "You do not need to hover over me." She was not happy.

"I'm not," I said. "I offered to help because you are going for a big farm and I have the experience to help." I could see in her face that she didn't believe me for a minute, but she didn't say any more.

In the end, I think she was happy I was coming. We got in the truck. It was filled with petrol. "Henry, I see we have a full tank. Anything I should know?" I asked.

Henry laughed. "Don't worry; we didn't kill anyone. Nachman and I fooled a kid at the station into thinking we were Polish military and that he would have to answer to the Nazis if he didn't fill the tank. We made sure he saw our weapons. We had no issue."

We drove off. This farm was about twenty kilometers away. I was not exactly sure where it was, but Henry seemed confident. There was definitely some flooding along the roads, and we had to slow down going through some puddles because we did not know how deep they were. Luckily we had no problem getting through.

When we arrived, Henry said, "Turn left here."

I turned onto a dirt road but could not see anything. "It's down this road two kilometers," he said. "Shut your lights."

I did, and finally we arrived. There was a large barn on the left and a house on the right. The house had lights on. I killed the engine, and we coasted down the hill in front of the barn door. The three of them got out and went into the barn. I stayed outside and stood guard with my rifle loaded and cocked. They started bringing out boxes and cans.

"There's a lot here," said Henry.

Suddenly, I heard shouts from the house in German. "Someone's out there!" I heard.

I ran to the door and yelled, "They're coming; let's go!" As I got back into the truck, I heard shots from behind. I couldn't see who was shooting, and I couldn't tell how many were shooting. I was facing away from the house, and the rest of the team was still in the barn. I started the truck. I moved forward and turned the truck around. When I turned on the lights, I saw at least five men moving toward the barn, shooting into the building through windows. I pulled up in front of the door. I turned on the lights and started shooting out the side widow of the truck. I hit one of the shooters, who was leaning through a window. I could see the door open behind me in the mirror and heard the three team members climb into the truck.

"Let's go!" Henry shouted. I hit the gas. Now they were shooting right at me. I heard the glass shatter from a bullet that came through the windshield, but I was not hit.

I turned up the road and headed away from the farm. I hit one of the shooters, who jumped in front of the truck. I kept going. As we drove away, I continued to hear shooting, seeing through the mirror that the back of the truck was open.

I heard Miriam's voice. "He's bleeding."

"Who?" I yelled back.

"Mr. Herschell," yelled Henry. "Just drive."

I did. I was bleeding too, but I was cut from the broken glass not a gunshot, so I drove as fast as I could. It took about forty-five minutes to get back to camp. I jumped out of the truck and ran around the back. Miriam was crying. When she saw me, she yelled, "He's dead!"

Everyone heard us and gathered around. Nachman came over and started crying when he saw his father dead from gunshot wounds. We carried Mr. Herschell's lifeless body out of the truck. Nachman's sister and mother fell over him and cried uncontrollably.

Miriam said, still crying, "I tried to stop the bleeding, but he was hit twice, and I couldn't help him. I am so sorry."

We always knew this could happen but never believed it would. We talked big about preferring to die fighting, but the reality was hard to live with.

Naomi saw blood on my face and came over. "You're hurt," she said.

"I'm OK," I said, but she was already gone. She brought me a wet cloth and started wiping me off. "Thanks," I said. I took the towel and held it to my face. This was terrible, but I couldn't help thinking that this was in fact better than being loaded on a train for who knew what. This was no less painful for Nachman and his family.

Henry came over. "We should take him back to his house and clean him and stay with him. It's time to be Jewish again."

Nachman agreed, and we brought him home and took care of him. The Fishers came and took Mrs. Herschell to their home. Everyone was in shock, but we had to go on.

CHAPTER 16

She's Gone

We spent the next several hours cleaning the body the best we could do with what few materials we had, finding some bedsheets to wrap him in. I went home to sleep, leaving Ari and Joel to stay with the body. We wanted to give him the dignity he deserved. We would have to figure out the burial tomorrow.

The next morning, we all went to see Nachman and his sister and mother. I didn't count, but I think everyone in the camp was there to see them. I wanted them to know that Mr. Herschell was a hero. He was in good shape. He had every reason to be with us. Any of us could have been killed that night. It was so sad, but they knew he preferred to die this way instead of being a slave. We all were prepared to give our lives so the rest of our families could survive.

Henry and I went over to see how bad the truck was. I knew the windshield was smashed. There was glass all over the cab. There were bullet holes on both sides. It's amazing we all weren't killed. The good part was that the truck was running. We cleaned out the glass. There was no way to get a replacement for the window. We would have to make do or steal another truck. This was our connection to the outside world.

Henry said, "If we are seen driving this thing without a windshield, we will definitely be stopped and caught. We have to get another truck." He was right, but I had no idea how we would pull that off.

At that point Nachman walked over to us. "We discussed the burial. There is no way we will be able to bury him in the cemetery. We need to find a spot nearby here where we can dig a grave."

Henry said, "We are here to help."

I said, "If you want, we can go now and find a spot and help you dig the grave."

"The sooner the better," Nachman said.

We stopped working on the truck. We grabbed some shovels and went looking for a spot for a grave. I grabbed Benjamin and Yossel on the way. The area around the camp was thick, and there was plenty of land in all directions. It wasn't hard to find a spot. Nachman wanted to have him buried by day's end, and the five of us were able to dig the grave in a few hours.

We let everyone know we would meet at dusk, and Jonah agreed to officiate. Everyone in camp came to the burial. Jonah spoke wonderfully about a man he didn't know, but he used my theme that he was a hero. We were put in this position by the evil in the world, and any or all of us may meet the same fate. We were soldiers in an army with a mission of survival. Others who knew Mr. Herschell spoke about his life and family, who were very emotional. Frankly, my mind was wandering, thinking about what we were doing and how we could find allies rather than making blind attacks that could wind up getting us all killed. Also Kozlowski was coming tonight. How much should we tell him? Probably nothing.

On the way back from the funeral, I walked with Jonah, who was in pain and moving slowly. I said, "Maybe we should rethink this idea of attacking farms at gunpoint. There may be others like the farmer we met the other night who would be willing to help us. I would like to get a small team to go out in daylight and try to find farms that are still run by Poles, not taken over by Germans, and see what we can arrange. We can always go back to the attacks."

He looked at me strangely and just said, "What are you going to do about the truck?"

"I don't know yet," I responded. "Probably steal another one."

Jonah then said, "I think asking for help is just as dangerous, and they will be able to identify you. It might be good to do a little more reconnaissance to see who lives in the farms we are attacking. Clearly this was a well-armed group of German men. If you see they might be friendly, you may want to try to talk to them. I think going after the biggest farm was a mistake. Those are probably the ones that the Germans will focus on."

"Fine," I said. "We will plan better. I will talk to Henry and Nachman when he is able, and we will adjust. Meanwhile we will see what Kozlowski has for us tonight."

When I got back, Momma and the girls were putting together food to bring to the Herschells. Although we were fugitives living like animals, we could be civil and take care of our neighbors in pain. I tagged along as they went to pay a shiva call. There were so many people visiting we had to wait to get in to their hut to see them. Nachman came out to see me, so we took a little walk. "How are you doing, my friend?" I asked.

He responded, "I knew this could happen when he insisted on going, but it hurts. He was a great father and a great man. I really looked up to him. I will miss him terribly." He was choked up. "Mom is worried that I'll be next. She knows we are all in danger, but she is a mother first. Why did Henry go for the biggest farm? Germans took over the farm, and they were heavily armed."

I replied, "Jonah said the same thing. We talked about being more careful about picking our targets. As soon as you are ready, we should talk to Henry. We also have to figure out what to do about the truck."

"Give me a couple of days," he said. "I need to make sure my mother and sister are settled and understand that I have to get back to work and cannot sit shiva as we normally would."

"That's fine. Henry, Benjamin, and I will meet Kozlowski."

We took the truck to the meeting spot just before midnight. We were hoping to hide the missing windshield and hoped he didn't notice that the truck was shot full of holes, but Kozlowski was standing there as we drove up. He had his lights on when we arrived, and we were exposed.

We got out of the truck to his uncontrollable laughter. "Look at you guys, a bunch of common criminals! Look at the mess you made. You are the talk of the Pysznica police. The Nazis are coming down hard on us. Someone killed two German settlers last night in a robbery at a farm. They were in a gun battle, but the robbers got away. Now they expect us to solve the case. I never thought you guys would have the guts to commit robberies and murders. I should turn you in, except you are still my best customers."

Henry asked, "Do they have any idea who we are?"

"No," he replied. "All they know is they shot up a Polish military truck and think they hit at least one of the robbers."

"They killed one of us," I said. "Do you know where we can get a replacement truck?" He thought for a minute. "Take mine."

"Yours?" we all said at the same time.

"He replied, "Yeah! I got this from a lot where surplus Polish military and police vehicles were being kept. They will never miss it. Besides, if I tell them I found the truck abandoned with no sign of the culprits, maybe we can get them off our backs, and I will make some points at headquarters. This I will do for free, but you have to buy everything I have in the back."

We climbed in the back to look at what we were buying. There wasn't really that much. Clearly Kozlowski was losing his ability to get more supplies. There were some clothes we could use, some food, including pork that we would not eat, but as Benjamin said, "Let's make a deal with him. The truck is worth all of this." We agreed. He actually didn't overcharge us. It seemed that he was excited about solving the crime of the century. We would have to be much more careful with our second chance.

The next day, we spent the morning explaining how we "fixed" the truck. Nachman came over and said, "I heard the news. Are you sure Kozlowski won't turn us in?"

"Honestly, I don't know," I responded. "He was so excited that he could turn in the truck and still take our money. He is loving this. That being said, once he cannot sell us anything, then we could be in trouble."

While we were talking, Miriam came over. "Can I talk to you in private?" she asked.

"Sure," I said.

We took a walk away from the camp. We had not been alone much since we set up the camp. There was no time for love, but the feelings were still there.

Finally, we stopped and Miriam turned to me and said, "I'm leaving."

That came as a surprise. "What does that mean?" I asked. "Where are you going?"

She replied, "I'm taking Shlomo, and we're going to the Dombecks'."

"How can you leave us now?" I asked very selfishly.

She got angry. "Do you remember what happened the other night? I was pretty shaken up. When my mother saw me, she immediately decided I should go. Shlomo is scared. I told her I want to stay with them. This is where I belong, but I'd be lying if I said I wasn't scared. This is all about surviving. I have an opportunity to take Shlomo and give us a better chance of living through this nightmare. If it wasn't for Shlomo, I would not go, but maybe I can find other families that will take some of us in." She began to cry. "This is the hardest thing I have ever had to do. I don't want to leave you either. Momma and I told Papa this morning. He agreed. He knows this is not the best place for any of us and immediately took Momma's side. You have to tell me it's all right and that I will see you and them again."

"Wait a minute. How do you know they will still take you in? A lot has happened, and they might not even be there anymore."

"I don't," she said. "That's why you are going to take us there and make sure they will take us in."

"Now I'm sorry we got a new truck. I'm kidding. I will get you there, and yes, I will find you whenever this is over. We must believe that life will get back to normal someday. We all have to find a way to get to the end of this. When do you want to go?"

"Today, as soon as possible," she said.

"We will go soon," I said, "Let's go back. You need to get ready and say good-bye."

I was very sad to see her go. So was her family. Poor Shlomo, eight years old and having to leave his mother. He and Miriam adored each other. They spent every spare moment together. They sang songs, and she taught him about the world that she knew. I had to fight to get her attention. She said she loved me, but I knew she loved him more. Now they would be together, and we all hoped they would be on a path to a better life. The good-byes were tough. There was a lot of crying. Ruth, Pearl, and Mr. and Mrs. Goldin were all hugging and kissing endlessly. All the camp residents came out to say good-bye. Even Nachman and family came out from their mourning to wish Miriam and Shlomo well. They would be missed by everyone, but no one would miss them more than me. I stood in the background and took in the scene, but I could not help but think that this was probably the end of us, even though I would never tell her.

They brought out four bags with their belongings. The bags were sewn together by Miriam from leftover material she gathered from the dress shop. She was truly talented and creative. They were all different and would serve them well on their trip. We got in the truck, and it was finally time to leave.

It was still light out, and I thought it was dangerous to go in daylight, but Miriam insisted. She did not want to show up in the middle of the night and let them think she was some sort of criminal. We headed toward Rozwadow. Then I found out the real reason she wanted to go in daylight.

"I want to go by our old house," she said.

"Ah," I said. "I did the same thing the other day."

She replied, "I know where the Dombecks live. It's not that far out of the way."

Shayna and Jonah had always talked about the house they built in 1936. Jonah bought the land for an investment some years before and was proud that he had been able to build a beautiful home for the family. When we arrived, I saw it was in fact beautiful. It was large and had three stories. On the right side, it had a tall spire that came to a point, and it had a large front porch. As we drove by, we saw two young boys kicking a football around.

"They are probably German, the children of thieves who drove us from our home," said Miriam angrily.

"Is that our house?" asked Shlomo, thinking that was where they were moving.

"Not anymore," she said, putting her arm around him and squeezing him tight, trying to keep from crying.

"Let's go see the Dombecks," I said.

We drove up to the house. It was smaller than the Goldins' former home, but it was nice and well kept. It was a two-story wood-frame house with a small garden in the front.

"I will go in alone and talk to them," Miriam said.

"Shlomo and I will wait in the truck," I replied.

Miriam took a deep breath and got out of the truck.

She went up to the front door. I could see her knock on the door. After about thirty seconds, the door opened. A woman answered the door. After a few seconds, they hugged and Miriam went in and the door closed.

⅄ ⅄ ⅄

"Miriam," said Mrs. Dombeck, "I am so happy you are alive! I went back to get our dresses, and they said you were gone. They were angry that you disappeared. They said you would be hunted down and killed. Stephania is working, but she will be happy to see you. What brings you here?"

I took another deep breath. "I want to take you up on your offer to take me in. We have a hiding place, but it is not safe, and my family wants me to see if this is a better place for us to stay, if your offer is still good."

"We?" said Mrs. Dombeck.

"I brought my eight-year-old brother, Shlomo. We have to stay together."

"Where is he?" she asked.

"Outside with the man who brought us here."

"Can I meet him?" she asked.

"Yes." I got up and walked out to the truck. "Shlomo, come with me," I said.

"Are you staying?" asked Meyer.

"I don't know yet," I said. "She wants to meet Shlomo. Let's go."

We went back into the house.

"Shlomo, this is Mrs. Dombeck. Say hello."

"Hello," he said quietly.

"He's adorable," said Mrs. Dombeck.

"He's a good boy. He's quiet and won't be any trouble," I said.

Mrs. Dombeck thought for a minute. "This is very dangerous for us. My husband worked for the armaments factory in Stalowa Wola that was destroyed by the Germans. He lived through the bombing but was taken to Germany to work in an armaments factory in Berlin. He is sending us money, but we have no idea when we will see him. I am going to take you in, but it is still illegal to help Jews. We are supposed to turn you in and have you arrested. No one can know you are here. Come with me, and I will show you the room in the basement."

It was small, but it was dry and a big improvement over the hut in the woods. It had two small beds, a small cabinet with drawers, and a closet. I said enthusiastically, "This will be great. Thank you so much. I will help clean the house, cook, and even make you clothes if you have a sewing machine and can get me fabric and thread."

"It will be good to have you here," she said. "We may take you up on your offer. Go get your things, and welcome."

Shlomo and I went out, but Meyer and the truck were gone. While we were trying to figure out what happened, he drove up.

"There were two policemen walking down the street, so I decided to take a ride so they would not get suspicious," Meyer said.

"We are staying," I said.

He replied, "I will help you get your bags out of the truck." He didn't dare go in the house. Two Jews were all this woman could handle. It was time for him to go. We looked at each other. "I'm going to miss you," he said.

"I love you," I responded.

We knew we should not show affection in public and draw attention to ourselves.

Meyer climbed back in the truck and drove away. Shlomo and I went into the house and down to our room. I was so sad. What would happen to all that I loved?

"Mimi, what are we going to do here?" asked Shlomo.

"Live," I said. "Momma and Papa sent us here to be safe."

Shlomo replied, "I miss them. I want us to all be together. Will the Nazis find us here?" He had some understanding of what was going on. He knew there were lots of soldiers taking over our country and that they wanted to find us because we were hiding from them. He was there when they killed Leibish. He did not see what happened but knew Leibish was dead. He went to the funeral, but he never reacted too much. I don't know how much he understood about death. Maybe he was being strong for the rest of us.

"Would you like to sing a song?" I asked. Momma used to sing us Yiddish lullabies, and on Shabbos, Papa would sing songs with the boys after lunch, so there was a lot of music in the house. We sat and sang all the songs we knew. We were off key, and we laughed at how bad we were, but we had fun.

Suddenly, I heard some voices from upstairs, but I couldn't make out what was being said. "Shh," I said, not knowing if we should be scared. As I got up to go see what was going on, I heard footsteps coming down the stairs.

"Miriam!" said a high, shrieking voice. It was Stephania, home from work. She ran over and gave me a big hug. "I'm so glad you're here," she said. "And who is this handsome young man?"

"Tell her," I said to a shy Shlomo.

"My name is Shlomo," he said proudly. "I'm eight."

We all laughed.

I had to admit that it was strange to have this girl who never even looked in my direction at school suddenly be my best friend. Somehow I could not help but be suspicious, but at the same time, I was thankful that they took me into their home.

Stephania said excitedly, "Let's go upstairs. I want to show you my room. You come too, Shlomo."

We went upstairs. She had a lovely room with lots of pretty frills and things. She had lots of dolls that she must have played with as a little girl. She was about twenty-one now and working in a textile mill.

"I can't believe you are here!" she said, still excited. "We are still planning the wedding. My fiancé is Russian, a handsome young man named Yuri, whom I met at work. We are trying to find a date, and hopefully this silly war will be over soon."

What a different world she was living in. This silly war was killing my people, driving us into slavery, and making us hide in the woods to stay alive.

I just smiled and nodded as she continued, "I am so happy you came to stay with us. We went back to the shop to ask you to make my wedding dress, and you were gone. Now you are here and can make the dress."

"I would love to," I replied. "That is the least I can do for taking me in."

"That's great!" she shrieked even louder. "Do you ever want to get married? Do you have a boyfriend?"

"Yes," I said. "His name is Meyer, but I am not sure I will ever see him again."

"Why not?" she asked. "Did he leave you?"

She had no idea what was happening outside her little frilly room. I guessed I had to explain. "Being Jewish is against the law. We all have to find ways to survive. We hope someday we will be back together. What kind of dress do you want?"

That got her off the subject. She would much prefer to talk about herself anyway. I was happy to listen. It was a distraction. She described the most ornate and of course frilly dress imaginable.

"Can you get a picture?" I asked.

"I saw it in the newspaper." Then she ran downstairs to get it. She was up in a flash. It was long with lots of lace and beads and a big flair at the bottom.

I looked at it carefully. After studying it for a few minutes, I said, "This is a very detailed and complicated dress. I know I can make something close to this. I will draw out a pattern, and you will have to get me material and all the lace and beads."

She ran out to the top of the stairs. "Mommy!" she yelled. "She can make the dress."

This would take months with all the detail work, and I hoped they would let us stay here long enough to finish it.

Mrs. Dombeck came upstairs and said, "Are you sure you can make this? It is so expensive to buy. I told her to look for something less fancy."

"I can make it," I replied. "It will take a lot of material, and maybe we can eliminate some of the detail, but it will be beautiful and fit her perfectly. She will look beautiful. I will do it for letting us stay here, so you don't have to pay me for the work."

Mrs. Dombeck seemed annoyed that her daughter was getting her way. They must have argued over the dress. "It is going to be hard to get all of the material with the war going on," she said. "I will write to my husband and see if he can get it in Germany."

Perfect, I thought, this will take forever.

"Thank you, Mommy!" Stephania screamed, and they hugged.

Mrs. Dombeck broke the hold they had on each other. "Let's go down and prepare dinner. Miriam, can you help me?"

"Yes," I responded.

Shlomo and I went down with her while Stephania stayed upstairs, still in the clouds, studying the picture of her future dress.

"She is very spoiled, I know," Mrs. Dombeck said as if she needed my approval.

"She is happy, and it is nice to see," I said, trying to be understanding. "I have seen nothing but sorrow and death since the Germans came into our world."

She took my hand. "I want to help you. Will you eat my food? I know you have rules."

"Yes, we have strict rules about what we can eat, mixing milk and meat, how animals are slaughtered, but it has been harder to keep our laws since the war started. Don't worry; we will find what to eat from what you have. Vegetables work great. You are so generous and kind for taking us in. We will not be a burden to you."

Stephania came down to eat when the food was ready. She could not stop talking about her dress, her fiancé, and her wedding. I thought this might be worse than sleeping in the mud with my sisters. I was thankful dinner ended, and when it got dark, we were able to sit out back and let Shlomo run around a bit to get some of his restless energy out before bedtime. This was certainly safer and cleaner than where we were, but we both missed the family, and I already missed seeing Meyer constantly. Frankly, I also missed being part of the fight, even though there was death all around and it felt like we were all doomed. The night of the battle, I shot randomly at the faceless enemy, but I am sure I would feel differently when faced with actually killing someone, and I was thankful that I would not be faced with that now.

CHAPTER 17

The Fight Goes On

"ARE THEY SAFE?" ASKED JONAH, when I returned.

"Yes," I replied. "There was some discussion, some nervousness, but the lady of the house took them in. They took their things and disappeared into the house, and I drove off."

Jonah said, "They will be better off. All the older people, including your mother, have come to me and want us to stop the robberies and find another way. No one wants a repeat of the other night. Your idea of trying to get support of the local farmers is still the best chance we have of surviving without more violence. We probably need three or four other farms to help us. Then we can stop buying from your friend Kozlowski."

I protested. "No. We cannot cut Kozlowski off completely. We need to keep him close. He knows more or less where we are, and I don't fully trust him to keep our camp a secret. Also he knows what is happening in the outside world, which is useful. We will try to keep our spending to a minimum, but first I will take Benjamin, Henry, and Nachman back to the Dudek farm to see if they know others who will help us."

"That's a good start," replied Jonah. "I will talk to the others and see if they know anyone we might try."

The next morning, I talked to Benjamin and then went out to find Henry and Nachman. Since we were all confined to the small camp, it was never hard to find anyone. The boys were happy to go out on a peaceful mission, but we agreed to load the truck with weapons just in case. In fact, we agreed to always take weapons when we left the camp.

As we got close to the Dudek farm, Benjamin said, "Let me go in alone. I don't want to alarm them."

Henry said, "What if they are gone and you are faced with German occupiers?"

Benjamin replied, "Then you be prepared to shoot if I get in trouble, but I am not bringing a weapon to their door."

"Good," I said. "We will stand behind the truck, ready to shoot if you get in trouble."

When we arrived, everything looked normal and quiet. We all got out quietly, and Henry, Nachman, and I took positions around the truck where we could see the front door. Benjamin went up to the front door of the house and knocked. The door opened slightly, and we could see a gun barrel sticking out but could not see who was behind it. I was about to step out and yell something to distract the shooter, when I saw the gun barrel drop and Mr. Dudek walk out to greet Benjamin, putting his free hand on his shoulder. They spoke for a minute, then Benjamin waved at us to come into the house. I breathed a sigh of relief.

Henry said, "You boys go in. I will stay out here and keep a watch out for any trouble."

Nachman said, "Let's leave the guns in the truck. Benjamin was right not to take any into the house."

Nachman and I went in. We followed Mr. Dudek into the kitchen, where Mrs. Dudek was putting up a pot of coffee. "Sit down," said Mr. Dudek. "I am sorry about the gun, but the police were here a couple of days ago and told us about the shooting at one of the farms in town. They told us to be prepared for attacks. I figure you boys know something about what happened, but I am better off not knowing anything, so don't tell me. Besides, I am still expecting the Nazis to show up one day, and I am not leaving this farm without a fight."

"Good for you," said Benjamin.

"Yes," I said. "We would certainly help you anyway we can."

"Well, I have been gathering up some supplies for you," said Mr. Dudek as Mrs. Dudek began pouring coffee. "I had a feeling you were going to come by soon. I have it waiting in the barn."

Benjamin got up and spoke. "That is terrific. We really appreciate everything you have done for us. In fact, we wanted to ask you if you know anyone else who is sympathetic to our situation or is just fighting the occupation? There is no sense in fighting people who may be friendly to our cause."

Mr. Dudek stared at us thoughtfully for what seemed like an eternity but was really only a few seconds. Then he spoke. "I have two close friends who are farmers that I work closely with. They were also visited by the police, and they are on guard looking for robbers. They know about you, and I think they would help as well. Their names are Garek Rykaczewski and Milek Pilcicki."

"When can we go meet them?" I asked.

He responded, "Why don't I go talk to them? You come back tomorrow, and I will let you know what they say."

"Mr. Dudek," I said, "we are in a desperate situation. If the Nazis find us, they will kill us. We have women, children, and sick people in the camp. We need food and supplies, and we will stop at nothing to get enough for all in the camp. If you know people who can help us, we would like to solve this today and let the people at camp know that we have found generous, wonderful people to help us. Can we come with you to introduce ourselves?"

He responded, "I don't want to leave Magda here alone. I would take her with me to see our friends."

I thought for a second. "How about if Benjamin and I go with you? Henry and Nachman can stay here with Magda and make sure she is safe."

Magda spoke for the first time. "I will make them lunch, and I will feed you all when you get back."

"That sounds good to me!" Henry chimed in, and we all laughed.

Surprisingly, Mr. Dudek agreed. I think he was nervous that he was leaving his beloved wife with criminals, but he got his keys. Benjamin and I went with him out to his car.

The first stop was the Pilcicki farm. It was just two kilometers east. It was larger than Dudek's, and we saw three men working out in the field as we drove up. "Milek is out there with his sons," Dudek said. "Let me go over and tell him what we want." He got out of the car and walked over to where they were working. We couldn't hear what was being said, but arms started flailing and they were getting animated. They started walking toward us, so Benjamin and I got out of the car to greet them. As they got close, we could start to hear what was happening.

"How can you help these filthy Jews!" screamed the elder Pilcicki. "They are criminals and deserve to die."

"They are people, like us, and are being killed by those filthy occupiers. The Nazis are ruining this country!" Dudek shouted back. "The Jews are just trying to live their lives."

As they approached one of the sons shouted, "Get off our property, miserable vermin!"

The elder Pilcicki said, "We have to live with the Nazis now. If they want to kill these cockroaches, why do we care?"

At that point, the other son spit on Benjamin. "Get out, filthy pigs."

Benjamin lunged at him, grabbed him by the throat, and forced him to the ground. He was smaller than his foe but caught him by surprise and had the upper hand. "I wish I had brought my gun. I would put a bullet right in your head, stupid bastard!" he shouted as he was choking him.

I ran over and pulled Benjamin off him and held him tight. I didn't want to lose Dudek's help in the process.

"Good idea!" yelled the other son. "Let's take care of this problem for the Nazis." Then he turned and ran toward the house, presumably to get a gun.

I turned to Dudek. "Let's get out of here."

He nodded, and we all got in the car and took off. "I had no idea that they would react this way," Dudek said. He shook his head and was clearly distressed. "I knew I should have come alone. I would have gotten the same reaction, but we could have avoided all of this."

"Everyone is reacting differently," I replied "We have always been hated in Poland for being different. Now that the Nazis are targeting us, some Poles like you are seeing things differently, but for others, it is confirming what a lot of Poles have felt all along. Thank you for modifying your views and helping us."

"I may have to pay them a little visit some night," said Benjamin under his breath, clearly still angry.

"No, you won't," I replied, trying to be forceful. "We will only attack if absolutely forced to. This is about survival. We are not criminals."

Dudek said nothing and continued to drive, probably wondering if he was making a mistake helping us.

After about ten minutes of silence, Dudek finally spoke. "We are almost at the Rykaczewski farm. This time I will park on the road. You will stay in the car, and I will go in alone."

I was concerned about sitting on a road unarmed, but it was hard to argue with him.

"All right," I said, "but we will find a wooded area nearby and stay off the road. We do not want to be recognized. Enough people in town know us from the lumberyard and know we are Jewish."

"Understood," said Dudek. He dropped us off on the road outside the property instead. We found a wooded area to hide, and he continued down the road to the farm entrance.

"Benjamin," I said, "you have to learn to control your emotions. We can't let outsiders know what we are thinking. At some point, we may want to hit that farm, but we do not want them to know it was us. Now they will."

"Fine, but I may pay them a little visit anyway," Benjamin said with revenge on his mind.

I just said, "You know how I feel."

We sat quietly for about thirty minutes until we saw Dudek's car pull up slowly, as he was looking for us. We walked out of our hiding spot. He stopped and we got in.

"How did it go?" I asked.

"We're going back," he said. "They want to meet you. They will help, but they want to hear it from you."

We drove to the entrance of the farm. There was an older but well-kept barn. There were several horses grazing in the field and a chicken coop attached to the barn with about a dozen chickens clucking away. The house was small but also very nice, with flowers blooming all around the entrance. It was welcoming, and we hoped the inhabitants were as well.

Dudek knocked on the front door. Mr. Rykaczewski came outside. We were introduced, and Mr. Rykaczewski said, "I have been in your lumberyard. I knew your father. He was a good man. What happened to all of you?"

I responded, "Our father died months before the war. I was in the army, and my family continued to run the business. When the war broke out, I came home, and we were made slave laborers in our own lumberyard. Later when we learned we would be removed from our homes and be taken away, my family and about thirty others decided it would be better to live in hiding instead of being taken captive. We are living by our wits, and we need help with food and supplies to survive.

Our friend Mr. Dudek agreed to help us and offered to come see you, so we are asking for your help."

Rykaczewski replied calmly, "I understand you originally came to the Dudek farm armed and ready to steal what you could before he offered to help you. Then we heard from the police that a band of partisans robbed a German-held farm and killed two people. I don't want to be part of helping criminals."

I responded somewhat truthfully, "It's true that we went to Dudek's with the idea that we would rob the farm. We didn't want to hurt anyone, but we felt we had to protect ourselves. Then we heard about another band of partisans that got caught at the German-occupied farm. They were attacked by a group of armed Germans, and one of them, a father of two, was killed in the attack. We decided that it would be better if we could find people who were sympathetic to our cause and would help, which is why we came to Dudek today. We wanted to see if he knew anyone else who might help. He brought us to you. We do not want to hurt anyone, but we will protect ourselves if we have to."

Rykaczewski thought for a second. "Look, I have a wife and two daughters. I want them safe. I will help you with supplies as much as I can, but I want you to make sure no partisans show up to hurt us."

I replied, "Thank you so much. We are in touch with the other partisans, and we will let them know that your farm and family are off limits. Honestly, the Nazis are a bigger threat to you than a few Jews."

"I understand, but you are desperate, and I have to be sure I can trust you. I have no love for the Nazis, but if they suspect we are feeding you, I will have to stop."

"We understand, and we thank you again."

"Come back in two days, and I will have some supplies for you."

We shook hands and left.

"You were lying back there, weren't you?" asked Dudek once we got on the road.

"What do you mean?" I asked, knowing full well what he meant.

"The cuts on your face give you away," he said. "You were in some kind of battle."

I confessed. "I was driving. The windshield was shot out, and I got cut. They were well armed and shot first. We shot in defense and killed two of them as we left. My friend Nachman's father was on the team and was killed. We decided we were going down the wrong path. That part is the truth and is why we came to see you."

"Thank you for that," he said. "I want to know who we are dealing with. I don't think I would be any different in your place. I'll think about who else might help. Benjamin, you have to promise me you will leave the Pilcickis alone. I doubt that I will be dealing with them again, but I don't want to be responsible for violence. Benjamin?"

"Yes, I'll leave them alone," said Benjamin softly.

When we got back to the house, we heard laughter coming from the kitchen. Mrs. Dudek had made a feast of Polish sausage and other foods forbidden to Jews. Nachman and Henry were stuffing their faces, and Mrs. Dudek was enjoying watching them make pigs of themselves. "Come in, boys," she said. "There is plenty for everyone."

I was very hungry, and we all sat down as she was serving us. "I hope you had as much fun as we did," said Mrs. Dudek joyfully.

"I don't think so," said Mr. Dudek. "Nachman, I was sorry to hear about your father."

"You told him?" Nachman looked at me, surprised.

"I told him everything," I said proudly.

"Told him what?" asked Mrs. Dudek. "What happened to your father?"

"He died recently," said Nachman.

"I am so sorry," she replied. She was chubby with red cheeks. She was upbeat and wanted everyone around her happy. For a moment, we were all very happy and full.

After we ate as much as we could, Mrs. Dudek gave us each a package with food and told us to come back anytime. Henry and Nachman had loaded up the truck with their offerings, and we went back to camp. Everyone was happy except Benjamin. He was taking this much too personally. As far as I was concerned, we had a successful trip. There were good people out there who would risk helping us.

On the ride home, I filled Henry and Nachman in on the incident at the Pilcickis'.

"Why didn't you let me kill the bastard?" cried Benjamin. "They are as bad as the Nazis who killed Chava!"

"They didn't kill Chava," I replied. "You have to put this behind you. The important thing is that we protect the rest of our family."

"Fine," said Benjamin, but I wasn't convinced that he'd let it go.

The next few weeks went by pretty smoothly. We found another sympathetic farmer who was a friend of someone whom Henry had known. We kept Kozlowski appeased with small purchases, and no one needed to take any bigger risks than necessary.

We all took turns patrolling the camp at night to make sure there were no surprise visits. One afternoon, Naomi came and asked me, "Where is Benjamin? Momma is looking for him, and we cannot find him anywhere." We walked around the camp, and he was not there. Naomi continued, "He was on watch last night. Something could have happened to him."

"All right," I said. "Let's get everyone together and search the woods around the camp."

We got everyone together and split, searching in all directions for several hours until dark. We all came back empty-handed. There was no sign of him anywhere. No clues, footprints, clothing, bloodstains, nothing. That night, I couldn't help but wonder if he had just had enough and wandered off or if he visited the Pilcicki son who spit on him. He hadn't mentioned it after that day, but that did not mean he forgot.

There was no way I could drop in and see if they saw him, but maybe Dudek knew something. I would pay him a visit the next day.

At first light that morning, I hopped in the truck and took off to visit Dudek. When I arrived, Magda was serving breakfast. That woman could cook.

"You're early," he said.

"Come have some eggs," said Magda.

"Why not?" This was a treat for me. "I'm not here for supplies. Benjamin is missing, and I am afraid he may have gone to visit the Pilcickis. He was so angry that day."

"I have not heard a thing," said Dudek. "I'll be happy to pay them a visit to see if they know anything."

"I want to go with you," I insisted.

"No, you wait here," he replied. "I will be back in an hour." He got up, got his hat, and left in a flash.

"He's always running somewhere," said Magda, annoyed. At least she had me to feed for a while. She continued as she poured me a cup of coffee. "So I never did hear what happened that day at the Pilcickis'."

I had a feeling Dudek didn't tell her much. He probably wanted to keep her innocent from what was going on outside their little world. "My brother got into a little argument with one of the sons over there," I said. "Nothing too serious."

She responded, "I'm not surprised. Those boys have always been wild and hard to control. Their mother died when they were young, and their father was always working, so they raised themselves most of the time."

Great, I thought. If Benjamin did show up there, he would have a tough fight on his hands.

True to his word, Dudek was back in an hour. "They haven't seen him," he said immediately.

"No sign of him?" I asked, perplexed.

"Nothing," he replied. "Everything seemed normal over there. Both boys were there, and it was business as usual. They asked me if I was still helping the Jews, and I said, 'No, I don't trust them now,' so the less they know, the better."

"I'm surprised," I said. "I was sure that's where he must have gone. I have no idea where else he could be. Thank you for checking and all your help."

"I'll see you in a few days," said Dudek cheerfully. "I should have a good shipment for you this week. I am sure you will find Benjamin soon, safe and sound."

"Thanks," I said and left.

I drove through town and the shtetl to see if there was any sign of him. There was nothing. In fact, I saw no one who looked even remotely Jewish. It was as if the Jewish community of Pysznica never existed. Now I had to go back to camp and explain to Momma that her son was missing and I had no idea what had happened to him.

CHAPTER 18

A New Path

THE MATERIAL FOR STEPHANIA'S WEDDING dress arrived by post in a big box. It also came with a large envelope from her father in Germany addressed to her mother. Mrs. Dombeck read the letter and then gave it to Stephania to read. The arguing began right away. Mr. Dombeck was asking them to come to Germany. He felt that he would be stuck there indefinitely, and he wanted to be with his family. He sent work visas and travel documents for both. They were to sell the house and move to Germany as soon as they could.

"What about my wedding?" Stephania screamed. "What about my fiancé? I'm not leaving him, and he won't come to Germany. We have plans." While they were arguing, I was wondering what would happen to me and Shlomo if they moved. Would we go back to the camp? What else could we do?

Finally, the screaming died down. Mrs. Dombeck said, "We need to think about this. You should marry Yuri. He is a good man from a good family. Maybe you can live here and I will go to Germany and be with your father. We must sell the house so we can afford a nice place in Leipzig. Let's think about this. In the meantime, Miriam, you can start working on the dress."

"And we can finalize all the wedding plans," Stephania said, all excited.

"Yes," said Mrs. Dombeck, "but I'm afraid your father may not be able to get permission to leave Germany to attend. We will see."

The next day I got to work on the dress. They set up their sewing machine in our room. I would be stuck in the basement until I finished this thing. I had been working on the pattern for weeks from the pictures she had given me and knew exactly what I needed to do. Now that I had the material, I could begin. It was a beautiful white satin material, nicer than anything I had ever seen in Poland. Mr. Dombeck must have paid dearly for this. He had clearly always spoiled his little girl, and this was no exception. He also sent some lace and beading, but we would need more.

Shlomo wanted to go outside. I couldn't keep him locked in the basement all day and night. Over the past few weeks, I had let him go outside and play in the neighborhood. He befriended a couple of the boys on the street. I sat him down and spoke to him. I hoped he would be careful about what he said to anyone outside the house.

"Shlomo," I said sternly, "you should not talk to any strangers outside the house, especially adults. They cannot know anything about us, who we are, where we come from, why we are here, and especially that we are Jewish. No one can know. I know you want to play with those two boys down the street. You can, but if they ask you any questions, we are visiting our cousins, the Dombecks, and we come from the Russian side of Poland. Do you understand?"

"Yes, Mimi," he responded. "I know we are hiding because we are Jewish, and I will not tell anybody anything."

He had been playing with those boys a lot, and everything seemed to be fine, but I was very worried someone would find out, so I would talk to him every day to remind him who we were and why we were there. He was a good boy, sweet and loving. He hugged me every morning and every night, and I loved it. I wanted to live, and I wanted him with me forever.

The wedding was set for Saturday, September 19, 1942, a little less than five months away. That meant that we were at least welcome here until then. It wouldn't take me that long to make the dress, so maybe I could stretch that out with all the intricate beading she wanted. About three weeks later, I was ready to give Stephania her first fitting. She had not bothered me too much about my progress. She was clearly busy with her mother making other arrangements. There was a location for the big event, food, flowers—all a cause for screaming and arguments. I rather enjoyed that they forgot that I existed.

When I came upstairs with a basic dress and asked if I could try it on her, Stephania squealed with joy.

"Where should I stand?" she shouted. "What should I do?"

"Let's make some room in your living room," I responded. We moved two chairs and a table, and then I handed it to her and said, "Put it on." I had taken her measurements when I made the pattern, but I made it especially big so I could tailor it.

"Do you think I'm a cow?" she cried. "Look how big this is."

I started to laugh, and so did her mother, who I think understood. "Just stand over here and let me see," I said.

She was very pretty with a nice figure. She was going to make a lovely bride. I started pinning from the top. It would be tucked in at the waist, fitted around her hips, and then flare out at the bottom. Once I had it pinned, I told her to look in their hall mirror.

"You have to imagine the extra material cut out, and it will fit you perfectly," I said before she could start complaining.

"I hope so," she said, "but I think I want it sleeveless. It will still be summer in September, and I will look better with my shoulders and arms showing."

The dress had short sleeves and a high back, but I could make that change. A Jewish woman would never wear such a thing. We covered up for modesty, especially once married, but she did not care about modesty.

"I can do that," I said, "but once it is done, we cannot go back."

Now it was time for the argument. Mrs. Dombeck started. "Why do you want to change now? I like the dress the way it is. It is beautiful and shows class. You are getting married in church, and making it sleeveless makes you look like a whore."

Oh boy, here we go.

"I don't care what you think!" she screamed. "I want Yuri to think I am the most beautiful bride in the world. I don't want him to think he is marrying a nun!"

This went on for about ten to fifteen minutes. Along the way, I had an idea but waited while I was enjoying the fight. Finally, I interrupted. "I have an idea."

Stephania snapped at me. "It better be what I want." This girl had no respect.

I continued, "How about if the dress is sleeveless, and I make a short-sleeve jacket that you can wear in the church and then take off for the party."

"I agree to that," said Mrs. Dombeck.

"Not me," Stephania snapped back. "I want him to see me for the first time without the jacket."

I tried. The fighting continued. I knew Mrs. Dombeck would give in eventually, but she was worried about the priest. I thought I would try one more idea.

"How about if I make a shear shawl? He can see through it, but you will be covered to respect the church, and then you can get rid of it."

"Maybe," said Stephania quietly but not really accepting it.

"I'll make it; then you can decide," I said, as I had had enough of these two.

Stephania went up to take off the dress. After she was out of sight, Mrs. Dombeck said, "Thank you, Miriam. She's impossible. I like your ideas."

Stephania was down quickly. I grabbed the dress and went back to work.

The work kept me busy, but I couldn't help thinking about what might be happening at the camp. How were my parents and sisters doing? I missed seeing Meyer, even hearing his voice in my head, reassuring me everything would be all right. When I wasn't working on the dress, I was helping Mrs. Dombeck cook and clean the house. I think I was becoming the daughter she wished she had. She was very nice to me. She gave me some of the clothes she didn't wear anymore. She wanted me to try things on, and if they fit, she wanted me to keep them. I was very thankful, and she felt needed and respected instead of shunned and yelled at, as she was by her real daughter. She wanted me to tell her about my life, but I did not tell her much. I did tell her a bit about Meyer. Unfortunately, I felt like more of a slave than a daughter, being given some crumbs for all the work, but it was better than getting caught. There were times when I was alone with Shlomo in the house. I always took the chance to sit down and read the newspaper, which was brought to the house every day. I wanted to see what was happening outside my basement room. It was always filled with news of German victories throughout Europe. There were pictures of Nazis in Czechoslovakia, even France. I was curious that there was nothing about Russia. Maybe Nazis were not winning there. I couldn't help but think that we should have pressed on and gone to Russia. Maybe the Russians were kinder to the Jewish people. Maybe they would win and save us all. I had hope.

Three more weeks went by, and I had a dress ready for the next fitting. Stephania was asking almost daily now. When she got home from work, I was in the kitchen with Mrs. Dombeck. We were getting ready to start dinner. I left the dress hanging on the door in the living room. We waited for the shriek, and we both came out together.

"It's beautiful," she declared as she grabbed it and ran upstairs to put it on.

She came down the stairs slowly, as if she were entering a great palace and she was the new princess with everyone looking at her. The dress fit her well, her bare arms and shoulders showing off her white skin and long neck. It was a good choice for her, even if it lacked the modesty her religion required. When she reached the floor, she twirled around to show off the flared bottom. She was clearly pleased. I called her to the middle of the living room, where we once again cleared away the table and chairs. I asked her to stay still. I needed to make some adjustments to take in the bust so it would hold up, tighten the waist a bit, and make the dress slightly shorter. I still needed to add the lace and beading, very intricate work that would take several more weeks. The dress was now plain but very elegant. I would've been thrilled to be married in a simple, unadorned dress like this. I preferred it to the ornate dress she wanted, but I was happy to accommodate her.

"Where is the shawl?" asked Mrs. Dombeck.

I responded, "That will be easy, and I am saving it for the end, but I need the sheer material to make it."

"I can get that here," she said.

Stephania surprisingly didn't say a word. She clearly loved the dress and was busy looking at herself. A thank-you would've been nice, but I didn't expect it. Mrs. Dombeck was very appreciative, and that was good enough.

I told Stephania, "I have the adjustments and would like to get the changes made and start the lace and beading."

"Do I have to take it off?" Stephania asked.

Mrs. Dombeck chimed in. "Take it off, and let's have dinner."

Stephania strolled up the stairs. Just as she reached the top, the front door flew open, and Shlomo ran in, crying, "Mimi! Mimi!" He ran to me and gave me a big hug.

"What happened?" I asked. I pulled him off me. He was disheveled and dirty. His shirt was ripped, and he looked like he had been in a fight.

"I'm sorry, Mimi," he cried. "I didn't mean it. It just came out."

"What came out?" I asked. I had no idea what he was talking about. I continued, "Just calm down, and tell me what happened." I took him downstairs so we would have privacy. By then, he had stopped crying.

"I was playing with my two friends, and I told them I was Jewish." He started crying again. "I know you told me not to tell them, but they asked me why I didn't go to school with them. I didn't know what to say, so I told them I went to a different school because I was Jewish. As soon as they heard that, they started yelling how it was all our fault that the Germans came and how we were ruining Poland and had to be killed. Then they started punching me. I fought back, but they pushed me on the ground and were punching me more. I got loose and ran home. I'm sorry."

"It's all right," I said and gave him a big hug. It was hard to believe that young boys could hate already. They were taught to be haters by their parents, and if they told the adults, we could be in for trouble. "Let's go up and eat dinner." I took him by the hand, and we went upstairs.

I debated about what to tell the Dombecks as we sat down to eat.

"So what happened?" asked Mrs. Dombeck.

"Shlomo got into a fight with the two boys he has been playing with. He will be all right." I was hoping this would go away. I would keep Shlomo inside from now on, and maybe the boys would not mention it to their parents.

When we finished dinner, Shlomo and I stayed in the kitchen and helped clean up. Suddenly there was a knock at the door. Mrs. Dombeck went to get it. There was a man's voice. I went to the door to listen.

"My son came home and told me you have Jews living here," he said angrily. "We can't have Jews living here. If the Germans find out, who knows what they will do."

"We have a young girl here with her eight-year-old brother," said Mrs. Dombeck. "She is working for us, making a wedding dress for my daughter, then they will leave. She is just here to work."

The man at the door became angry. "I don't care what they are doing here! It's illegal to hide Jews. If you don't send them away, I will turn you in to the police, and you will be arrested and sent away."

"How can you do that?" she said. "They are people, just like us. They are trying to live and are being treated badly. They are not hurting anyone; they are just trying to survive."

He got even angrier. "Jews are filthy vermin that are ruining the country and need to be exterminated. If you don't see that, maybe you should be turned over to the Nazis."

"Fine," she said. "If I send them away, will you leave us alone?"

"Yes," he said. "I don't want police crawling around here, and I won't let my children be around Jews."

"I will tell them," she said dejectedly. "Now leave."

He did. She closed the door and started to cry. Shlomo and I came out of the kitchen. "I heard," I told her.

She gave me a hug. We were both in shock.

Just then Stephania came bouncing down the steps with the dress draped across her arm. "I can't wait to see this when it's finished. Yuri is going to love the way I look in this!" She was taken aback when we didn't react. "What happened? You look like the world is ending."

"It is, for us," I said sarcastically.

"Miriam has to leave," her mother said.

"Where are you going?" Stephania asked in a panic.

"I don't know," I replied.

Mrs. Dombeck told her, "The neighbor found out we have Jews living here, and they threatened to turn us in."

"To hell with them!" she cried. "She is staying here and finishing my dress!"

Mrs. Dombeck stood up, and as her face filled with blood, she yelled, "Are you crazy? No one cares about your stupid wedding! If the police come here and find out they are here, we will be in deep trouble. Miriam has to leave, and we are going to Germany to be with your father!"

Stephania got up and got into her face. "I'm not going to Germany! I am marrying Yuri and staying here!"

Mrs. Dombeck yelled right back, "You're a grown woman, and you can do what you want. I may as well give your work papers to Miriam and take her to Germany!"

They both stopped yelling and looked at me. "Where will you go?" asked Mrs. Dombeck.

"I guess back into hiding with my family," I responded. "I don't even know what is happening with them."

Stephania seemed to wake up out of her wedding stupor and said, "Why don't you take my papers? I will marry Yuri and take his name. You can go to Germany and be Stephania Dombeck. They'll never know you are Jewish."

"I think that is a great idea," said Mrs. Dombeck.

"I can't go without Shlomo," I said.

"He does not need papers," she said. "He's a minor. You can take him under your custody. You will not be questioned."

"I have to think about this," I said. "Maybe I can get a job as a seamstress and finish your dress."

We all laughed. I took the dress and Shlomo, and we went downstairs. This would be a sleepless night.

"Do you miss Momma and Papa?" I asked Shlomo as we were getting ready to go to sleep.

"Yes, and Tsippi and Pearl too. I miss Leibish the most."

I began to cry. I missed him too. I was afraid we were all in the same danger. "Maybe we should go on an adventure to a new place," I said. "Just me and you. That could be fun, right? What do you think?"

"I don't know," he said.

He was eight years old, and I was looking to him for answers. I was confused and scared. I put him to sleep. I would tell him stories and sing songs to get him to fall asleep. He finally dozed off. I tried to sleep but couldn't. I could not get it out of my head. I tossed and turned all night trying to figure out what we should do.

When morning came, I could see the daylight coming through the crack in the basement door. I got up, went upstairs, sat on the living room couch, and continued to agonize about what would be best for us. How could we survive? Either way, we would be hiding—in a camp in the woods with family or under assumed identities in the heart of the Nazi world? Not a great choice. My heart said go back home to family and Meyer. About an hour later, Mrs. Dombeck came down and saw me.

"Rough night?" she asked.

"Yes," I said, "I need to go see my parents."

"I understand," she said. "You never told me where they are."

"You're right," I responded. "They are hiding with a group of other Jewish families. I have not heard anything from them. I must see if they are all right, and I need to talk to them. Thank you so much for offering the papers, but I feel like I should be with them."

Mrs. Dombeck sat down next to me and said, "I think you will do better in Germany as a young Polish working girl. Hiding is no way to live."

"I will be hiding no matter what I do," I replied.

She thought for a minute. "I have a friend with a car who can take you to see them. It's Sunday, and he is off from work. Talk to them. Then you can decide. The offer stands."

"Thank you," I said. "You have been so good to me."

"It's the right thing to do," she said. "We Poles are not all the same. I don't understand why people are afraid of you. I will never understand it."

"Me neither." I shrugged.

After breakfast, she went to see if her friend could take us. Twenty minutes later, she was back with her friend. He was about the same age as my parents, late forties, maybe fifty, tall with gray hair. "This is my friend Jerzy," said Mrs. Dombeck. "He grew up with my husband, and he is a good friend. He will be happy to give you a ride. This is Miriam."

"Hello, Miriam. Anna asked me to give you a ride, but she didn't tell me where," said Jerzy.

Anna? She had never told me her first name.

Mrs. Dombeck chimed in. "That is because I don't know."

Did she tell him I was a Jew? I should have told her not to. "Just outside Pysznica," I said reluctantly.

"Perfect," said Jerzy. "I'll take you now. Do you need me to wait for you?"

"No," I said. "I should be able to get a ride back. Thank you for taking us. I will get my brother, and we will go."

Shlomo was in the kitchen. Mrs. Dombeck followed me in and said, "I didn't tell him who you were except a friend of Stephania who is staying with us. I don't want to take any chances. Are you sure you can get a ride back?"

"Not really, but I hope so," I said. "I can't let him take me all the way, and I don't know how long it will take. I don't want to get him in trouble."

She gave me a hug and said, "OK, good luck."

I didn't know what kind of car he was driving, but it was large and quite fancy. He seemed very proud of it. Shlomo was very excited and sat in the back by himself. He kept moving from side to side, opening all the compartments in the back. I sat in the front.

"Nice day for a drive in the country," he said.

"Sure," I said. He had no idea how desperate I was. "What do you do?" I asked.

"I'm a doctor in Stalowa Wola," he replied.

That explains the fancy car, I thought. "That's very nice," I said.

"What about you?" he asked, just making conversation.

I had to be careful. "I'm a seamstress," I said. "I am making a wedding dress for Stephania as a wedding gift."

"Wow," he said. "That's great. I am sure my wife would give you some business."

I replied gratefully, "Wonderful, but I need a few weeks to get the wedding dress finished." I would be gone long before that.

"So where exactly are we going?" he asked as we arrived in Pysznica.

"Just stay on this road about five kilometers outside town," I said. I had to find a place he could leave us that was not suspicious, a house, store, or something. As we got closer, I recognized the area closest to where the camp was. As we went by, I saw a farm stand on the road and said, "This is it. Let us off at the farm stand."

"Here?" he said.

"Yes," I said. "I want to get something for my friends, and then we can walk." He did not quite understand but agreed. He pulled over at the farm stand. "I think I will pick up some flowers for my wife while I'm here," he said.

"Great," I said. Just great. I must get rid of this guy. I helped him pick out a nice bouquet.

He paid and said, "Are you sure I can't take you the rest of the way?"

"No, this is great," I responded. "Thank you so much. It was very kind of you to bring us here."

"Anytime," he said. He got into his car and drove off, finally.

I didn't want to be identified. Luckily everyone seemed to be minding their own business. I grabbed Shlomo's hand and said, "Let's go find Momma and Papa." We walked down the road. Traffic was light, but a few cars came by. As soon as I saw no one was coming, we ducked into the woods. Shlomo kept running ahead. He knew exactly where to go. He was smart and sweet, and I loved having him with me.

When we arrived, everything seemed normal. Henry was the first to see me. "Miriam?"

Everyone looked up. Henry, Nachman, Meyer, and Papa were having a meeting.

Shlomo screamed, "Papa!" and ran to give him a hug.

I was right behind him. I wanted a hug from him too. Then I looked at Meyer. He was smiling. So was I. We embraced.

"I missed you so much," I said. "I didn't think I would ever see you again."

"I knew we would," he said.

Momma, Pearl, and Ruth came over. It was a great reunion. Shlomo was in his glory. His other big sisters were making a fuss over him. He began to run, knowing they would chase him.

"Momma, Papa, I need to talk to you," I said, ending the fun. We walked into the hut and sat down where we could. I didn't remember just how terrible our new home was with its dirt floors and the wooden structure sagging after being exposed to the elements for months. I had to admit, living in a well-kept home made me see just how difficult life in the woods was.

"We have to leave the Dombecks' house," I said and began to tell them about how the neighbors found out there were Jews living in the house and threatened to have Mrs. Dombeck and Stephania arrested if they didn't make us leave. I left out the part about Shlomo telling the neighborhood kids and getting into a fight.

"So you are back here to stay? What happened to your clothes?"

"I haven't decided if I am staying," I said. I continued to tell them the story of the wedding plans, the dress, and how Mr. Dombeck was stuck in Germany. "He sent them working papers and train tickets to Leipzig to be with him. Stephania is getting married and plans to stay in Poland. They offered me her work papers and train ticket with the idea that I would go to Leipzig as Stephania Dombeck, where I could work and live. I can take Shlomo under my custody, and I would raise him. I would change his name to Samuel Dombeck and send him to school in Germany. I don't want to leave you and the family, but I wanted to know what you thought."

Papa stood up and took my hand. I stood up, and he put his arm around my shoulder. "You must go to Germany," he said. "Look how we live. Like caged animals. We have to hunt for food. The hut is falling apart, and we have no way to fix it. We could be discovered at any moment, and I hate to think what they will do to us."

"Yes," said Momma. "Go and live your life. But Shlomo stays here with us."

"No!" I protested. "You heard what Papa said. This is no way to live, not for me and not for him. He has a better chance to live a long life if he comes with me."

"No!" she said. "He will slow you down. He will tell someone you are Jewish, and that will be the end of both of you. You must go yourself, forget who you are and where you came from, and live your life."

If she only knew why we were here today. She was right of course. I had a better chance by myself. "But it has been wonderful to have him with me. He is so good and sweet. It makes me so much happier to have him with me. I love him so much."

"Momma's right," said Papa. "You are better off on your own. That is final."

I shouldn't have told them. I should have just stayed here, but I knew they were right. I had to go. It was settled. "I need to see Meyer and say good-bye," I said. "He will want to take me back."

Meyer was sitting outside waiting for me to come out. "Let's walk," I said. Once we got out of the camp and into the woods, I said, "I'm leaving for good."

"What?" he asked.

I told the story once again. "I love you very much," I said, "but this is not possible. It's not our time. Our job is to live, and my future is in Germany, not here and not with you."

Meyer took my hand and said, "You left me once. Now you're telling me you came back just to leave again? I thought you were coming back to stay. I promise you this: I will find you someday and marry you."

"You're a romantic fool. We will never see each other again. Move on. I need you to take me back to the Dombecks'," I said coldly.

We were finished, even if he was a dreamer. I was not. He was clearly hurt. We walked back to camp in silence.

I still had to break the news to Shlomo. When we got back, both our families were waiting to say good-bye. Apparently, everyone was talking about the idea of taking an assumed identity. "What kind of papers do you need to be someone else?" asked Pearl.

I responded, "I don't have them with me, but she has an identification card that just says her name and her parents' names and is issued by the Polish government. It also has her picture, which I can pass for. I didn't know this document existed. She also has a work permit that will allow me to enter and work in Germany."

"Do all Poles have these papers?" asked Naomi.

"I think they all have their identification cards, but the work papers came from her father, who works in Germany, so I think those are special."

Ruth said, "I went to school with you. I remember some of the girls I talked to. Maybe there is a way to get some more people to give up their papers."

"Maybe," I said.

Suddenly, Shlomo came running and jumped into my arms. "Momma says I can't go with you."

"No, sweetheart," I said, tearing up. "You have to stay here with Momma and Papa."

"But I want to go on the adventure with you. I want to be with you." He started crying, and so did I. Momma came over and picked him up.

I was crying hysterically. "I don't want to leave him here," I said, trying to stop crying.

"Go," she said. "He's staying with us."

I put my arms around them and told them both I loved them. It took a while to say good-bye to everyone, but finally Meyer and I got in the truck and left the camp and my past.

CHAPTER 19

The Adventure of Life

⅄ ⅄ ⅄

DURING THE RIDE BACK TO Rozwadow, Meyer was quiet. I knew I had spurned him, but he should understand we had to part and that I still loved him. "Why so quiet?" I asked.

"Benjamin is missing," he replied.

I did not expect this.

"What?" I said. "What happened?"

"We don't know" was the reply. "He left one night without a word. I thought he was going to exact revenge on an anti-Semitic farm family we met. He got into a fight with one of their sons, and he vowed to get revenge. We checked, but they have not seen him. We do not know if he is alive or dead. We don't know if he has been captured or if the camp is in danger of being discovered."

"I thought you were angry at me," I said.

"No, I know what you have to do," Meyer replied. "We will wait to be together."

When we arrived, I moved over to him, and we kissed passionately for a long time. This would be the last moment of warmth and happiness I expected to feel for a long time. After a while, Meyer looked at me and said, "Go, before I run away with you."

"Why don't you?" I asked, tongue in cheek. "You can be my servant who carries my bags." We laughed. "Wait here," I said. "I will get Shlomo's clothes for you to take back."

When I knocked on the door of the house, Mrs. Dombeck answered, clearly upset. "Come in and close the door," she said. "Another neighbor came here wanting to know if I had Jews living here. I told her there was no one living here except me and Stephania. The whole neighborhood was talking about this, and everyone is scared that the Nazis will come here looking for Jews. This is unbelievable how something so unimportant can become such an issue."

I replied angrily, "It's important to me. It's life and death. I've decided to go to Germany and become Stephania Dombeck." It was hard to hear those words coming out of my mouth.

"That is a good decision," she said nervously. "When can you leave?"

"I guess on the next train to Leipzig, but I don't know when that is."

"I hate to say this to you, but I think it's best for all of us if you leave now. I prepared a package for you. It has Stephania's papers, the train pass, and some cash. There is also a note with a name and address for you. My husband knows a manager at the Hotel Fuerstenhof. He should be able to help you with a job. Just tell him that you are my daughter."

"My things are packed, and the man who brought me here will take me to the train station," I replied, feeling rushed to leave but grateful for her help.

"Hey, where's Shlomo?" she called as I was headed downstairs.

"My parents wanted him to stay with them," I said. "They thought he would be trouble for me."

She came down to help me with my bags. "They are right, you know," she said.

"I know," I replied, "but I loved having him around."

She helped me get the bags to the truck. I introduced her to Meyer. "So," she said, "this is the young man you're in love with." I had told her our story during one of our many mother-daughter talks in the kitchen, talks I knew she preferred over those with her own daughter. Meyer didn't say anything but turned red with embarrassment.

"I don't want to hug good-bye out here, you understand," she said with embarrassment of her own. "I'll be in Leipzig after the wedding. Please look me up. Besides, I want to introduce my husband to his new daughter."

I wasn't sure if she meant that, but I thanked her for all she had done for me and got back in the truck.

"What just happened?" asked Meyer.

"You are taking me to the train station," I replied. "I will explain on the way." As we pulled out, I said, "People are so afraid of us. I don't think they know who we are, just that we are different. They think they need to hate us so they can be part of normal society. They have always hated us, but now hate is the normal way of life. It's the policy of the government, and people will follow blindly and turn in anyone who shows us kindness. I don't want to have children in this world."

Meyer dismissed me. "The only thing that matters right now is that you get on a train as Stephania Dombeck and hide that you were born a Jew."

"Do you think I am wrong?" I asked, annoyed.

"There is no wrong," he said. "We must survive, or we will disappear. When this is over, you will be there to help the Jewish people grow again."

"You promised to find me when this is over," I responded. "I expect you to be there when this is over."

Just then, we arrived at the station in Stalowa Wola. He waited while I went in to find out when the next train to Leipzig was leaving. I had some decent travel clothes, thanks to the Dombecks' hand-me-downs. I was scared to death to walk into the crowded train station. There were police outside and in. There were also some German soldiers milling around. Meyer parked out of sight, and I walked into the station, standing tall, with my new identity at the ready. I took a deep breath, walked up to the ticket window, and asked when the next train was leaving for Leipzig. The clerk asked to see my rail pass. I showed it to him. He looked at it a long time. "This was issued in Germany," he said.

"Yes," I said. "My father sent it to me so I can join him in Leipzig."

The line behind me was getting longer. A police officer came over. "Is there a problem?"

"No," said the clerk, "just a little confusion."

The policeman looked at me.

My God! I knew him! And he knew me. He went to my school, and now he was a policeman. I knew he recognized me from the way he looked at me, and he knew I was Jewish.

Suddenly he smiled and said, "Sorry to have bothered you." He walked away, thank God. "The next train to Krakow is in three hours," said the clerk. "You can switch to the Leipzig train there. Here are your tickets."

I turned around and walked out as fast as I could without running. I thought I had an angel of God looking over me at that moment. This was going to be scarier than I thought. Once I left the station, I could start to breathe again. I walked to where Meyer was sitting in the truck and got in.

"How did it go?" he asked.

"Good," I said, "except I am scared. How am I going to be Stephania? I already had to explain to the clerk and a policeman, who I know recognized me."

"You will get used to it; you have to," he said.

"I'm still shaking," I said. "The train is in three hours."

"I will stay with you until you have to go," he said.

We sat there quietly for a while. Finally, Meyer broke the silence. "Do you ever wonder what life would be like without the war? I think we would be married by now and maybe have a child."

"You're such a dreamer," I said dismissively. "First, I would never have met you. I would still be living in Rozwadow, where there were lots more eligible men than in little Pysznica."

He looked at me a bit hurt and said, "So lucky for me the Nazis showed up and sent you my way, eh?"

"Yes, lucky for you," I said but then slithered to his side and give him a big kiss on the cheek. "Lucky for me too. I love you very much, but now I am leaving and will never see you again. I am angry about that."

He put his arm around me and said quietly, "I choose to believe this will end someday, and I will find you and marry you."

"I will pray for that every morning when I awake and at night before I go to sleep," I replied.

"Me too," he said, and we continued to sit there for a long time.

Finally, Meyer looked at his watch, the only thing he kept from his army days, and said, "It's time for you to go. The train will be boarding soon."

I had not felt at peace for many months, but I did being held in his arms at that moment. "I don't want to go," I said. "Kiss me one more time."

He did and held me tight for a long time. I got out of the truck, sad to say good-bye to him, sad to say good-bye to my beloved Shlomo and the rest of the family. I was truly on my own.

The nerves were coming back. I had to get on that train. As I was walking back to the station, I saw Meyer drive by. He didn't acknowledge me. He just drove by. It was dangerous for him to even be on the street. I walked past two Nazi soldiers. They both stared at me from head to toe. They didn't say anything. I didn't know if they thought I looked like a Jew or if they just liked the way I looked in Stephania's dress. I hated Nazis.

As I got to the platform, the train was in the station unloading from its last trip. There were police and Nazis scrutinizing people coming off the train, checking a few for tickets and papers. An older couple attracted some attention and were escorted off the platform. I wondered who they were and why they were being questioned. Were they Jews trying to get to Russia? It was hard to think of anything else.

Finally, it was time to board. I started to get on a middle car when I heard, "Fraulein!" I stopped and turned around. "Where are you going?" said the German officer.

I understood his German, although I was not fluent. Growing up speaking Yiddish, much of which was derived from German, helped me understand. I responded in Polish. "I am going to Leipzig."

"A young lady traveling by yourself?" he said. "Let me see your papers."

I showed him the ticket and the identification. He looked at the picture and looked at me. This was the first test. He said, "You know, if I saw you on the street, I would swear that you were a Jew, but your papers are in order." He handed back the papers and I got on the train. He offered to help me carry my bags on the train. He was just flirting. It made me want to puke, but it worked. I was so relieved. I realized at that moment I would have to become fluent in German, but I had a good start. I also realized that a young woman on her own would attract unwanted attention from men. I would have to be careful so as not to be discovered.

The train pulled out of the station. It was scheduled for five hours to Krakow and then another six hours to Leipzig, with time in between. I would arrive at my destination sometime tomorrow morning.

As the train moved out of the station, my thoughts were with those I loved. I felt leaving was a mistake. I missed everyone and had no idea if I would see them again, but I was committed. As the hours passed, Miriam Goldin moved further into the background of my mind, and my thoughts moved to the future and how I was going to live as Stephania. How would I speak? How would I repress my Jewish identity? Would I be expected to act like a Christian? Go to church? Were the Nazis Christians? I had never been in the Christian world, other than my little exposure in grade school. I had no idea what I was going to do or say.

Finally, we arrived in Krakow. I had never been this far from home. It was a much bigger station. There were lots of platforms with different trains going to different destinations. I was so sheltered. I had no idea.

I went inside to find out when the next train was leaving. It was leaving in about ninety minutes, at 2200 hours. I found a seat in the far corner of the station, where I could see the board with the train arrival and departure schedule and the rest of the room. I just sat and watched people go by for a while. Suddenly I felt a panic go through my system, a chill of sorts. Not only was I leaving Poland for the first time in my life but I was going *Germany*! I was going into the heart of the evil Nazi world. All the questions started going through my mind. How would I survive surrounded by Nazis? Then I saw a line forming in front of two windows. I walked up just to see if this was something I was supposed to do.

I asked the couple at the end of the line, "Excuse me, what is this line for?" They were German and were struggling to understand my Polish. I asked the question again, trying to use German without giving away my Yiddish roots.

The man spoke in German. "German customs."

"Where are you going?" asked his female companion in Polish.

"Leipzig," I replied.

"Then you must go through customs, just as we are," she said.

"What is your business in Germany?" asked the man rather gruffly.

I replied carefully. "I am joining my father, who is on a permanent work visa in Leipzig."

"He must be a loyal patriot of the Fatherland," he declared proudly.

"Yes, very loyal," I replied.

"My name is Marta," she said. "This is Heinrich. We work for the Third Reich, helping Germans settle here in Poland. We are on our way back to Berlin to report on our efforts."

My God, these people are responsible for us leaving our homes. If I'd had a gun, I would've shot them on the spot. "How is your effort going?" I asked as if I didn't know.

"It was a great success," she boasted. "We have brought in hundreds of German settlers. We moved many Polish families to better housing, finding them great jobs. The only problem has been the Jews, who come and steal from the good people. When they are all caught, they will be taken care of."

I could imagine what she meant by "taken care of." Thank God they were on a different train. I didn't think I could contain myself for the six-hour train ride.

Meanwhile the line was moving. As we got closer, I could see that officers were checking everyone's baggage and papers. I was careful to avoid taking anything that would give me away. I did have some old jewelry that I might need to sell at some point. I discreetly took it out of my bag and put it in a pocket on my dress.

The couple in front of me passed through in a matter of seconds without a bag search. Clearly they were known by the authorities. Now it was my turn.

"Show me your papers," said the customs officer. I gave him everything, including the work visa. "Your name?" asked the officer.

I thought a second and took a breath. "Stephania Dombeck."

"Address?" he continued.

I had memorized every detail of Stephania's life and had no problem answering.

"Reason for your travel?" He was not letting up. "Your address in Germany?"

I had no place to live there yet, but I needed to tell him something or he would be suspicious.

I responded, "Hotel Fuerstenhof."

Suddenly he was staring at my identification card. "This picture is not a good likeness. When was it taken?"

"About two years ago," I said, now very nervous. "I have changed a lot since then."

He looked at me and said, "You are much prettier now. You can go."

I smiled at him and said, "Thank you." One more Nazi pig I would've liked to have shot!

While I was being questioned by him, some Nazi frau went through my bags, and everything was piled up on the floor. I just repacked and moved on. Once I got through, it was time to get on the train. The good news was that the scrutiny was over. I showed the conductor my ticket and found a seat in a berth near the front of the train. It was not very crowded, but a woman and two men were sitting in there. The two men were staring at me and the other woman.

Once the train was on its way, one of the men got up and said, "You two look Jewish."

I looked at the other woman, and she looked at me. Now I was scared.

He said, "Unless you give me your money and jewelry, we will tell the Germans, and they will take you off this train."

The other woman immediately took off a watch, a bracelet, and a necklace she was wearing and gave it to him. All I had on was a ring my mother gave me. I gave it to him but left the other jewelry I had in my pockets hidden. He and the other man got up and left the berth. The other woman left behind them. I was afraid to sit there alone, so I got up and walked to the next car, not seeing any sign of the two men or the other Jewish woman. There were a few soldiers roaming the car, so I looked in one of the berths. There was an older couple sitting there, so I went in and sat down. They were polite and friendly. I introduced myself, found a blanket, covered myself, and fell asleep.

The train was about an hour and a half late, arriving at about 0530. I awoke just before the train pulled into the station. It was starting to get light. I got off the train. The station looked very much like Krakow. I was in a big city. Another line was forming. I got on. I went through customs much more easily this time. I had my story straight, and the agents didn't look too interested in stopping anyone. I walked out into Central Leipzig. I grabbed a city map as I left the station. When I got outside, I saw Mullerpark across the street. I carried my bags over and found a bench to sit on. It was now daylight. The park was lovely and had beautiful flowers all around. You would never know there was a war going on. I guess they were winning after all.

I opened the map to see where the Hotel Fuerstenhof was. For once, luck was on my side. The hotel was only about seven or eight blocks from where I was sitting. I needed a place to clean up so I could go meet the manager and ask for a job. There was the Park Hotel across the park. I could rent a room for a night and hopefully use that to find a place I could afford if the job worked out.

I dragged myself and my bags into the lobby of the hotel. It was old but clean. They had rooms available but wanted me to pay in advance. I had zlotys, and they were willing to exchange them into deutsche-marks. I paid them for a night. It was expensive, but I had to get my bearings. The room was small. It had a double bed, a small chair, a table with a lamp on it, and one picture of the city on the wall. The bathroom was also small but had a bathtub. That was where I was headed. After my bath, I felt totally refreshed. There was an iron and ironing board in the room. I pulled out all the dresses I had and ironed them out. I put one on, and I looked as professional as possible. Around 0900, I headed out the door with all my papers and the letter from Mrs. Dombeck.

It took about fifteen minutes to walk the few blocks to the Hotel Fuerstenhof. I walked up to the front desk and asked for Herr Vogt in the best German I could say.

"Who should I say is here to see him?" asked the desk clerk.

"Stephania Dombeck."

"Please sit down in the lobby," she said and then promptly disappeared.

I sat and looked around. This was a very fancy hotel. The lobby was tremendous, with fancy crystal chandeliers hanging everywhere. There were beautiful paintings all over the walls. Everyone in the lobby was dressed up beautifully. I clearly stuck out in my old clothes.

About thirty minutes went by. The clerk was back at the front desk. I did not want to call attention to myself, so I did not ask her where he was. For the first time, I realized that if there was no job here, I would be poor and alone very quickly, a Jew in the place we are hated the most, the middle of Germany. Suddenly, a tall, very handsome gentleman came up to me.

"Fraulein Dombeck?" he asked.

"Yes," I said, standing up.

"I am Herr Vogt. Please follow me," he said. He led me to a group of offices on the second floor. "Please sit down," he said as we walked into a small office with his name on the door. He spoke first. "Your father tells me you would like to work in our beautiful hotel."

"Yes, Herr Vogt," I replied. "I want to be here near him, but I do not want to be a burden on him." I didn't know how much Mr. Dombeck had told him and whether he knew I wasn't really his daughter.

"That is fine," he said. "What skills do you have we can use?" he asked.

"I am a seamstress," I said confidently. "I specialize in women's dresses."

"We are not a dress shop," he said, a bit annoyed. "We are a top luxury hotel, catering to wealthy businessmen. The only openings I have are for cleaning girls, maids. You clean the rooms to the high standards of our hotel. However, the more I think about it, we have many calls for repairs to torn clothing from our guests. We usually send them out to a tailor, but perhaps you could make the repairs in addition to your cleaning duties."

"That would be great," I said enthusiastically. "I can make torn seams look like new and can patch anything. I also am very good at cleaning. I always helped Mother clean around our house."

He thought for a minute and said, "Well, as a favor to your father and because you can sew, I would like to offer you the job. You will be paid fifty marks per month."

"Thank you," I replied. "I accept. Now I can look for a place to live."

"Live?" he asked. "Aren't you living with your father?"

Oh, no. How do I explain this? I started stuttering, "Eh, my father lives a bit far from here, and he has a small flat. I am grown, and I want to live on my own." I had no idea where Mr. Dombeck lived or what he lived in, and I hoped that Herr Vogt didn't know either. My heart was pounding.

Suddenly he started to laugh. Now my heart was racing. "I have a daughter your age." He chuckled. "The minute she turned twenty-one, she had to go out on her own. She is in Berlin now. Well, if it helps, the hotel has a dormitory about ten blocks from here, where many of the girls who work here live. If you like, you can live there while you work here, and we will take a few marks a week out of your pay. It's nothing fancy, but it's cheap and clean."

"Really?" I was amazed that this was working out. "When can I move in?" I asked.

"Let me introduce you to the maid supervisor, and we will set you up," said Herr Vogt.

We went down the freight elevator three floors to the basement. We went into the laundry area, where the linens and towels were being washed and dried. There was a lot of activity, as maids were scurrying around filling their carts, heading upstairs to clean the rooms and get ready for the next arrivals. Vogt told me to wait while he went into the supervisor's office and closed the door.

About ten minutes later, he came out with a short, squat woman with a mean-looking face. "Stephania," said Vogt, "this is Frau Reiniger. She oversees all maid services."

She sneered at me as if she knew I was a Jew. "You will report here at oh seven hundred tomorrow morning. You will be taken to the dormitory, where you will leave your clothes, then come back here for training." She turned, returned to her office, and closed the door.

"She is like a mother to all the girls," said Vogt.

I just shook my head.

"I will show you out," he said. "I also arranged for you to have an area in the laundry to work if your sewing skills are needed. We have an old sewing machine, which we will set up. I will show you the laundry."

I went back to my hotel room happy that I had a job and place to live but scared. Every word I said must be measured. I thought that the nasty maid supervisor was not happy that I was imposed on her without a choice. God forbid she found out who I was. I picked up some food on my way back and stayed in my room all night.

I arrived at the Hotel Fuerstenhof basement laundry at 0645, and Frau Reiniger was already in barking orders at three young women. Suddenly she turned and said, "Come with me!" I picked up my sacks. She led me out a back door and began to march down the street as if she were a well-trained soldier. My sacks were heavy, and she made no attempt to help or even slow down to acknowledge my burden. I was determined to keep up with her. I would not let her get the best of me. We reached the dormitory in about twenty minutes. It was an old building. We climbed three flights of stairs. There were bedrooms with two beds in each. There was one bathroom on the floor.

When we reached the room where I would stay, she looked at me and said, "This is your room. Come back to work in one hour."

My roommate was not in. I went in and unpacked. Afterward, I walked around the building. There were several girls walking around getting ready for work. I did not speak to anyone, but as I looked at the faces of these girls, I came to believe some of them looked like they had Jewish faces and were hiding in plain sight just like me. I now had hope.

CHAPTER 20

Trust No One

⅄⅄⅄

When I got back from dropping off Miriam, the camp was filled with tension. Everyone seemed to be arguing about what to do. With Benjamin suddenly missing and Miriam finding a way to hide her Jewish identity, everyone seemed inspired to find another solution.

Momma was talking to Rivka and Naomi. "Go!" she said. "There is nothing for you here. I can take care of myself. Go and find a way to survive. It will be easier to be on your own."

Rivka protested. "Don't be silly. I'm not leaving you. We have to take care of each other."

"I think Momma may be right," said Naomi. "I have been talking to Ruth, and she knows some people in Rozwadow who might be willing to help us get papers."

"Then go!" Momma said insistently. "What about you, Meyer?"

"What?" I said. "I am staying here. This camp is my responsibility, and I am not leaving until I find Benjamin."

Momma began to cry. "I can't bear to lose any more children. I wish your father was here."

All I could do was hug her. I didn't know what to say. Tears were rolling down my cheeks as well. I had to find out what happened to Benjamin.

Kozlowski had cut us back to once a week. He was running out of black-market supplies, which were harder to come by, but he was due the next night. Maybe he knew something. People in the camp were panicking. Naomi and Ruth were getting ready to leave, along with Henry's sister. They would take their chances on their own. The others wanted to stay with their families. Henry was staying with his mother. No one questioned which was the right decision; we had no idea—except Momma, who was sure we were all better off on our own.

Henry was taking the girls to Rozwadow. We hoped they would find their way to safety.

The next morning, Nachman, Yossel, and I hit the road to try to find Benjamin. Yossel thought that maybe he was going for revenge against the Pilcicki boy but changed his mind and just left and went on his own. I would've been surprised if he did that, just leaving us to wonder what happened. We felt the first place to look around was the Pilcicki farm. Maybe they were lying to Dudek. We decided to go directly there and hope that we didn't need to use force. They wouldn't be happy to see us, but we decided to just knock on the front door.

When we arrived, something seemed strange. There were two men walking in the field, but they were not the men we saw last time we were there. Yossel stayed in the truck. Nachman and I went to the front door of the house and knocked. A woman answered. She spoke Polish but with a heavy German accent.

"Mrs. Pilcicki?" I asked.

"No," she said.

"Isn't this the Pilcicki farm?" I started to see the picture.

"No," she said. "We just moved in. I don't know where the people who lived here before moved."

"Was there anyone here or any other strangers here when you moved in?" I asked. It must have sounded like a stupid question.

"No," she said.

The two men were walking over to see what was going on. We decided to get out of there.

"Thank you," said Nachman. We got into the truck and left before the two men reached the house.

Nachman said, "It looks like being loyal to the Nazis didn't help the Pilcickis."

"It looks like you are right," I responded. "Let's go see if the Dudeks are still there. I wonder if Benjamin came here after we did, only to find that the Pilcickis were gone and he left. But to where?"

We drove over to the Dudeks', and to our surprise, Mr. Dudek answered the door. "Hello, boys," Mr. Dudek said in his usual cheerful voice. "C'mon in; I'm sure Magda would like to feed you something."

"I'm afraid we don't have time to stay," I said. "We are still looking for Benjamin. We went to the Pilcicki farm to take another look and found out that they are gone. There are Germans living there."

"Oh God, I had no idea," said Mr. Dudek, quite distraught. "I haven't been there since last time you were here. Do you have any idea what happened to them?"

"None," I said.

"I guess maybe we are too small to worry about, but they have not been here since I saw you. Have you checked the police and train stations?"

"No," I said. "It's not a good idea for us to show up at the police, but maybe we can drive past police stations between here and Stalowa Wola and see if we find anything. We will also check the train station, but I was there yesterday and saw nothing unusual."

"Good luck," said Dudek. "I hope you find him safe."

"I can't thank you enough," I replied.

We hugged, said good-bye, and left.

We took a ride through Pysznica but saw nothing unusual. There were more German soldiers milling around than usual, but that just meant we should move on and not be seen. If he was going to go somewhere, he would be smart to stay off the trains and go on foot, but we had to look in the obvious places, so we headed toward Stalowa Wola, stopping in every town along the way. We had no idea where he could have gone, but we kept looking, stopping in restaurants and asking people if they saw someone of his description. If we saw police or soldiers, we went the other way. This was no way to investigate a missing person, but we were determined to keep looking. After many hours, we wound up at the Stalowa Wola train station. We walked around for a long time, hoping for some kind of miracle, like seeing Benjamin waiting on a platform for some train, but there was no sign of him. Actually, I had a fantasy that Miriam had second thoughts of leaving and that I would find her perplexed, waiting for me at the station, and we would go off together, but that was just another disappointment for me to suffer.

Finally, after a whole day on the road, it was time to head back to camp, empty-handed, with no more answers about what happened to Benjamin than when we left that morning.

We headed straight back to the camp, and as we carefully turned off the road and into the woods, we could smell burning wood. As we got closer to camp, we could see smoke. A panic set in to my stomach as we drove up.

Yossel screamed, "My God, they found us!" He was right. The huts were mostly burned to the ground, and there was not a soul to be found.

"Look!" cried Nachman. There were two bodies lying in the mud next to his hut on the far side of the camp. We ran over. It was Kozlowski and Benjamin. Kozlowski was in a pool of blood, dead and beaten, with bullets in his head. Benjamin was moving but hurt.

"Benjamin!" cried Yossel.

"Yossel," he said softly.

"It's me, Meyer, too," I said.

He was barely alive. His legs were mangled, obviously broken. He had been beaten severely. He was also bleeding from his abdomen. There was a jug of water in the rubble of Nachman's hut, and he brought it over. Benjamin drank a little but could not move.

"Can you tell us what happened?" I asked. "Where is everyone?"

He began to speak softly, obviously in great pain. "I was caught. I went to see that Pilcicki bastard but was seen by two Polish policemen. I was carrying my guns and had no papers, so they arrested me. I was recognized as a Jew from the lumberyard. They brought me to a house outside town where a German patrol was stationed and left me there. They beat me, trying to get me to confess to killing the two Germans at the farm, you know. I told them nothing, I swear. I didn't know what exactly happened, but I agreed to nothing. They seemed to know there were partisans hiding in the woods somewhere but had no idea where, and I swear I did not tell them anything." He began to cry. When he shifted his body a little, he grunted loudly. He was in great pain.

I knew we couldn't move him. Yossel brought some towels and blankets. We tried to tie up a towel and put pressure on the area that was bleeding. We covered him with one blanket, folded up another, and propped his head up.

Benjamin spoke again after taking another sip of water. "They kept asking the same questions over and over. 'Why did you kill those farmers? Who else was with you? Where are they hiding? Where did you get the guns?' I told them I didn't know what they were talking about. I was alone, just trying to live my life. I told them I was in the army and the guns were mine. Every time I answered, they beat me some more. One of those Nazi bastards, a big guy with a mean look on his face, hit my leg with a pipe. I could feel the bones shatter. The pain was terrible, but I did not cry out. Finally, they left, and I fell asleep. All I know is they woke me up some time later and started asking the same questions again. More beatings. Then they left again. This went on all night. When I woke up this morning, I heard some commotion. The police showed up with Kozlowski. I overheard them telling the Nazis that Kozlowski was drunk in a bar last night, bragging to those around him that he knew where there were Jews living in the woods and that he was making a fortune selling black-market goods to them. He was complaining that the black market was drying up because of all the Germans moving in. He got into a fight with some men at the bar, and the police came and broke it up. They were going to let him go since he was a cop, but then someone told them that he was selling black-market goods to the Jews, and they arrested him for questioning."

Benjamin closed his eyes. I thought he died for a moment, but he nodded off for a few seconds and then woke up.

Then Yossel asked, "Why did they bring one of their own to the Nazis?"

Benjamin said, "They are all crooks dealing in the black market, and they sacrificed one of their own to take attention away from themselves. They dropped him off and told the Nazis he knew where the Jews were hiding. They brought him in to see me. He took one look at me and said, 'I know him. His name is Benjamin. He is one of a whole group of Jews hiding in the woods near Pysznica.'

"'Where?' asked one of the Nazi officers.

"Kozlowski replied, 'I'm not sure exactly. I just met them and sold them goods.'

"They didn't believe him and started hitting him. These were brutal bastards who truly enjoyed inflicting pain. Kozlowski said, 'I'll show you where I meet them. They can't be too far.' They beat him some more. After a while, they left us alone and went outside. When they left, I started yelling at him, 'You can't tell them where we are hiding! They will kill us all!'

"Kozlowski was scared. 'If I give them what they want, they will let me go. They would rather kill a few Jews. They don't want a Polish cop.'

"After a couple of hours, they came for us. They got Kozlowski on his feet, but they had to drag me outside because of my broken leg. There were several trucks filled with Polish police. There were also more Nazis, maybe a hundred altogether. They threw me into the back of one of the trucks, while they put Kozlowski in the front seat. I knew where we were going. That son of a bitch Kozlowski took them right to our meeting place. They dragged me out of the truck and screamed at me, demanding I tell them where the camp was. I refused. That Nazi bastard with the pipe came over and smashed my other leg. This time I screamed, but I swear I did not tell them. I think I passed out for a while. They sent a patrol looking for the camp and found it. They sent the police to surround them. They dragged me and Kozlowski to the front of the line and then attacked. There were bullets flying, and everyone was running in different directions. I saw Momma running away, and they shot her."

Benjamin started to cry. "She was still alive. They brought her to the middle of camp with me and Kozlowski watching. They eventually gathered everyone up. They had Momma and Rivka. They had Mr. and Mrs. Goldin, Pearl, and little Shlomo. They had everyone else who stayed in the camp. They told everyone to march. They were headed back toward the meeting area. They started dragging me and Kozlowski but dropped us and left us here. One of the policemen shot Kozlowski in the head twice and then shot me in the stomach, spit on me, and left. A little while later, I heard gunshots."

Suddenly, I heard gunshots. I jumped up, startled. I looked around, and it was Nachman putting more bullets into Kozlowski.

"You bastard! You thought they would let you go!"

Benjamin was bleeding through the towel, and I knew it was only a matter of time. I called Yossel away from Benjamin. "He's dying. Stay here with him. Nachman! Let's go to the meeting place and see if we can find anyone."

We left the truck and walked, as we didn't want to attract attention in case they were still there. As we walked down the path that was now our neighborhood, I became very nervous about what we would find. We arrived at the clearing that was our meeting place with Kozlowski, and it was very quiet. It was worse than I feared. Bodies were everywhere.

No one moved. It didn't take me long to focus on someone who looked familiar.

It was Momma. She was facedown in a pool of blood. I turned her over. She was dead, shot twice through the chest. I yelled, "No!" I held her close to me and cried. I closed her eyes and held her for a long time. Those bastards had no shame. Nachman found his mother dead, and I heard him screaming. This was beyond belief. I always knew this could happen, but why was I still alive? I left them at the mercy of these butchers while I rode around looking for Benjamin. Now they were all dead. Rivka, where was Rivka? She would never leave Momma's side. I got up and looked at the other bodies. Near Momma was Jonah Goldin. He had been riddled with bullets. I bet he tried to fight back. I didn't see Rivka. I went over to Nachman. He was so distraught.

"She was so sweet. She didn't deserve this. I shouldn't have left her."

I bent down and whispered, "Where is your sister?"

He got up, and we both looked around. His sister was not to be found. Neither was Rivka. Nachman said, "It looks like they murdered all the older adults. None of the younger partisans are here."

We decided to look at all the bodies. They were all dead, but he was right. It was all the older adults. Henry's mother was there but no sign of Henry. The only one we could not find was Shayna Goldin. Young Shlomo was not there either.

"I think you're right," I said. "The young people can work. They took them. I'll bet they took Mrs. Goldin because of Shlomo. I have no idea why they would let them live."

We were both in shock. "How are we going to bury all these bodies?" asked Nachman.

"I don't know," I said. "I have to tell Yossel and Benjamin. I'm going back."

"All right," said Nachman. "I'll stay here."

I ran back through the woods, crying all the way. I had so much anger built up inside me. How could they murder women? What was wrong with these people? These were mostly other Poles. They were as bad as the Nazis.

When I got back to what was left of the camp, Yossel was lying over Benjamin's body, crying.

"Yossel," I said.

"He's gone," Yossel cried.

I leaned down next to him and cried more. How do I tell him his mother is dead too? "We were talking," said Yossel. "He asked where you were. I told him you went to the meeting place to look around. When I finished the sentence, he just stared at me. He was dead. I was talking to my dead brother."

We cried together and embraced. He was all I had left. We had to stay close. Suddenly he pushed me away. "What did you find?"

"More death," I replied, not wanting to tell him. He asked anyway.

"Momma? Rivka?"

"Not Rivka," I replied, giving him the good news first. "Momma's dead."

We both fell to our knees and embraced. He cried out, "Not Momma! I want to see her."

We wrapped Benjamin's body in the blankets and walked back to the meeting spot, a place now filled with death. We walked arm in arm, holding each other up. We were both in shock now, only thinking about this profound loss. When we got back, Nachman was sitting and talking to his mother. Yossel gasped when he saw the multitude of dead people he knew. Then he saw Momma exactly where I had left her. He dove to the ground, screaming in pain. I let him have his moment alone with Momma. I didn't know what to do next. I just stood there.

Nachman came over. "What if our sisters escaped and are looking for us?"

I responded, "Wouldn't they have gone back to the camp, knowing we were coming back?"

Nachman said, "Maybe they ran away and were afraid to be found."

I replied, "Maybe we should look around. Even if they are being held prisoner, maybe we can find them."

"We have to do something," he said. "Maybe we can save them."

Yossel overheard the conversation. "We have to try to save Rivka."

I knew she had to be captured because she would never leave Momma, but he was right; we had to try. We had to do something with the bodies. We positioned the bodies so they were facing the same way. There were ten bodies altogether. Three couples, Mr. and Mrs. Fisher, Mr. and Mrs. Levine, and Mr. and Mrs. Wachtel. We put the couples together, as they would be buried together. We put the other three women next to each other—Momma, Nachman's mother, and Henry's mother—then we put Jonah on the other side. Each of us had bursts of crying episodes. Each time, we had to stop what we were doing, comfort the other, and then get back to the task at hand.

It was late, and we were exhausted. We walked back to camp. It still smelled of burning wood. We didn't dare spend the night in the camp. Who knew if the police would take another look? We searched the camp for supplies. We took blankets, shovels, and any food we could find and loaded them into the truck. That would be our home for a while. We also searched for any other weapons and ammunition but found nothing. We would keep what we had. We left the camp. We would come back only to bury bodies, nothing else.

As soon as we saw daylight, we were up and ready to hit the road. We would follow the same route we took to try to find Benjamin, rolling through Pysznica and slowly searching each town until we got to Stalowa Wola.

It had been several hours since the attack. If they were wandering around the streets, they might not have gone far. If they were captured, they could be anywhere. After driving around Pysznica for an hour, we saw no sign of any military activity other than the usual police walking the streets. We felt like the best place to look would be the train station. As we approached the Stalowa Wola station from the west, there was a train leaving the station headed east. It was freight train of boxcars and other railcars. As we approached the station, there was a mob of people, police, and soldiers. There were men, women, and children crowding into the station. Many of them were obviously Jewish, dressed in traditional clothing. The officials had their guns drawn. These people were captured and being transported somewhere. We drove slowly past the station to see if we could see a familiar face, especially Rivka, but none could be found. As we drove to the other end of the station, another train of freight cars was pulling in. They were clearly transporting these people somewhere in freight cars like animals to some unknown place. We were horrified.

Nachman said, "Let's go into the station and look."

"We have no papers," I reminded Nachman. "If we walk in there, we will be captured and on the next train ourselves. And what if we find your sister or Rivka or Henry? If they haven't been able to escape, how will we?"

"We have to do something," said Yossel.

I replied, "I'm afraid all we can really do is watch. Maybe they have not been brought here yet. If we see them, maybe we can do something." We felt helpless. We thought about going in, guns blazing, but that would be committing suicide, and we would probably get other people killed as well.

So, we sat and watched. Another train pulled in. Two more hours went by. More prisoners were marched to the line. No sign of anyone we knew. The crowd began to thin. We could see some of the people entering the train. They were crowding them into these freight cars. When they were full, the doors were shut. There were no windows, just slits on top, probably air vents. What were they doing to these people? After a while, the line in front of the station was gone. We could not see all the cars, but they must have continued to load these poor people. We were close enough to see but not close enough to hear the crying and screaming that must have been taking place. We sat in silence and watched this atrocity, not fully understanding what was going on. Finally, the train pulled out. The streets around the station were empty. The police and soldiers were gone, and we saw no sign of our loved ones. We all were in shock.

"I hope none of them were on those trains," said Yossel as I started the truck. I could not help having visions in my head of Rivka being stuffed into one of those awful boxcars, of Shayna Goldin and poor little Shlomo holding on for dear life.

We headed back to Pysznica and found a new spot off the road in the woods to camp out. I slept some but had horrible nightmares. All the death and murder I had seen was somehow eclipsed by the vison of men, women, and children being loaded onto a train like cattle. In fact, cattle were treated better. Who could survive being stuffed into a box with no air or room to move? A bullet through the heart was a better way to die.

We still had a job to do. We had to bury our loved ones and comrades. There were twelve bodies and three of us with shovels. It was overwhelming. We decided to start with our loved ones, our beloved mothers, our dear brother. I added Jonah to the list. I expected to see Miriam again, and I wanted her to know that her father was taken care of. We brought Benjamin to the meeting place. We left Kozlowski to the elements. We would never come back to the camp.

We buried four bodies that day. We were starving. We were out of food and water. During this ordeal, none of us ever thought about our own survival. Now we would have to before we could finish honoring our comrades.

CHAPTER 21

The Selection

⅄ ⅄ ⅄

THEY WERE KILLING US; THEY were gathering us up and shipping us like animals to who knew where. Was the whole purpose of the Nazi invasion of Poland to kill the Jews? It felt that way to me. Our jobs were now to stay alive and free.

"I think it's time to visit the Dudeks," said Nachman. "I could use a homemade meal from Mrs. Dudek."

Yossel and I agreed. We headed over to their farm. They were the friendliest, most sympathetic people, and we could always count on them. After the last few days, we couldn't wait to see the Dudeks' round faces and happy smiles.

As we approached the farm, our hopes were shattered. The Dudeks were there, but they were being escorted into a car by the local police. The Germans finally caught up to them. Their farm was small, but they were being moved. We had to back out of their road before we were seen. These were good people. They took us in when no one else would. Were they ousted for helping us? I hoped we were not the cause of them being relocated away from the little farm they loved.

Our last hope for an easy solution was the Rykaczewskis. That was our next stop. When we arrived, everything looked normal. We pulled up. Nachman stayed in the car. Yossel and I went out and knocked on the door. Garek answered.

"You're alive," he declared. He looked around and came outside. He continued, "The police came here this morning and told us all of the partisans were killed or captured. They know we were supplying you and warned us we would suffer if we helped any Jews. The Dudeks are losing their farm. We can't help you. You must leave now before you are seen." With that, he went inside and shut the door. He was scared.

We went back to the truck. Now what?

We still had some money, so we could try to find a market where we would not be recognized. We could not go into town. There was a farm stand outside Stalowa Wola. We headed there. The plan was simple. When we arrived, Nachman and Yossel would stand on either side of the truck to look out for potential trouble while I would get the food. We would leave the guns hidden in order not to draw attention. If there was trouble and they could not get my attention, they would escape and I would be on my own.

We parked on the road next to the farm stand. We stepped out of the truck, but before Nachman and Yossel could take their positions, two police wagons pulled alongside the truck and two policemen from each vehicle jumped out, pointed rifles at us, and yelled, "Halt! Stand still with your hands in the air."

We complied, totally surprised. Where did they come from? Were they following us and I didn't see them? Did they know who we were? We had been so careful about where we went and how we did things. One of the officers ordered me into one wagon, and Nachman and Yossel were ordered into the other wagon. I got in. There were other young men in the wagon who looked like they had been arrested. The cop got in with us. "Why have I been arrested?" I asked, suspecting that they knew we were Jewish and were going to turn us over to the Nazis.

"Silence," ordered the guard.

I thought it was odd that they didn't ask me for identification. The other men didn't look particularly Jewish. I was totally confused about what was going on. Each seat in the wagon was filled, so I assumed they were finished picking people up and were headed to the destination, whatever that might be.

There were no windows in the van, so I had no idea where we were headed. It was sinking in that after months of hiding in the woods and surviving by our wits, we were captured so easily. I was still wondering how they came out of nowhere to surprise us.

About an hour later, the wagon stopped. We were ordered out. The sun was in my eyes. The other truck was behind us, and Nachman and Yossel came out. The answer of our arrest soon became apparent. They needed young men for a road crew. We were lined up, with guns pointed at us, and an officer spoke.

"You have been brought here to work. You are prisoners of the Third Reich. You will be given work and be fed meals. If you work hard, you will be released when the project is completed. We are building a new road, and you will be told what to do."

I made my way to where Yossel and Nachman were standing. "This is unbelievable," said Yossel.

"We were in the wrong place at the wrong time," said Nachman.

I replied, "We have to be careful not to tell them who we are."

Nachman said, "I don't think they care who we are. They just want us to work."

At that moment, the guards came over and told us to be quiet. They lined us up, and we began to march. It was fall but unusually hot. We came to the site of the project. There were men with pickaxes and shovels. We were brought to the line to get right to work. We were the cleanup detail, clearing all the rocks and debris that the crew had managed to create that morning. The sun was bright, and we were already hungry and thirsty. After several hours, they gave us a break with water and some food. It was like manna from heaven. After fifteen minutes, it was back to work until dark.

We were expected to camp out with the other prisoners, with armed guards all around. We were exhausted and, in a way, happy to comply. Our only option was to escape and then try to survive on our own. Sadly, we were prisoners but not of the Nazis. The Poles just wanted workers, even if just to follow Nazi directives.

I guessed there were about forty workers altogether. We bunked in an area that had been prepared with some blankets. I was exhausted and welcomed sleep. At some point in the middle of the night, I was awoken by gunshots. Yossel and Nachman jumped up, as I did, along with half the camp. Two workers had tried to escape. One was shot. I didn't know if he was dead. The other seemed to get away, and there was a lot of commotion of guards getting in a police wagon to give chase. Another guard came over and told us to get back to sleep. He said everything was under control, and anyone trying to escape would be shot. Well, if there was any question about our captors' resolve to keep us here working, that was answered.

We labored hard over the next couple of days. It was hard, but it gave me time to think about losing all that was important to me—Momma, Benjamin, my sisters, Miriam, our entire way of life. Yossel and I were all that was left of that life, and we were barely surviving. I wondered if Miriam had survived the trip to Germany and what she was doing.

Suddenly my daydreaming was interrupted. We were ordered to line up along the road. Walking down the road were three Nazis whose uniforms I recognized as Gestapo. I had seen them before. They visited me in the lumberyard, looking for the killer of the Nazi who killed Chava. They looked at each face in the line.

When he got to me, he recognized me and smiled. "You are Juden." Then he announced to the group, "We are looking for three Juden criminals who were missing from a partisan group we captured. This is one of them."

One of the other Nazis pulled me out of the line and hit me on the head with a nightstick, just enough to buckle me to my knees.

"Stop!" yelled a voice down the line.

"Yossel, no!" I said and then held back.

"Here is number two." The Gestapo officer reveled.

Then one of the other prisoners cried, "He is Juden. He came with the other two," pointing to Nachman. They grabbed Nachman. They and three Polish policemen walked us back to the base camp, where they had their vehicles. "Did you think you could hide from us?" said the Nazi pig who gave me a beating back in the lumberyard. "I knew you were a criminal the first time I saw you, and now you will pay for running away from your comrades like little children."

How did they know we even existed? Did someone in the camp tell them about us? Dudek? Garek! He must have told them we visited and who we were. That was the only way they could have known. How they found us was a complete mystery. Either way, it didn't matter. They were about to shoot us. Yossel must have thought so too. Nachman and I had military training and knew to keep our mouths shut, but Yossel did not.

"You're all murderers!" he shouted.

One of the Polish cops pulled out his nightstick and beat him with it. Nachman and I picked him up and held him as we walked. When we got to the base, there was a high-ranking German officer talking to the construction supervisor.

One of the Gestapo went to talk to him. He looked over and pointed at Yossel. I couldn't hear them, but I imagine that he told him why he had to be held up. Now I began to think they were not going to kill us. I was right. They ordered us into the back of one of the Nazi cars, and off we went. Yossel could walk on his own. I had a feeling we would find out where they had taken the other Jews. Maybe I would find Rivka. One guard was driving while the other was pointing a gun at us the whole time. I assumed we were headed to the train station in Stalowa Wola for transport, like all the others we had seen lined up. Instead we rode past Stalowa Wola and headed north toward Lublin. After a while, I got the nerve to ask the guard pointing the gun at our heads where were we going.

"Krasnik," the guard responded, surprisingly. "There is a new Budzyn labor camp in a big industrial area, and you will be among the first Juden workers. We have been assigned there as guards, so if you work, you might live awhile." He and the other guard laughed hysterically. We weren't laughing.

About an hour later, we drove north of Krasnik and past a large factory. A few minutes later, we arrived at a gate with armed guards. One of the guards came over to the car, and our driver showed them papers, which I think were their orders to join the guards at the camp. Then he explained that they had captured prisoners and were ordered to bring us with them. The gates opened, and we were driven in. Once we were on the inside of the gate, another armed guard opened the door and yelled at us to get out of the car. We did, and the car drove off unceremoniously.

We stood in a large courtyard that was mostly empty except for a few German guards and some Jewish prisoners who were working to clean the debris from the camp. A guard came over to us and ordered the three of us to walk toward a nearby building. We were taken in. A clerk sat at a desk. We were told to line up. I was in front.

"Name!" he ordered.

I had no reason to lie anymore. "Meyer Marcus."

"Town!" he stated, looking down and writing in his book.

"Pysznica," I replied.

"Occupation!" was next.

I responded, "My family owned and managed a lumberyard."

The clerk looked up, quite impressed. "You will be assigned to work in the lumberyard near the factory," he said enthusiastically. It looked like they had a need met.

"My brother here also was with me in the lumber business," I volunteered.

"Go to the next room," he said. He wasn't taking suggestions from me.

I went into the next room. A German SS officer sat near a bunch of strange-looking metal instruments. There were metal blocks with sharp metal spikes protruding. I was told to sit in a chair next to the officer. He placed my left hand on the table palm down and pulled out one of the strange instruments that was dipped in ink, placed it on my wrist, and pressed until the skin was broken and it was bleeding and painful. I could see the letters *KL* emblazoned on my wrist.

I was told to step outside. As I walked out, Yossel came in next. I stood outside under guard. After a while Yossel came out. I assumed we were waiting for Nachman to come through. While we were waiting, I asked the guard what KL meant.

He looked around and just said, "Konsentrationslager." It was the first time I had heard the term "concentration camp."

In a few minutes, Nachman came out, also holding his wrist. We were branded by the Nazis like cattle, their farm animals that they could do with what they pleased. The officer outside ordered us to stand in a straight line. It was just the three of us, but he felt he had to exact discipline. He ordered us to march. We did not know the consequences of disobeying. The yard was a long and narrow rectangle. Each corner had a guard tower with armed guards. Along the sides were one-story buildings that were connected at two of the corners. There were other similar buildings scattered throughout the camp, with two roads cutting across the camp along the way. These were barracks where no doubt the prisoners like us were housed, but again there were very few prisoners in sight. Some of the officers were Ukrainian soldiers who were sympathetic to the Nazis and had joined the militia. They had a reputation for brutality even beyond that of the Nazi soldiers.

We reached one of the buildings toward the back of the camp. The German officer took us inside. "Find an empty bunk," he said. "Be ready to be counted at oh five hundred tomorrow." He left.

The room was a long and narrow dormitory. There were endless wooden crates that were supposed to be beds, four high. Wooden boxes with no padding and no blankets. This was our new home, a prison where proud men would work with little food and sleep. It smelled of death. And for good reason. Yossel tapped me on the shoulder. I turned around, and he pointed down the hall. There were two men lying on the floor on top of each other. We made our way to them, and clearly they were dead. Half-naked and thin, they obviously did not make it to be counted today and were left to rot.

We walked outside to get some air. We dared not say anything to the guards or we might wind up on top of them. We just waited, trying to be inconspicuous. I think we were all in shock. There was nothing to be said. I didn't know what to say. There was no hope, only servitude. We were slaves before, but this was a new level. We were slaves and caged animals whose only purpose was to serve the master and then die when we could not service anymore.

We sat there for a long time, being ignored, until we noticed a commotion at the far end of the camp. A guard came over and led us to the source of the commotion. The prisoners were returning from work. They were marching into the camp, singing some unrecognizable song. They were wearing their civilian clothing. Some were wearing the garb of traditional Jews. Some, like us, were in more conventional clothing. They were likely all Jews.

Well, maybe not all Jews. This time, it was my turn to tap Yossel on the shoulder. He looked at me. I pointed toward the back end of the procession. There was a tall blond man in tow. It was Szweda, the wealthiest landowner in all Pysznica, our landlord and friend. He was also an admitted homosexual and apparently also a target for slavery.

His substantial land holdings were clearly of no consequence. He was now a slave. We were told to go to the back of the line. As we walked, I estimated there were a total of about five hundred prisoners. We stood in line for about an hour, slowly moving ahead. At some point, I realized there was food at the end of the line.

The meal consisted of cabbage soup and a hunk of bread. It was awful and not very satisfying but certainly enough to keep us alive for another day.

After the meal, we were ordered to the barracks. As we walked back to find our place, Szweda stuck out like a sore thumb. Yossel and I ran over to see if we could talk to him. Nachman had no idea where we were going but followed us.

"Szweda!" I called.

He looked around. He recognized us but showed no emotion. "Look what has become of us," he said.

"How long have you been here?" I asked.

"A few weeks," he answered. "I was transferred from another camp. I have been a prisoner for about a year. They took everything from me, beat me, nearly killed me. I wish they had. This is no life for a human being. Be careful of the Ukrainians. They are the worst. They'll kill you if you look at them the wrong way."

"What do they have you doing?" I asked.

He replied, "They have an old munitions factory they are converting to making German airplanes. Most of us are laborers preparing the factory for production. Have you been given a job?"

"Yossel and I are going to a lumberyard of all things. They seemed to be happy we were experienced," I said.

"That's good," he replied. "You will do well here if they need you."

There was some talking going on among the inmates, but it was short lived. Everyone was going to their bunks. Szweda went in, so we walked down to where we were assigned. As we got to the entrance, four prisoners were carrying the dead bodies out to a cart and then were ordered to push the cart back toward the front of the camp. What would they do with the bodies? We went in with the others. Nachman saw someone he knew and talked to him. The area we were in was not that crowded. Everyone seemed to be settling in the bottom two rows of the bunks. A few climbed to the top. Clearly this camp was built for many more prisoners. The men were not very talkative. They were tired and hungry, and some of them looked sick and in pain. It was obvious that more would die soon.

We found bunks on the second level, and Yossel and I settled in. Nachman bunked near his other mate. I guess he had had enough of us for a while. All we could do was try to sleep. I was determined to live through this.

At 0500, the screaming started. Guards came rattling though the barracks with sticks, banging on the beds to let us know it was time to line up outside. Everyone scrambled outside. Looking around, I saw that these men were suffering. Coughing and wheezing, these men were slowly dying from disease and starvation. Once they got us outside, the guards started taking inventory of the prisoners. I say inventory because they ran the camp like a business. We were assets on the shelf they would use to build their war machine. Once the inmates were all accounted for, the guards turned around and left. We were told to stand at attention. There were two guards watching the whole camp!

"What is going on?" I asked the man next to me.

"Breakfast for the guards," he said. We stood there an hour, waiting for the guards to have their breakfast.

When they returned, we were ordered to form two lines. We began to march toward the entrance to the camp. One of the guards barked some order I did not understand. Suddenly everyone in line began singing some German work song I had never heard. Really? These men, starving and exhausted, would be further humiliated by having to sing a song praising the German fatherland? In the time it took me to process what was going on, I felt a blow to my head from a guard's nightstick.

He yelled, "Sing!"

I sang.

We marched about thirty minutes to the entrance of the factory being converted to make airplanes. Most of the prisoners went out of line into the plant. We were looking for the lumberyard, so we stayed in line. That was the right decision. We continued the march around the back of the plant to find a large lumberyard. One of the guards came over and told us to follow him. We did, along with four others.

In the yard, we learned it was being managed by local Poles. When they learned we knew the lumber business, they were thrilled. It turned out they were displaced farmers who were working for the Germans at a trade they knew little about. Yossel and I saw an opportunity to make this work to our advantage. We worked throughout the day. The plant needed finished wood to make tables and chairs, and we had plenty of inventory to cut and prepare to specifications provided by the German engineers, who knew exactly what they wanted.

Near the end of the day, the yard manager came over and introduced himself. "My name is Janek Turko. I see you know what you are doing. I want you to help me manage this place. Please come with me."

We followed him into the office and into a back room. He continued, "The Nazis give us little compensation for our work, but they do give us food. We know they are starving you. We can share some of our food if you have something to give us. We will feed you some now. But we know many of you have money and jewelry they left with you. Have something now, but if you want more tomorrow, you will have to pay."

We were hungry. They had some bread and a small amount of meat and potatoes that they shared with us, and we were thankful for the little extra sustenance.

Janek spoke again. "Do not tell anyone about our arrangement. We will all be killed."

"We understand," I said.

He was right. Yossel and I held on to some money, gold rings, and chains we could carry discreetly. The Gestapo and SS officers did not take anything from us when we were captured and brought to Budzyn. "We will share what we have for food," I said.

Janek shook our hands, and we went back out to the yard with some food in our bellies. We felt like an angel of God was watching over us.

CHAPTER 22

Budzyn

⅄⅄⅄

AT THE END OF THE day, we marched back to camp with a secret we guarded with our lives. We were the lucky ones. The little bit of added food we got at the lumberyard helped greatly. As the days passed, the routine was the same. I could almost see the men getting thinner by the day. There was disease, and the odor of the men at night seemed to get progressively worse. Combine starvation along with the brutality of the guards, and the result was death.

Shooting of prisoners that were weak and not pulling their weight was a regular occurrence. The Ukrainian guards took pleasure in murder, even for the slightest infraction or looking at them the wrong way. I could not understand how the Nazis expected to get the work done with a dying workforce.

Most of the original inhabitants of the camp were Jewish residents of the Krasnik Ghetto. It was cleaned out when Herman Goring Worke took over the munitions plant shortly after the occupation of Poland. Many of the residents were killed except those men who were fit to work.

The routine was the same every day, seven days a week: up at 0500, march to work, meal break, more work, meal break, bedtime. The only break in the monotony was a beating for doing a bad job or a shooting or hanging of a prisoner and being thankful it wasn't me.

Sometime toward the end of 1942, a new group of prisoners arrived. As they marched into the camp, the odd thing was that they were wearing Polish army uniforms. We were all lined up outside the bunks one morning at our usual 0500 roll call when they arrived. There were several hundred. I estimated about four hundred. There were lots of empty bunks, so I knew it was a matter of time before new inmates arrived. The Nazis were very efficient.

While we stood there watching the guards reviewing the names, I saw a familiar face. I was sure it was him. Yitzchak Lubin. He had been missing in action but obviously was taken prisoner and survived to this point. He was very thin, and his face looked gray and drawn, but I was sure it was him. Somehow I would have to find him again and tell him of his father's kindness to the Goldins, his heartbreak over his missing son, and his unfortunate death.

When the counting was over, the commandant came out to address the group. His name was Oberscharführer Otto Hantke, an SS officer. He was not visible very often, but whenever I saw him, he was having someone beaten or shot. He liked to pull the trigger himself.

He spoke to the group in a loud, clear voice and in Polish. "You have been selected and brought here to work at finishing the aircraft factory here at Budzyn. You will work alongside all the other workers in this camp. You were soldiers, prisoners of war, but you were brought here because you are Jews, and you will not be treated differently than Jewish pigs should be treated. You will have no special privileges and will be kept alive only to work for me." He then looked at one of the guards, who went into the crowd and dragged out one of the prisoners. He was in the general vicinity of where Yitzchak was standing, but it wasn't him.

"On your knees, pig!" shouted Hantke.

The prisoner just stood there, so two guards hit him in the back of the legs. The prisoner fell flat on his face. Hantke pulled out his revolver and shot him twice in the back of the head. He lay there in a pool of blood, dead. The message was clear, and nothing else needed to be said.

The guards lined us up as usual, with the new group in the rear, and off we went for our daily drudgery. When we returned and lined up for our evening meal of watery soup and a small hunk of bread, I saw an opportunity to maneuver myself to where Yitzchak was standing. I tapped him on the shoulder. He turned and looked perplexed. He didn't recognize me.

"It's Meyer," I said quietly.

He hugged me tight. I saw a guard starting to come over, so I pushed him away and said, "Don't show emotion. We have a lot to talk about."

We went back to moving down the line. As we walked, I explained where we could meet inside the barracks after it was time to sleep. We could sneak around within the building without getting caught. Once we got our food, we went our separate ways.

After the meal, we were ordered back to the barracks until it was time to lie in our bunks and the doors were locked. I sneaked out of the bunk and went to the designated meeting place. There was an open area between the buildings inside where we could meet and talk.

Yitzchak came within minutes. "It's so good to see you, Meyer," he said, sincerely excited to see me. "I have been a prisoner for three years. I was caught and became a prisoner of war after the initial attack. At first, all POWs were lumped together and were treated humanely. It was only recently that they tried to weed out the Jews. It was in my military records, and I was singled out. All the Jewish POWs from Poland and some from Germany were gathered together. I was held in Lublin for a while, and then we were marched here, and here we are. What about you?"

"I escaped and went home," I responded.

"Really?" He was shocked. "Did you see my father?"

"Yes," I said. "He was a wonderful, kind man."

"Was?" he asked.

I didn't realize I'd gone right to the point. "Yes," I said. "He died a hero, shot by Polish police under orders of the Nazis. He was defending a slow-moving man who was being harassed by the police." I could see tears forming in his eyes. I continued, "I want you to know that he took a displaced family into your home and saved them from certain death. He was a hero and a great man. You should be very proud of him."

"Thank you for telling me, Meyer," he said.

I could tell he wanted to be alone with his thoughts. We shook hands and went back to our bunks.

Day after monotonous day went by as we toiled on behalf of our captors. The best time for me and Yossel was working in the lumberyard. We knew the work and were appreciated by our Polish supervisors. As the factory was getting built out, the demand for wood products cut to order was steady. In the yard, our Polish overseers were tough and demanding, occasionally beating us with sticks and whips when we did not work fast enough. In private, they explained they needed to impress the Germans with their toughness but knew we could do the work and they would not hit us hard. It was a game we played to keep the Nazis happy.

In the office, they slipped us food and water to keep us in reasonable health. Janek got to the point where they stopped charging us for the extra food. In fact, he took a liking to Yossel and gave him a new jacket and hat that Yossel had seen Janek wear and took a liking to. He was told it was the latest fashion from Germany. Yossel wore it proudly the rest of the day. He marched back to camp with a little extra energy in his step and sang a little louder. An act of kindness aimed at a Jew was rare indeed, and it meant a lot to Yossel.

We marched to the factory, where the rest of the workers joined the procession. That day, Szweda happened to come out and was marching next to us. He noticed Yossel's new clothes. "Where did he get that?" Szweda asked.

"A gift from our Polish overseer," I replied.

"Tell him to get rid of it," he said and marched ahead.

I didn't understand what he was upset about, so I ignored him.

I should have listened. The next morning, we lined up outside the barracks to be counted. As one of the Ukrainian guards walked by, he stopped to look at Yossel. "What are you wearing?" he asked, grabbing his new jacket.

"This is my jacket," Yossel replied.

The guard grabbed Yossel by the back of the neck and pushed him out to the middle of the yard. Two other guards came over to see what was going on. "Where did you get this jacket and this hat?" demanded the guard.

"It's mine," declared Yossel.

The guard pulled out his nightstick and hit him on the back of the neck. Yossel fell to one knee and popped back up.

"Again, where did you get this?" yelled the guard.

Yossel hesitated. "From someone outside the camp." He was trying to protect Janek's identity. I hoped they would take the jacket from him and that would be the end of it.

The guard then circled around him and said, "You must be a rich Jew to buy such a nice jacket. Take it off!"

Yossel took it off and dropped it on the ground.

"Take everything off!" demanded the guard.

He did and stood totally naked before the entire camp. It was cold. He was undernourished, and he was shivering. One of the other guards began going through his clothes and found his remaining zlotys and some gold chains we had divided up before we got to the camp.

At that point, I started walking toward the scene, not knowing what I would do if I got there. The third guard saw me and walked toward me with his pistol drawn.

"Where are you going?" he shouted.

"That is my brother," I said, hoping it might distract them.

"Then watch," said the guard, raising his pistol to my head.

The guard, now humiliating Yossel, shouted to the crowd, "Look what happens to rich Jews who think they can buy everything!" He ordered Yossel to march and led him around the cold, dreary camp, totally naked, while the guard with a gun in one hand was waving the money and chains he had found with the other. It was the most humiliating thing I had ever seen. More guards joined in during the march, laughing and yelling, "Dirty Jew!" and "Ugly Jew!" and other anti-Semitic phrases. After marching him around, they came back to where his clothing was lying. I hoped this was the end of this episode.

They ordered him to stand at attention. The guards stood there, laughing at him. One of the other Ukrainian guards pulled out his revolver and shot Yossel in the stomach. The other guards then started shooting at him up and down his naked body. He fell down dead, with blood spraying on some of the guards. Meanwhile, the guard pointing the gun at me just calmly said, "Go take him away."

I just stood there in shock. I couldn't believe he was dead over something so stupid. I ran over to the body. He was shot almost beyond recognition. I was too shocked to cry. I looked up and saw Nachman, Szweda, and Yitzchak, who had volunteered to help me carry him. We knew too well where we were going. There was an area outside the camp where dead bodies were dumped and later burned once any valuables were looked for and gold was extracted from teeth. I looked at Szweda and suddenly understood what he was saying, but it was too late.

We still had a whole day ahead of us. Janek felt horrible when I told him what happened. He really liked Yossel and thought he had done a good thing. Anyway, we had to work, so he assigned another one of the prisoners to work with me. I couldn't believe Yossel was gone. My last link to family. Would any of us survive this?

I went through the motions the rest of the day. As I lay in my hard, cold bunk that night, I began to cry. In my head, I prayed and said kaddish as I did every night, but now in addition to Momma, Chava, and Benjamin, I had to add Yossel. I also prayed for Naomi, who I had hoped had found her way. And what of Miriam? She was in my thoughts every day. I promised to find her when this was over. I didn't feel that this would ever be over.

There was no ability to grieve. It was back to drudgery and monotony the next day and trying to survive. I had to push my feelings of sorrow and hatred of my captors and their henchman aside and continue with the business of being a slave.

I became withdrawn as the weeks passed. I was truly alone for the first time since I arrived home from the army, with no mission or hope. The winter subsided, and the leaves began to bloom. More and more people began to fill up the camp. There were even a few women and children. Then one day in May, a whole new group arrived. They were ragged and downtrodden like the rest of us but had a very different story. As the first few days passed, I began listening to this new group. They had been part of a rebellion, an uprising. They were survivors of the Warsaw Ghetto.

I knew Warsaw had had the single largest population of Jews in all of Poland, hundreds of thousands. What I learned from these soldiers was that they had all been confined to a three-square-kilometer area known as the Warsaw Ghetto. Over time, the Nazis had sent many thousands of the inhabitants to labor camps. Somehow, they learned that some of the camps were not labor camps; the elderly and weak were being sent to extermination camps, where the Nazis were systematically killing Jews by the thousands every day. This was the first time I had heard that the Nazis were trying to eliminate and kill all Jews, and I now understood why they were starving all of us. Death was just part of their plan. I also feared for those who were missing and those who had tried to escape.

Did Miriam make it to Germany as Stephania, or was she captured and sent to an extermination camp? I had no way of knowing. I began to think that maybe being shot in the woods of Pysznica was a better fate than what else the Nazis had planned for us.

The Warsaw survivors spoke of their resistance toward the end. They had stopped the Germans from transporting any more residents temporarily. They had guns and grenades, and they killed German soldiers resisting capture. The Nazi army attacked them, burning down whole streets of houses, killing many of the resistors with flames and smoke. The rest were captured and sent to camps. There were hundreds who wound up in Budzyn, maybe a thousand.

We now had a new camp commander, SS Oberscharführer Reinhold Feix, who seemed more sadistic and murderous than Hantke. In the weeks following Yossel's murder, there seemed to be more beatings and murders of prisoners for no other reason than the whims of the guards and the oberscharführer. A few days after the Warsaw Ghetto captives arrived, the guards built a wooden structure in the middle of the camp, no doubt with wood that I cut at the lumberyard where I worked. It was a crude-looking platform. There were now somewhere between twenty-five hundred and three thousand workers in the camp. It was now crowded, and those who were weakened by the hard work and the lack of food were regularly murdered, not to mention the few who tried to escape.

One morning soon after the last group arrived, we were crowded in the middle of the camp, surrounded by the platform. There was a rope hanging from the top. It was a gallows, and something terrible was about to happen.

Oberscharführer Feix stood on the platform and began to speak. "A few weeks ago, the German army defeated a group of Jews who thought they could fight our power. When we cleaned out the filthy ghetto where you Jews liked to live, we found many valuables. Money and jewelry was being hoarded by the Jews. We need this to help the war effort. We know you Jews are rich and are holding money and gold. You will now give us everything you have. When the guards come around, you will give them everything."

Just then, one of the prisoners was brought up on the platform. I did not recognize his face, but I assumed it was one of the Warsaw Ghetto survivors. One of the guards put the noose around his neck, and they hanged him for all to see. Many in the crowd sighed and yelled. He was known to some of them.

Then Feix spoke out again. "If we find out you did not give us everything, you will be brought here and hanged. Now be ready to give the guards everything."

As the guards walked around with large containers, many of the prisoners filled the tubs with all kinds of money, rings, chains, and everything that they had hidden on their persons. Meanwhile, as this was going on, they brought another prisoner to the platform and hanged him. This went on for at least two hours. As the guard who was collecting from the group I was standing with, my bunkmates, came closer, I could see that not all of them were giving up their belongings. When they claimed they didn't have anything, the guards just moved on. Others were clearly scared of being hanged and emptied their pockets immediately. As I watched, another man was hanged. When the guard came to me, I just shook my head and said I had nothing. I lied. I had a long gold chain that I cut off pieces from to buy food and some money. I knew that if I had nothing, I could not survive long on what they fed us, and it would be better to be hanged than die a slow, painful death. The guard moved on.

In the end, they filled up three trucks with the spoils of what they collected. I lost count of how many men were hanged. It was a horrible show of strength and sadism that I knew was designed to make us lose what little hope we had. Something was keeping me going forward. It may have just been the survival instinct; it may have been my need to find out what had happened to my sisters, or maybe it was the promise

I made to find Miriam after this was over. All I knew was that I was going to do what I could to survive this.

Finally, Feix and his henchmen were satisfied, and we were lined up to go to work. There was no singing that day. Even the guards thought they had extracted enough from us. We were totally exhausted, and the mood was somber.

The monotony went on for several more months. In September, a new commandant arrived, Fritz Tauscher. He believed prisoners should look like prisoners, so he issued an order that all inmates should wear uniforms. Each prisoner was given a gray-and-black-striped shirt and pants. One size fit or didn't fit all. All the prisoners were very thin by then, so this uniform hung loosely on everyone. Everyone's clothes were taken away, including those of the army prisoners of war. Everyone now looked the same. We had no individual identity. We were cattle.

Eventually, winter came, and then the new year of 1944. Those who were working inside survived better than those who were working outside in the camp or on the roads. The barracks had no heat but were stuffed with warm bodies, which seemed to be enough at night. As the camp grew, the work was spread out to different tasks. Now the factory was producing airplanes, and the lumberyard remained busy. Although I worked outside most of the day, I could come in the office to warm up. When I was inside, Janek was now sharing news of the war that he had heard. The Nazis were having a difficult time fighting the Russians. The Germans were being repelled, and the Russians were making advances, even in Poland. There was some optimism that the Russians would defeat the Nazis and liberate us. That was welcome news. There was hope once again.

You could tell when a prisoner was in poor health. There was coughing throughout the night and bloodstains everywhere. Even when someone was sick with fever, he was forced to line up and march to work. Sometimes he collapsed and died on the way. Sometimes he was dead when the call came for the morning lineup. I was numb to it all. I was alive, and that was all that mattered. The best I could do was pray for the Russians to liberate us before we were all dead. I had no idea if the Russians treated Jews any better than the Nazis, but it certainly could not be worse.

Winter was over, and spring arrived. There were still stories that the Russians were moving closer and the Nazis were losing ground. Finally, in May, we heard they were moving on Lublin, only fifty kilometers away. I felt the end of the Nazis was coming. One morning, we lined up and were told we were not going to work. We were to march to Krasnik. When we arrived in Krasnik, there were trains, trucks, and all kinds of transports. We were being evacuated. They were not waiting for the Russians. We were leaving. They certainly did not have enough vehicles to take all of us away. We had lost many to disease and murder, but there were still over two thousand people there. They started loading the trains. They were stuffing people in like animals. There was no room to breathe. When they could not push any more into the boxcar, they closed the doors and started filling the next one. Finally, the cars were full, and the train left. I was toward the back of the line. We were told to move toward the trucks. I was loaded into a troop carrier. I was stuffed in with as many people as they could get in. I had no idea where we were going, but since we were in a truck, I was hoping it was a shorter distance.

We drove for a couple of hours. I think I fell asleep for a while. It was hot in the truck, and I was squeezed in between the other men. When I woke up, we rode for another hour, and then we arrived. We literally fell out of the truck. When I looked up, I saw we were in Mielec. I knew Mielec. It was less than one hundred kilometers from Pysznica. What I didn't know was that there was a Mielec concentration camp. It looked very much like Budzyn, about the same size. As we walked in, there was a sign reading, *Arbeit Macht Frei*, "Work Makes Free." They had been telling us all along that if we worked hard, we would be free. We all knew it was a lie.

CHAPTER 23

Incognito

It had been many months since I came to Leipzig. The hotel was relying more and more on my seamstress skills, and Frau Reiniger treated me with much more respect than the other girls. I worked hard and did double duty, continuing to clean rooms when the sewing ran out. I pushed my Jewish identity deep into the background, but at night in the dark, I wept and dreamed about the day I could live freely and find my family. I wondered if Meyer would remember me. I missed him.

I made friends with three girls at the dormitory. One was Polish, from Krakow, named Minka, and the other two were sisters from Czechoslovakia, Giselle and Katarina. After a few months, we all learned fluent German, although we spoke with accents. Minka was tall, very thin, and statuesque, a real beauty. She always wore long dresses, she said, to hide being so tall. Giselle and Katarina were shorter and a bit heavier. Giselle was two years older but did not look much like her sister. We moved our rooms so we could be near each other. We learned to speak German together and helped each other become fluent. We became inseparable. We went everywhere together—the market, walks in the park, and museums when we had some time off. We told our stories to each other. All of them were taken from their families and transported to Germany to work. Of course, I told the story of my parents, the Dombecks. My father was there in Germany while my mother was selling the house and expected there soon. They told their stories too. Minka was from Wroclaw. Her family were merchants and were told that they could keep their store if she would join a group of other young women who were going to Germany to work. Giselle and Katarina had similar stories, except they were from a small town outside Prague.

We got along very well. We seemed to have the same views on the world and the horrors of this war. When I looked closely at them, I got the sense they were Jewish girls, trying to survive like I was. As we got to know each other, there were slips—a Yiddish word here and there, something about holidays. We were all Jewish girls living under assumed names, but no one dared to speak the truth. We all knew it, but clearly we felt that we should live our assumed lives and keep our identities hidden. I agreed that was the right thing to do.

One morning, I was mending a man's suit jacket and trousers that had been torn the night before. The bellboy told me the story when he brought me the suit. A businessman from Berlin was drinking hard at the local beer hall down the street. He started proposing to all the women. One of the husbands was not happy and beat him up pretty good. A brawl started, and the police had to break it up. They dragged him back to the hotel, and he was sleeping it off.

While I was mending the pants, Frau Reiniger came into the area of the basement where I was working with a policeman. "This is Officer Moller," she said.

The cop looked at me and said, "Please come with me."

What was this? I got up and followed them out without saying a word. I was scared. How did they find out I was a Jew? I did not speak of it, not even with the girls. Officer Moller and I proceeded as Frau Reiniger stayed behind. We walked toward the train station. Were they sending me to a labor camp? Moller said very little. He mentioned the cold weather. He did not say I was under arrest or what was happening. I was too scared to say anything. Besides, I had no idea what he knew about me.

We walked a few blocks along the Trondlinring toward the station but then turned left and walked three more blocks where there was a police station. This was not good. I followed him inside. He brought me to a locked door. He opened the door with his key. We walked down the hall to another locked door. He opened that door. We went inside the room, which had a table and a few chairs. He said, "Wait here," and left with the door locked behind me.

Well, this was it. I began to think about Meyer and all the plans we talked about for the future. He promised to find me, but there might not be anything to find. I thought I would see Leibish soon. What about Shlomo? Was he OK? Time was passing. It was a least an hour since he sat me in there, locked up.

Suddenly, the door burst open. Moller walked in. Two other cops came in behind him with a man, his hands behind his back in handcuffs. I had no idea who he was. What did this have to do with me?

Moller spoke. "This man was caught stealing from a nearby butcher shop yesterday. He does not speak German, only Polish. Can you translate for us?"

My heart sank into my stomach. It was not about me. I was so relieved.

"Of course," I said.

"Good," said Moller. "Ask him what he is doing in Germany."

I did and explained to Moller, "This man was transported here by the German army from his farm near Lublin, which was confiscated. He, his wife, and his two daughters were told they would be put to work in Germany. After a few months, the work stopped, and he and his family have been living in the nearby park for the past two weeks, stealing food to survive."

Moller, who was clearly the lead cop, told me to ask him where they could find his wife and children. The prisoner was not willing to tell him, for fear of what would happen. Moller said, "Tell him that we cannot have people living in the streets of our beautiful city and robbing local businesses. You will be put in a shelter, and we will contact the military, who will reassign you."

I repeated Moller's comments in Polish. The prisoner asked me in Polish, "Do you think I can believe them?"

I replied, "I really do not know, but I think you will be better off if you are together."

"What did he say?" asked Moller.

"He wanted advice. I told him to trust you."

"Good," said Moller. "Ask him if he is a Jew."

I did.

The prisoner replied, "No!" and he spit on the floor. "The Jews are scum, and the reason we are here."

Now I didn't care if the Nazis killed him and his family.

"Then you will be fine," said Moller.

I knew he was lying, but I told the prisoner what Moller had said.

The prisoner thought for a minute. "They are on the far side of the train station near the northern entrance."

"We are finished here," said Moller.

The other two cops took the prisoner out of the room. "You are free to go," he said to me. "Frau Reiniger said you would be very helpful, and you were. I would like to call on you again if we need a Polish interpreter. We have people here now from many countries since the war."

"I am happy to help," I said, wishing not to see the inside of this police station again. He showed me to the door, and I walked speedily back to the Fuerstenhof, still shaken from the scare they put into me.

I went back to work. I picked up the suit I was repairing. I could not help thinking about the man who robbed for his family. I would do the same for mine. Now they were being taken off the street. Would they be cared for, or would they suffer for his crime? The Nazis seemed to need an endless supply of workers, so chances were they would be shipped somewhere and forced into some type of labor. It would not be good either way. What a horrible world we lived in, but regardless of what happened to them, it was worse to be a known Jew. I considered myself lucky to be able to hide by looking right into their eyes.

That night after work, the four of us got changed and took a walk to the park near the train station. As we walked into the park, I began to tell the story of my morning visit to the police station and how I was surprised that I was asked to interpret for a Polish prisoner. I was now the official police interpreter of Polish to German. That got a laugh. I also told of the family who was living in this park and about the father who got arrested for stealing food.

Minka stopped, turned to me and said, "You must have been scared to death that you would be discovered."

I looked at her, not knowing what to say. This was the first open acknowledgment that I was Jewish. Finally, I said softly, "Yes, I was scared to death," and then I turned forward and started walking.

Minka stopped walking, and so did we. "I'm tired of hiding my identity," she declared. "My name is Esther, and I am a Bais Ya'akov teacher from Krakow."

"Shhh," I said, "are you crazy?"

"No," she said, "I want to talk about my real story. If I can't talk to you, who can I talk to?" She was very proud to be Jewish. The Bais Ya'akov schools were started in Poland as an all-girls school for Jewish Orthodox girls. In the traditional Orthodox world, girls were not required to study the Torah or Talmud. They were to learn to create a kosher home as well as other domestic duties. The Bais Ya'akov schools were developed in Poland after World War I to address the growing pressure from the government for all children to have a formal education. Orthodox parents could send their daughters to an Orthodox all-girls school and not have them mix together with non-Jews the way I did in Rozwadow.

We agreed to tell our stories but not our real names. We agreed that we would keep our identities secret, even if our lives were in danger. We even formed a secret society, the Partisan Ladies of Leipzig. We would die for our secrets, but we would also die for each other. I told my story of being chased from my home and being taken in by the wonderful Mr. Lubin. They listened to the story of the murder of my brother Leibish and the sadness of leaving Shlomo. But what they couldn't get enough of was the story of how I fell in love with Meyer.

"What was he like?" they asked.

"What did you do together?" they asked.

"Why did you leave him?" they wanted to know.

I gave them all the details they wanted but couldn't totally explain why I left him at the train station that day. Was I just obeying my parents, or was I too scared to go back with him into the woods? I didn't want to answer. Minka, or Esther as we now knew her, was so beautiful but had gone to and taught at Bais Ya'akov. Her parents had formed a shitach, an arranged marriage, but when the war broke out, the family of her betrothed fled, and her marriage with it. She was separated from her parents and sent here. She had no idea what happened to them. She escaped and joined the partisans. They arranged for her to purchase the identity and papers of a Polish girl named Minka, and she was transported here with a group of non-Jewish Poles ordered to come to work in Germany.

It turns out Giselle and Katarina were not sisters after all. They were friends and lived in a shtetl near Prague. They also were chased from their homes and were separated from their families. Katrina watched as her parents were murdered and her two brothers were captured and sent off to prison. She escaped, and she and Giselle were also able to obtain false identities as sisters and come here to hide together. It was comforting but also disturbing to know that others from other places in Europe were having the same experiences. We were now closer than ever, sisters in a secret society forever bound together. We all started to cry until we realized we were attracting attention. We composed ourselves and walked back to the dormitory.

In the weeks that followed, I had a few requests from the police to translate. It was usually the same story. Polish men and women had come to Germany either by force or voluntarily only to find little work and had resorted to crime. The Germans looked down at the Poles as inferior and just a local nuisance. I had always experienced being treated badly as a Jew but was surprised that Christian Poles were treated badly as well. During a particularly busy Sunday afternoon while I was cleaning rooms, preparing for the week ahead, Frau Reiniger found me and told me I had a visitor. I assumed it was another visit from the police. When we went down to the employee entrance, I was shocked to see a well-dressed woman.

"Surprise!" said Frau Reiniger.

"Momma!" I cried and ran over to hug Mrs. Dombeck.

"My sweet Stephania," she said, "I missed you so."

I was worried for a second that she had told them who I was, but she didn't. In fact, she seemed genuinely happy to see me.

When I looked up, Herr Vogt was standing there smiling broadly. "Why don't you two go out for a coffee?" he said. "I'm sure Frau Reiniger can manage without you for a couple of hours."

Reiniger was not happy but reluctantly agreed to let me spend some time with my long-lost mother.

"I'll be back soon," I said, and off we went.

"I'm surprised to see you," I said as we walked to the local coffeehouse. "I've moved to Leipzig with Mr. Dombeck, just as we planned," she replied. "Stephania was married in the church. Mr. Dombeck got a leave of absence and attended. It was a beautiful wedding. Stephania is very happy, and I was able to sell the house and move here a few weeks ago."

"That is very nice," I said.

She continued, "I miss our little chats. I am so sorry you had to leave so suddenly. How have you been getting along here?"

"Good," I said. "Herr Vogt received me very kindly and gave me this job, thanks to your husband's kind recommendation. My seamstress skills have come in handy."

"You are an excellent dressmaker!" exclaimed Mrs. Dombeck. "We took the wedding dress you made to a shop in Stalowa Wola to have it finished, and the mistress was very impressed with your workmanship and design. It came out beautifully. Look, I have a picture."

"She's a beautiful bride," I said, but I was just admiring my dress. I should have married Meyer in such a dress.

Finally, the small talk was over, and Mrs. Dombeck got to the point. "I need a favor."

"Anything. What is it?" I replied.

She said, "I need Stephania's original identification papers back."

"I need them," I protested. "It's my only proof that I am here legally and not a Jew."

"I know," she said. "Stephania needs them to get her name changed legally. They agreed to perform the wedding but need her official papers to get her name changed. Once she has new papers, you can have them back. I will take them to her personally and will get them back to you in two weeks. I tried to get copies from the government office, but the Nazis have taken over and they will not allow new papers to be issued without the originals. We told them they were missing and nowhere to be found, but they said without the papers, she was in Poland illegally. I promise I will bring them back to you."

"I don't know what to say," I replied. "Without my papers, I could lose my job and even be arrested. It would be a death sentence for me."

"I'm sorry," she said sadly but sternly. "I must have them. If you do not give them to me, I will tell Herr Vogt who you are. I promise I will bring them to you as soon as I am done."

I had no choice. She got me this far. I could not risk being discovered. "I will give them to you," I said. I pulled them out of my purse and handed them to her.

"Thank you," she said. "I want you to know that I truly want to help you. I am assured this is just a formality. I will bring these to Poland myself. I have a temporary visa, and I promise to return in no more than two weeks."

We finished our coffee. We got up and hugged. My life was in her hands. I had no choice but to agree. I am not sure she would have turned me in because she would be arrested for helping me, but I owed her for taking me in and giving me this chance in the first place. I hoped I could stay hidden for two weeks and not need to show identification. We went our separate ways, and I went back to work.

When I returned, Frau Reiniger seemed to be waiting for me. "I have work for you to do. The wife of a Nazi officer staying at the hotel needs a dress altered for a gala tonight. You need to stay until it is finished."

Understood, perfect! Working with a Nazi with no papers. I was told to go to room 351. I knocked, and a very large woman answered. I announced myself. "I am Stephania, and I understand you need alterations on a dress."

"Come in; I'll put it on," she snapped.

A few minutes later, she walked out in what looked like a large sack. It was horrible. "What a lovely dress," I said.

She replied, "I have lost weight, and I need you to take it in."

I had to cough to keep myself from laughing. She was huge. She continued, "I want you to taper it so it shows off my new figure."

I was dying inside. "You have a beautiful figure. Your husband will love it," I said quite seriously. I had become a pretty good liar.

"Yes. We are going to a very important dinner dance tonight. All the top Nazi officials will be there. There is even a rumor that the führer himself will attend."

This dress was big enough that maybe I could sew a bomb in the lining and kill them all. She wouldn't even notice. I was daydreaming of singlehandedly ending the war.

I pinned the dress to show off her svelte body and told her I would be back in two hours for a fitting. "I must be ready by nineteen hundred hours, so get to work."

I did. This was not that big a job. She hadn't lost that much weight. I got to work and was back in her room at 1730. She tried it on again, and it fit well but needed to be lengthened a bit. I finished it and brought it back upstairs. This time her husband was there, ready in his dress uniform. He was rather handsome, fortyish. She must have blown up after the marriage. I thought he spent a lot of time at work. Anyhow, she took the dress and dismissed me without a thank-you or any acknowledgment for the work I had done. I was used to that and was happy to be out of their sight.

I was tired when I came back to the dormitory. The girls were in a panic, very upset. "What happened?" I asked.

Katarina jumped in. "Our little Bais Ya'akov girl decided to announce in the crowded street in front of the dormitory that she was Jewish."

"Why?" I asked, getting nervous myself.

Giselle replied, "We were coming back from the market. I was telling Katerina about the clerk who was trying to sell me and Minka roasted pork. He was very insistent. He had made it himself, and when we refused, he told us we were crazy."

Katarina interrupted. "Yes, and as we got to the front of the building, Minka screamed out that she wanted to tell him she was a Jew but didn't. Meanwhile several people on the street heard her and turned around. We ran inside in a panic. Now we're afraid someone will come after us."

"We have to stay calm," I said. "There are lots of girls here. It will be just a rumor that there are Jews here, if they report it at all."

I was panicking inside. I just gave away my papers. We stayed in all evening, but nothing happened. In the middle of the night, there was a commotion that woke us up. I went into the hall, and others were out there. I saw one of the girls coming up the steps. "What is going on?" I asked.

She replied, "There are police in the building asking for a tall, dark-haired woman. I think they are looking for Minka."

I could hear loud footsteps coming up the stairs. I ran into the room. "Wake up," I said. "There are police looking for Minka." They started getting up. I was in a panic. I crawled under the bed with my blanket and hid. We always said that we would protect each other, but I knew I could not identify myself. That would be a sure reason to arrest me.

The police arrived. "Please stand at attention," one of them announced. I knew Minka would stand out from the crowd and be recognized. "Are you a Jew?" one of the officers asked.

"Yes," she said proudly.

"Are there any other Jews here?" he asked her.

"No," she said. "Just me!"

They shuffled out. They didn't even ask to see papers for the others. I crawled out from under the bed. Katarina just stared in disbelief. "They took her," she said quietly. "What will happen to her?"

No one spoke. No one had an answer. There was little hope we would see Minka again. She was defiant, and now she would pay the price of being who she was. None of us were willing to pay that price, and I was ashamed. I had to believe the only hope of the Jewish people was for us to live and hope to be free someday.

Giselle, Katarina, and I agreed not to discuss our heritage again. I would be Stephania Dombeck. We were Polish and Czech women happily working for the benefit of the Third Reich. I waited for two weeks, but Mrs. Dombeck did not come back. Luckily, I had not been asked to produce identification. By then, I was well known among the police, so I would stay close to home. Winter was coming, and a chill was in the air.

One early morning, during the first week of December 1943, we were woken by a huge noise. The building shook, and we heard a constant barrage of explosions. We were being bombed. Everyone made it to the basement, where we held on to each other. I had heard rumors that the British had bombed cities in Germany, but there was not a clue that they could reach Leipzig. Was Germany losing the war? Of course, all we heard was that the glorious Third Reich was marching across Europe, gaining more and more strength. Our hope was that this was the beginning of the end and that we would be freed. The problem was, we were in Germany and being bombed. After about an hour and a half, the siren indicating the bombing had stopped sounded. We walked outside. Our building had not been hit, but we could see fires burning in the distance. We were told to go about our normal business. I went in and got ready to go to work. I was now sure that I would never see Mrs. Dombeck. If she came back to Leipzig, she would not venture out to see me with bombs dropping. If she was still in Poland, she would probably be stuck there. The Germans had more to worry about than some Jewish seamstress without identification papers.

CHAPTER 24

Mielec

THE CAMP WAS LAID OUT differently than Budzyn, but it was basically the same. The main difference was that the bunks were smaller and more crowded. I was numb. Yossel was dead, and Nachman and Szweda were nowhere to be found. I was now truly alone, surrounded by two to three thousand starving men, many of them sick.

The first morning was typical. Up at 0500. Line up outside the barracks. There was a large, empty yard in the center of the camp. We were lined up in a circle around this field. The new prisoners were ordered to wait while the rest marched out of the camp, presumably to their work stations.

A German officer rode up on his horse. He proudly announced that he was Oberscharführer Josef Schwammberger. "We are situated near the Heinkel factory, making bomber airplanes for our glorious Luftwaffe. Many of you have come from Budzyn, where some of you worked in the Heinkel factory. We want the experienced airplane mechanics for our plant. Tell the guards who you are." Then he turned his horse around and left. He was an imposing figure, sitting on that horse. He looked young, maybe thirty years old. He didn't get this command by being kind. I already knew to stay far away from the higher-ranking officers. They murdered people like me for fun.

I was surprised to find out that they built these camps around aircraft manufacturing plants. I never saw the inside of the Budzyn factory, but I knew that if I did not work inside the factory, they would put me to work on the roads or in the camp itself. That work was brutal. It was freezing in winter and hot in the summer. We were not dressed, and we were not fed. Men dropped dead in the middle of work, or if they were slow, they would be shot where they stood. I knew that I had a better chance of survival if I worked in the plant.

"Guard," I said as he walked by. "I work on airplanes." I was told to move to a line that was forming. These were other men who said they worked on aircraft. I had no idea if they were lying like me. Once the line was formed, we were told to march and sing the usual German work songs. This process had become very familiar to me.

As we reached the entrance of the plant, there was a big sign: "Heinkel Flugzeugwerke." This plant was operational. There were finished bomber planes in the yard. We went inside. There were different areas where various sections of the planes were being worked on by different crews. It was one big hangar. There were clearly Poles and Germans working alongside the Jewish prisoners. There seemed to be thousands of workers in the main manufacturing area. I could see some large pieces, such as the main cabin and large wings, being assembled. We were told to stand in the holding area, lined up side by side at attention. The tremendous roar of machinery noises was almost deafening.

A man with a clipboard came over to us and yelled in German-accented Polish over the noise. "I understand you are airplane factory workers from Budzyn. I need to know your specialty."

I had no specialty. I just thought they would put me somewhere where I could clean up or something. If they found out I was lying, they would kill me for sure.

Luckily they started at the far end of the line. I was in the middle. "Give me your name and specialty," he said.

I didn't pay attention to the names. My mind was racing. The first man said he was a mechanical engineer. There was no way I could fake that. The next man said he was an expert assembling engines. I could change the oil of my army motorcycle, but that was no airplane engine. The third man said he was a riveter. I could see men with riveting guns working at various positions on the outside of the airplane cabins. I began to wonder if I could do that.

Suddenly my daydream was interrupted by Herr Clipboard. "You! What do you do?"

"Riveter!" I declared proudly.

He moved on. I must be crazy or stupid.

Each man down the line announced a specialty. Most of the Budzyn prisoners worked on the airplanes. I was one of only a few who worked in the lumberyard. I began to think I was the only one faking it. It was too late to turn back now. Once we were all recorded, they divided us up by specialty, and a supervisor came over to collect us. There were six of us, and we were divided into two-man teams. We were brought into a room with a table and chairs. There were diagrams on the walls, blueprints of sections of the airplanes.

The supervisor stood in front of the room and introduced himself. "I am Gerek Nowak." He was obviously Polish. He continued, "I have been supervisor at this factory since before the war, and I am now solely dedicated to building Heinkel airplanes to the German specifications. I expect perfection from all my workers. The Nazis expect nothing less. These airplanes must be built quickly, and each rivet must be placed in the perfect position and sealed perfectly." I wished I knew what a perfect rivet looked like. He talked some more. "I know that all Jews are lazy and have bad work habits. You will be expected to work hard and make a perfect job, or you will be punished. Look at this diagram. You will be assembling the main wings. You and your partner will work together. One of you will measure and hold the sections of metal in place, and the other will use the gun to rivet the sections together. Do you have any questions?"

I had lots of questions, like, how does the rivet gun work? How do you measure the metal? I hoped my partner knew what he was doing. I kept my mouth shut. That was the extent of our training. I did not know the name of my partner, and he didn't know mine, nor did he care. They did not give us much time to chat.

We were marched to the supply area and told to get what we needed. I looked at my partner and just said, "I'm Meyer."

He said, "Zalman."

Well, that was a start. He went over and grabbed a rivet gun and a supply of rivets. "This should be enough to start," he said. I just shook my head and followed his lead. He knew what he was doing. "Do you want to measure and hold or install the rivets?" he asked. I chose the rivets, hoping that would require less precision. We began to march to the wing-assembly area. Lucky for me it was the end of the day, and the horn blew. We marched back to the supply area, put everything away, and formed the line to march back to camp. I got to see a little bit of the riveting going on, so I had some idea of how it worked. I would have tonight to think about it. I could not ask anyone, as I did not know whom I could trust. Zalman was not being friendly. Just another starving man trying to survive.

We marched back to camp to line up for our evening meal, more watery soup and a small hunk of bread. Somehow I was staying alive on this, although my uniform continued to get looser. I did not see Zalman that night. I spent the night trying to visualize the rivet gun and how I would use it the next day.

I fell asleep, and the night flew by. The morning lineup was here again. As I walked outside, I saw a group of prisoners carrying a dead man across the yard. Men dying of starvation and exhaustion had become a normal, everyday sight. Only slightly rarer was a guard or the commandant murdering someone for a minor infraction. Every time I saw a dead prisoner, I began to cry for Yossel. Momma, Benjamin, and my sisters were also in my thoughts daily. But today I had to become a riveter.

When we got to the plant, we picked up where we had left off. Zalman had already grabbed the supplies when I arrived. We were marched out to the wing-assembly area. We lifted the curved metal section and placed it on a table specially shaped for the task. Zalman made several marks about ten millimeters apart. He then went behind the table and placed the two sections together. I knew it was my turn to place the rivets in the gun, point it at the marked areas, and squeeze the rivets in place. I shot the first one. It did not go through all the way. I pulled the rivet out by hand and shot it again. It went through, but it was crooked, not fully flat. I went to the next section. The results were not much better. I did a few more. Zalman couldn't see what I was doing from his position, but suddenly the supervisor walked by and saw what I was doing. He ordered me to stop. Zalman came out from behind the station and looked at my sloppy work.

He began to protest. "I measured the areas perfectly, and I held them in place with precision. This man did the poor job."

Nowak took out his slide rule and measured the marks, and they were indeed perfect. The supervisor looked at Zalman and told him to remain at his station. I was ordered to follow him. I was marched outside behind the building where the finished airplanes were parked. Nowak called one of the guards over. He then started screaming at me, "Slimy Jew! I knew you cannot be trusted. Did you think we would not notice your treachery? Did you think we would not notice you trying to sabotage our airplanes so it would crash in midflight? I told you if you did not do a perfect job, you would be punished!"

He thought I had done this on purpose. He had no idea that I didn't know what to do. If they caught me lying, they would kill me. Sabotage just got a punishment?

"Strip, filthy Jew!" yelled the guard.

I removed all my clothes. It was cold. "Fall to your knees and bend over," he ordered.

I complied. I heard a snap and felt a sharp pain on my back and buttocks. I jumped up and turned around. The guard was holding a whip.

"Get back down, and don't move!" he yelled.

I did. He struck again. This one hurt more. The lashes continued. I screamed with each one. The pain was horrible and increased with each strike. I started to see blood dripping down between my legs. I had never felt so much pain. Tears were rolling down my face. Blood was forming pools beneath me. Finally, I fell flat on my face. The lashes continued. I was nearly unconscious when they stopped.

I heard the guard say, "That's twenty-five," and he walked away. I could not move. The pain was unbearable.

"Get up!" yelled Nowak. "This is what you get."

I could not move. Two guards came and lifted me to my feet. The pain grew more intense. The blood was everywhere. I fell unconscious.

When I woke up, I was in my bunk, it was night, and the barracks were full. I was alive but just barely. I tried to get up and off the bunk, but I screamed in pain when I tried to move. No one acknowledged me. They had their own problems. I would just be another bunkmate who died around them. I just lay still for the rest of the night, sleeping a bit but not much. At 0500, the guards came around to get us to the lineup. The pain was still horrible, but I knew if I did not get up, I would be shot on the spot. I dragged myself out for the lineup. Somehow I willed myself to march to the plant.

Nowak didn't seem surprised to see me. "I hope you learned your lesson. We need you on the line. Grab your supplies, and let's go."

I tried it again. This time with a new partner. I thought I was getting the hang of it. The rivets were flush and seemed to be a perfect job. When the quality inspector came around to look, he immediately called over the supervisor.

Nowak came over and looked at my work. They found some that were less than perfect. "Did you think we would not find this substandard work? Do you think we would let one of our crews fly in this garbage?" Nowak screamed.

"I'll fix them," I said softly.

"Take him outside," he said. "You will be taught what happens to saboteurs."

They killed so many for less. I had no idea why they did not kill me. They must be desperate for skilled labor.

I was told to strip again. The bleeding had stopped from yesterday, but I didn't think I could take more of this. The whipping started. This time, I knew what to expect. After two or three on the back, he moved down to my buttocks and my legs. They wanted me to live. They seemed to get more pleasure out of causing me pain than killing me. After they were done, I was conscious. I pulled myself up. I fell from the pain in my legs, but I dragged myself up and put my clothes on. The guard pushed me toward the door. They expected me to get back on the line. They were either easier on me this time, or I was stronger than before.

"You get one more chance, Juden," declared Nowak. "Now you will fix your mistakes and continue. If you try to sabotage us again, I will shoot you myself."

I limped back to the line, where my rivet gun and partner were waiting. He looked scared that they were going to blame him. But he surprised me. "You don't know how to do this, do you?" he whispered.

"I'm learning," I said.

"Just hold it straight and steady, and you will be fine," he replied.

By then, I knew what to do. We dug out the bad ones and replaced them. This was how I learned to be a riveter. I was now an expert, and when the quality control man looked at my work this time, he just moved on. I did not see Nowak again that day. When we marched back to camp that night, I felt I had just fought and won a battle. It was a small victory for me. I was in pain, and I moved slowly. I was in the back of the line, dragging behind. I got yelled at a lot, but they needed mechanics, and they let me lag. When I finally got to camp, I got in line for food. By the time I reached the end of the line, the meal period was over, and I got nothing. That was two days in a row. I crawled back to my bunk and went to sleep.

It took a few days for the wounds to heal and for me to be able to sit in a normal position and walk at a normal speed, although the pain never quite went away. I had lost more weight, and my uniform was hanging off me. I spent the next few weeks helping the Nazis build Heinkel HE 343 bombers. I was growing weaker and had no more money or gold to buy food. At least the work was keeping my brain busy. One night, while sitting and eating my watery cabbage soup, I heard a noise that sounded like a horse galloping across the yard. I stood up to see what was going on, like most around me. Oberscharführer Schwammberger's horse was indeed loose and running at full speed. It ran straight into the perimeter fence and was electrocuted. The fence was so powerful you could feel the charge if you got within five feet of it. The horse neighed but collapsed dead within a few seconds. The prisoners were lined up and ordered to stand at attention as Schwammberger arrived at the scene. I could hear him screaming at the guards.

"He was tied to the post! Some of these filthy pigs must have let him loose and killed him! I want them arrested!" Then he left.

The guards he yelled at ran back toward the commandant's office. I could not see if they arrested anyone, but the show was not quite over. Five men were brought to the field in the middle of the camp. We were ordered to line up around the field as we normally did each morning. Five men were marched to the middle. I did not recognize them, but undoubtedly these were unskilled workers. Schwammberger marched out, pulled his revolver, and shot each one to death personally, as if he were squashing a cockroach. I suspected that these men had nothing to do with his horse getting loose and electrocuted, but he seemed to relish having a reason to commit more murders.

When I got to Mielec, I had hope that the Russians were beating the Germans and we would be liberated, but after four months, I was losing hope. These were the longest months of my life so far. The pain in my back and legs was only matched by the pain in my heart, not only for my family but for the Jewish people. I knew the stories of persecution for thousands of years going back to the destruction of the temples but never paid too much attention to the details. We had fought, and we had survived. That was the past. Now I and all Jews were living through it again. I had no idea of anything happening outside this camp. Our survival was all we had to work for.

Finally, one very hot night in August, I was wakened by booms in the distance. I could hear the guards screaming and scurrying outside. We were not being directly attacked, but perhaps the Russians were on the march again. Work was normal over the next couple of days, but we continued to hear the bombing and shelling at night. We had no idea how far away they were.

The next morning at lineup, we were told we were not working. We were moving to a new location. I was reticent about what was next. As brutal as this was, I had a new skill and was being left alone. The Russians were clearly moving west and closing in on us. If they left us here, we would be saved. If we were moved, remaining under German control in a new hell hole, we would probably all die. We fell into line and marched. We headed to the Heinkel factory, but instead of going inside, we were stopped outside. A rail line crossed the plant property, and a long train of boxcars was waiting. This was our transport.

I waited in line as men were being loaded into these railcars two at a time like sheep. I had seen this before. It felt like waiting for death. I had seen men try to escape, only to be shot. That might be a better death than what was awaiting me, but what if I survived the trip? Where were they taking us? Would the Russians eventually catch up with them and defeat them, and we would be free? The possibility of beating this kept me and the two thousand others waiting in line docile and obedient.

Suddenly the line stopped, and the doors to the boxcars were shut. The steam engine of the locomotive began to huff and puff and started churning. The train began to move and pulled out away on its journey. We were told to stand at attention. At least two hours went by before another train arrived. Another hour went by as they started loading. As I moved closer, I could see how they were stuffing people into the cars, as many as they could get in, so no one could move or breathe. There were no windows, and I could only hope there was some way to breathe. Finally, it was my turn to climb in. It was as bad as I expected. I don't know how many of us were stuffed into that box, but the smell of death was all around us. Once they closed the doors and the heat set in, it was hard to breathe. There were a couple of small cutouts or vents at the top to allow air in, but that didn't seem to help much once we got moving.

I was lying across two other prisoners, and two were lying on my legs. No one moved or spoke. Grown men were crying and groaning. It would be a matter of will to survive this trip. There was some light in the car, but as nightfall came it was pitch-black. I tried to shift my body so as not to feel numb all over, but others around me groaned and tried to do the same, and it was truly unbearable. The smell grew worse by the minute. I was afraid to fall asleep, not knowing if I would wake up. Some were clearly suffocating under the pile of flesh. One man cried, "Where are they taking us?" No one responded, for no one knew. I must have fallen asleep for a while because when I opened my eyes, it was daylight, allowing me to see what was around me. I picked up my head and saw the man lying on my leg, lifeless. His eyes and mouth were wide open. He was clearly dead. I reached over and closed his eyes. I pushed him off my leg, but he plopped over onto someone else, who seemed not to care. I heard others crying that they had dead men on them.

As another day went by, suddenly we slowed down and stopped. After a long wait, the door to the boxcar was opened, and prisoners started to pile out. I crawled outside for the first time in two days. Not everyone made it outside. There were many dead. The fresh air and the warmth of the sun felt good. My arms and legs were numb, and I shook them. I looked down the track and saw a long brick building with a tower and a gate in the middle. I asked if anyone knew where we were. "Auschwitz" came a reply. There was talk of this place among the prisoners and the Poles alike throughout my experience at the labor camps. It was a place where thousands of Jews were being sent. There were rumors of mass exterminations, but no one could believe this was true. It looked ominous, huge, even from a distance. Then suddenly a guard told us to stop getting off. Auschwitz was full and could not accept any more prisoners. We were ordered to get back on.

I asked, "What about the dead men?"

"Get back on," came the order from the guard.

I complied. The door was closed, and the train began to move. The dead stayed with us.

Three more days and nights went by. No food, no water. More men dying around me. The first of the dead started to decay, and the smell was much worse than I thought possible. What drove me to stay alive I will never know. I was still young, only twenty-nine years old, but not nearly as strong as my former self. I had avoided disease, but there was sickness all around me except for those who were dead. There had been stops, presumably for fuel, and the hope that we had arrived returned, but I was disappointed each time. Finally, the train stopped once more, and I hoped this was finally the end. The doors opened. Those of us who could climbed out of the car. There were more dead now than alive, and some did not have the strength to move. I helped one man stand up and get off the car.

When I got out, we were in a huge facility with another sign saying "Arbeit Macht Frei." This was the greatest lie ever told. We had traveled so far that I didn't think we were still in Poland. I was right. We were in Germany, Dachau to be exact. We were fed. I felt numb, way beyond starving. We were given water and the usual cabbage soup. There was meat in the soup. I devoured all I could. I cried. I was alive.

CHAPTER 25

Dachau and the Finishing Pit

⅄ ⅄ ⅄

They wanted to know who we were and what we did. Those of us who made it off the train and were strong enough to work were ordered to line up in front of an administrative building. Once the line moved inside, I saw we were being registered. All they wanted were our names and skills. When it was my turn, I stated proudly, "Airplane mechanic, riveter." I was ordered to follow a guard who took me through a back door. The new prisoners were lined up in groups. I was led to a small group of about a dozen men. It appeared that the Nazis were still looking for laborers. The war was still on, but perhaps the Russians were pushing them out of Poland.

After all the prisoners were processed, we were marched to waiting transports. Our group was loaded into a military truck. We were leaving Dachau.

About an hour later, we arrived at our destination. We were lined up in another camp. It was an odd place. We were taken to a building that looked like a wooden tent. A Jewish man came in front of the group and began to speak in Yiddish. "I am David Gross. I am the kapo for this group. I will be your supervisor. You are in a subsidiary camp of Dachau in Kaufering. You will be marching each day to Landsberg to a new airplane factory where we will be building Messerschmitt ME262 fighter planes. These are the most advanced fighter planes in the world. You are the lucky ones and should be honored to work on such an important project. You will be working indoors and be rewarded for a perfect job. For a poor job, you will be punished. This is your bunk. It is very crowded, and you must find a place for yourselves."

It was very crowded. The bunks were wooden planks covered with straw along the sides of the wooden tent, slightly elevated from the floor. There were puddles on the dirt floor, and you could see holes in the roof. Every bunk was full. Some were being shared by two men. I found one with a small thin man and asked him to let me in.

"My name is Joseph," he said. "I have been waiting for someone to join me. I have been lucky to be alone this long. This place gets worse by the day. Where are you from?"

We struck up a conversation. He was Czech. He had been in Dachau for two years and worked on airplane-engine assembly. He looked sickly but was very talkative. His story was familiar. The Germans marched in and chased him and his family from their homes, killing many in the process and turning those who survived and who were strong enough to work into slave laborers. We talked into the night. I didn't remember falling asleep.

The next morning, it took about an hour and a half to march the six or seven kilometers to Landsberg. There was no visible plant. We were let into a gate that led into the side of a mountain. This factory was unmarked and underground. It was amazing. Once inside, I was impressed to see a huge factory floor, twice as large as the Heinkel factory in Mielec.

I was brought to the wing-assembly section. Now I was confident in my abilities. The wing-assembly team was gathered together. Only two of us were new, but we were all told that the expectation was that we would make twelve wings every workday. We went to work. This was a good team. We worked quickly, and I kept up with the expected pace. In the middle of the shift, we had a break for a meal. There was an area where the plant workers would line up to get food. I was unfamiliar with what was going on. The meal break was fifteen minutes. By the time I lined up and got near the food, the meal period was over and I had to get back to work. I would have to run to the front of the line to get anything to eat.

The work proceeded with German efficiency. We easily finished twelve wings in less than eight hours. Gross mentioned some reward. I wondered what that would be. At the end of the shift, the quality inspectors reviewed our work. The entire group had done a perfect job that day. We were each given one cigarette. I had never smoked. I had known a lot of smokers in the army. Maybe it was time to start.

During the march back to camp, several of the men who had earned a cigarette were given matches by the guards and lit up. They seemed in heaven and thrilled to have such a luxury. I decided to join them. The kapo came over to join me. I took a puff. It wasn't so bad.

Gross laughed at me. "Breathe it into your lungs." He had to teach me how to smoke. I did and immediately started coughing and getting nauseous. "You are white as a ghost." He laughed. By then, some of the other prisoners had joined in the laughter. We didn't laugh much, so I didn't mind being the butt of the joke.

"You want this?" I asked Gross. He took it from me, and that was the end of my smoking career, but I learned a valuable lesson. There was demand for cigarettes, and perhaps I could buy something I wanted with those I would earn in the future.

When the laughter died down, I remained alongside the kapo. "Why did they build this factory inside a mountain?" I asked.

"The Nazis are losing the war," he said without hesitation. "Their airplane production has been slowed to a crawl due to bombings of many of their factories throughout Germany by the Americans and the British. Now that the Russians are pushing the Germans back from Poland and Czechoslovakia, their only hope is to increase their production of fighter planes to fight back. The plant is built with walls made of concrete five feet deep to withstand Allied bombing. This is their only hope."

I now felt a sense of real hope for an end to this horror. I had no idea the Americans and British had joined the war. I had no news and knew only what I had heard about the Russians. The Nazis, who seemed invincible when they came across the Polish border, now had formidable enemies and could be defeated. I fantasized about sabotaging the wings I was working on, but I wanted desperately to live to see what the world would be like when the Nazi brutality ended and those murderers were caught and punished. I now had a little bounce in my step.

I started having dreams about Miriam. I was in a huge house, a building of some kind, with lots of rooms. I opened one door. The room was empty. I opened another door, and the room was filled with strangers. Another door, a room filled with Polish soldiers from my unit. The dream seemed to last for hours, but I know it didn't. Finally, I opened a door, and Miriam held her arms out to me. I woke up. It was morning, time to get to the lineup.

The dreams continued for months. So did the work. Each time we met our goal, we received a cigarette. Now I was saving them. Occasionally I traded them for a piece of bread or some additional soup. They were keeping me alive. The months went by. On September 1, 1944, I marked the day in my mind. It was five years since the Nazis invaded Poland. Winter came and so did 1945. The bunks at Kaufering were freezing. Even though we were fed somewhat better here than at my other camps, men started dying from being frozen and starving. Again, many of these were men working outside in the cold, and this was too much even for men who were young and strong when they were captured. Again, I was thankful for working inside and having cigarettes to trade.

Each day, we continued to produce wings for the fighter planes, but increasingly, we were not meeting our quota of wing assemblies. We were not getting enough material to complete twelve wings each day. It was subtle, but when we ran out of supplies, we stood around. It was noticeable. We didn't know why this was happening, and it was not for us to question. It didn't happen every day, but it started once a week, then twice.

Finally, as the weather started warming up, we began to have entire days where there was no work. One morning when we lined up, we were told that the plant was closed and we had no work. We were leaving Kaufering and going to the main camp at Dachau. We were lined up, but there were no transports—we were marching. It took an hour and a half when we first were driven from Dachau. I was guessing it was sixty or seventy kilometers. It would take most of a full day. There were so many sick and weak prisoners; it was clear that many of them would never live through this journey. I wasn't sure if I would. There were German guards everywhere. Some were wearing large backpacks and gear, and they were ready for the long march. Others were loading supplies into vehicles that would either meet us there or guide our journey. Some of the very sick and weak were pulled out of line and moved to the center of the camp. I had no doubt that this was the end of time for them.

We were told to move out, and so we did. I guessed that there were about one thousand prisoners marching. The spring rains had arrived, and it was going to be a wet journey. It didn't take long for trouble to start. After about two hours, three men near me collapsed. They were clearly sick and starving and just didn't have the strength to continue. Two guards came over and without hesitation shot them to death as they knelt over. This would truly be a death march. We were told to look forward and keep moving. I had seen so much murder and death that this didn't even jolt me. I just kept walking. What a terrible world this had become.

As the hours went by, we stopped several times. You could hear shots ring out from different parts of the lines. We would continue and pass dead bodies of prisoners along the way. One of those was Joseph, my bunkmate. I was surprised that he had made it this far, but he was full of life and was optimistic that he would see the end of slavery. I began to feel sick, and my legs began to buckle. I was determined to continue. I thought of the biblical story of Moses crossing the desert with nothing but a staff and his belief that God's strength was pushing him to continue. I had never questioned my faith in God before, but there was all this death among his chosen people. How could he let this happen or, worse yet, cause it to happen? Was it his strength pushing me, or was it my own? I had to continue to have faith to believe there was a higher purpose to this human disaster. The only way out of this was some divine power that would defeat the Nazi monstrosity.

Daylight came and went, but the rain continued to pour. I could not feel my feet, but I kept going. We continued to stop so the guards could shoot some more failing prisoners, but one of the stops we made was for vehicles setting up large steel barrels of soup. It was basically water with not much substance. We lined up. I had accumulated several dozen cigarettes during my time at the Landsberg factory and kept them in a pouch in the pocket of my uniform. I kept them dry. I offered one to the guard serving the soup. He reached to the bottom of the barrel where the soup was thicker. It had some meat, some vegetables. Others seemed to have taken notice. I saw some others chewing on the heartier soup, but most just had water. Those who were fortunate enough to have something to trade would always fare better than those who didn't. I thought about how I could help some of the others. I gave away a few of my cigarettes to men in the line behind me who had come this far but were struggling. I had no idea how long this would go on, and I had to be careful not to give away too many, to protect my own existence.

The march continued well into the night. We reached our destination sometime in the middle of the night. Even the horrible wooden plank bunks would be welcome. I had no doubt I would get some sleep.

But it turned out even the overcrowded shacks they called bunks were luxury compared to what they had in mind for us. We were directed into a series of trenches, muddied from the rain that had now finally stopped. I climbed down into one of the pits. It was filled with survivors of the Kaufering-to-Dachau death march. If one thousand prisoners started the day, maybe six or seven hundred made it the entire way. I could not see how many were in the pit. We were all standing bewildered about what we were to do here when Kapo Gross addressed us from just outside the bunker. "Men, you will be living and sleeping here now. There are no bunks available for us. The subcamps have been closed, and all the prisoners will be here. I am the kapo of this bunker and will be with you. There is no work, so this is where we will stay."

We all lay down in the mud. It was like being on the crowded train, one on top of the other, except we were outside. I may have slept an hour or two before it became daylight.

There was no lineup and no march to work. The sun was shining on us, and there was no relief. There were guards making sure no one left. We just milled around the pit. They meant to let us rot and die. They meant to finish us off. This became known as the Finishing Pit. Sometime in the middle of the day, they brought the same steel pots with the same soup. Luckily I still had cigarettes and could negotiate some of the heartier meat and vegetables from the bottom of the barrel. Again, most just got water and were starving. We all were thin, with distended stomachs. Many of us were near death.

As the days went by, I was alone with my thoughts, of being a child in cheder, in school, learning Torah, and living the life of an observant Jew. I thought about my father, who was so virile but died before all this started. I imagined that he was with Momma, looking down at me and somehow guiding me to get through this. I hoped Chava, Benjamin, and Yossel were at peace. I hoped someone other than me was still alive. And Miriam, would I ever see her again? She filled my dreams. I always saw her in the distance but could never get close. We did not speak but only gazed into each other's eyes.

I thought about being a child and swimming in the San River with my brothers and the other boys in the shtetl. We had a good life, carefree, filled with love and purpose. We knew what was expected of us, and war was the furthest thing from our minds.

We were fed once a day. Every morning, there was more death. One by one, they were indeed finishing us off. They did not remove the bodies. We slowly segmented the bunker so we could keep the dead men at one end while we slept. The kapo also segregated the sick. Typhus was common. It was amazing that we were not all sick. You could tell who was sick from the chills and fever. The sick had rashes on their faces and bodies, and many of the deaths in the pit were a result of untreated typhus.

I literally counted the days we were in the Finishing Pit to keep my mind active. It was four weeks to the day when we were ordered out of the bunker. They were evacuating the camp. Dachau was so huge that there was chaos, guards running all over the place. Piles of dead men left in the bunkers as far as I could see. This had to be a sign that the Germans were running. This was the center of the Third Reich. If they were running from here, was the end of the war near? Prisoners were being loaded into trucks and organized to march. I was in a group that began to march out of the camp. We were evacuating. We marched to the train tracks. We were loaded onto a train. This time, I was on an old passenger car that had its seats removed. We were stuffed like sardines in a tin can. As usual, I had no idea where we were going. Where could they hide if not in the center of Germany?

Sure enough, about two hours out of Dachau, I could hear airplanes overhead. Next thing I knew, bombs were dropping and exploding nearby. The train was not hit, but it stopped. There was panic among the guards and likewise the prisoners. Many of us jumped off the train and ran into the woods just along the track. This was the first time in three years I had an opportunity to escape. I would probably be shot, but the taste of freedom would at least be the feeling I felt at the end. I had no idea where to go, so I stayed close to the tracks. Once the bombing run ended, the guards came looking for us. We did not get far. Shots rang out behind me and a few others, and we stopped in our tracks. They spent the next two hours loading us back onto the train.

We began to move again. We rode all night. The next morning, the bombing started again. The train stopped again, and we all jumped off again. This time, some of us went deeper, hiding in the trees. It wasn't long before we were gathered up and put back on the train. I couldn't imagine why they bothered. They were on the run. These Nazi stooges were slaves to their orders. They were told to hold the prisoners, so that was what they did.

The train started up again. I didn't know if we were going east or west. Was it the Russians or the Americans making them run? Another few hours went by, and the roar of the planes was now louder. They were flying lower and made another bombing run. This time, it was a direct hit. The train derailed, and the car I was on twisted and turned on its side off the track. Somehow we all cushioned each other from the impact, and I was not hurt. The others near me seemed unhurt. We began to climb out the windows and the doors, which were now facing upward. We scattered. I ran with two other men into an open field. The planes were gone. We looked back, and the engine was on fire. A bomb must have hit it square. No one followed us. We turned and left. We were free, but we had to keep going. The guards were likely occupied with the damage or, better yet, killed in the bombing.

We walked through this field until we came to a road. It was deserted. At that point, I felt that no one would follow. We followed the road for a few kilometers. I could hardly believe what had just happened. I had been a prisoner for three solid years. I did not know what to do or say. We walked for an hour before I broke the ice.

"My name is Meyer," I said, hoping they would respond.

"Ephraim," said one of the men.

"Mendy," said the other.

We laughed, and Mendy started singing "Dovid, Melech Yisrael" ("David, King of Israel"), a song every Jewish child knew. We joined in. There were Jews alive. It was a miracle from God.

There were farms and homes along the road. As we were celebrating our freedom, a man came out of his house, holding up a rifle and pointing it at us. We stopped in our tracks. "Halt!" he said, long after we had already stopped. We raised our hands. He put his gun down and said in German, "Where did you come from?"

I spoke. "Our train was bombed. We are looking for food."

"Come here," he said. "Are you concentration camp prisoners?"

I looked at the others.

"Yes," said Ephraim. "We were at Dachau. We were evacuated onto trains, and it was bombed. We escaped."

"Americans," he said. "Come inside. My name is Klaus. You are welcome here. I left the German army. I deserted. They are murderous barbarians, and I have been hiding here since I left. They're losing the war. It's almost over. The American army is overwhelming us throughout Europe, and Russia is closing in from the east. You can stay here. I won't let anything happen to you so long as I am alive."

He lived alone but had stockpiles of food and weapons. We were saved.

CHAPTER 26

Liberation

THE FIRES BURNED THROUGHOUT THE city all day. We could hear the sirens of firetrucks and ambulances throughout the hotel. On my way back to the dormitory after work, I picked up the afternoon newspaper. The *LVZ*, the *Leipziger Volkszeitung* (*Leipzig People's Newspaper*), reported that hundreds of people had been killed and hundreds more were injured. Most of the buildings hit were industrial factories, presumably to weaken the German war machine, but schools, churches, and museums were also hit. Bombs coming from the sky meant we were all targets, or at least potential victims.

Until today, the papers had been filled with stories of conquest by the Nazi forces: the bombing of London, German soldiers marching down the Champs-Élysées under the Arc de Triomphe in Paris, the victories all along the eastern front deep into Russia. Now the British and Americans were bombing Leipzig? The Americans were in the war? Maybe Germany was not indestructible after all. I just hoped I lived to see them defeated.

Things quieted down after that for a while. The streets became active again, and the hotel filled up. Work was back to normal. Giselle, Katarina, and I started going out to cafés in the evening to hear what others were saying about the war. We started talking to an older retired couple from Berlin. They were traveling by train to Frankfurt to see their children and grandchildren. Their train was stopped in Leipzig because of American bombings around Frankfurt. They were told to spend the night here and that the train would continue the next morning.

"We are worried about our children and if we will get to see them," said the woman.

The man followed up with, "I am more worried about what the Americans, British, and Russians will do to us when they take over Berlin. It is only a matter of time. The government tells us we are winning, but our cities are getting hit hard. Even Berlin has seen lots of bombs raining on us. We were hoping Frankfurt would be safer, but there may be no safe place. Hitler stretched his armies too wide, and now we will all pay."

Giselle asked, "Were you in World War I?"

"Yes," he said, "I was in the army. We thought we could take over Europe, and we were wrong. It's hard to believe we did this again, but this time, the weapons are bigger and more powerful. They will destroy us."

I sat there taking this all in. It was true. Germany was losing the war. I asked, "When do you think this war will end?"

He responded, "Maybe a year, maybe less. I don't know. We have the whole world against us."

I was thrilled but did not show any emotion. As the girls were talking to them, my thoughts wandered to my parents. Would I see them soon? Was Meyer still watching over them in the woods around Pysznica? Shlomo must be getting big. I wanted to see Meyer. He was strong and made me feel safe. My heart ached for him. I was having weird dreams almost every night. My father would come talk to me to tell me Meyer loved me and would find me. Sometimes it was Momma and Shlomo, but they would always talk about Meyer. I missed them all terribly and wondered why they came to me and Meyer never did. I was afraid they were dead but felt they were angels watching over me.

One night I saw Meyer climbing a ladder. He climbed and climbed. Was I at the top of the ladder? I never found out. I woke up before he could reach me.

On the walk back to the dormitory, I couldn't help but get excited. "This may be over soon. We can go back to who we are and live our lives in peace. They say the streets in America are paved in gold. You can live free without any fear of anti-Semitism. This is where I will go after the war."

They both laughed at me.

"You're a dreamer," said Katarina. "The war is far from over, and remember what the Nazis did to Poland. They will not give up easily."

I just shut up and kept walking, but I believed God would save us or maybe the Americans would.

About two months went by with no new attacks. Perhaps they were right, and the Germans were getting back on the winning way. Then one morning, about 0400 in February, we were awoken by explosions. This time, they were far away but could be clearly heard. We emptied into the streets. I could see fires burning in several directions. It was a ring of fire that almost surrounded the city. That evening, the *LVZ* reported that more industrial factories outside the city were destroyed, but they were mostly reporting that the bombs were killing innocent women and children. Frankly I didn't care. They could kill all the Germans for all I cared. How many innocent lives, Jewish and otherwise, did they destroy with their hatred and hunger for power? These were the worst people on earth, and they should all die. I was so sad that they came in and destroyed the lives of my family and everyone I knew. I would never forgive them.

Life got back to normal after a few days. The *LVZ* told us that the Third Reich was pushing the evil invaders back. Nothing would happen for a while, and the hope for liberation was being pushed back into memory when more bombings occurred in May. This time, they hit in the city and outside. Many buildings were destroyed and then nothing and back to work. I was so frustrated and saddened by the ups and downs that I just buried myself in the work.

The summer came and went, and the bombings came and went. More buildings were destroyed, and hundreds of people died each time, but the Nazis were firmly in control. I prayed every morning and every night for the end of the war.

Christmas was something I had heard about as a child in school but learned to ignore while the Poles celebrated the birth of Jesus and came to school with new clothes. I never had to experience it until I came to Germany. Here it was different. People celebrated cautiously. There was not much talk of Jesus, and the Christmas trees in the hotel had swastikas on top. They did not even notice that the three of us did not participate. Some of the girls in the dorm exchanged gifts. One girl who was so sweet and friendly handed out little chocolates to everyone in the dormitory.

As 1945 came in, the bombings intensified. We all spent a lot of time in the basement of the hotel, and the guests stopped coming. At the end of February, we were told the hotel would close temporarily while repairs were made, due to damage from a bomb that fell across the street. We were told that we could stay in the dormitory rent free while the repairs were made. In February, the bombing intensified. There were always deaths caused by the bombings, but most people could reach shelters and the damage was mostly to buildings and roads. The train station was bombed heavily, and the rails stopped running. By March, we knew it was just a matter of time. We could hear explosions in the distance, different than the bombs. These were the sounds of cannons and big guns like I heard when the Nazis invaded Poland. Germany was being invaded and would be defeated soon. My prayers and those of my friends were being answered.

Finally, on April 18, 1945, a day I would never forget, American soldiers marched into Leipzig. There was gunfire in the streets and large explosions. We all went into the basement. There were loudspeaker announcements that everyone should stay inside. A few days went by, and things seemed to quiet down.

One afternoon, about a dozen of the women in the building, including me, Giselle, and Katarina, could not take being cooped up and left. We ran toward the hotel on the Trondlinring, a major thoroughfare in the city. Most of the women stayed back, afraid to go outside. We saw American soldiers patrolling the streets with rifles drawn. I was so excited I ran up to one very handsome man to welcome him, when he started screaming at me in English, which I had never heard before. Another soldier came over and spoke German. He told us to go home and stay there. They were still securing the area, and it was dangerous to be on the street. As soon as he said that, the sound of gunshots rang out, and we ran into the hotel, which thankfully was open.

There was a skeleton staff just keeping the place clean. Herr Vogt ran out to see us. "What are you girls doing here?" he asked.

I responded, "We came out to see what was going on. We heard the Americans were here. We heard shots and were told to go inside."

The girls were all talking behind me.

"You will stay here tonight," he said sternly. "We will open up some rooms, and there is some food in the pantry."

We found some bottles of wine in the pantry and decided to celebrate. We toasted to the Americans and the defeat of Germany. Suddenly, to my surprise, Katarina held up her glass and began to speak in Yiddish. "Here is to my poor parents, murdered by these Nazi bastards."

Giselle and I looked at each other. The other girls looked at Katarina in shock. I just turned back to Katarina, shrugged my shoulders, and said, "L'chayim."

Giselle said, "L'chayim," and we drank to her parents. Now that the Americans were here, who would they turn us in to? The three of us found a suite with a living room and a great big bed. We felt like princesses, and we drank and taught each other Yiddish songs from our youth. We drank into the early morning. At some point, I just fell asleep. Next thing I knew, it was morning, and I woke up with a big headache. I was on the couch but did not see the girls. I walked into the bedroom, and it looked like the girls made it into bed before they passed out.

It was quiet outside. I walked out on the terrace and saw American soldiers patrolling the street. They won and were in control. I ran in and yelled, "Wake up!" The girls were groggy but started waking up. We were all hungover. "I think the war is over!" I declared.

I took a bath and felt a little better. While I waited for the girls to get ready, I watched from the balcony as people began to come out onto the street. I could not wait to see what the conquerors would do to these animals who had tried to exterminate my people.

"Let's go!" I yelled out.

"Calm down!" Giselle yelled back.

I shut up. I was just excited. They were finally ready.

We went outside and walked toward the train station. When we got to the site that had been bombed heavily, I was shocked by what we saw. There were stands set up around the park where American soldiers were handing food packages to any German who got in line. In one area, they were handing packages to men wearing Nazi and police uniforms. I could not believe my eyes. Why were they being so nice to these murderers? They should be killing these bastards. I saw a group of soldiers standing together talking. I was so angry that I went right up to them and started yelling in Polish, "Why are you being so nice to these murderers? They killed us, made us slaves, and are the worst people on earth!"

Giselle and Katarina followed me and tried to calm me down. Suddenly one of the soldiers came up to us and responded in Polish, "Are you Jewish?"

The question shocked me. I was used to hiding my identity and wasn't sure if Americans treated Jews any differently than Nazis. Katarina made the decision for us. "Yes, we are Jewish," she said. "We are living under Polish papers hiding our identities."

"Kat, stop!" I yelled. I didn't trust anybody. This was what I had learned over the last five years.

"Follow me," said the soldier. Were we now captured?

We followed the soldier, who did not identify himself, across the park. Standing there talking to a small group of men and women was a man in uniform wearing a yarmulke.

"Chaplain," said the soldier, "these ladies would like to talk to you." The man I thought had just captured us turned around and left.

"Hello, ladies. My name is Rabbi Dembovich. Do you speak Yiddish?"

Tears began to come from all three of us. "Yes," I said, when I caught my breath.

"Please come with me," he said and led us into a nearby tent. "Please sit down," he said.

We did.

He wanted to hear each of our individual stories, where we were from, what we knew about our families, and whether we wanted to go back. We each had stories of brutality and slavery. Yes, I wanted to go back to find my parents, Shlomo, and of course Meyer. Then Rabbi Dembovich stood up and spoke to us. "I know you have been through a lot, but there are things that we have discovered about the Nazis and the Jewish people as we have liberated the captured territories that you may not know. First, the war is almost over. The Allied armies, mostly the United States, Great Britain, and Russia, now have control of all the territories the Nazis invaded, including Poland and Czechoslovakia, most of which is now controlled by Russia. We have found many camps, concentration camps, with hundreds of thousands of starving and tortured Jewish men and women and the remains of hundreds of thousands more. The Nazis meant to exterminate the Jewish people, and they came pretty close."

Even watching what they did to us, I never imagined such a horror.

The rabbi continued, "The Allied armies and the United Nations are now just setting up displaced person camps, DP camps, where people affected by the war can come and use our resources to find their surviving family and friends. There are DP camps for all kinds of people. I am working at a DP camp for displaced Jews. You are welcome to join me. You will be living with others, many of whom are sick, having just been liberated from the concentration camps. You all are healthy, and you can help us care for the sick. We have kosher food, and you can live a Jewish life once again."

We all agreed to go.

We ran back to the dormitory, packed our bags, said our good-byes, and headed back to the park. None of us were sorry to leave. We spoke only Yiddish now and were looking forward to being with other Jewish people again, living in freedom.

When we got back, Rabbi Dembovich led us to a military bus. We got on. There were six others on with us. It looked like there were other Jews hiding in Leipzig. While we rode, his words sank in: "exterminate the Jewish people." Did anyone survive?

It was a long ride. We stopped to get some food and then traveled all night. It was hard to sleep on the bus, but I managed a couple of hours. The morning sun shined in my eyes and woke me up. The first thing I saw was a sign for Stuttgart. When we arrived at the DP camp, I couldn't take my eyes off a banner that hung at the entrance. It was a blue Jewish star and a picture of a menorah with some English words I could not read. I would learn later that it was the American Jewish Joint Distribution Committee. The camp was run by the American army, but the Joint Distribution made the camp Jewish. They brought kosher food, gave classes, set up synagogues, and had counselors to help us learn to be Jewish again. The camp itself was in the city. There was a DP center surrounded by older apartment buildings that would be the home for the survivors. It was rough and crowded, but no one cared. We were free to be who we were.

The girls and I settled into one of the apartments. They were crude and dirty, but we washed down the floors and made the beds. It was not as nice as our dormitory but certainly better than my shack in the woods around Pysznica. Once we were settled, we took a walk around the camp area. The most shocking was the condition of many of the men and women who were arriving. They were so thin and drawn they looked like they were starving. They were skinny, with their bones sticking out almost like walking skeletons with stomachs that stuck out like a football. Many had to be carried on stretchers or wheeled in. There were people with missing limbs or other physical injuries. They had come out of the concentration camps that Rabbi Dembovich spoke of, barely alive. As we watched them unload transports, Rabbi Dembovich came up and startled us.

"Hello, ladies," he said.

I jumped as I was staring at the new arrivals.

"What do you think of our little camp?" he asked.

"It's horrible," said Giselle. "Look at these poor people."

"This is how you found them?" I asked. "In the concentration camps?"

"Yes," he said, "the ones who could work were starved, near death. The men and women who could not work were killed. We found as many dead bodies as those who were alive. I will ask you to report to our medical facility as soon as you can. We need volunteers to help our doctors and nurses bring these people back to health."

We followed the group to see where they were being taken. The medical facility was in fact a hospital taken over by the army. The group that just arrived was just a drop in the bucket. There were maybe a thousand former prisoners being attended by doctors, nurses, and other volunteers. We were immediately put to work, setting up beds and feeding patients. I was feeding a poor woman who was a prisoner in Buchenwald. She told me her story of torture, how the Nazis pulled all her teeth out to get the gold that was in her mouth. She was very sick with fever, and I had to push her to eat the apple sauce I was given. As we were talking, we were interrupted by a very handsome man wearing a white coat.

"I am Dr. Berger," he said in German but with an American accent. "I am an American army medic, and I need to examine this patient."

"Your German is very good," I said, standing up to get out of his way.

"My parents were German and left before World War I and settled in New York," he said. "That's where I grew up and went to school." He looked at me and smiled and then turned to the patient.

He pulled out his stethoscope and began his examination. He took her temperature and checked her quite thoroughly. When he finished, he looked at me and said, "Her lungs are filled with fluid. Her fever is at a very high level. I will get her some penicillin, but I am afraid she may not make it. Please try to make her comfortable."

The next day when I came to see her, she was gone. Dr. Berger came up to me and told me she had died overnight. I was so sad that this poor woman had survived the horror of the war and died after she was saved. This was not fair.

Then, to my surprise, the good doctor asked me if I would have supper with him. "I would like to learn more about you," he said. "How about tonight?"

"Sure," I said. "I will meet you outside your building at six."

He was smooth, but I liked him. I pulled Katarina and Giselle aside and told them the news. They were excited and giddy.

"Nice, an American doctor!" said Katarina. "What does he look like?"

"He's tall," I said, bragging a little. "He has thick brown hair and blue eyes. He's not Meyer, but he'll do in a pinch." That got a big laugh from the girls.

Giselle chimed in. "Maybe he will take you to New York with him."

"What about Meyer?" asked Katarina. "All you did the whole time in Leipzig was talk about him."

"I'm not getting married," I snapped back. "I'm just eating. Besides, I don't know if Meyer is alive or dead. Herr Doctor is very handsome and very nice."

Giselle responded, "We'll wait up for you. We want to hear all about it. What's his first name?"

I was stumped. "You know, I never asked. I guess that will be my first question. Let's go back. I have to figure out what to wear."

I picked out the newest dress I made for spring. It was yellow and white. It was the first time in a long time that I cared what I looked like. The girls said I looked beautiful. I went outside, and he was waiting for me. He looked different in his uniform. I had only seen him in his white coat.

"Good evening, Miriam," he said as he took my hand and wrapped it around his arm. We began to walk.

"I never told you my name," I said, surprised he knew it.

"I overheard you telling one of the patients," he said and smiled. "My name is Jonah, in case you were wondering."

"That's my father's name," I said, and a tear came to my eye.

"What happened to him?" he asked.

"I don't know," I said. "My parents sent me off once I got the opportunity to get a Polish identity. When I left, they were hiding in the woods with a few other families."

We arrived at our destination. "This is the Officer's Club," he said. "This is where we eat. They have kosher food for the Jewish personnel." He said hello to a few of the officers, some doctors and some just military. He introduced me, but I was nervous, and for the life of me, I don't recall one name. We sat at a small table for two.

"So tell me about New York," I said. "I have two uncles there and some cousins, none of whom I have ever met."

"I live in a place called Queens," he said. "My parents came to the United States around 1910, and my father worked in retail shops on the Lower East Side of Manhattan. He saved every penny and started buying and selling houses with a friend. He and my mom then had me and my younger brother. He sent me to college and medical school, and here I am. New York has a very big Jewish community, and we can live and work as Americans and be observant Jews as little or as much as we want. It has been shocking to see what has happened to the Jews of Europe. We had little knowledge of what was happening here. Have you looked through the survivor lists for your family?"

"The what?" I asked.

He replied, "Every person who the Allied armies have found alive in the camps or those who have made themselves known to us are placed on a list so you can search for any surviving family members."

"Really!" I shrieked with excitement. "Where is this list?"

"Rabbi Dembovich should have told you," he said. "He can show you where to go. Also, he can try to find your relatives in America to let them know you are all right." After that, he talked about his family, friends, and hopes and dreams after the war, but all I could think of was telling the girls about the list and seeing whom I could find. I wondered if Meyer was alive.

"Are you all right?" he asked.

"Sorry," I replied. "I was just thinking about who I would find." There was no need to tell him about Meyer.

Dinner was quite good. I had a vegetable soup and then roasted chicken and vegetables, with a nice glass of wine. We had coffee and some sort of sponge cake. We walked back to the barracks.

"You are lovely and nice, and I would like to see you again," he said.

"I would like that," I said.

He was very nice and seemed sincere. I liked talking to him and hearing about what life was like in New York. I still thought about Meyer, but I would look for him tomorrow.

He leaned over, kissed me on the cheek, and said, "Good night."

I said, "Good night," and went inside.

"That was quick," said Giselle, as soon as she saw me.

"Did he dump you already?" Katarina laughed.

"No," I said. "He wants to see me again. What did you expect? We can't leave the camp area yet. We went to the officers' dining room. They live better than us. We were served like being in a fancy restaurant. We had a nice chat. The real news is that the army has a list of survivors that they have found. We can look for our families."

"Did he tell you that?" asked Giselle.

"Yes," I said, "Rabbi Dembovich should have told us."

"Why wouldn't he tell us?" asked Katarina.

"How do I know?" I was annoyed. "We'll find out tomorrow."

First thing the next morning, we were up early and went looking for Rabbi Dembovich. He was having breakfast with a group of concentration camp survivors in the DP center cafeteria. I went over and whispered in his ear, "We would like to talk to you after breakfast." We sat down and had some eggs and coffee.

As we got up for our second cup of coffee, we heard, "What can I do for you ladies?" from a cheerful Rabbi Dembovich.

"We understand you can help us find our families," I said sternly.

"We get lists of men and women who are liberated in various camps and towns, not only Jews but all prisoners," said the rabbi. "We also have a list of anyone who has registered with a DP camp, like yourselves. I thought I would give you a few days to get acclimated, but perhaps that was a mistake. There are literally tens of thousands of names, and more come in every week. We have not had time to sort them, so to find anyone, you must search through all the names. Also, we do not know if it is complete. We don't know the accuracy of the British and the Russian records. The other thing we can help you with is finding and contacting any relatives you have in the United States."

"When can we start?" asked Katarina.

"You can start this afternoon," said the rabbi.

We spent an anxious morning working with some of the patients in the infirmary. Jonah came over. "I had a nice time last night."

"Me too," I said.

"Maybe we can take a walk later," he said.

I replied, "I'm going over to look at the names of the survivors later, and I will probably be tied up with that tonight. Maybe another time."

"Sure," he said, "but I don't give up so easily."

I laughed. "That's good. I would be disappointed if you did."

After our shift, we went to the rabbi's office. He was ready for us. He brought us into a room with shelves of books. There were hundreds of them. There were two soldiers in uniform sitting at a desk binding the latest shipment of papers into notebooks.

"How can we help you lovely ladies?" asked one of them.

Rabbi Dembovich intervened. "These ladies are survivors who are trying to find their families. I told them you would help them."

The officers stood up and said in unison, "We sure will."

Rabbi Dembovich said, "Good hunting," and left.

Giselle and Katarina started giggling like schoolgirls. They liked these guys. I might never find out anything. We wrote down all the names of the people we were looking for. I included Meyer, along with my parents, brother, and sisters on my list. The books were organized by country of where people were found or registered. We focused on Poland, Czechoslovakia, Germany, and Russia. That was a lot and would take us days.

I tried to get the attention of one of the men, who was focused on Katarina. "Excuse me," I said. He turned around, and Kat gave me a dirty look. "I have two uncles in New York I want to contact."

"Names?" he asked.

"Nathan and Israel Goldin," I replied.

"Address?" he asked.

"I have no idea," I said. "They are my father's—Jonah Goldin—brothers, and they live in New York. Israel is a kosher butcher. That is all I know."

"We will try our best," he replied.

The rabbi overheard the conversation as he came in to check on us and said, "If he is a butcher, he will be in the Orthodox union. I know someone in New York who may be able to help."

We spent the next several days searching through the names.

In the evenings, Dr. Jonah would call on me, and we took walks in the spring air. He talked about some of his patients. He was saving lives, and he was thrilled to tell me about them. He wanted to hear every detail of my search. I finally had to confess that I had fallen in love with a soldier in Poland who had helped my family survive the early days of the war. I was looking for him but had not found him yet.

"Don't be angry with me," he said, "but it would not upset me if you don't find him."

"Don't you get upset, but I'm still looking!" I replied.

He laughed.

"I also did not find my parents or little brother, but I think I may have found one of my sisters. There was a Ruth Goldin registered in Munich. I am writing her a letter to see if it is her."

"Well, that's exciting," he said.

"I still have some looking to do," I replied, showing my sadness.

He wanted to kiss me good night, but I asked him not to.

I could not sleep much that night, thinking of why I could not find the rest of them. Was Meyer dead? Was Ruth the only survivor besides me? I was determined to keep looking.

CHAPTER 27

L'Chaim (To Life)!

⅄ ⅄ ⅄

We stayed with Klaus several days, about a week. We ate. We slept. We slowly regained our strength. I had a low-grade fever, something I picked up along the way, but it cleared up in a few days. It was eerily quiet along the road where Klaus lived. We began to take walks and get some spring air as we regained our strength. Klaus had gone out to find some more food. We were eating everything he had. When he came back that day, he had something besides food. A local German newspaper, dated May 2, 1945. The headline read, "Chancellor Dead, Committed Suicide." The article said Adolf Hitler was found dead in his bunker where he was hiding from the Allies, along with his wife, Eva Braun. He shot himself, and she took poison. The war was truly over. All four of us drank whiskey and celebrated. We taught our new friend Klaus to say l'chaim!

I was never much of a drinker but got really drunk that night and passed out in Klaus's living room. I woke up in the middle of the night sometime, dragged myself up to the bedroom I was sharing with Mendy and Ephraim, and passed out again.

I awoke to a low rumbling sound. We all got up and looked out the window. We saw a military truck moving slowly down the road outside the house. It had an American flag on the top of the cab.

"Americans!" cried Ephraim.

There was a whole division moving down the road.

I said, "Let's put our prisoner uniforms on and let them know we are here." We got dressed as fast as we could and ran outside. On the way out, Mendy grabbed the newspaper with the "Chancellor Dead" headline. We started waving our arms and the newspaper as they went by. Suddenly a small personnel carrier pulled over, and two American officers came out to talk to us. They spoke English, but we started yelling, "Polish, Dachau."

They seemed to understand. They pointed to the truck.

"I think they want us to go with them," I said to Ephraim and Mendy. We gestured that we wanted to go but had to go into the house. We went inside and gathered up some of the clothes that Klaus had given us. We said good-bye to Klaus, thanking him for taking us in and being so kind. We jumped in the back of the open vehicle, and the driver took off, soon catching up with the rest of the convoy.

The vehicles moved slowly down the road. Every one of the soldiers we could see looked very serious, even somber. The trains the Nazis put us on had taken us north from Dachau, up near Nuremburg. We continued north, arriving at a huge military base outside Frankfurt am Main. We were immediately brought to a hospital, where we were checked by several doctors.

I was told I weighed ninety pounds, or forty-one kilograms. I was a shadow of my former self. This was after eating for the last few days. They kept us for two days, taking pictures of us, X-rays, and giving us all kinds of tests. The last morning, they gave us some new civilian clothing and an officer came by and asked us to go with him. They took us to a building, five stories high. When we got inside, we were separated, and I was taken to a small room with a table and chairs. Two officers came in, and one introduced himself, speaking Polish.

"My name is Lieutenant Jones; this is Lieutenant Johnson. We are translators, and we would like to ask you a few questions about your experiences during the war. First, I want to tell you that we are here to help all the people affected by the war get healthy and try to find their families. I understand that you were a prisoner in Dachau Concentration Camp. Is that correct?"

"Yes," I replied.

He continued, "The division that picked you up had just visited your camp, and we have all been shocked by what we have seen there. The death, the brutality of what the Nazis have done to the Jews and others is unspeakable. The highest level of our military command has ordered every soldier in Germany to visit at least one camp like Dachau to see what has happened here. We would like to hear from you how you came there and how you escaped to where we found you."

They sat there with a notebook and pencil and began to write as I recounted my story from the day my army unit was attacked by the blitzkrieg. I told about going home to be a slave laborer for the Polish police and the Nazis. I told them of the murders of my poor sister Chava, my mother, and of course my brothers, Yossel and Benjamin. Finally, I described my last three years in captivity, how I survived, and how I was freed by the bombings of the American air force, for which I was very grateful. "Thank you for saving us from this horror," I said as a tear ran down my face.

"So what do you want to do now?" he asked.

I thought for a minute. "I don't know," I said. "I would go back to Poland and try to find any family members who still may be alive."

"I would not suggest that," said Lieutenant Johnson. "The Russians control that area, and if you go there, you may not be able to leave. You should give us the names, and we can help try to find any who are alive, but the Russians are not very open with information."

"Actually," I said, "I want to find Miriam."

"Who's Miriam?" he asked.

"The girl I fell in love with in Poland before I was captured," I said. "She was living under Polish papers. Last time I saw her, I put her on a train. She was going to Leipzig to work at a hotel."

"That sounds like a plan to me." Lieutenant Jones laughed. "You can stay with us for a while. We have a big shot coming to visit us in a few days. You may want to stay at least until then."

The interview was over. The three of us were reunited and brought to a barracks, where we were assigned a bed. We were given free reign of the camp and could walk around. It was huge. There were thousands of American and some British soldiers. It was like a city. We even got to watch an American baseball game. We had no idea what was going on. We were just happy to see people laughing and having fun.

Over the next few days, the soldiers were cleaning the base, building a stage, and getting ready for the big shot to arrive. The funny thing for me was that not only were we not asked to do the work, but they were apologizing for getting in our way. We felt like kings. They cleaned our rooms and fed us until we begged them to stop.

Finally, the day was here. Above the stage there was a big sign: "Welcome General Eisenhower." We had no idea what this meant or who was coming. We tracked down Lieutenant Jones in the office where we met him. He explained, "General Dwight D. Eisenhower, the commander of all Allied Forces in Europe, now the military governor of the US Occupation Zone. His headquarters were in Frankfurt am Main, and he is coming to talk to the troops about the occupation of Germany. You can thank him for leading us to beat the Nazis. He is the one who wants to make sure everyone knows what happened to the Jews of Europe."

Now, that was a big shot, I thought.

On a late afternoon in early June, a helicopter landed. About an hour later, the soldiers began to march in formation and take their positions in front of the stage. We found some room in the middle of the pack. He was introduced, and the men began to cheer. We screamed and tried to be the loudest. We were thrilled to see this great hero. He spoke for about thirty minutes. We had absolutely no idea what he said. In fact, we were so far away, we could not even see his face. We could hear his voice, and when the men and women of the base applauded, so did we. When they cheered, so did we. At the end, they cheered the loudest, and we screamed as loud as we could. It didn't matter. These men and women saved us from the horror of the Nazis, and all I wanted to do was find Miriam, marry her, and take her to America. I now had a purpose in life.

We were in a bunk with some other Jewish survivors. I overheard a conversation about a Jewish Community Center that was being established in Frankfurt. Some were headed there that night, so we decided to join them. We were free to come and go from the base, and we could walk to a train headed into the city. The trains were now free throughout Germany, so we could travel as we wished.

The Jewish Center was a two-story building in a neighborhood where most of the buildings were destroyed by bombings. We walked in, and there were about twenty-five men and women just socializing. There was music playing, and a few were dancing. This was great. I never imagined this would be possible. Just a few weeks ago, Jewish men were dying all around me. Now they were dancing with Jewish women. Mendy and Ephraim immediately got into the spirit of things. They approached a couple of the ladies and seemed to be doing pretty well. I just sat and drank a cup of coffee. I enjoyed watching the proceedings. There was still a curfew in effect, so the evening ended around 2100 hours. On the trip back to the base, everyone was delighted. They would have this social twice a week, so we were ready for the next one, which would be Saturday night.

Friday morning, we were walking to breakfast when we saw a sign in Hebrew: "Shabbos Service at 1930 hours in the Social Hall." I had not even thought of observing Shabbos in a long time. The world had changed so much since the war began, and me with it, but the idea that I could sit in shul again and have Shabbos lifted my spirits so high. So many died, but they could not kill Shabbos. I couldn't wait.

I had a decent shirt and pair of pants that Klaus had given me, so I dressed and walked over to the social hall. There were about twenty-five or thirty men gathering to pray. About half were soldiers. Who knew there were Jewish-American soldiers? The rest were "guests" like me, freed from the camps. There was a small wooden case sitting on a chair in the front of the room, which I assumed held a Torah, something I had not seen in several years. There were rows of chairs lined up with a curtained wall, presumably a mechitzah, behind which the women would sit tomorrow morning. I grabbed a yarmulke and a siddur from the bookcase and sat down.

Right on time, one of the soldiers came up in front of the room and began to sing "Shalom Alechem." He encouraged us to sing along. Maybe it was years, but I didn't need to open the book. I remembered every word that I had learned as a child. We were welcoming Shabbos, and I was in disbelief that I was sitting in shul. Looking around while we were davening, I could see that many of the soldiers were not that knowledgeable in reading Hebrew, but the camp survivors were mostly like me, Orthodox, and had most of the service memorized.

Afterward, the soldier who had led us came over to a few of us and spoke in German. "I am Rabbi Levine. I am the Jewish chaplain at this base. Please come tomorrow, and if you like, we can have a minyan every day. We also have Shabbos dinner prepared next door, and you are all invited."

It was delightful. We all intermingled. I sat next to a soldier who tried to teach me the English words for all the different foods being served, gefilte fish, matzah ball soup, and roasted chicken. I knew I would have to learn English to live in this new world and when I went to America, which was now my greatest desire.

When I got back to the bunk, Ephraim and Mendy were standing outside talking about Saturday night.

"Why didn't you come to shul?" I asked.

They looked at each other, and Mendy said to me, "Truthfully we have no interest in praying to a god that would allow this to happen to his Chosen People. There clearly is no God, and we will no longer pretend there is a man in the sky that controls everything."

"The Nazis took everything away from me, my family and the woman I love," I snapped, "but the fact that I can sit and worship in the traditional way that I learned as a child gives me hope that the future will be better than the past." I went inside to be alone with my thoughts.

The next day at services, I reveled in my return to Yiddishkeit. I sang as loud as I could when they took out the Torah. When the rabbi spoke, I completely ignored him. I was daydreaming about being a boy in shul with my father and brothers. I thought about Miriam and wondered again if she was alive and if I could find her. Life on the base was quite wonderful, but I knew it could not last long; I would need to move on soon. Meanwhile the boys were excited about going to the Jewish Center in Frankfurt that night. I was happy to go too. It was fun to be among people who had lived through hell, trying to get back to a normal life.

When we arrived that night, the crowd was even bigger. Ephraim, Mendy, and I sat at a table near the entrance so we could see the comings and goings of the people. The other people at the table were talking about what to do, to go to America or Palestine. No one wanted to stay in Germany or go back to Poland or certainly not Russia. Suddenly the two girls from the other night walked in, and the boys rushed over to greet them. They disappeared for a while, but I saw them on the dance floor soon. There was a jukebox playing some popular dance music. I was talking to a couple about how impressed I was with the Americans when the boys and their girlfriends came over to introduce me.

"This is our friend Meyer," said Mendy. "We all escaped Dachau together."

"My name is Sara, and this is Golda," she said as she held her hand out to shake mine.

Golda spoke. “We hear you are looking for your girlfriend. We also came here on Polish papers and worked in a factory for the Germans until the Americans came. Where do you think she is?”

I replied, “Last time I saw her, I dropped her at a train station headed for Leipzig. She had papers under the name of Stephania Dombeck. She was promised a job. That was before I was captured in ‘42. I have no idea if she is alive or dead.”

“Stephie?” cried a girl standing at the other side of the table. “I knew her. I worked with her at the Hotel Fuerstenhof in Leipzig. I had no idea she was Jewish. I left there when one of the workers was discovered to be Jewish and was taken away. That was over a year ago, but Stephie was a seamstress and very well liked. She was fine.”

“That’s her,” I said. “I didn’t know the name of the hotel, but she was an excellent seamstress.”

“That is so sweet,” said Sara. “I can’t believe you were so in love. Maybe she is still there. How great would it be if we could find her and be there to see you get back together after three years! Why don’t we all go help you find her? The trains are free, and there is nothing for us to do here. Leipzig is in the American Zone, so we will be safe.”

“I don’t want to go to Leipzig,” said Ephraim.

“Me neither,” said Mendy. “This is a great place. There is great fun here, and Frankfurt is a bigger city with great opportunities.”

“It will be a great adventure,” said Golda. “I’ll go. It’s so romantic.”

“I think it’s a great idea,” I said.

“You’re all meshugga, crazy,” cried Mendy.

“Let’s go tomorrow,” I said, half joking.

“Perfect,” said Golda. “I’m ready to get out of here.”

We agreed to meet at the train station at 1000 hours.

On the way home, Ephraim said, “Thanks a lot, Meyer. I liked those two.”

I laughed. "It looks like I stole both your girlfriends without even trying."

Mendy replied, "Eh, there's plenty fish in the sea. Good luck with those two. I think they are crazy anyway. I'll bet they don't even show up to the train tomorrow."

"We'll see," I said. "Either way, they got me excited about finding her."

I was up early the next morning. As nice and comfortable as living with the US Army was, it was time to go. I packed what little I had and headed for the train station. I said good-bye to the boys. I also stopped at the administration office to let them know I was leaving. I was free to go. When I got to the station, there was no sign of the girls. I expected that I was going alone anyway. I checked the schedule, and a train was leaving for Leipzig just after noon. When I walked back out to the center of the station, I heard someone call, "Meyer!"

Sure enough, Sara and Golda were standing there. I was surprised to see them but happy also.

"You came," I said.

"Of course we came," said Golda.

"Did you think we were lying?" Sara asked.

"Of course not," I lied.

"We wouldn't miss this," said Golda. "We're bored here, and this will be exciting."

We got in line to board the train. You didn't need a ticket; you just got on board. There were a lot of people looking for a free ride. The girls found two seats and sat next to each other. I had to go to the next car to sit. That was fine. The train left exactly on time; German efficiency was still in effect. It was scheduled for six and a half hours. I put my head back and tried to sleep. I dreamed that I was on the train to Dachau, stuffed with people, all dead. I was the only one alive, and I couldn't move. I looked around again, and they were all skeletons. I was sinking under them all.

I woke up startled. I opened my eyes wide and was determined not to sleep anymore. I stood up and took a walk. The girls were talking nonstop. I went over to say hello.

"So tell us about this Miriam you love so much," said Golda.

I told them the story of how the Goldins came to Pysznica after being chased from their home and how I was immediately drawn to her at first sight. I talked about sneaking away and spending as much time together as we could because we had no idea if we would live through another day.

"That's so romantic!" cried Sara.

I could see that we were keeping some of the other passengers awake, and they were staring at me. I could read their minds: "Please shut up!"

"I think I'll go back to my seat and try to sleep," I said.

I went back to the other car and sat down. The train made a few stops along the way, but then the announcement was made: "Next stop, Leipzig station." I gathered my things and hoped the ladies did the same.

They did. I saw them get off the next car. I waved, and they walked over. I had no idea where this hotel was, so I grabbed a city map of Leipzig, hoping I could find it. I didn't know where to look. After a few minutes, Sara tapped me on the shoulder.

"It's a fifteen-minute walk east of here."

"How do you know that?" I asked, annoyed.

"We asked the man at the information desk," said Golda indignantly. "You men are all alike."

I looked back down at the map and found the train station and the hotel right in the middle. "Oh, I found it," I said.

They just shook their heads.

We headed out of the station and onto the street. I was starting to realize that I might find her still working there. That would be great. I was getting excited. It seemed longer than fifteen minutes, as I was getting very anxious.

"I am looking for Stephania Dombeck," I announced to the woman at the front desk. "I believe she works here as a seamstress."

She looked at me very politely and replied, "Please have a seat in the lobby, and I will get someone who can help you."

We did and watched the people coming and going, mostly businessmen in suits with briefcases. There were some families as well, with children. I wondered if they were displaced from their homes or just visiting relatives. We sat quietly for about twenty minutes until we saw a distinguished, well-dressed man speak to the lady at the front desk, who was pointing at us. I stood up as he walked over.

"May I help you? My name is Herr Vogt, and I am the manager of this hotel."

I shook his hand and said, "My name is Meyer Marcus, and I am a close friend of Stephania Dombeck from Poland."

He looked at me and replied, "It looks like you had some difficulty during the war."

"Yes," I said, annoyed that he would comment on my appearance. "I was in the Polish army and was recently released from a prisoner-of-war camp."

"Please come with me," said Herr Vogt. I asked Sara and Golda to stay in the lobby. He led me to the second floor of the hotel, into his office, and shut the door. He spoke once we sat down. "Stephania resigned suddenly several weeks ago, packed her things, and left without saying good-bye. I was quite annoyed since I gave her the job as a favor to her father, whom I knew from business, so I rang them up to ask them what happened. I spoke to Mrs. Dombeck, who explained that Stephie was not Stephie at all but a Jewish girl whom they took in and gave her their real daughter's identity. I should have been angry because that could have put all of us in danger, but the truth was, she was a great worker and we were lucky to have her. I later found out we had several Jewish girls working for us under false identities. It is truly a tragedy what we Germans did to your people. I feel proud that we could help in some small way. Now who are you really?"

"My name is really Meyer Marcus," I said. "Miriam and I were in love back in Poland, but the war split us up. I knew she came here to work as Stephania, and I stayed back and tried to stay with our families, most of whom were murdered by Nazis and Poles. I spent three years in concentration camps and was recently released from Dachau. Once I got some strength back, I came to see if she is alive. She is all I have."

"She is very much alive," he said, "but I have no idea where she is. Mrs. Dombeck used to come to visit her, so they may still be in touch. Let me call them." He looked up their number in his file and dialed the phone. It rang for quite a while until he hung up. "Let me give you their address," he said and wrote it down. "They live just outside the city in the town of Taucha. Here is the address."

"Thank you," I said and stood up.

He stood and said, "I hope you find her. Good luck." He walked me back to the lobby. We shook hands.

"What happened?" asked Golda, dying to know.

"She's not here," I replied as I walked out the door.

"Where are we going?" asked Sara.

"Back to the train station," I said, already annoyed with all the questions.

"I'm hungry," said Sara.

I stopped walking. "You know, so am I. Let's stop at a café, and I'll explain the whole thing."

It was night, and we had nowhere to stay. We ate, and I told them of my conversation with Herr Vogt. When we got to the train station, we saw there was a late train to Taucha. Maybe we could find a cheap hotel there. We arrived around 2300 hours and found a place to stay. The girls shared a room, and I had my own.

I was up early the next morning and went out for a cup of coffee. When I got back, I showed the address to the man at the front desk, who gave me a street map and showed me where the Dombecks were located. We could walk. It was a small town and a nice day. I got tired of waiting, so I knocked on their door. Golda answered. They were almost ready.

"Why don't you go find out where they live and get some coffee?" she said.

"Already done," I replied.

I could hear Sara from the bathroom. "I'm not going anywhere without coffee."

"All right," I said. "I'll meet you in the lobby."

After about a half hour, they came down. We went back to where I had my coffee, and we all had some. I was anxious to get moving, but it was nice having company. I honestly had not asked too many questions of them, but I was curious as to why they were so carefree and willing to tag along with me, so I asked, "Where are you from? Do you have family that survived?"

Golda spoke. "Both our parents are dead. We are sisters from a small village near Kracow. Our mother was Jewish but not our father. We did not observe Jewish rituals or holidays. We lived and worked among the Poles. When the war broke out, we didn't see much of a problem because we frankly hid our Jewish heritage. That was the way my parents wanted it. As the anti-Jewish feelings grew, the police found out about my mother. They arrested her. My father went to the police to protest, and they were both shot. We were told by one of the police what had happened and were told to run away. We did, bought Polish identities, and came to Germany to work. We have nowhere to be and will find our way as we always do, but now we are here to help you find your long-lost love, so let's go."

We walked about five kilometers, following the map and directions the clerk at the hotel gave me. The Dombecks lived in a second-floor flat in a building right next door to a church. I knocked on their door. It opened. It was Mrs. Dombeck.

"I am Meyer," I said.

Before I could say any more, she said excitedly, "I know who you are. Come in!"

CHAPTER 28

Reunion

⅄ ⅄ ⅄

"You're alive; it's a miracle!" she declared. "You look like you have been through a lot. It's unbelievable what has happened. The bombs fell all around us. We were spending our nights in the basement of this building. Somehow they missed us. I want to go back to Poland. My daughter, the real Stephania, is pregnant, and I want to be with her when she has the baby. They are stuck in Poland. The Russians won't let anyone in or out, and we can't see her."

She was going on and on, and I had to interrupt. "Mrs. Dombeck," I said, trying not to be rude, "do you know where Miriam is?"

She stopped her diatribe, looked at me, and said, "Stuttgart."

"Really? How did she get there?" I asked, wondering why she didn't tell me that in the first place. She knew why I was there.

She looked at me, annoyed for interrupting her, and said, "I just got a letter from her that you should read." She stood up and went into the kitchen. She was gone about five minutes, then came out, saying, "I put on a pot of coffee. Here." She handed me the letter, folded in an envelope.

"I'd love a cup of coffee," said Golda. Both girls stood up and walked into the kitchen with Mrs. Dombeck.

"It was brave of you to let Miriam live with you and give her your daughter's papers," said Sara, starting a conversation with Mrs. Dombeck.

I pulled out the letter, and it was definitely Miriam's handwriting. I began to read.

Dear Mrs. Dombeck,

I hope you and Mr. Dombeck are well and have come through the war safely. I hope Stephania is doing well. Is she still in Poland? I had to leave my job suddenly and did not even tell Herr Vogt. I hope you can let him know that I meant no harm. I am happily living in a Jewish Displaced Persons Camp in Stuttgart. I met a rabbi in Leipzig who brought me here. I am now Miriam Goldin again. I do not have to hide anymore. I cannot thank you enough for what you did for me. You saved my life, and I can never repay you.

So far I have found one sister who is alive in Germany. I do not know what happened to everyone else. Meanwhile, I met a young American doctor who seems very interested in me, and we have been seeing a lot of each other. I like him very much but still think of Meyer often. He is not on any list of survivors, and I must assume he is dead. I will move on with my life. Who knows? Maybe I'll be living in America soon. That is where I want to go. I could not believe how nice the American army was to the Germans after the war ended. They say they will help all the people and help rebuild the parts of Europe that were destroyed by war. They are welcoming to everyone and are very sympathetic to the suffering that occurred to the Jewish people. These are truly great men and a great country.

Please stay in touch. I will let you know if I move, but in the meantime, I will stay here in Stuttgart.

Gratefully yours,

Miriam

"Girls, we have to go!" I yelled out. I walked into the kitchen. They were laughing and talking away. "We have to go," I said again.

"Why?" asked Sara. "We are having such a nice time."

"Because Miriam has a new boyfriend," said Mrs. Dombeck.

"Really?" asked Golda.

"An American doctor," said Mrs. Dombeck.

"Oh, Meyer, you are in trouble," said Golda, laughing.

"Let's go," I said sternly.

Golda gulped down her coffee, and the girls stood up.

"Good luck, Meyer," said Mrs. Dombeck. "She loves you; don't worry."

We all hugged Mrs. Dombeck good-bye.

"Thank you for everything," I said.

"Walk faster," I said. They were strolling along.

We hopped on a local train from Taucha back to Leipzig. I was very nervous about seeing Miriam, but I wanted to surprise her. I couldn't wait to see her. We got back to the Leipzig train station late that afternoon. The next train to Stuttgart was not until 2000 hours. That meant we had hours to kill.

The girls wanted to walk around town and see the sights. I was so anxious that after over three years I might finally be reunited with the only woman I had ever loved. I was going to let them go, but I needed a distraction, so I tagged along with them. The area around the Leipzig train station was a fashionable area, but many of the shops were closed. Sara and Golda went into every shop that was open to look around. We found a big clothing store, and they were very excited. While they went in, I just stood outside and watched the people going by. There were American soldiers in small groups scattered around the area. They were staying out of the way of the people. Businessmen were walking to their next appointments, and local residents were trying to go about their business. The occupation seemed to be working. After what seemed to be an hour, they came out with shopping bags.

"What did you buy?" I asked, shocked that they had money to buy anything. I certainly did not.

"Oh, just some clothes, shoes, and things," said Golda.

I just shook my head, and we moved on. We stopped for some food and got back to the train station well ahead of the time we needed to board. The trip would be eleven or twelve hours. There were lots of stops between here and Stuttgart. I hoped I could sleep.

Shortly after we left the station, I did fall sound asleep. When I woke up, my head was foggy. I had just awoken from a dream where I was going from room to room, thinking I was about to find Miriam. The train was moving fast. I sat there just wondering what she would look like. Had she changed? What would she think about how I looked? I certainly did not look the same. What about this American doctor boyfriend she spoke of? Was this serious? Was I too late? I was anxious to see her.

We were still a few hours away. My mind drifted back to my train ride between Mielec and Dachau, lying on the floor of a boxcar surrounded by bodies, some alive, some dead. As I started thinking back to that, I began to shiver, and I was sweating. I felt sick.

Sara, who was sitting across the aisle, saw me shaking and asked, "Are you all right?"

"Yes," I said and pulled myself together. I got up, went to the bathroom, and washed my face. I looked in the mirror and shook my head. I could not believe I had lived through this. I was now sitting in a comfortable seat surrounded by well-dressed men and women. It was as if the war never happened. I wished that it had been a dream. But it did happen. Most everyone I knew and loved was dead. I hoped someone else lived through this. I had to focus on the future. I had to find Miriam.

As we pulled into Stuttgart, I began to get very nervous. Sara and Golda popped up.

"Let's get her," said Golda.

I had the address, and we had to take a trolley to get there. This time I asked directions.

The camp was in Stuttgart-West. An hour later, we got off the trolley right in front of the DP center. This was the address Miriam used as the return address on the letter. There was an information desk, and they easily gave me the apartment location where she was. It was a few short blocks from the center. We walked there briskly. The girls were just as excited as I was. We climbed the stairs to the third floor. We got to the door of apartment 34. The door was slightly ajar. I hesitated for a moment.

Sara and Golda marched right in, and I heard one of them say, "Are you Stephania Dombeck?"

After a few seconds, I heard a soft voice reply, "Ah, yes."

"Then we have something for you," she said, and the girls stepped aside, leaving me face to face with Miriam. She was sitting on a chair at the table with a mouthful of herring, her face turned to me in total shock.

I laughed, as she didn't know what to do. Finally, she spit it out onto her plate as she began to cry. She stood up and came running into my arms.

"You look beautiful," I said, "exactly the same as when I saw you last."

She pushed me away and replied, "You look horrible. What did they do to you?" Then she pulled me close again and kissed me.

"I just got out from the concentration camp," I said. "I am still getting back to normal." I knew my face and body were still swollen, even though I was now eating well.

"I don't care. I thought you were dead," she said. "I could not find you on any list. "We have a lot of catching up to do."

"Well, our work is finished here," said Golda.

Sara and Golda came over and both hugged me and then Miriam.

"We are off for our next adventure," said Sara, and in a flash, they were gone.

"Who were they?" asked Miriam.

"A couple of real angels I met in Frankfurt who brought me to you."

"Frankfurt?" she asked. "We do have a lot to catch up on. How did you get out of Poland? What happened after I left? What happened to everyone? I can't find anyone except Ruth."

"Let's go get some coffee, and I will tell you everything," I said, realizing I would have to tell her all that I knew.

We walked down to the street, and she led me a few blocks away to a café. We were both quiet on the walk. I was thinking about how I would tell her what happened after she left, and she was probably thinking about how to tell me about her doctor boyfriend. We sat down at an outside table and ordered coffee.

"Remember how I told you Benjamin was missing when I dropped you at the train station?" I began.

"Yes," she said. "What happened?"

I recounted that while I was looking for Benjamin, Kozlowski told the authorities the location of the camp. I told her how I found Kozlowski dead and Benjamin near death but able to tell me what happened. I had to tell her that when I got to the place we used to meet Kozlowski, I found many dead bodies, including her beloved father, shot to death along with my and Nachman's mothers. "They killed all the older people except your mother, probably because she was with Shlomo. Pearl was also with them. I don't know what happened to them, but they were captured and probably sent to a concentration camp."

"You mean they could have survived?" asked Miriam hopefully.

"You said you found Ruth," I said. "She left the camp with Naomi, believing they could find Polish papers."

"Yes," said Miriam, "I found her on a list of survivors in Munich. I am waiting to get a letter back."

"My sister Rivka was also missing," I said. "Maybe we can look for her and Naomi. I buried your father and my mother before we were captured. He was like my family too."

Miriam began to cry again and squeezed my hand. It felt good to be with her again. Just then, the coffee arrived. She wiped the tears from her face.

"How did you find me anyway?" she asked.

I pulled out the letter she wrote to Mrs. Dombeck. "I made a little trip to Leipzig looking for you." She laughed a bit, and then I got serious again. "What is this about an American boyfriend?"

She smiled and said, "Well, he's a doctor, Jewish, and wants to take me to America."

"So?" I asked stupidly, not knowing what to say.

"So," she replied, annoyed, "I was considering it until you showed up alive. I thought you were dead. Why weren't you on any list?"

I replied, "I don't know. I was on an American army base, but there were only a few of us."

It was like we never left each other. We could talk for hours. I told her my story of getting captured with Yossel and how he was killed and I survived. I told her of the beatings, the train rides, the Finishing Pit, and finally my liberation. By evening, we seemed to be all caught up. We walked back to her building, when just outside we met a man she knew, holding flowers.

"Hello, Jonah," she said. "This is Meyer, whom I told you about."

I shook hands with him, not realizing that this was the boyfriend.

"Meyer, why don't you go to the DP center and see about a place to stay?" Miriam said. "I need to talk to Jonah for a bit."

"Sure," I said, totally ignorant of what just happened.

As I walked away, it hit me. This was the American doctor, my new enemy. I turned around, but they were gone. There wasn't much I could do; it was her decision. I kept thinking about why she wanted to talk to him suddenly. I had little to offer except the connection we had before we separated. He was a handsome doctor who could give her a great life in America. I was a beat-up prisoner who had nothing. There was not much hope.

I walked back to the information desk at the DP center and asked about a place to stay. The man at the counter was an American soldier and was very kind to me, offering me a couple of options. I chose to stay in a flat in the building next to Miriam's. There was another man staying there, but there was an extra room. He gave me some papers to show the roommate and a key.

"Is there any work in the area I can do?" I asked.

The officer told me that many merchants in the area were hiring survivors, and there were signs in the next room from people looking for help. I grabbed a couple of flyers and headed to see my new apartment. It was on the first floor of the building. It was fine, two bedrooms and a living room with a kitchen. I had my own room for the first time ever. I was beginning to feel human again. My roommate was out, so I would have to meet him later. I would look for work tomorrow, but it was time to find Miriam. I cleaned up the best I could.

"Where have you been?" Miriam asked when she opened the door.

"I got my own room," I said. "It's great. Tomorrow I will look for work. I wanted to give you time to see your boyfriend."

"Thank you," she said. "We had such a lovely time together." Then she walked close and yelled, "You're an idiot! I dumped him. I love you. I was dying when I thought you were dead." She came over, kissed me, and held me close. I kissed her back. We were together again.

"We are free, and we will make a life together," I said very happily. "As soon as I get some money, we will get married."

I spent a few days looking for work. I met a jewelry wholesaler who told me that there was a shortage of watches and gold jewelry in

Leonberg, only about ten kilometers away. That sounded crazy, but he said he would give me items to sell there and I could pay him when I got back. That seemed even crazier to me, but I picked out several nice watches and gold chains, bracelets, and earrings. I took the train to Leonberg and went into a few jewelry stores. I sold out in a matter of a couple of hours. Apparently, they couldn't get deliveries fast enough, and they had a lot of demand. I started going back and forth every other day and started making money.

Miriam received a letter from her uncle Israel in New Jersey. She had two uncles and several cousins who were all excited that she was alive, and they wanted her to come to the United States. We made plans to go as soon as we could make it happen. We would get married there in front of her family and start one of our own.

We went to the American consulate to apply for immigration. The line was very long. We had to stay in line for hours outside. It looked like everyone in Germany wanted to become American. When we finally got to the immigration clerk, we learned that there were restrictions on immigration to the United States. The good news was that I could get legal immigration status as a concentration camp survivor. The bad news was that I could not bring a fiancée. I could, however, bring a wife. If we wanted to go to America, we would need to marry in Germany. That was all right with me, but Miriam was sad that the wedding would have to be private.

I continued to buy and sell jewelry until one day when I learned that Leonberg was flush with watches and jewelry, and I was stuck with my inventory. I went back to Stuttgart, not knowing what was next. I had put aside a beautiful diamond ring and watch for Miriam. Today was as good a day as ever. I went to see her.

"It's time," I said and put on her ring and watch. She hugged me and cried. We were married the next day by Rabbi Dembovich in front of two witnesses he had recruited from patients Miriam had worked with at the hospital. When I smashed the glass, I smashed my past. I had a future that millions of my fellow Jewish men and women would not have. I was going to live it to the fullest in their honor and in honor of my family and every man I saw murdered with my own eyes. I had no guilt for living, but I would never forget those faces.

AUTHOR'S NOTE

This is a fictional tale based on the stories told to me by my parents. Their love story and experiences during the Holocaust defined their lives and mine in many ways. There were fourteen real members of their families when they came together in 1939 shortly after the war broke out. Four survived. Miriam and Meyer came to America shortly after they were married in 1946. They each had a sister who survived. Meyer's sister settled in New York state and Miriam's in Buenos Aires, Argentina.

They each had families and lived rich, meaningful lives to a ripe old age. They always remembered the family members and all martyrs who lost their lives during the Holocaust. They taught their children to never forget.

My parents lived through hell so I could live the American dream, which I did. This book is a thank you to them. The stories they told me were of unbelievable horrors and of unshakable love. That part is true, even if the details had to be fictionalized.

ACKNOWLEDGMENTS

I WANT TO THANK THE following people who were instrumental in making this book a reality: Sandy Birnbaum, my wife of forty years and best friend who died tragically way too young just before I began writing the book but who helped me formulate the idea for it and also helped me grow as a man, a husband, and a father of four great daughters; Gilda Winters, my sister, who knows way more about my family history than I do; Marielle Messing, my daughter, who gave me ideas, advice, and encouragement; Ronnie Himmel, my first cousin, who was told a completely different story than I but gave me some great ideas, including the character of Szweda, whom I had never heard of; Audree Burg, who encouraged me to write every day and made me let her read it as I went along—she told me it was great even when I knew it wasn't; and Doris Kearns Goodwin, who, by some amazing coincidence, I randomly sat next to at a bar in a South Florida restaurant. She was very engaging and in a twenty-minute conversation gave me months of inspiration and encouragement.

48894609R00183

Made in the USA
Middletown, DE
30 September 2017